PUTTIN' ON OLE MASSA

PUTTIN' ON OLE MASSA

The Slave Narratives of
Henry Bibb,
William Wells Brown, and
Solomon Northup

Gilbert Osofsky,
Editor

HARPER TORCHBOOKS
Harper & Row, Publishers
New York, Evanston, and London

For
my kids, Lisa and Judith,
and all kids who ask why?
and how?

PUTTIN' ON OLE MASSA

Printed in the United States of America.

First HARPER TORCHBOOK edition published 1969 by Harper & Row, Publishers, Incorporated, New York, N.Y. 10016.

Library of Congress Catalog Card Number: 69-17285.

Heart of what slave poured out such melody
As "Steal away to Jesus"? On its strains
His spirit must have nightly floated free,
Though still about his hands he felt his chains.
Who heard great "Jordan roll"? Whose starward eye
Saw chariot "swing low"? And who was he
That breathed that comforting melodic sigh,
"Nobody knows de trouble I see"?

—From "O Black and Unknown Bards,"
by James Weldon Johnson

Contents

Introduction

Puttin' On Ole Massa:

The Significance of Slave Narratives

> "The only weapon of self defence I could use successfully, was that of deception."
>
> *Narrative of the Life and Adventures of Henry Bibb, An American Slave* (New York, 1849), p. 17.

> "Ever after I entertained the first idea of being free, I had endeavored so to conduct myself as not to become obnoxious to the white inhabitants, knowing as I did their power, and their hostility to the colored people. The two points necessary in such a case I had kept constantly in mind. First, I had made no display of the little property or money I possessed, but in every way I wore as much as possible the aspect of slavery. Second, I had never appeared to be even so intelligent as I really was. This all colored people at the south, free and slaves, find it peculiarly necessary for their own comfort and safety to observe."
>
> *The Narrative of Lunsford Lane, Formerly of Raleigh, North Carolina* (Boston, 1848), p. 31.

The slave narratives are tales of bondage and freedom written or told by former slaves. There are many thousands of such narratives if one includes the stories of fugitives collected by antislavery advocates and published in the abolitionist press, or those gathered for publication in nineteenth- and twentieth-century documentary accounts. Brief descriptions of slavery from the mouths of those who lived it appear in many nineteenth-century books, such as William Still's *The Underground Rail Road* (1883), Levi Coffin's *Reminiscences* (1876), Benjamin Drew's *North-Side View of Slavery* (1856), Lydia Maria Child's *Isaac T. Hopper: A True Life* (1854), Wilson Armistead's *A Tribute for the Negro*

(1848). The WPA slave-narrative collection in the Library of Congress runs to seventeen volumes.[1] Perhaps most remarkable of this extensive literature are the four-score full-length autobiographies of slaves published before the Civil War. These books are the main focus of this essay.[2]

A literature so diffuse obviously varies widely in style, purpose, and competence. Some books are works of enduring value from a literary as well as "protest" perspective. The autobiographies of Frederick Douglass, Henry Bibb, and Solomon Northup fuse imaginative style with keenness of insight. They are penetrating and self-critical, superior autobiography by any standards. The quality of mind and spirit of their authors is apparent.

Because the best narratives reflect the imaginative minds of the most gifted and rebellious slaves, their value as reliable sources for the study of slavery has been questioned.[3] To doubt the relevancy of autobiographies written by exceptional slaves, however, is a specious argument in its inception. The great slave narrative, like all great autobiography, is the work of the especially perceptive viewer and writer. In describing his personal life, the sensitive and creative writer touches a deeper reality that transcends his individuality. Frederick Douglass, for example, was certainly an exceptional man, but his autobiography has much to teach us about the slaves around him, his friends and enemies on the plantation and in the city, and many other typical aspects of American slavery. Douglass is gibingly critical of the weaknesses of many of his fellow slaves. He derides those who adopted the master's code of behavior, those who fought for the baubles and goodies used as rewards and bribes, and those who dissipated their energy in wild

[1] Federal Writers' Project, "Slave Narratives: A Folk History of Slavery in the United States from Interviews with Former Slaves" (Typescripts, Washington, D.C., 1941), 17 vols.; Norman R. Yetman, "The Background of the Slave Narrative Collection," *American Quarterly,* XIX (Fall, 1967), 534–553; Benjamin A. Botkin, *Lay My Burden Down: A Folk History of Slavery* (Chicago, 1945).

[2] Two invaluable doctoral dissertations in the field of American literature provide an overview of the subject: Charles H. Nichols, Jr., "A Study of the Slave Narrative" (doctoral dissertation, Brown University, 1948); and Margaret Young Jackson, "An Investigation of Biographies and Autobiographies of American Slaves Published Between 1840 and 1860: Based upon the Cornell Special Slavery Collection (doctoral dissertation, Cornell University, 1954). Each contains a solid bibliography.

[3] This question has arisen with deadening regularity each time I've lectured on the subject. The argument generally made is that men like Douglass were so unusual that their experiences emphasize only the atypical aspects of slavery.

sports and drinking bouts during holidays.[4] Douglass presents a many-sided depiction of the slave experience—his is no papier-mâché book or antislavery tract. The historians who fail to use such a book or the narratives of a Bibb, a Brown, a Northup, or a Samuel Ringgold Ward because they are "exceptional" men might as well argue that Claude Brown and Eldridge Cleaver are unsuitable commentators on today's ghetto. To exclude the "exceptional" is to eliminate all strong autobiography as a distortion of the events of its time. Yet it is these writers whose books are most likely to interpret reality with insight and clarity.

The majority of slave narratives, like most autobiographies, are more parochial and weaker in literary quality. Many are confused. A blatant illustration is the rambling memoir of that delightful character William Grimes ("Old Grimes"), who escaped from Georgia, settled in New Haven, and became a handyman and general factotum to students at Yale. In his poorly organized tales, ends of stories precede beginnings, detailed descriptions of many jobs (horse trader, barber, gambler, waiter, laborer, pimp, grocer) and of his legal difficulties are presented in confusing bits and pieces, and at one juncture an unexplained wife arrives on the scene.[5]

Volumes compiled to raise money in the North for the purchase of relatives in slavery, such as the autobiographies of Lunsford Lane and Noah Davis, were written hurriedly and hawked from door to door.[6] As their books demonstrate, these authors were men of unusual ability and integrity, but they had little time for leisurely reminiscing or training in literary style. Lane, for example, worked around the clock to raise money for the food and freedom of his family. He simultaneously sold tobacco, pipes, and lumber, ran a hauling service, and labored as a domestic. Another author of a narrative, Davis, was a slave shoemaker and preacher who learned letters by copying customers' names from the shoes he repaired and passages from the New Testament. Their life stories abound with accounts of their own response to slavery and the

[4] Frederick Douglass, *Life and Times of Frederick Douglass* (New York, 1962), pp. 145–148.

[5] William Grimes, *Life of William Grimes, the Runaway Slave* (New Haven, 1855).

[6] *The Narrative of Lunsford Lane, Formerly of Raleigh, North Carolina* (Boston, 1848); Rev. Noah Davis, *A Narrative of the Life of Rev. Noah Davis, A Colored Man: Written by Himself, At the Age of Fifty-four* (Baltimore, 1859).

experiences of others. The very shortcomings of their books as literature in part testify to their authenticity as historical sources. The style of their books is a product of their schooling.

A number of slave narratives are of such doubtful validity that they may be shelved at the start. When the authenticity of a "memoir," *The Narrative of James Williams* (1838), dictated by one black man to the Quaker poet John Greenleaf Whittier, was questioned, Williams was nowhere to be found. The book was withdrawn from publication. Williams seems to have been a free Negro who culled stories from neighbors and invented others for a little ready cash. The antislavery press is full of warnings against such bogus fugitives. Two other books, *The Slave: Or the Memoirs of Archie Moore* (1836) and *The Autobiography of a Female Slave* (1856), were works of antislavery fiction.[7] The first was written by the American historian Richard Hildreth; the second was composed by Mattie Griffith, the white daughter of a Kentucky slaveholder. Such potential hoaxes led to careful investigation of the stories fugitives wrote for publication. Narrators were subjected to detailed questioning by committees of knowledgeable people; letters were written to former masters and neighbors for corroboration. A tale so seemingly improbable as the life of Henry Bibb led to an extensive correspondence with white Southerners, all of whom verified Bibb's account—the improbable was the real.[8] Solomon Northup's fantastic experiences were verified by a basketful of legal documents.

Because few slaves were literate enough to write their names, much less their autobiographies, and were thus forced to rely on amanuenses, usually abolitionists, scholars have rightly wondered where the slave's experience began and that of the antislavery recorder left off. Some have maintained that the typical slave narrative is so doctored that all are suspect as sources. Ulrich B. Phillips, for example, believed that most narratives "were issued with so much abolitionist editing that as a class their authenticity is doubtful."[9]

We should be wary of such sweeping generalizations that assign the majority of surviving books to the trash heap. Phillips cited the reminiscences of Josiah Henson as a prime instance of an unreliable

[7] C. H. Nichols, Jr., pp. 1–10.

[8] Henry Bibb, *Narrative of the Life and Adventures of Henry Bibb, An American Slave, Written by Himself* (New York, 1849), pp. i–x.

[9] Ulrich B. Phillips, *Life and Labor in the Old South* (Boston, 1929), p. 219.

slave narrative. My own analysis indicates that in the early editions it is an honest autobiography. Henson became a leader among the fugitives in Canada and received widespread coverage in the antislavery press. Many abrasive news stories resulted from his serious break with the Garrisonian abolitionists on the question of emigration to Canada but none questioned the authenticity of his autobiography. Also, the portions of his book that provide descriptions of incidents of his public career have proved authentic when checked against other sources.[10] In one of the most jolting passages in the slave-narrative literature, Henson describes how he, as a black driver, transported an entire group of fellow slaves through free territory in Ohio to a Kentucky plantation. He was repeatedly told all were legally free as soon as they touched Ohio soil, and crowds of free blacks in Cincinnati tried to convince him to remain—some showered him with curses—yet Henson pushed on, convinced that his integrity and self-esteem required him to do his master's bidding. "My pride was aroused in view of the importance of my responsibility, and heart and soul I became identified with my master's project of running off his negroes," he wrote. When Henson became a free man he admitted a deep sense of guilt in having obeyed these orders. Few men have had better cause to assign such disagreeable memories to the furthest reaches of their minds; yet this story, in all its hideous candor, is recorded in Josiah Henson's memoir. No scholarly or social purpose is served by assuming such narratives, *a priori*, to be unreliable sources.[11]

The most obviously false accounts readily give themselves away. The Preface to the life of the militant black abolitionist and fugitive slave J. W. Loguen, for example, relates how the author who recorded Loguen's experiences invented transitional incidents to tie together what seemed to him a disjointed account.[12] He gave an appearance of coherence to his story and destroyed its credibility in the process. Elleanor Eldridge's amanuensis, after the manner of third-rate contemporary fiction, spiced her book with imaginary and gushy romances. Innumerable paragraphs exhort the reader to sympathize with the trials of the lowly as they would with the meander-

[10] See the following issues of *The Liberator,* which deal with many aspects of his career and also include descriptions of his journeys to England, which coincide with materials in the autobiography: April 11, November 7, 1851; July 2, 1852; June 11, 1858.

[11] Josiah Henson, *Father Henson's Story of His Own Life* (Boston, 1858), pp. 48–54.

[12] *The Rev. J. W. Loguen as a Slave and as a Freeman: A Narrative of Real Life* (Syracuse, New York, 1859), p. iv.

ings of kings and queens.[13] In other lurid tales of suffering and woe and torture, cruelty after shocking cruelty appears with such deadening regularity that one easily recognizes the presence of a morality play, not the record of a human life. What the nineteenth century called "shame-shame" is pervasive in many narratives. Such clearly false or doctored accounts are excluded from this essay.

Nevertheless, the simple stories of slave life in most narratives, with their unembroidered descriptions of plantation activities, camp meetings in the woods, and many other aspects of daily routine, are striking in the consistency of themes that appear among individuals who lived on widely separated plantations, in different states, and in different decades. A coherent pattern of slave life emerges in these diverse testimonies, yet most of our present historical accounts of slavery exclude or underestimate the significance of these themes. Our histories have been written primarily from the surviving manuscript records of slaveholders and therefore tend to reflect the concerns and biases of the master caste. The witnesses who wrote or dictated narratives must be heeded if a balanced account of the history of slavery in the United States is to be written.

II

To understand the narrative literature it is important to keep in mind the relative ease of *occasional* escape from the plantation. The narratives are replete with stories of slaves who ran off to hide in woods and swamps, thereby escaping slavery for at least some portion of their lives. The frequency of such stories in slave autobiographies makes clear that running away was a common means of black protest and rebellion against slavery.

Repeatedly slaves speak of leaving in fear of sale or transportation to the Deep South, or as a means of protest against unusually brutal and unjustified physical punishment, or in an attempt to find friends, husbands, wives, children, and parents who were sold to a new master or sent to a different section of the country. It was not only possible for slaves to escape and hide out for long periods of

13 *Memoirs of Elleanor Eldridge* (Providence, 1847).

time, but the more skillful could also remain away almost as long as they chose. All the narrators are wise in the ways of nature, knowledgeable in animal lore and in techniques for foraging and living off the land. They often arranged to contact friends and family on the plantation to supply them with food on secret visits.

Many stories illustrate these themes. One was recorded by Lewis W. Paine, a white man, who was sent to prison for trying to help Samson, a giant slave, escape from Georgia:

> When [Samson] stayed out as long as he wished, he would send word to master that he would "come in," provided he would not punish him. . . . No one knew where he was, except a few of his faithful companions. He kept hid during the day, only venturing out at night, in order to procure necessary supplies. He was out about three months before he came to me. Those who are not acquainted with southern life will think this strange. But it not infrequently happens that they stay out for years in that way. There are large tracts of land, covered with heavy timber, containing not only deep and unpenetrable swamps, but caves, holes, shelving rocks and banks. In these they secrete themselves during the daytime, venturing abroad only by night, in pursuit of food, and such articles as they may need, or to see their brother slaves who they can trust. If they intend to "stay out" long, they prepare some way to cook, and by taking fowls, and once in a while a pig, they make out very well. . . . But if they are going to tarry long, they depend on such things as they can get, or others may give them.[14]

A Louisiana slave told of a fugitive who hid in a large hole in a dense forest. He gathered trees, leaves, and branches to protect himself not only from discovery but from storms and wild beasts. (A number of narrators allude to coming upon packs of wolves.) The fugitive clubbed birds and animals to obtain food and occasionally slipped back to the plantation where his mother gathered provisions for him. He continued to live in this manner "until freedom came" and finally emerged from the forest so covered with hair that he looked to others like the animals among whom he had lived so long.[15]

John Little, who later became a successful farmer in Canada,

[14] Lewis W. Paine, *Six Years in a Georgia Prison* (New York, 1851), pp. 28–29. See also Kenneth M. Stampp, *The Peculiar Institution: Slavery in the Ante-Bellum South* (New York, 1956), pp. 109–124.

[15] James B. Cade, "Out of the Mouths of Ex-Slaves," *Journal of Negro History*, XXII (April, 1935), 322.

stayed in the woods for two years. A powerful slave, Aaron, avoided being captured for a year. Another slave named Aaron Siddles hid out for five months. William Street hid for eight months. Another lived in the woods for five years before capture by a patrol—and then escaped again.[16] Moses Roper, the slave son of a plantation owner who once ran away to find his mother after being flogged, said, "It must be recollected that when a person is two miles from a house, in that part of the country, that he can hide himself in the woods for weeks, and I knew a slave who hid for six months without discovery, the trees being so thick." Roper later slipped out of bondage on a merchant ship.[17] Fugitive John Thompson wrote that few slaves of his acquaintance knew of "the friendly guidance of the north star" but all were aware of the potential tactical value of swamps and bushes.[18] Henry Bibb, an escape artist equal to Houdini who seemed able to come and go almost at his own discretion, put the case neatly when he said, "Among other good trades I learned the art of running away to perfection. I made a regular business of it, and never gave it up. . . ."[19]

One of the most illustrious slaves in American history, Nat Turner, took to the woods after his revolt collapsed and devised ingenious ways of avoiding capture. He burrowed into the earth, skillfully camouflaged his hideout with materials gathered in the forest, found ways to round up food, and emerged only at night. Though the entire slave South was on the lookout for him, Turner lived in this way—comfortably, he said—for about eight weeks. He was finally discovered by accident when a hunting dog strayed into his hideaway for a piece of meat. If Nat Turner could remain hidden for so long with an army of searchers on his trail, less valuable prey had an even better chance to go undetected.[20]

16 Benjamin Drew, *The Refugee, or the Narratives of Fugitive Slaves in Canada: A Northside View of Slavery* (Boston, 1856), *passim.* The story of the slave out for five years is in *The Liberator,* October 1, 1852.

17 Moses Roper, *A Narrative of the Adventures of Moses Roper . . . .* (London, 1840), p. 59.

18 John Thompson, *The Life of John Thompson, a Fugitive Slave: Containing His History of Twenty-five Years in Bondage, and His Providential Escape* (Worcester, Mass., 1856), pp. 27–28.

19 Henry Bibb, p. 15.

20 *The Confession, Trial and Execution of Nat Turner, The Negro Insurgent* (Washington, D.C., 1910), pp. 13–14.

The relative ease of occasional escape *within* the plantation South must be contrasted with the difficulty of escape to freedom in the North. Narrators tell us that most slaves on plantations lacked a sense of geography and a knowledge of the outside world. Even a man as inquisitive as Frederick Douglass admitted that there was a time in his life when he hadn't heard of the North; he learned about the abolitionists only by accident.[21] One of John Brown's admirers and followers, James Redpath, who interviewed numbers of slaves, expressed amazement at their lack of geographical knowledge. Redpath met slaves who had never heard of Europe, did not know their own states, and could not tell him the terminus of the railroad that ran by their own locality.[22]

When a Boston visitor asked Henry Watson why he didn't try to leave the plantation, Watson "told him, with a laugh, I knew not where to go. . . . He informed me of . . . the great anti-slavery movement . . . a subject which I was entirely ignorant of before. . . ."[23] When Leonard Black landed in New York City he asked a man if there was such a place as Boston. "I was so ignorant I knew not whether Boston was a State or city," Black recorded. "In fact, I scarcely knew there was such a place. Slavery is as ill adapted for obtaining this kind of knowledge as all other kinds."[24] Henry Banks recalled he heard of a free country "somewhere" but wasn't sure where it was.[25] When the kidnaped Peter Still returned to Philadelphia after a lifetime of slavery, he was told by his brother, black abolitionist William Still, that their mother lived in New Jersey and they would go together to visit her. Peter hesitated to believe him because he had never heard of New Jersey.[26] On Henry Bibb's first escape he was befriended by a black man in Cincinnati who said the abolitionists would help transport him to Canada. Bibb was unbelieving: "This was the first time in my life that ever I had heard of such people," he wrote. "I supposed that

21 Frederick Douglass, pp. 81–87.

22 James Redpath, *The Roving Editor: Or, Talks with Slaves in the Southern States* (New York, 1859), pp. 65–66, and *passim.*

23 Henry Watson, *Narrative of Henry Watson: A Fugitive Slave* (Boston, 1848), p. 34.

24 Leonard Black, *The Life and Sufferings of Leonard Black: A Fugitive from Slavery* (New Bedford, Mass., 1847), pp. 33–34.

25 *The Refugee*, pp. 75–76.

26 Kate E. R. Pickard, ed., *The Kidnapped and the Ransomed: Being the Personal Recollections of Peter Still and His Wife 'Vina,' After Forty Years of Slavery* (Syracuse, New York, 1856), pp. 247–251.

they were a different race. . . ." Bibb aptly called slavery "the graveyard of the mind."[27]

Many narrators blame such ignorance on practiced deceit by their masters; they argued that the master caste consciously exploited slave ignorance and gullibility for its own advantage. There is abundant evidence in the narratives to demonstrate at least the partial truth of that charge. One slave asked his master who abolitionists were, and was told that they rounded up slaves for sale in Deep South markets.[28] One of Harriet Tubman's major tasks during the Civil War was to counsel plantation blacks that it was safe to board Northern gunboats.[29] Numbers of slaves had been encouraged to believe that Yankees were cannibals who looked upon them as tasty morsels. The memoirs of the sharp-witted Lewis Clarke record a convincing illustration of this fear.

> I will not forget all the horrid stories slaveholders tell about Canada [Clarke wrote]. They assured the slave that, when they get hold of slaves in Canada, they make various uses of them. Sometimes they *skin* the *head*, and wear the wool on their coat collars—put them into the lead-mines, with both eyes out—the young slaves they eat; as for the red coats, they are sure death to the slave. However ridiculous to a well-informed person such stories may appear, they work powerfully upon the excited imagination of an ignorant slave.[30]

Leonard Black said derisively that "Slaves are taught ignorance as we teach our children knowledge."[31]

In the deepest sense the entire South was a prison house, and all white men, solely because of their skin color, were prison keepers.[32] By law and custom every white was permitted to stop any black along the road and ask him to present his pass or freedom papers or explain why he was away from the plantation. To collect the reward on a fugitive or perhaps claim the person of a slave whose master could not be located must have been enticing bait for the poor whites who patrolled the Southern countryside. A good

[27] Henry Bibb, pp. 50–51.

[28] *The Kidnapped and the Ransomed*, p. 247.

[29] Sarah Hopkins Bradford, *Scenes in the Life of Harriet Tubman* (Auburn, New York, 1869), pp. 38–41.

[30] *Narratives of the Sufferings of Lewis and Milton Clarke, Sons of a Soldier of the Revolution. . . .* (Boston, 1846), pp. 40–41.

[31] Leonard Black, pp. 50–51.

[32] The prison analogy is also used in George M. Frederickson and Christopher Lasch, "Resistance to Slavery," *Civil War History*, XIII (December, 1967), 315–329.

catch not only seemed a fulfillment of one's communal responsibility but also might mean instant wealth. The most thrilling passages of slave autobiographies deal with strategies fugitives used for handling or avoiding such confrontations with whites. Andrew Jackson wrote that he "learned to look on every white man as my foe, and dared not pass near to any one."[33] Lewis Clarke described slave anxiety in even contemplating escape to the North: "All the white part of mankind, that he [the slave] has ever seen, are enemies to him and all his kindred. How can he venture where none but white faces shall greet him?"[34]

Further, slaves had to avoid "guards," both black and white. Most slaves and free blacks in the narratives were willing to assist fugitives, but certain black Judases sabotaged the escape plans of many. Henry Bibb's schemes were exposed at least four times by black traitors; the escape plans of Leonard Black, Frederick Douglass, and John Little were revealed by fellow Negroes, Black's by his closest friend. Little was betrayed by a free black who received a ten-dollar reward for his service. James Adams of Virginia said he feared to tell even his father and mother of his plans to leave.[35]

The escape of three slaves as described by black Garrisonian William Wells Brown to the New England Anti-Slavery Society was a dramatic example of such treachery. One of the three, who was nearly white, had impersonated the master of the other two, but when they had traveled far away from home territory, the white slave claimed the other two as his property and sold them. "He had not black blood enough in him to make him honest!" Brown said.[36] When free blacks captured such men they took care of business. One black worker in the employ of Southern slaveholders was tarred and feathered in Washington, Pennsylvania.[37] Another from Kentucky was bombarded with boulders and brickbats in Detroit and finally locked in prison for his own safety. "Kill him," "murder the villain," the crowds shouted. One powerful black woman said she was determined to have "his heart's blood."[38]

The dominant mechanisms of control in the slave society made

33 *Narrative and Writings of Andrew Jackson of Kentucky* (Syracuse, 1847), p. 15.
34 *Narratives of Lewis and Milton Clarke*, p. 31.
35 Leonard Black, pp. 22, 25, 29; *The Refugee*, pp. 19, 205.
36 *The Liberator*, June 4, 1858.
37 *Ibid.*, August 29, 1856.
38 *Ibid.*, September 17, 1858.

possible a social system which permitted a measure of occasional freedom. If the experiences of slave narrators are in the least way typical, large numbers of slaves were on the move from Saturday night through Sunday and during such holidays as Easter, Christmas, and July Fourth. These were times to visit wives, husbands, lovers, children, and friends on neighboring plantations. This leniency of control acted as a necessary emotional outlet for the entire regime. The master caste would not have permitted such wanderings unless it could be certain that the man or woman who departed Saturday night would be back in the quarters the next day. "It becomes a matter of mutual interest for each [master] to protect his neighbor's 'rights' in order to render his own more secure," the black Andrew Jackson commented. Whenever he passed whites along a road, Jackson was asked: "Where do you belong, nigger?" "Whose boy are you?" "Where are you going, nigger?"[39] Another slave said that under these conditions "it is almost a matter of impossibility for a slave to escape."[40]

This barrier to escape poses a limitation of the use of slave narratives as sources. Most though not all of the books were written by men and women who were closest to free territory and who escaped from the Border States, not the Deep South: few escaped permanently from plantations in Louisiana, Mississippi, and Alabama. Solomon Northup, Henry Watson, Peter Still, and Henry Bibb all describe parts of their lives spent in the heartland of the cotton-producing South, but these accounts are not typical. It is unfortunate for comparative purposes that we have so few descriptions of slavery as slaves saw it in the Deep South. The efficient slave control that choked off routes of escape also blocked history's access to full understanding of black bondage in America.

Successful fugitives passed through chinks in the wall of the closed society. It was an article of lore, repeated in most slave autobiographies, that the best time to plan a permanent escape was on a Saturday night or during some holiday when slaves were on the move on visits and fugitives were, therefore, least likely to be detected. Even to conceive the possibility of escape under these conditions required a special quality of mind: imagination, independ-

[39] *Narrative of Andrew Jackson*, p. 10.

[40] *Narrative of Henry Watson*, p. 32. Note the similar comment of Philip Younger in *The Refugee*, p. 249: "Escape from Alabama is almost impossible,–if a man escapes, it is by the skin of his teeth."

ence, cunning, daring, and a sense of self-pride. It required a strategic appearance of obedience to their masters, like seeming most satisfied at the moment they were most discontented. ("At that time, of all times, he must appear best satisfied with slavery, least anxious for freedom. . . .")[41] It called for the use of subtle psychological weapons. It demanded all the shrewdness and practiced deceit one finds in such abundance in the rich folklore of Old John, the symbolic slave hero who mastered the art of tricking "Ole Massa," of fooling him, of "puttin' him on."

III

The narratives permit a measure of access to the privacy of the mind of a slave and the conversations that took place in the slave cabin. No adequate analysis can be made of the much debated question of the impact of slavery on the personalities of bondsmen without hearing the stories slaves told one another when their owners were not around. As such they are crucial evidence of the ideas that passed through a slave's consciousness, his mind, if not his mouth. Such stories, crammed with aggressive humor—and wit is one of mankind's most useful aggressive tools[42]—reveal the difficulty of enslaving a man's mind as one has enslaved his body. Lewis Clarke, a slave who recorded much of this inside humor, said he would not vouch for the truth of many anecdotes, but they were tales "slaves delight to tell each other."[43] Many of the tales are surely apocryphal in a technical sense—they probably refer to things slaves wished to say as well as to the things they said.

Some slaves undoubtedly felt loyalty and affection for their owners, but the stories of fugitives describe even this relationship as one of ambivalence. Slaves often held two overlapping attitudes: a willingness to accept life with an owner who treated them fairly,

[41] Samuel Ringgold Ward, *Autobiography of A Fugitive Negro: His Anti-Slavery Labours in the United States, Canada and England* (London, 1855), p. 162.

[42] Sigmund Freud, "Wit and Its Relation to the Unconscious," in Dr. A. A. Brill, ed., *The Basic Writings of Sigmund Freud* (New York, 1938), pp. 697–702; Donald C. Simmons, "Protest Humor: Folkloristic Reaction to Prejudice," *American Journal of Psychiatry*, CXX (December 1963), 567–570.

[43] *Narratives of Lewis and Milton Clarke*, p. 114.

an *entente cordiale* rather than a feeling of serious devotion; and a private sense of irreverence for many of their master's ideas. This irreverence was the subject of much slave humor.

Peter Randolph, one of sixty-six slaves emancipated on the death of their owner, told a story he had overheard on his plantation in Virginia. The following conversation is said to have occurred between the slave Pompey and his master, as the slaveowner prepared to fight a duel:[44]

> Pompey, how do I look?
> O, massa, mighty.
> What do you mean "mighty," Pompey?
> Why, massa, you look noble.
> What do you mean by "noble"?
> Why, sar, you just look like one *lion.*
> Why, Pompey, where have you ever seen a lion?
> I see one down in yonder field the other day, massa.
> Pompey, you foolish fellow, that was a *jackass.*
> Was it, massa? Well you look just like him.

It is quite unlikely that this confrontation took place as Pompey remembered it, but it is not unreasonable to assume that he wished it had, or thought of saying such things, or told other slaves like Randolph that he had replied in this manner. That the slaves told such stories to one another is a clue to their state of mind—and there are numbers of similar examples in the narrative literature.

Lewis Clarke of Kentucky recalled meeting two slaves sent out to dig a grave for their departed owner and recounted their conversation at the gravesite:

> Two slaves were sent out to dig a grave for old master. They dug it very deep. As I passed by I asked Jess and Bob what in the world they dug it so deep for. It was down six or seven feet. I told them there would be a fuss about it, and they had better fill it up some. Jess said it suited him exactly. Bob said he would not fill it up; he wanted to get the old man as near *home* as possible. When we got a stone to put on his grave, we hauled the largest we could find, so as to fasten him down as strong as possible.[45]

[44] Quoted in Margaret Young Jackson, pp. 232–233.
[45] Quoted in *ibid.*, pp. 234–235.

And another from North Carolina, remembered by Lunsford Lane: One evening, Derby, a slave of the state treasurer, passed by to tell of the funeral of another respected state officer. The family of the deceased was greatly pleased that Derby had voluntarily placed crape on his hat as a sign of mourning—"they thought it envinced great consideration for the family and friends, and for which he deserved great praise." Derby told his black friends that his motives were misunderstood and "he would be glad to have kept it upon his hat until they were all as decently placed beneath the sod as Secretary White, if that would aid him in securing his freedom."[46]

Slaves on Solomon Northup's Louisiana plantation referred to their master privately as "hogeye" and "hogjaw"—[47] hardly terms of endearment. Another slave, "Faithful Jack," recalled a supposed conversation he had with his master at the deathbed. "Farewell, massa!" he told his buddies he had said. "Pleasant journey: you soon be dere, massa—[it's] all de way down hill!"[48] Others remembered refusing to be buried in the same grave as their owners in fear of the devil, "Old Sam," taking the wrong body.[49]

The ultimate in irreverences was the occasional letter fugitives sent to former masters after they had successfully "taken the long walk." Jackson Whitney made his "feet feel for Canada" when his master attempted to sell him after having previously agreed to let Whitney buy himself out of slavery. Whitney told William Riley, his former master, that he could now put his "conscience in his pocket"—a variation of the expression "to put a slave in one's pocket," which meant "to sell a slave." The slave informed his previous owner that he was now working for another fugitive from Kentucky whose farm was large, productive, and "so level that there are not hills enough on it to hide a dog. . . ." The country was not cold and barren, as he had been told, but beautiful and fertile. Whitney only wished his master could see how enjoyable his life was. He also said he knew the Lord would punish Riley for forcing him to abandon his family. The letter concluded: "You must not

46 Rev. William G. Hawkins, ed., *Lunsford Lane or Another Helper from North Carolina* (Boston, 1863), p. 84.

47 *Twelve Years A Slave: Narrative of Solomon Northup* (New York, 1853), pp. 197, 220.

48 Quoted in Margaret Young Jackson, pp. 304–305.

49 *Narratives of Lewis and Milton Clarke*, p. 119.

consider that it is a slave talking to 'massa' now, but one as free as yourself. . . . I pretended all the time that I thought you or some one else had a better right to me than I had to myself, which, you know, is rather hard thinking."[50]

A slave who settled in Windsor, Canada West, wrote her mistress that she loved the white children she had nursed so faithfully but she appreciated "breathing free air" more. When safely out of the country, a young man returned by mail the keys to his master's storehouse.[51] Milton Clarke taunted his owner with a note from Oberlin telling him not to worry too much about his ex-slave or the loss of the two hundred dollars a year Clarke paid him for the right to hire his own time (find self-employment): "he had found by experience he had wit enough to take care of himself, and he thought the care of his master was not worth the two hundred dollars a year which he had been paying for it, for four years; that, on the whole, if his master would be quiet and contented, he thought he should do very well."[52]

IV

A considerable portion of most slave narratives deals with the methods of escape. The narrative literature probably acquired some of its popularity in the 1840's and 1850's because of the excitement of these tales. The melodrama and romance of the escape —the elements that Harriet Beecher Stowe skillfully weaves into *Uncle Tom's Cabin*—are less significant, however, than the evidence of the demands of courage and imagination required for execution of a successful escape plan. Such shrewdness and guile were characteristic of slave response in other less dramatic aspects of the plantation experience. For many slaves deception was a socially useful weapon of survival.

A number of the most impressive stories of practiced deceit deal with stealing food. As Eugene D. Genovese has shown in his brilliant analysis of the plantation economy, it was difficult to sup-

50 *The Weekly Anglo-African*, July 23, 1859.
51 *The Liberator*, January 5, 1855.
52 *Narratives of Lewis and Milton Clarke*, pp. 47–48.

ply bondsmen with a nutritionally balanced diet that would satisfy the body needs of hard-working laborers.[53] Slaves who were hungry, therefore, stole food; others undoubtedly also found thieving satisfying as a form of aggression and revenge. Inventiveness was necessary if one was to avoid detection. Aunt Peggy, for example, was an artist at stealing little pigs. One day the "Philistines were upon her" as she was boiling her catch in a large kettle. Peggy put a door on the kettle, seated her daughter on the door, covered the young girl with a heavy quilt, and told the inquisitive overseer the child had a heavy cold and was taking a steam bath. Andrew Jackson described how slaves stole pigs, skinned possums, buried the pig's hide, and told anyone who asked that they were eating possum. Others stole turkeys and chickens but left enough feathers scattered about to make it appear the foxes had done it. Some stole potatoes and drove hogs into the field and called master to show him all the damage the animals had done. There are literally hundreds of such tales in the narratives.[54]

Cunning and intelligence had to be concealed. Numbers of slaves who appeared *too intelligent* were sometimes difficult to sell: they were assumed to be troublesome. A man as perceptive and enterprising as Lunsford Lane devoted as much effort to hiding his abilities as he did to raising money to buy his family out of slavery. Lane always wore shabby clothing and looked very poor, as he hid every penny he earned. He told no one but his wife how much money he had saved.

> Ever after I entertained the first idea of being free [Lane explained], I had endeavored so to conduct myself as not to become obnoxious to the white inhabitants, knowing as I did their power, and their hostility to the colored people. The two points necessary in such a case I had kept constantly in mind. First, I had made no display of the little property or money I possessed, but in every way I wore as much as possible the aspect of slavery. Second, I had

53 Eugene D. Genovese, *The Political Economy of Slavery: Studies in the Economy and Society of the Slave South* (New York, 1965), pp. 44–46.

54 "The slaves on Col. A's plantation had to provide and prepare the supper for the expected vast 'turn out,' which was no light matter; and as slaves like on such occasions to pattern as much as possible after their master's family, the result was, to meet the emergency of the case, they *took*, without saying, 'by your leave, sir,' some property belonging to their master, reasoning among themselves, as slaves often do, that it can not be *stealing*, because 'it belongs to massa, and so do we. . . .' " Steward, *Twenty-two Years a Slave*, p. 29. Charles H. Nichols, Jr., pp. 123–124; Narrative of Andrew Jackson, pp. 27–28; Ward, *Autobiography of a Fugitive*, pp. 175–177; *Narrative of Solomon Northup*, pp. 129–130.

> never appeared to be even so intelligent as I really was. This all colored people at the south, free and slaves, find it peculiarly necessary for their own comfort and safety to observe.[55]

Some of the best stories of artifice were told by Solomon Northup. As a black driver, he once supervised the punishment of three slaves caught stealing melons. When the master drove off for a while Northup released his captives from the stocks but made sure they were back before the slave owner returned. "Aha! Ye haven't been strolling about much to-day," the master said when he came back. Northup was so dexterous in the use of a whip he was able to throw the lash within a "hair's breadth of the back, the ear, the nose, without . . . touching them." He pretended to flog, and the slaves acted as though they were seriously injured: "Uncle Abram, with an appearance of honesty peculiar to himself, would declare roundly I had just whipped them worse than General Jackson whipped the enemy at New-Orleans."[56]

References to a secret slave communications system appear in many narratives. Some, like Douglass, talk of double meanings in songs, but most just mention the fact that the system existed. Andrew Jackson wrote that slaves "have a means of communication with each other, altogether unknown to their masters, or to the people of the free states." John Thompson said the same thing. The fugitive blacksmith who became one of the most influential black clergymen in the North, J. W. C. Pennington, wrote: "The telegraph, which by the speed of lightning carries news from one end of this land to another, does not more certainly report news than the slaves do one to another."[57]

One slave said a "lie is often so useful to them, and the truth so often disastrous, and their aptness at a lie is such, that they take in sustaining it an air of assurance and tranquility which imposes on strangers. . . ."[58] Henry Bibb, the undoubted master of them all, repeatedly described deception as his only armor: "The only weapon of self defence that I could use successfully, was that of deception. It is useless for a poor slave, to resist the white man in a

[55] *Narrative of Lunsford Lane,* p. 31.

[56] *Narrative of Solomon Northup,* pp. 129–130, 226–227.

[57] *Narrative of Andrew Jackson,* p. 15; *Life of John Thompson,* pp. 62–63; J. W. C. Pennington, *A Narrative of Events of the Life of J. H. Banks, An Escaped Slave, From the Cotton State of Alabama, in America* (Liverpool, 1861), p. 20; *Scenes in the Life of Harriet Tubman,* p. 40.

[58] *Narrative of Andrew Jackson,* p. 29.

slaveholding State. Public opinion and the law is against him; and resistance in many cases is death to the slave, while the law declares, that he shall submit or die."[59]

Thieving and deception as forms of aggression seem to be normal human responses to unjust treatment and confinement; one finds them beyond the limits of the southern plantation. A fascinating parallel development took place among Americans of Japanese descent in their years of imprisonment in so-called "relocation centers" during World War II. Here was an ethnic group that historically put the highest premium on honesty, that ritualized just standards of public behavior, that had the lowest rates of criminality of all minority groups not only in the United States but in Hawaii and Canada as well. In the psychic pressure cooker of mass imprisonment, however, traditional forms of behavior simply evaporated. In one desert camp at Poston, Arizona, building materials were stolen with abandon. Lumber was taken from contractors, wire was clipped from refrigerators, cement was robbed from the stockpile of items used to build a school. The longer the Japanese were incarcerated the bolder their pillaging became.

And the explanations they used to define their behavior were similar to those used by slaves. The Japanese-Americans insisted they were only "borrowing" items that justly belonged to them; that they were wards of the government and entitled to a fairer share of government services; that the people as well as the physical material might both be looked upon as "property" of the government and therefore incapable of theft from one another. "The residents, with their tongues in their cheeks called this 'borrowing,'" a historian of Poston recorded, "and rationalized that the material had been bought for their use, so they were not really stealing, but only putting it to a more immediate purpose. . . ."[60]

When the Canadian-Japanese community was forcibly uprooted in the same years about half the population was resettled in abandoned mining villages and refurbished ghost towns. Here too traditional social controls and mores underwent rapid and radical change. The Japanese immigrants had historically prided themselves on taking care of their own economic needs, of avoiding public charity and

59 *Narrative of Henry Bibb*, p. 17.

60 Alexander Leighton, *The Governing of Men: General Principles and Recommendations Based on Experience at a Japanese Relocation Camp* (Princeton, New Jersey, 1945), p. 148.

institutions. In all the countries to which the Japanese migrated it was customary for them to contribute more money to community funds than they ever withdrew from them. In the Canadian "interior settlements," the ghost towns, these standard social values were reversed. A premium was placed on cunning, cheating and deception. As public expenditures were adjusted to income, many Japanese refused to make honest disclosures of their wages and savings; they took an "exceedingly hostile" view to all government officials and argued that the government was responsible for their plight and therefore had to assume the burden of their maintenance. "In pre-evacuation days it was considered a disgrace for a Japanese to accept relief," sociologist Forrest E. La Violette wrote. "With evacuation, acceptance was made easy by the belief that such help was owed them by the government, and if it were denied to them, the applicants would become extremely hostile."[61]

Fugitive slaves honed the art of pretense into a sharp-edged tool of self-defense. There are innumerable stories of women who pretended to be men and men who made wigs of horses' manes to dress as women, or wore false beards. An amazing use of disguises permitted William and Ellen Craft to get to Boston, and their story became familiar throughout the North.[62] Numbers of light-skinned slaves passed for whites, some audaciously stopping at the best restaurants and hotels to exchange gossip on the price of land, cotton, and slaves. A man like Douglass simply pretended to be free and got away with it.

A number of fugitives—some successfully, others not—used elaborate devices to escape. Some had themselves packed in crates or barrels and shipped north. One man tied himself to the underside of a night passenger train. Those pursued by bloodhounds sometimes put red pepper on their limbs or dug into graves and used the dust on their bodies to throw off their human scent. A fugitive in desperate need of a skiff tore off a wooden gate and floated down a river. Some intentionally asked directions of suspicious whites and made sure to go the opposite way. Slaves in port towns stowed away on ships. John Little and his wife traveled only at night and were so afraid to light a fire they ate only raw meat.

61 Forrest E. La Violette, *The Canadian Japanese and World War II: A Sociological and Psychological Account* (Toronto, 1948), p. 106.

62 William Craft, *Running a Thousand Miles for Freedom, or the Escape of William and Ellen Craft from Slavery* (London, 1860).

One group of fugitives escaped in the winter on a sleigh. Forced to ford a stream, they dismantled the sleigh and built a makeshift bridge. Stories of daring and courage were legion. William Johnson refused to turn back, despite frostbitten feet, until he was safe in Canada. Numbers of men who carried pistols and bowie knives vowed to kill anyone who tried to stop them. Some fought desperately for their lives when confronted; one man cut open his captors with a scythe. Men who escaped to the North sometimes returned for their wives, and at least one woman came back for her husband.[63]

A number of sensitive antebellum commentators recognized their courage and hailed the fugitives as men of great imagination and valor. "They are among the heroes of our age," Charles Sumner wrote. "Romance has no stories of more thrilling interest than theirs. Classical antiquity has preserved no examples of adventurous trial more worthy of renown."[64]

Thomas Wentworth Higginson declared that it was his solemn conviction, from

> years of intercourse with fugitive slaves, that if the truth could be fairly told to-day, we white Anglo-Saxons on this continent must yield the palm of native heroism to the negro. I tell you, that if you had seen and heard the things some of us have seen and heard you would think so too. . . . Go among the thousands of refugees in Canada, hear their simple story, talk with the men and women, learn what they have gone through in their efforts to escape, seven times seven repeated, more than once, and you will learn of courage which puts to shame the puny efforts of us who call ourselves men of courage here and now. There is not a great deed in history, there is not an act of self-devotion . . . there is not one single item in the long catalogue of self-consecration in the ages which I cannot match with some act as heroic and noble, done by an African. . . .[65]

In an essay titled "Physical Courage" for the *Atlantic Monthly* Higginson further explored the theme.

> These men and women, who have tested their courage in the lonely

[63] The antislavery press recorded these stories in each issue. My examples are from *The Liberator*, July 11, 1851; September 3, October 1, 1852; August 19, 1853; January 5, 19, 1855; April 4, May 9, October 3, 1856; June 19, September 11, 1857; August 27, 1858; March 25, 1859; April 27, 1860; and also *The Refugee, passim.*, for numerous others.

[64] *The Liberator*, October 22, 1852.

[65] *Ibid.*, May 28, 1858.

> swamp [he said], who have starved on the prairies, hidden in the holds, clung to locomotives, ridden hundreds of miles cramped in boxes, head downward, equally near to death if discovered or deserted—and who have then, after enduring all this, gone voluntarily back to risk it over again, for the sake of wife or child—what are we pale faces, that we should claim a rival capacity with theirs for heroic deeds?[66]

V

Ingenuity, deception, courage, and aggressive humor also pervade the stories of slave religious attitudes and behavior. Some of the most impressive passages in the autobiographies deal with the slave's quest for meaningful spiritual guidance.

Many fugitives were men of piety and unbending social standards. Lunsford Lane's father, Edward, was noted as "a man of prayer," and his son as well. Lunsford read scripture with regularity, attended church as often as he could, and was Puritanical in personal behavior.[67] Noah Davis, William Troy, R. S. W. Savrick, Alexander Hemsley, Dan Josiah Lockhart, Daniel West, Eli Johnson, and Josiah Henson were slave preachers, "professors," "exhorters." Davis believed the Lord revealed himself to him and "called me to talk to sinners." Henson was such a skillful evangelist that he could proselytize the most "callous and indifferent" souls who heard him. Austin Steward was a religious zealot, a True Believer—the pages of his autobiography ooze weighty homilies. He moralized on "rude music," gaming, and the nefarious liquor trade. As a freeman he wrote a pamphlet showing how consumption of alcoholic beverages led down the road to perdition.[68]

Many narrators went to school to become clergymen after they acquired their freedom: J. W. C. Pennington, Peter Randolph, J. W. Loguen, Josiah Henson, Noah Davis, Samuel Ringgold Ward.

66 [Thomas Wentworth Higginson], "Physical Courage," *Atlantic Monthly*, XIII (November, 1858), 732.

67 *The Liberator*, February 26, 1858.

68 *The Refugee, passim.*; Josiah Henson, p. 57; Austin Steward, *Twenty-two Years a Slave and Forty Years a Freeman* (Rochester, 1857); *Narrative of Lunsford Lane; Narrative of Noah Davis.*

Perhaps the most well-known fugitive of his generation, Anthony Burns, is a perfect case in point. The attempt to free Burns after he escaped to Boston in 1854 and the subsequent battle to return him to slavery electrified the North. Burns, as a slave, was a devout man, a Baptist preacher who tried "to lead his fellow-servants to a knowledge of the Redeemer." When Burns acquired his freedom he delivered a speech in the Reverend Dr. Pennington's church in New York City in which he described how Christ came to him as a young boy. "Until my tenth year I did not care what came of me," he said, "but soon after I began to hear about a North, and to feel the necessity for freedom of soul and body." Burns went on to Oberlin for a religious education, was ordained and settled in St. Catherine's, Canada West, as the spiritual leader of Zion Baptist Church.[69] Within this context one also thinks of the intensely religious frame of mind of such people as Harriet Tubman, Sojourner Truth, and Nat Turner. Harriet Tubman, for example, said she prayed all the time about "my work, everywhere, I prayed, an' I groaned to de Lord."[70]

It is essential that this sense of piety among slaves be separated as a concept from the attitudes bondsmen expressed toward the kind of religious fare they often received on the plantation. For centuries slaves had been admonished to put to memory and soul those portions of the sacred books which advised servants to be especially obedient to their masters.[71] Henry Watson paraphrased the typical sermon he heard at Vicksburg (before Grant):

> Suppose you do not deserve it, or at least do not deserve so much punishment for the fault you committed, you perhaps have escaped a great many more, and are at last paid for all. Or, suppose you are quite innocent of what is laid to your charge, and suffer wrongfully in that particular thing; is it not possible you may have done some other bad thing which was never discovered, and that Almighty God, who saw you doing it would not let you escape without punishment some time or another? And ought you not in such a case to give glory to him, and be thankful that he would rather

69 *The Liberator*, July 7, 1854; March 9, December 14, 1855; February 22, May 9, 1856, August 13, 1858; August 30, 1861; August 22, 1862.

70 *Scenes in the Life of Harriet Tubman*, p .14.

71 See the eighteenth-century hack sermon reprinted in Gilbert Osofsky, ed., *The Burden of Race: A Documentary History of Negro-White Relations in America* (New York, 1967), pp. 39–44; and also Luther P. Jackson, "Religious Instruction of Negroes, 1830–1860, with Special Reference to South Carolina," *Journal of Negro History*, XV (January, 1930), 72–114.

> punish you in this world for your wickedness than destroy your soul for it in the next? But, suppose that this even was not the case,—a case hardly to be imagined; and that you have by no means, known or unknown, deserved the correction you have received, there is this great comfort in it, that if you bear it patiently and leave your cause in the hands of God, he will reward you for it in heaven; and this punishment you suffer unjustly here, shall turn to your exceeding great glory hereafter.[72]

That Watson neither distorted the tone nor intent of the spiritual verbiage passed down to him and other slaves is illustrated by the following catechisms for bondsmen—the first from South Carolina,[73] the second from Mississippi:[74]

> Who keeps *snakes* and all bad things from hurting you?—*God does.*
>
> Who gave you a master and a mistress?—*God gave them to me.*
>
> Who says that you must obey them?—*God says that I must.*
>
> What book tells you these things?—*The Bible.*
>
> How does God do all His work?—*He always does it right.*
>
> Does God love to work?—*Yes, God is always at work.*
>
> Do the good angels work?—*Yes, they do what God tells them.*
>
> Do they love to work?—*Yes, they love to please God.*
>
> What does God say about your work?—*He that will not work shall not eat.*
>
> Did Adam and Eve have to work?—*Yes, they were to keep the garden.*
>
> Was it hard to keep that garden?—*No, it was very easy.*
>
> What makes the crops so hard to grow now?—*Sin makes it.*
>
> What makes you lazy?—*My own wicked heart.*
>
> How do you know your heart is wicked?—*I feel it every day.*
>
> What teaches you so many wicked things?—*The Devil.*
>
> Must you let the Devil teach you?—*No, I must not.*

> Q. Are not servants bound to obey their masters?
>
> A. Yes. The Bible exhorts servants to be obedient to their masters, and to please them well in all things, not answering again.
>
> Q. If the master be unreasonable, may the servant disobey?
>
> A. No. The Bible says, "Servants, be subject to your masters with all fear, not only to the good and gentle, but also to the forward."

72 *Narrative of Henry Watson,* pp. 30–31.
73 *The Liberator,* June 16, 1854.
74 *Ibid.,* July 17, 1857.

Q. What does the Bible say to servants on this subject?

A. They are to obey, not with eye-service as men-pleasers, but as the servants of Christ.

Q. If servants suffer unjustly, what are they to do?

A. They must bear it patiently.

Q. Ought servants to rebel against the authority of their masters?

A. No. It is a sin against God and man.

Q. Should servants ever run away?

A. No. If they do, they sin against God and man.

Q. How do we know this?

A. The Bible tells us that the apostle Paul found a servant who had run away from his master, and he sent him home.

Q. Why did not Paul conceal him, that he might be free?

A. Because he would not make religion a cloak for injustice.

The narrators tell us some slaves accepted such gospel, but they also say considerable numbers of bondsmen thought such preaching was hypocritical perversion of holy scripture. White preachers were described by one slave as men with "God in the face, and the devil in the heart.[75] Independently of one another, and from different sections of the South, many slave narrators also recorded these sermons in order to mock them. Andrew Jackson, Harriet Jacobs, John Thompson, Frederick Douglass, Peter Randolph, Lunsford Lane, and Solomon Northup, independent of one another, ridiculed the supposedly devout preacher and slaveholder as hypocrites. In his earliest years as an antislavery lecturer Frederick Douglass convulsed Northern audiences by derisively mimicking sermons he had listened to: "Oh, consider the wonderful goodness of God! Look at your hard, horny hands, your strong muscular frames, and see how mercifully he has adapted you to the duties you are to fulfill! . . . while to your masters who have slender frames and long delicate fingers, he has given brilliant intellects, that they may do the thinking while you do the working."[76] Harriet Jacobs said that after listening to a sermon on obedience, "We went home highly amused at brother Pike's gospel teaching, we determined to hear him again."[77] Peter Randolph recalled the Sunday Jem Fulcrum fell from his seat in the congregation onto the floor. Minister Shell

[75] *Life of John Thompson*, p. 64.

[76] Part of Douglass's spoof sermon is reprinted in Benjamin Quarles, *Frederick Douglass* (New York, 1948), p. 363.

[77] Quoted in Charles H. Nichols, Jr., p. 143.

believed he had preached Brother Jem into ecstasy but all the slaves knew that Jem had fallen asleep.[78]

And here is a classic illustration of the tension of conflicting ideas within one culture. All commentators, including the evangelists who came South after the Civil War to set up schools for the freedmen, refer to the towering religiosity of slaves. The fervency of a black prayer meeting shocked white fundamentalists who had spent their lives drumming up a camp-meeting enthusiasm in the North. Slave soldiers who fought with Thomas Wentworth Higginson killed by day and sang hymns at night like some Cromwellian army. All the Yankee teachers mention older people who made heroic sacrifices to learn English to read scripture. The earliest and most flourishing black institution to arise in the ashes of the Civil War was the church—many led by black men who had been recognized by slaves as preachers in antebellum days.

What all this points to is the fundamental truth that many slaves, repulsed by indigestible spiritual admonitions to embrace their suffering, sought guidance elsewhere. Some confined their religion to their private lives and transformed it into an institution which the master caste might notice, or poke fun at, or bring visitors to see, or try to stifle—but which flourished nonetheless. In place of listless sermons black preachers offered slave congregations soul-shaking and personally satisfying spiritual messages. The gospel, as preached in the more formal slaveowner-dominant Christian services, "was so mixed with slavery," a freedman suggested, "that the people could see no beauty in it, and feel no reverence for it."[79] Nancy Howard said she prayed for her owners because they didn't know how to read scripture right.[80] One magnificent confrontation occurred in the Massachusetts legislature between the fugitive and black abolitionist Lewis Hayden and a slaveholder. "The gentleman speaks of religious privileges and the gospel we enjoy," Hayden said. "Yes—the missionary and the slave priest stand up side by side and say 'Servants, obey your masters,' and such like gospel is all we hear. But as soon as a slave begins to feel himself near a man, he wants a free gospel."[81]

The narrators describe a variety of masterful tactics improvised

[78] Rev. Peter Randolph, *From Slave Cabin to the Pulpit* (Boston, 1855), pp. 198–199.
[79] *Ibid.*, p. 196.
[80] *The Refugee*, p. 51.
[81] *The Liberator*, March 2, 1855.

by slaves to satisfy their spiritual hunger, to release their emotional energy, to experience the "whole gospel," the "free gospel." On one Louisiana plantation slaves would attend the standard service in the morning and then assemble in one another's cabins in the afternoon for an all-black gathering, with a black pastor. Most of the stories that have come down to us refer to slipping away at night and holding meetings in the secrecy of the woods. Here is one description:

> The slaves did not have churches as we have now. They made arbors of small pine trees. Some of them didn't have arbors. When they wanted to sing and pray, they would steal off into the woods. . . . Whipping did not stop them from having meetings. When one place was located they would find another. . . . All of them would sing and pray." [And another]: "Most of the times . . . the slaves held their meetings in the woods under . . . arbors made by them. . . . Sometimes the slaves would steal away at night and go into cane thickets and pray for deliverance. . . ."[82]

It was important to keep these prayer meetings concealed. Often women would wet down old quilts and rags to prevent sound from carrying in the distance, and hang them on trees and bushes to create the atmosphere of a room. Behind these drapes, slaves would huddle to pray and sing. At some meetings, the slaves lay prostrate with their faces close to the ground, "so that no sound could escape to warn the master or the overseer." Another was described in this way: ". . . the slaves would steal away into the woods at night and hold services. They would form a circle on their knees around the speaker who would also be on his knees. He would bend forward and speak into or over a vessel of water to drown the sound. If anyone became animated and cried out, the others would quickly stop the noise by placing their hands over the offender's mouth." Pots full of water were placed on the ground or in doorways "to prevent their masters from hearing them."[83]

The most comprehensive account I have read of a secret prayer meeting appears in the autobiography of Peter Randolph:[84]

> Not being allowed to hold meetings on the plantation, the slaves assemble in the swamps, out of reach of the patrols. They have an

[82] James B. Cade, "Out of the Mouths of Ex-Slaves," *Journal of Negro History*, XXII (April, 1935), 328–329.

[83] *Ibid.*, 330–331.

[84] *From Slave Cabin to Pulpit*, pp. 202–203.

> understanding among themselves as to the time and place of getting together. This is often done by the first one arriving breaking boughs from the trees, and bending them in the direction of the selected spot. Arrangements are then made for conducting the exercises. They first ask each other how they feel, the state of their minds, etc. The male members then select a certain space, in separate groups, for their division of the meeting. Preaching in order, by the brethren; then praying and singing all round, until they generally feel quite happy. The speaker usually commences by calling himself unworthy, and talks very slowly, until, feeling the spirit, he grows excited, and in a short time, there fall to the ground twenty or thirty men and women under its influence. Enlightened people call it excitement; but I wish the same was felt by everybody, so far as they are sincere.
>
> The slave forgets all his sufferings, except to remind others of the trials during the past week, exclaiming: "Thank God, I shall not live here always!" Then they pass from one to another, shaking hands, and bidding each other farewell, promising, should they meet no more on earth, to strive and meet in heaven, where all is joy, happiness and liberty. As they separate, they sing a parting hymn of praise.

The simplest Bible stories, put to memory, passed on through oral tradition, through folklore and folk tales or in the form of songs, were transformed into moral lessons that helped explain and ease the day-to-day burden of bondage. Harriet Tubman, Nat Turner, Denmark Vesey, and many others regularly referred to biblical tales that seemed relevant to their lives—the stories of Moses and Egypt, Pharaoh and the plagues, Daniel, the river Jordan, Jonah, Joseph and the crucifixion—and read comforting or illuminating messages from these parables.[85] One slave wrote that if God didn't punish his master for inflicting such distress on him and his family, "then there is no use of *having* any God, or *talking* about one. . . ."[86]

Satan, "Old Sam," was a living presence, active in life, an ever-present manipulator of human destiny, a being looked upon with awe and fear, and one who must be placated. He seems a syncretic deity, a blend of the Old Testament dissembler and some African spirit—like Anansi the spider, or the Afro-Brazilian Exú, or the Haitian Legba.[87] These deities regularly toy with man's fate and

[85] Charles H. Nichols, Jr., pp. 140–142.

[86] *The Weekly Anglo-African*, July 23, 1859.

[87] Susan Feldman, ed., *African Myths and Tales* (New York, 1963); Melville J.

have a comic as well as tragic aspect to their characters. William Wells Brown recorded a humorous song, sung by slaves about the devil during the Civil War, that suggests these themes:[88]

If de Debble do not ketch
Jeff. Davis, dat infernal retch,
An roast and frigazee dat rebble,
Wat is de use of any Debble?

Elements of the demonic and superstitious fused with slave religion. Witches, as in African and European folklore, were said to ride people at night, and entered into the stories slaves told one another. Slaves had faith in dreams and messages from the Lord. The archetype of such conviction was Harriet Tubman, who lived only partially in the world of her present and mostly in some trancelike contact with what she conceived as the eternal verities. The writer who recorded her autobiography mentions dozens of dreams revealing Harriet Tubman's prescience: "She is the most shrewd and practical person in the world, yet she is a firm believer in omens, dreams and warnings. She declares that before her escape from slavery, she used to dream of flying over fields and towns, and rivers and mountains, looking down upon them 'like a bird,' and reaching at last a great fence, or sometimes a river, over which she would try to fly. . . ." Tubman said she dreamed repeatedly of John Brown and his sons in the form of serpents and had premonitions of their doom on the very day of the Harpers Ferry attack.[89]

Harriet Tubman's faith in the spiritual guidance of dreams was shared by even the most sophisticated and wordly of the narrators. Douglass, Bibb, Lewis Clarke, Josiah Henson, and Peter Still visited local wise men, conjurers, and healers when especially troublesome personal or sexual problems needed resolving. (Bibb's use of the toad as a love charm parallels similar rites of Afro-Brazilian

Herskovits, *Life in a Haitian Village* (New York, 1937), p. 142; Edison Carneire, *Candomblés da Bahia* (Bahia, 1961), p. 75.

88 William Wells Brown, *The Negro in the American Rebellion: His Heroism and His Fidelity* (Boston, 1867), p. 113.

89 "Not long since, the writer, on going into Harriet's room in the morning, sat down by her and began to read that wonderful . . . description of the heavenly Jerusalem in the two last chapters of Revelation. When the reading was finished, Harriet burst into a rhapsody which perfectly amazed her reader—telling of what she had seen in one of these visions, sights which no human imagination could have conceived, it would seem, unless in dream or vision. There was a wild poetry in these descriptions which seemed to border almost on inspiration. . . ." *Scenes in the Life of Harriet Tubman*, pp. 56, 79–80, 82–83.

sexual magic.)[90] They also had faith in dream interpretation, as illustrated by Clarke's candid discussion of his own spectral fears:

> The slaves uniformly prefer to be buried at the greatest possible distance away from master [he wrote]. They are superstitious, and fear that the slavedriver, having whipped so much when alive, will, somehow, be beating them when dead. I was actually as much afraid of my old master when dead, as I was when he was alive. I often dreamed of him, too, after he was dead, and thought he had actually come back again, to torment me more.[91]

This truth speaks to one of the central themes of Stanley Elkins' important book, *Slavery*. Elkins suggests that slaves found models of behavior and authority, "significant others," in the master caste.[92] The narrators say the models were more likely to be other slaves. Many plantations had some powerful black slave whose courage others respected, whose overwhelming physical presence coupled with a sense of self-esteem was admired by the other slaves. Slave preachers and storytellers and local healers skilled in root medicine or capable of interpreting one's dreams, were also admired: men like Lunsford Lane, who was so adept at healing through herbs and roots that fellow blacks called him "Doctor," or the fugitive Harry Thomas, who practiced medicine in Canada, and Alfred T. Jones, who opened an apothecary shop.[93] If even a modicum of truth resides in the abundant folklore of slavery collected since the end of the Civil War, there must have been thousands of such individuals on the plantations.

One must also include as models the black drivers, and the many patriarchs and matriarchs, the older Uncles and Aunties, who appear throughout slave autobiographies. Slaves generally felt deference and respect for the aged on the plantation, a reverence similar to that found among many African tribal groups. The older person stands symbolically between this world and the next—to do injury to him is to tempt the wrath of the shades; to respect him is partially to assure a gracious welcome for yourself in the nether world. One such patriarch was Frederick Douglass's Uncle Isaac Copper. "His remedial prescriptions embraced four articles," Douglass wrote.

[90] Gilberto Freyre, *The Masters and the Slaves* (New York, 1967), p. 289.
[91] *Narratives of Lewis and Milton Clarke*, p. 119.
[92] Stanley M. Elkins, *Slavery: A Problem in American Institutional and Intellectual Life* (Chicago, 1959), pp. 103–139.
[93] Hawkins, *Lunsford Lane*, pp. 194–195; *The Refugee*, pp. 152, 305.

"For diseases of the body, Epsom salts and castor oil; for those of the soul, the Lord's Prayer and hickory switches!"[94]

To fail to see these many social types, these black "significant others," is to blind oneself to the facts of the slavery experience. The most crucial problems of a man's life were resolved by fellow slaves of special gifts. The slave narrators leave no record of slaves' counseling with their masters about their deepest hopes. To satisfy the mind and body, as well as the spirit, it was necessary to turn elsewhere.

VI

These are the most striking central themes of the narratives, but they are far from the only ones. Every subtle and banal aspect of the slave regime is somewhere touched upon and illuminated by these autobiographies. Music, dancing, and laughter are discussed as means to lighten the burdens of a toiling life. Northup said he couldn't survive without his blessed fiddle: "Had it not been for my beloved violin, I scarcely can conceive how I could have endured the long years of bondage. Often, at midnight, when sleep had fled . . . and my soul disturbed and troubled with the contemplation of my fate, it would sing me a song of peace."[95] Douglass, too, played the violin, and others played banjoes, drums, and other instruments. A moving illustration of this idea is embodied in the memoir of John Little, who laughed and danced with chains on:

> They say slaves are happy, because they laugh, and are merry [Little commented]. I myself and three or four others, have received two hundred lashes in the day, and had our feet in fetters; yet, at night, we would sing and dance, and make others laugh at the rattling of our chains. Happy men we must have been! We did it to keep down trouble, and to keep our hearts from being completely broken: that is as true as the gospel! Just look at it,—must not we

94 Quoted in Margaret Young Jackson, p. 163.
95 Osofsky, *The Burden of Race*, pp. 26–27.

> have been very happy? Yet I have done it myself—I have cut capers in chains."[96]

Numerous slaves talk of their perpetual war to prevent debasement. The powerful, the self-willed, those whose spirits could not be broken and who sometimes repulsed physically all attempts to whip them, presented the ultimate challenge to the mystique of the all-powerful master caste. The more the pressure of debasement was applied to some, the more rebellious they became. This is especially evident in the common stories fugitives tell of learning to read and write. Austin Steward vowed to teach himself letters after his master destroyed his spelling book and whipped him for having it. Peter Still maneuvered his way into a Sabbath school in Lexington despite his owner's opposition to "getting learning." Northup, who knew how to write, contrived a pen from old duck feathers and ink from the bark of a maple tree. James W. Sumler hid his books in a hayloft and came there on Sundays. Leonard Black bought a book and his master found him with it and burned it. "You black son of a bitch, if I ever know you to have a book again, I will whip you half to death," Black quoted his owner as saying. He went right out and acquired another.[97]

The burning went two ways. W. C. Nell, a black Garrisonian and historian, told of a conversation he had with a female fugitive in Canada. She learned to read by taking books from the family library and stealthily returning them. When they couldn't be put back without arousing suspicion she tossed them into the kitchen fire. As she explained it, she "evinced a *burning* desire for knowledge."[98]

This struggle over letters must be seen within the broader context of the strategic and psychic importance of controlling learning. Slaveowners certainly hesitated to foster education for such obvious reasons as preventing bondsmen from writing passes and freedom papers. A subconscious and more meaningful question in control of language is also at stake. Through the ages, in the most widely divergent cultures, the right to proscribe letters or command a man's

96 Quoted in Margaret Young Jackson, pp. 83–84.

97 *Narrative of Noah Davis*, p. 17; *Life of Leonard Black*, pp. 18–19; Steward, *Twenty-two Years a Slave*, p. 83; *The Kidnapped and the Ransomed*, pp. 40–41; *The Refugee*, p. 97; *Narrative of Solomon Northup*, pp. 229–230.

98 *The Liberator*, January 5, 1855.

name is understood as the power to subordinate—the "word" has quasi-magical, mystical connotations. The right to control it is the power to order reality, to subjugate man himself. Conquerors and conquered have both understood this truth.[99]

An interesting comparative example is found in the history of naming rituals among American Indians. Indian children often received secret names at birth. As long as adults retained responsibility for the youngsters, the names remained hidden. At puberty, however, girls and boys were permitted to pass into psychological as well as physical adulthood by selection of new names—ones reflective of personality or prowess. These personal choices remained sacred thereafter, though new names might be added as life progressed and people changed. This linguistic ritual symbolized the right of each person to choose his own being; to have a name that mirrored his manhood.

The variety and complexity of such Indian names confused many whites. Missionaries, government officials, census takers, lawyers, traders, and land agents tidied up their records and account books by arbitrarily shortening or changing the names of their charges. "He Who Causes Fear" and "Brave Chief" suddenly became Indian Joe or Bob. These anglicized labels ignored the cultural significance of naming. Some Indians, ashamed of their newly acquired designations, rejected them. Others covertly retained their meaningful names for tribal rituals and feasts as whites continued to know them only by their anglicized names. One scholar noted, "The English name was not to be used on serious occasions." John Collier claimed that the persistence of a sense of self was the most impressive theme of American Indian history.[100]

Strikingly similar experiences took place in slavery. The concept is evident in stories slaves tell of their sense of loss in not knowing

[99] William F. Murphy, "A Note on the Significance of Names," *The Psychoanalytic Quarterly*, XXVI (1957), 91–106; Ingeborg Flugel, "On the Significance of Names," *British Journal of Medical Psychology*, X (1930), 208–213; Mary Fuller, " 'The Naming of Names' in Indian Folk Belief," *Asian Folklore Studies*, XXIV (1965), 63–79; *The Basic Writings of Sigmund Freud*, p. 825.

[100] Hope Holway, "The American Indian and His Name," *The Chronicles of Oklahoma*, XLIII (Autumn, 1965), 340–345; Harold E. Driver, *The Indians of North America* (Chicago, 1961), pp. 469–470; Lewis H. Morgan, *Ancient Society* (Cambridge, Mass., 1964), pp. 73–75; T. M. Pearce, "Naming Customs Among Southwest Indians," *New Mexico Folklore Record*, II (1963–64), 33–37; John Collier, *Indians of the Americas* (New York, 1947).

their birth dates. To deprive one of such vital information is to cloud his sense of self.[101] One also finds it among former slaves who insist on selecting their own names as free men. Douglass and Wells Brown permit their family names to be changed at will, but both refuse to relinquish their given names. For them "Frederick" and "William" signified their sense of being, their manhood. Black nationalist Martin R. Delany had a similar experience. His biographer summarized Delany's attitude toward his name:

> Regarding it as not legally belonging to his family and suspicious of its having been borrowed from the whites . . . he expresses himself always as though it was distasteful to him, recalling associations of the servitude of his family. With these associations clinging to it, his pride revolts at retaining that which he believes originated with the oppressors of his ancestors . . . [and] he eagerly awaits the opportunity for its erasure.[102]

This relation of selfhood to learning also helps explain a major trend of Reconstruction social history. Yankee teachers sent South to build school houses in the 1860's and 1870's were greeted enthusiastically by the freedmen. Makeshift schools were jammed with pupils. It was common to note the awe with which youngsters regarded the mastery of penmanship, or to comment on the similar attitude of older folk. One Quaker teacher wrote that "Men come home tired with their labors, sit in their door-ways, with their open books, till the dusk drives them to the fire-light and are joined at their fire-sides by their little ones, with whom they 'Stumble along right smart.' "[103] As Harriet Beecher Stowe said, the former slave "rushed not for the grog-shop but for the schoolroom—they cried for the spelling-book as for bread."[104] J. W. Alvord of the Freedmen's Bureau said it was impossible to overestimate this "thirst for knowledge." Slaves spoke of the "wonderful power" in letters, the "mysteries of literature," and the rewards that flowed from control of the written word. One observer thought they envisioned

101 "Like most of my brothers in bondage, I have no correct account of my age. Slaves keep the birth of their children by the different seasons of the year. Children often ask their parents their age. The answers is, 'this planting corn time, you are six, or eight, or ten. . . .' " *Narrative of Henry Watson*, p. 5.

102 Frank A. Rollin, *Life and Public Services of Martin R. Delany* (Boston, 1883), p. 15.

103 Henry L. Swint, ed., *Dear Ones At Home* (Nashville, 1966), pp. 62–63.

104 Osofsky, *The Burden of Race*, pp. 158–159.

education as a "sort of talisman."[105] These slaves hungered not only for knowledge but also for a sense of self. By crowding the schoolhouses they were laying claim to their manhood as well as to their McGuffey's Readers.

Many other suggestive themes in these books call for further investigation on the part of scholars: the many class- and color-conscious hatreds that divided slaves among themselves; the discussion of slavery's debasement of their *masters* and corruption of whites generally; the pattern of use and abuse of black women as field hands and as sexual partners; the role of the white mistress on the plantations. The image of blessed, genteel, white Southern femininity must find some place for the woman who tried to kill Moses Roper because he looked too like her husband, or for the ladies the Clarke brothers referred to as she-wolves, screech owls, and she-bears.

A further consideration of major importance is the length of time slaves remained with a single owner or on one plantation. It is the exceptional fugitive who lived on one place all his life. On the contrary, it was typical to have three, five, and sometimes more masters in the course of one's servitude. It is not necessary to posit evil intent on the part of the master caste to understand this. Families weren't destroyed capriciously. But the slave autobiographies explain that the disruptions were caused most often by indebtedness—and subsequent forced sales—and secondly by divisions of estates upon death. Some of the most heroic sections of the narratives deal with attempts of husbands and fathers to keep their families intact in the face of these realities. If the disruption so evident on the plantations that fugitives describe was typical of the entire slave South, it is certainly necessary to modify the image of a relatively stable plantation experience for most bondsmen.

The narratives are essential sources for the study of slavery for all these reasons. One can understand more clearly now why they were a popular literature more than a century ago.

> The fugitive slave literature is destined to be a powerful lever [an antebellum commentator wrote]. We have the most profound conviction of its potency. We see in it the way and infallible means of abolitionizing the free states. Argument provokes argument, reason

105 Henry Lee Swint, *The Northern Teacher in the South, 1862–1870* (New York 1967), p. 72.

> is met with sophistry; but narratives go right to the heart of men. We defy any man to think of patience or tolerance of slavery after reading Bibb's narrative. . . . Put a dozen copies of this book into every school district, or neighborhood in the free states, and you might sweep the whole north on a thorough-going liberty platform for abolishing slavery, everywhere and everyhow.[106]

VII

The volumes reprinted here are chosen for reasons of judgment and preference. They are fascinating slave narratives. Northup, Brown, and Bibb, as their autobiographies demonstrate, were men of creativity, wisdom and talent. Each was capable of writing or telling his life story with sophistication. Brown and Bibb wrote their books with their own hands, Northup dictated his memoir to an amanuensis. Brown and Bibb became leading figures in the anti-slavery movement immediately upon their escapes. Brown was a well-known novelist, playwright, and professional lecturer. He was one of the most militant and astute Garrisonians in the country. Bibb settled in Canada, helped establish a colony for fugitives and free blacks, and edited the influential *Voice of the Fugitive* until his untimely death at the age of thirty-eight in 1854. Northup was less active in the organized antislavery movement, but he too toured the country telling people of his days of bondage.[107] These three books differ from one another in style and content, yet exemplify the slave-narrative literature in its most representative forms.

GILBERT OSOFSKY

University of Illinois, Chicago

106 Quoted in Charles H. Nichols, Jr., pp. 241–242.

107 A recent study of the Northup volume attests to its authenticity. See: Sue Eakin and Joseph Logsdon, eds., *Twelve Years a Slave* (Baton Rouge, 1968), pp. ix–xxiv.

A Note on the Usefulness of Folklore

> "I fooled Old Master seven years, Fooled the overseer three. Hand me down my banjo, and I'll tickle your bel-lee."
>
> B. A. Botkin, ed., *Lay My Burden Down: A Folk History of Slavery* (Chicago, 1945), p. 3.

At many points in this essay on the narratives I was tempted to include corroborative materials from the rich folklore of slavery found in the *American Journal of Folklore*, the *Southern Folklore Quarterly*, *Midwest Folklore*, the many state folklore journals, the varieties of slave memoirs and collections of slave folklore that have appeared since the late nineteenth century, and the published works of such scholars as B. A. Botkin, Richard Dorson, J. Mason Brewer, Arna Bontemps, Sterling A. Brown, Howard W. Odum, Newbell N. Puckett, and many, many others. As the published antebellum narrative literature itself has been questioned as a useful historical source, I chose not to further cloud the issue by suggesting that historians take seriously another type of traditionally overlooked source—traditionally overlooked by professional historians, that is.

I would just like to make two suggestions. The first deals with the budding and, I hope, proliferating trend among scholars to stretch their imaginative reach by studying materials that never enter a manuscript archive. Anyone interested in working-class history, or the attitudes of the "masses" to any given question, must devise techniques to analyze actions and institutions of people who left few written records of their feelings. It hardly needs emphasis here that the majority of slaves were not permitted to enter the schoolhouse. If one is ever to know about their visions, their quests, their "mind," it is obviously necessary to turn to the oral record: the songs, spirituals, and folk tales that were collected in the nineteenth century and remain alive at this very moment. There are innumerable difficulties in using such sources—the specialists in folklore have been writing about them for generations—yet if the question is of vital importance, as it undoubtedly is, I would suggest that historians at least peek into the plethora of books on the usefulness and meaning of folk materials. Here is another example where the arbitrary lines separating the disciplines become a hindrance to deeper understanding. Folklorists collect stories, analyze hundreds of variations on a single theme, and compile motif indexes, but rarely search for the historical meaning of their evidence. Historians have a tendency to be overcautious about all such materials but anxiously hope to find meaningful generalizations that are applicable to the past. Perhaps there can be some meeting of the minds between the fields.

Second. In going over some of the material myself, I have been impressed by the way in which so much of the *tone* of late nineteenth- and twentieth-century black folk stories and jokes about slavery simply repeat the substance of recorded slave humor of the 1830's, 1840's, and 1850's. They seem to supplement, not call into question, the basic materials one finds in the narratives. Perhaps we have here the continuation of an oral tradition whose roots are centuries old.

A case in point are the anecdotes of "Old John." Stories about this slave trickster collected in Michigan, Texas, North Carolina, Mississippi, and elsewhere, and in each decade since the end of the Civil War, generally emphasize a single theme: the ability of Old John (and obviously Brer Rabbit, too) to outwit his master; to use wit, guile, and cunning, as real slaves did, to turn a situation to his own advantage. In one of my favorite tales, Old John is pitted against a powerful opponent. John's master wagers a few thousand dollars that John can whip the most powerful black man on a neighboring plantation. When John arrives at the battleground, he finds his opponent chained to an iron stake, scratching and pawing the dirt, a bull in human form ready to pounce on his enemy. What strategy can he devise to handle such a threatening situation? John walked over to his mistress and slapped her in the face. His opponent immediately pulled up the stake, ran away, and the bet was forfeited. The enraged master asked John to justify his action and the folk hero replies: "Well, Jim knowed if I slapped a white woman I'd killed him, so he ran," and John's master carried off the prize.[1]

Another: John has a passion for onions and busily steals them from his master's garden each night. When the master suspects there is a thief around he asks John to catch him. John returns with the culprit, a skunk, and tells his master if he doesn't believe

[1] Richard Dorson, *Negro Folktales in Michigan* (Cambridge, Mass., 1956), pp. 55–56.

that the varmint was the crook "he could smell the skunk's breath" himself.[2]

One final illustration: John and master go fishing and pass the time with a little idle banter. John tells his owner that his cane has "three ends" and that he can prove it. Master replies that if John can show him the three, he can have his freedom. John picks up the cane and points to each end, and then he throws the walking stick into the river and said that that was the cane's "last end."[3]

And though John is the most universal symbol of slave resistance in the folksay, he is not the only one. The substance of Old John tales is repeated throughout slave humor. Consider the marvelous story of the hogs who died of "malitis." On one plantation there were seven fat hogs and seventy lean slaves, the storyteller recalls. Old Master was "mighty stingy" and was preparing to eat the "porkers" himself. One day he discovered they died of "malitis," and fearing the meat was tainted he decided to distribute it all to the slaves. What was the mysterious plague? A former bondsman described it this way: "One of the strongest Negroes got up early in the morning, long 'fore the rising horn called the slaves from their cabins. He skitted to the hog pen with a heavy mallet in his hand. When he tapped Mister Hog 'tween the eyes with that mallet, 'malitis' set in mighty quick. . . ."[4]

I cite these few illustrations because I found them strikingly similar to the varieties of printed stories I came upon with such regularity in the narrative literature and in the antislavery press, and which I used to develop the central themes of my essay. Is it not surprising that the documented evidence of the Jacksonian years is repeated with richness and clarity in the twentieth century? I suspect the presence of an enduring oral tradition that has much to teach us of the "mind" and "personality" of slaves, and of the way humor was used to keep men sane under the most trying of human conditions.

A quarter century ago B. A. Botkin wrote that such tales "provide an invaluable source of knowledge of the lives and thoughts of

[2] John Q. Anderson, "Old John and the Master," *Southern Folklore Quarterly,* XXV (1961), 195; Fred O. We'don, "Negro Folktale Heroes," *Texas Folklore Society Publications,* XXIV (1959), 170–189.

[3] John Q. Anderson, "Old John and the Master," *Southern Folklore Quarterly,* XXV (1961), 195–196.

[4] B. A. Botkin, "The Slave as His Own Interpreter," *The Library of Congress Quarterly Journal of Current Acquisitions,* II (1944), 42.

thousands who once were slaves. Plantation life is pictured here in its multiplicity of folkways and folk notions, as seen by field hand, house servant and artisan, against varied backgrounds of Southeast and Southwest, tidewater and inland, lowland and upland regions." These anecdotes, Botkin said, are no less important for the study of slavery than analyses of bondage as an economic institution.[5]

And what was true in the 1840's and 1940's remains valid today.

[5] B. A. Botkin, "The Slave as His Own Interpreter," *The Library of Congress Quarterly Journal of Current Acquisitions*, II (1944), 42.

Acknowledgments

I again wish to express my indebtedness to the marvelous staff at Howard University's Moorland Collection: Mrs. Dorothy B. Porter, Mrs. Virginia S. Spencer, Mrs. Ethel M. Ellis, and Mrs. Cornelia R. Stokes. They located rare materials for me and microfilmed or Xeroxed many of the narratives.

I also wish to thank my perceptive and (sometimes) hard-working research assistant, Irving Himelblau. He has had a very enjoyable year criticizing my work. Heidi Taube Marks, as usual tried and true, did a "sterling" job of proofreading. I also appreciate the help and imaginativeness that Robert Lewis has brought to this and other research projects that are still in the works.

Narrative of the Life and Adventures of HENRY BIBB,

An American Slave

Written by himself

with an Introduction
by Lucius C. Matlack

INTRODUCTION

by Lucius C. Matlack

From the most obnoxious substances we often see spring forth, beautiful and fragrant, flowers of every hue, to regale the eye, and perfume the air. Thus, frequently, are results originated which are wholly unlike the cause that gave them birth. An illustration of this truth is afforded by the history of American slavery.

Naturally and necessarily the enemy of literature, it has become the prolific theme of much that is profound in argument, sublime in poetry, and thrilling in narrative. From the soil of slavery itself have sprung forth some of the most brilliant productions, whose logical levers will ultimately upheave and overthrow the system. Gushing fountains of poetic thought, have started from beneath the rod of violence, that will long continue to slake the feverish thirst of humanity outraged, until swelling to a flood it shall rush with wasting violence over the ill-gotten heritage of the oppressor. Startling incidents authenticated, far excelling fiction in their touching pathos, from the pen of self-emancipated slaves, do now exhibit slavery in such revolting aspects as to secure the execrations of all good men and become a monument more enduring than marble, in testimony strong as sacred writ against it.

Of the class last named, is the narrative of the life of Henry Bibb, which is equally distinguished as a revolting portrait of the hideous slave system, a thrilling narrative of individual suffering, and a triumphant vindication of the slave's manhood and mental dignity. And all this is associated with unmistakable traces of originality and truthfulness.

To many, the elevated style, purity of diction, and easy flow of language, frequently exhibited, will appear unaccountable and contradictory, in view of his want of early mental culture. But to the thousands who have listened with delight to his speeches on anniversary and other occasions, these same traits will be noted as unequivocal evidence of originality. Very few men present in their written composition so perfect a transcript of their style as is exhibited by Mr. Bibb.

Moreover, the writer of this introduction is well acquainted with his handwriting and style. The entire manuscript I have examined and prepared for the press. Many of the closing pages of it were written by Mr. Bibb in my office. And the whole is preserved for inspection now. An examination of it will show that no alteration of sentiment, language, or style was necessary to make it what it now is, in the hands of the reader. The work of preparation for the press was that of orthography and punctuation merely, an arrangement of the chapters, and a table of contents—little more than falls to the lot of publishers generally.

The fidelity of the narrative is sustained by the most satisfactory and ample testimony. Time has proved its claims to truth. Thorough investigation has sifted and analyzed every essential fact alleged, and demonstrated clearly that this thrilling and eloquent narrative, though stranger than fiction, is undoubtedly true.

It is only necessary to present the following documents to the reader to sustain this declaration. For convenience of reference, and that they may be more easily understood, the letters will be inserted consecutively, with explanations following the last.

The best preface to these letters is the report of a committee appointed to investigate the truth of Mr. Bibb's narrative as he has delivered it in public for years past.

REPORT

OF THE UNDERSIGNED, COMMITTEE APPOINTED BY THE DETROIT LIBERTY ASSOCIATION TO INVESTIGATE THE TRUTH OF THE NARRATIVE OF HENRY BIBB, A FUGITIVE FROM SLAVERY, AND REPORT THEREON:

Mr. Bibb has addressed several assemblies in Michigan, and his narrative is generally known. Some of his hearers, among whom were Liberty men, felt doubt as to the truth of his statements. Respect for their scruples and the obligation of duty to the public induced the formation of the present Committee.

The Committee entered on the duty confided to them, resolved on a searching scrutiny, and an unreserved publication of its result. Mr. Bibb acquiesced in the inquiry with a praiseworthy spirit. He attended before the Committee and gave willing aid to its object. He was subjected to a rigorous examination. Facts—dates—persons—and localities were demanded and cheerfully furnished. Proper inquiry—either by letter, or personally, or through the medium of friends was then made from *every* person, and in *every* quarter likely to elucidate the truth. In fact no test for its ascertainment, known to the sense or experience of the Committee, was omitted. The result was the collection of a large body of testimony from very diversified quarters. Slave owners, slave dealers, fugitives from slavery, political friends and political foes contributed to a mass of testimony, every part of which pointed to a common conclusion—the undoubted truth of Mr. Bibb's statements.

In the Committee's opinion no individual can substantiate the events of his life by testimony more conclusive and harmonious than is now before them in confirmation of Mr. Bibb. The main facts of his narrative, and many of the minor ones are corroborated beyond all question. No inconsistency has been disclosed nor anything revealed to create suspicion. The Committee have no hesitation in declaring their conviction that Mr. Bibb is amply sustained, and is entitled to public confidence and high esteem.

The bulk of testimony precludes its publication, but it is in the Committee's hands for the inspection of any applicant.

A. L. PORTER,
C. H. STEWART,
SILAS M. HOLMES.

DETROIT, *April* 22, 1845. Committee.

From the bulk of testimony obtained, a part only is here introduced. The remainder fully corroborates and strengthens that.

[No. 1. An Extract] DAWN MILLS, FEB. 19th, 1845.

CHARLES H. STEWART, ESQ.

MY DEAR BROTHER:

Your kind communication of the 13th came to hand yesterday. I have made inquiries respecting Henry Bibb which may be of service to you. Mr. Wm. Harrison, to whom you allude in your letter, is here. He is a respectable and worthy man—a man of piety. I have just had an interview with him this evening. He testifies, that he was well acquainted with Henry Bibb in Trimble County, Ky., and that he sent a letter to him by Thomas Henson, and got one in return from him. He says that Bibb came out to Canada some three years ago, and went back to get his wife up, but was betrayed at Cincinnati by a colored man—that he was taken to Louisville but got away—was taken again and lodged in jail, and sold off to New Orleans, or he, (Harrison,) understood that he was taken to New Orleans. He testifies that Bibb is a

Methodist man, and says that two persons who came on with him last Summer, knew Bibb. One of these, Simpson Young, is now at Malden. * * *

Very respectfully, thy friend,

HIRAM WILSON.

[No. 2.] BEDFORD, TRIMBLE CO., KENTUCKY.

March 4, 1845.

SIR:—Your letter under date of the 13th ult., is now before me, making some inquiry about a person supposed to be a fugitive from the South, "who is lecturing to your religious community on Slavery and the South."

I am pleased to inform you that I have it in my power to give you the information you desire. The person spoken of by you I have no doubt is Walton, a yellow man, who once belonged to my father, William Gatewood. He was purchased by him from John Sibly, and by John Sibly of his brother Albert G. Sibly, and Albert G. Sibly became possessed of him by his marriage with Judge David White's daughter, he being born Judge White's slave.

The boy Walton at the time he belonged to John Sibly, married a slave of my father's, a mulatto girl, and sometime afterwards solicited him to buy him; the old man after much importuning from Walton, consented to do so; and accordingly paid Sibly eight hundred and fifty dollars. He did not buy him because he needed him, but from the fact that he had a wife there, and Walton on his part promising every thing that my father could desire.

It was not long, however, before Walton became indolent and neglectful of his duty; and in addition to this, he was guilty, as the old man thought, of worse offences. He watched his conduct more strictly, and found he was guilty of disposing of articles from the farm for his own use, and pocketing the money.

He actually caught him one day stealing wheat—he had conveyed one sack full to a neighbor and whilst he was delivering the other my father caught him in the very act.

He confessed his guilt and promised to do better for the future —and on his making promises of this kind my father was disposed to keep him still, not wishing to part him from his wife, for whom he professed to entertain the strongest affection. When the Christmas Holidays came on, the old man, as is usual in this country, gave his negroes a week Holiday. Walton, instead of regaling himself by going about visiting his colored friends, took up his line of march for her Britanic Majesty's dominions.

He was gone about two years I think, when I heard of him in Cincinnati; I repaired thither, with some few friends to aid me, and succeeded in securing him.

He was taken to Louisville, and on the next morning after our arrival there, he escaped, almost from before our face, while we were on the street before the Tavern. He succeeded in eluding our pursuit, and again reached Canada in safety.

Nothing daunted he returned, after a lapse of some twelve or eighteen months, with the intention, as I have since learned, of conducting off his wife and eight or ten more slaves to Canada.

I got news of his whereabouts, and succeeded in recapturing him. I took him to Louisville and together with his wife and child, (she going along with him at her owner's request,) sold him. He was taken from thence to New Orleans—and from hence to Red River, Arkansas—and the next news I had of him he was again wending his way to Canada, and I suppose now is at or near Detroit.

In relation to his character, it was the general opinion here that he was a notorious liar, and a rogue. These things I can procure any number of respectable witnesses to prove.

In proof of it, he says his mother belonged to James Bibb, which is a lie, there not having been such a man about here, much less brother of Secretary Bibb. He says that Bibb's daughter married A. G. Sibly, when the fact is Sibly married Judge David White's daughter, and his mother belonged to White also and is now here, free.

So you will perceive he is guilty of lying for no effect, and what might it not be supposed he would do where he could effect anything by it.

I have been more tedious than I should have been, but being anxious to give you his rascally conduct in full, must be my apology. You are at liberty to publish this letter, or make any use you see proper of it. If you do publish it, let me have a paper containing the publication—at any rate let me hear from you again.

Respectfully yours, &c.,

SILAS GATEWOOD.

To C. H. STEWART, ESQ.

[No. 3. An Extract.] CINCINNATI, *March* 10, 1845.

MY DEAR SIR:—Mrs. Path, Nickens and Woodson did not see Bibb on his first visit, in 1837, when he staid with Job Dundy, but were subsequently told of it by Bibb. They first saw him in May,

1838. Mrs. Path remembers this date because it was the month in which she removed from Broadway to Harrison street, and Bibb assisted her to remove. Mrs. Path's garden adjoined Dundy's back yard. While engaged in digging up flowers, she was addressed by Bibb, who was staying with Dundy, and who offered to dig them up for her. She hired him to do it. Mrs. Dundy shortly after called over and told Mrs. Path that he was a slave. After that Mrs. Path took him into her house and concealed him. While concealed, he astonished his good protectress by his ingenuity in bottoming chairs with cane. When the furniture was removed, Bibb insisted on helping, and was, after some remonstrances, permitted. At the house on Harrison street, he was employed for several days in digging a cellar, and was so employed when seized on Saturday afternoon by the constables. He held frequent conversations with Mrs. Path and others, in which he gave them the same account which he has given you.

On Saturday afternoon, two noted slave-catching constables, E. V. Brooks and O'Neil, surprised Bibb as he was digging in the cellar. Bibb sprang for the fence and gained the top of it, where he was seized and dragged back. They took him immediately before William Doty, a Justice of infamous notoriety as an accomplice of kidnappers, proved property, paid charges and took him away.

His distressed friends were surprised by his re-appearance in a few days after, the Wednesday following, as they think. He reached the house of Dr. Woods, (a colored man since deceased,) before day-break, and staid until dusk. Mrs. Path, John Woodson and others made up about twelve dollars for him. Woodson accompanied him out of town a mile and bid him "God speed." He has never been here since. Woodson and Clark saw him at Detroit two years ago.

Yours truly,

WILLIAM BIRNEY.

[No. 4.] LOUISVILLE, *March* 14, 1845.

MR. STEWART.—Yours of the 1st came to hand on the 13th inst. You wished me to inform you what became of a boy that was in the work-house in the fall of '39. The boy you allude to went by the name of Walton; he had ran away from Kentucky some time before, and returned for his wife—was caught and sold to Garrison; he was taken to Louisiana, I think—he was sold on Red River to a planter. As Garrison is absent in the City of New Orleans at this time, I cannot inform you who he was sold to. Garrison will be in Louisville some time this Spring; if you wish me, I will inquire of Garrison and inform you to whom he was sold, and where his master lives at this time.

Yours,
W. PORTER.

[No. 5.] BEDFORD, TRIMBLE COUNTY, KY.

C. H. STEWART, ESQ.,

SIR.—I received your note on the 16th inst., and in accordance with it I write you these lines. You stated that you would wish to know something about Walton H. Bibb, and whether he had a wife and child, and whether they were sold to New Orleans. Sir, before I answer these inquiries, I should like to know who Charles H. Stewart is, and why you should make these inquiries of me, and how you knew who I was, as you are a stranger to me and I must be to you. In your next if you will tell me the intention of your inquiries, I will give you a full history of the whole case.

I have a boy in your county by the name of King, a large man and very black; if you are acquainted with him, give him my compliments, and tell him I am well, and all of his friends. W. H. Bibb is acquainted with him.

I wait your answer.

Your most obedient,
March 17, 1845. W. H. GATEWOOD.

[No. 6.] BEDFORD, KENTUCKY, *April* 6th, 1845.

MR. CHARLES H. STEWART.

SIR:—Yours of the 1st March is before me, inquiring if one Walton Bibb, a colored man, escaped from me at Louisville, Ky., in the Spring of 1839. To that inquiry I answer, he did. The particulars are these: He ran off from William Gatewood some time in 1838 I think, and was heard of in Cincinnati. Myself and some others went there and took him, and took him to Louisville for sale, by the directions of his master. While there he made his escape and was gone some time, I think about one year or longer. He came back it was said, to get his wife and child, so report says. He was again taken by his owner; he together with his wife and child was taken to Louisville and sold to a man who traded in negroes, and was taken by him to New Orleans and sold with his wife and child to some man up Red River, so I was informed by the man who sold him. He then ran off and left his wife and child and got back, it seems, to your country. I can say for Gatewood he was a good master, and treated him well. Gatewood bought him from a Mr. Sibly, who was going to send him down the river. Walton, to my knowledge, influenced Gatewood to buy him, and promised if he would,· never to disobey him or run off. Who he belongs to now, I do not know. I know Gatewood sold his wife and child at a great sacrifice, to satisfy him. If any other information is necessary I will give it, if required. You will please write me again what he is trying to do in your country, or what he wishes the inquiry from me for.

Yours, truly,

DANIEL S. LANE.

These letters need little comment. Their testimony combined is most harmonious and conclusive. Look at the points established.

1. Hiram Wilson gives the testimony of reputable men now in Canada, who knew Henry Bibb as a slave in Kentucky.

2. Silas Gatewood, with a peculiar relish, fills three pages of foolscap, "being anxious to give his rascally conduct in full," as he says. But he vaults over the saddle and lands on the other side. His testimony is invaluable as an endorsement of Mr. Bibb's truthfulness. He illustrates all the essential facts of this narrative. He also labors to prove him deceitful and a liar.

Deceit in a slave is only a slight reflex of the stupendous fraud practiced by his master. And its indulgence has far more logic in its favor than the ablest plea ever written for slave holding, under ever such peculiar circumstances. The attempt to prove Mr. Bibb in the lie is a signal failure, as he never affirmed what Gatewood denies. With this offset, the letter under notice is a triumphant vindication of one whom he thought thereby to injure sadly. As Mr. Bibb has most happily acknowledged the wheat (see page [166],) I pass the charge of stealing by referring to the logic there used, which will be deemed convincing.

3. William Birney, Esq., attests the facts of Mr. Bibb's arrest in Cincinnati, and the subsequent escape, as narrated by him, from the declaration of eyewitnesses.

4. W. Porter, Jailor, states that Bibb was in the workhouse at

Louisville, held and sold afterwards to the persons and at the places named in this volume.

5. W. H. Gatewood, with much Southern dignity, will answer no questions, but shows his relation to these matters by naming "King" —saying, "W. H. Bibb is acquainted with him," and promising "a full history of the case."

6. Daniel S. Lane, with remarkable straightforwardness and stupidity, tells all he knows, and then wants to know what they ask him for. The writer will answer that question. He wanted to prove by two or more witnesses the truth of his own statements; which has most surely been accomplished.

Having thus presented an array of testimony sustaining the facts alleged in this narrative, the introduction will be concluded by introducing a letter signed by respectable men of Detroit, and endorsed by Judge Wilkins, showing the high esteem in which Mr. Bibb is held by those who know him well where he makes his home. Their testimony expresses their present regard as well as an opinion of his past character. It is introduced here with the greatest satisfaction, as the writer is assured, from an intimate acquaintance with Henry Bibb, that all who know him hereafter will entertain the same sentiments toward him:

DETROIT, *March* 10, 1845.

The undersigned have pleasure in recommending Henry Bibb to the kindness and confidence of Anti-slavery friends in every State. He has resided among us for some years. His deportment, his conduct, and his christian course have won our esteem and affection. The narrative of his sufferings and more early life has been thoroughly investigated by a Committee appointed for the purpose. They sought evidence respecting it in every proper quarter, and their report attested its undoubted truth. In this conclusion we all cordially unite.

H. Bibb has for some years publicly made this narrative to assemblies, whose number cannot be told; it has commanded public attention in this State, and provoked inquiry. Occasionally too we see persons from the South, who knew him in early years, yet not a word or fact worthy of impairing its truth has reached us; but on the contrary, every thing tended to its corroboration.

Mr. Bibb's Anti-slavery efforts in this State have produced incalculable benefit. The Lord has blessed him into an instrument of great power. He has labored much, and for very inadequate compensation. Lucrative offers for other quarters did not tempt him to a more profitable field. His sincerity and disinterestedness are therefore beyond suspicion.

We bid him "God-speed," on his route. We bespeak for him every kind consideration.

H. HALLOCK,
President of the Detroit Lib. Association.
CULLEN BROWN, *Vice-President.*
S. M. HOLMES, *Secretary.*
J. D. BALDWIN,
CHARLES H. STEWART,
MARTIN WILSON,
WILLIAM BARNUM.

DETROIT, Nov. 11, 1845.

The undersigned, cheerfully concurs with Mr. Hallock and others in their friendly recommendation of Mr. Henry Bibb. The undersigned has known him for many months in the Sabbath School in this City, partly under his charge, and can certify to his correct deportment, and commend him to the sympathies of Christian benevolence.

ROSS WILKINS.

The task now performed, in preparing for the press and introducing to the public the narrative of Henry Bibb, has been one of the most pleasant ever required at my hands. And I conclude it with an expression of the hope that it may afford interest to the reader, support to the author in his efforts against slavery, and be instrumental in advancing the great work of emancipation in this country.

NEW YORK CITY, *July* 1st, 1849.

AUTHOR'S PREFACE

This work has been written during irregular intervals, while I have been travelling and laboring for the emancipation of my enslaved countrymen. The reader will remember that I make no pretension to literature; for I can truly say, that I have been educated in the school of adversity, whips, and chains. Experience and observation have been my principal teachers, with the exception of three weeks schooling which I have had the good fortune to receive since my escape from the "grave yard of the mind," or the dark prison of human bondage. And nothing but untiring perseverance has enabled me to prepare this volume for the public eye; and I trust by the aid of Divine Providence to be able to make it intelligible and instructive. I thank God for the blessings of Liberty—the contrast is truly great between freedom and slavery. To be changed from a chattel to a human being, is no light matter, though the process with myself practically was very simple. And if I could reach the ears of every slave to-day, throughout the whole continent of America, I would teach the same lesson, I would sound it in the ears of every hereditary bondman, "break your chains and fly for freedom!"

It may be asked why I have written this work, when there has been so much already written and published of the same character from other fugitives? And, why publish it after having told it publicly all through New England and the Western States to multiplied thousands?

My answer is, that in no place have I given orally the detail of my narrative; and some of the most interesting events of my life have never reached the public ear. Moreover, it was at the request of many friends of down-trodden humanity, that I have undertaken to write the following sketch, that light and truth might be spread on the sin and evils of slavery as far as possible. I also wanted to leave my humble testimony on record against this man-destroying system, to be read by succeeding generations when my body shall lie mouldering in the dust.

But I would not attempt by any sophistry to misrepresent slavery in order to prove its dreadful wickedness. For, I presume there are none who may read this narrative through, whether Christians or slaveholders, males or females, but what will admit it to be a system of the most high-handed oppression and tyranny that ever was tolerated by an enlightened nation.

HENRY BIBB

I

Sketch of my Parentage.—Early separation from my Mother. —Hard Fare.—First Experiments at running away.—Earnest longing for Freedom.—Abhorrent nature of Slavery.

I was born May 1815, of a slave mother, in Shelby County, Kentucky, and was claimed as the property of David White Esq. He came into possession of my mother long before I was born. I was brought up in the Counties of Shelby, Henry, Oldham, and Trimble. Or, more correctly speaking, in the above counties, I may safely say, I was *flogged up;* for where I should have received moral, mental, and religious instruction, I received stripes without number, the object of which was to degrade and keep me in subordination. I can truly say, that I drank deeply of the bitter cup of suffering and woe. I have been dragged down to the lowest depths of human degradation and wretchedness, by Slaveholders.

My mother was known by the name of Milldred Jackson. She is the mother of seven slaves only, all being sons, of whom I am the eldest. She was also so fortunate or unfortunate, as to have some of what is called the slaveholding blood flowing in her veins. I know not how much; but not enough to prevent her children though fathered by slaveholders, from being bought and sold in the slave markets of the South. It is almost impossible for slaves to give a correct account of their male parentage. All that I know about it is, that my mother informed me that my father's name was JAMES BIBB. He was doubtless one of the present Bibb family of Kentucky; but I have no personal knowledge of him at all, for he died before my recollection.

The first time I was separated from my mother, I was young and small. I knew nothing of my condition then as a slave. I was living with Mr. White, whose wife died and left him a widower with one little girl, who was said to be the legitimate owner of my mother,

Editor's note: Bibb's *Narrative* was first published by the author, at 5 Spruce Street in New York City, in 1849.

and all her children. This girl was also my playmate when we were children.

I was taken away from my mother, and hired out to labor for various persons, eight or ten years in succession; and all my wages were expended for the education of Harriet White, my playmate. It was then my sorrows and sufferings commenced. It was then I first commenced seeing and feeling that I was a wretched slave, compelled to work under the lash without wages, and often without clothes enough to hide my nakedness. I have often worked without half enough to eat, both late and early, by day and by night. I have often laid my wearied limbs down at night to rest upon a dirt floor, or a bench, without any covering at all, because I had no where else to rest my wearied body, after having worked hard all the day. I have also been compelled in early life, to go at the bidding of a tyrant, through all kinds of weather, hot or cold, wet or dry, and without shoes frequently, until the month of December, with my bare feet on the cold frosty ground, cracked open and bleeding as I walked. Reader, believe me when I say, that no tongue, nor pen ever has or can express the horrors of American Slavery. Consequently I despair in finding language to express adequately the deep feeling of my soul, as I contemplate the past history of my life. But although I have suffered much from the lash, and for want of food and raiment; I confess that it was no disadvantage to be passed through the hands of so many families, as the only source of information that I had to enlighten my mind, consisted in what I could see and hear from others. Slaves were not allowed books, pen, ink, nor paper, to improve their minds. But it seems to me now, that I was particularly observing, and apt to retain what came under my observation. But more especially, all that I heard about liberty and freedom to the slaves, I never forgot. Among other good trades I learned the art of running away to perfection. I made a regular business of it, and never gave it up, until I had broken the bands of slavery, and landed myself safely in Canada, where I was regarded as a man, and not as a thing.

The first time in my life that I ran away, was for ill treatment, in 1835. I was living with a Mr. Vires, in the village of Newcastle. His wife was a very cross woman. She was every day flogging me, boxing, pulling my ears, and scolding, so that I dreaded to enter the room where she was. This first started me to running away from them. I was often gone several days before I was caught. They would abuse me for going off, but it did no good. The next time they flogged me, I was off again; but after awhile they got sick of their bargain, and returned me back into the hands of my owners. By this time Mr. White had married his second wife. She was what I call a tyrant. I lived with her several months, but she kept me almost half of my time in the woods, running from under the bloody lash. While I was at home she kept me all the time rubbing furniture, washing, scrubbing the floors; and when I was not doing this, she would often seat herself in a large rocking chair, with two pillows about her, and would make me rock her, and keep off the flies. She was too lazy to scratch her own head, and would often make me scratch and comb it for her. She would at other times lie on her bed, in warm weather, and make me fan her while she slept, scratch and rub her feet; but after awhile she got sick of me, and preferred a maiden servant to do such business. I was then hired out again; but by this time I had become much better skilled in running away, and would make calculation to avoid detection, by taking with me a bridle. If any body should see me in the woods, as they have, and asked "what are you doing here sir? you are a runaway?"—I said, "no, sir, I am looking for our old mare;" at other times, "looking for our cows." For such excuses I was let pass. In fact, the only weapon of self defence that I could use successfully, was that of deception. It is useless for a poor helpless slave, to resist a white man in a slaveholding State. Public opinion and the law is against him; and resistance in many cases is death to the slave, while the law declares, that he shall submit or die.

The circumstances in which I was then placed, gave me a longing desire to be free. It kindled a fire of liberty within my breast which has never yet been quenched. This seemed to be a part of my nature; it was first revealed to me by the inevitable laws of nature's God. I could see that the All-wise Creator, had made man a free, moral, intelligent and accountable being; capable of knowing good and evil. And I believed then, as I believe now, that every man has a right to wages for his labor; a right to his own wife and children; a right to liberty and the pursuit of happiness; and a right to worship God according to the dictates of his own conscience. But here, in the light of these truths, I was a slave, a prisoner for life; I could possess nothing, nor acquire anything but what must belong to my keeper. No one can imagine my feelings in my reflecting moments, but he who has himself been a slave. Oh! I have often wept over my condition, while sauntering through the forest, to escape cruel punishment.

No arm to protect me from tyrants aggression;
No parents to cheer me when laden with grief.
Man may picture the bounds of the rocks and the rivers,
The hills and the valleys, the lakes and the ocean,
But the horrors of slavery, he never can trace.

The term slave to this day sounds with terror to my soul,—a word too obnoxious to speak—a system too intolerable to be endured. I know this from long and sad experience. I now feel as if I had just been aroused from sleep, and looking back with quickened perception at the state of torment from whence I fled. I was there held and claimed as a slave; as such I was subjected to the will and power of my keeper, in all respects whatsoever. That the slave is a human being, no one can deny. It is his lot to be exposed in common with other men, to the calamities of sickness, death, and the misfortunes incident to life. But unlike other men, he is denied the consolation of struggling against external difficulties, such as destroy the life, liberty, and happiness of himself and family. A slave may be bought and sold in the market like an ox. He is liable to be sold off to a distant land from his family. He is bound in chains hand and foot; and his sufferings are aggravated a hundred fold, by the terrible thought, that he is not allowed to struggle against misfortune, corporeal punishment, insults and outrages committed upon himself and family; and he is not allowed to help himself, to resist or escape the blow, which he sees impending over him.

This idea of utter helplessness, in perpetual bondage, is the more distressing, as there is no period even with the remotest generation when it shall terminate.

II

A fruitless effort for education.—The Sabbath among Slaves. —Degrading amusements.—Why religion is rejected.—Condition of poor white people.—Superstition among slaves.— Education forbidden.

In 1833, I had some very serious religious impressions, and there was quite a number of slaves in that neighborhood, who felt very desirous to be taught to read the Bible. There was a Miss Davis, a poor white girl, who offered to teach a Sabbath School for the slaves, notwithstanding public opinion and the law was opposed to it. Books were furnished and she commenced the school; but the news soon got to our owners that she was teaching us to read. This caused quite an excitement in the neighborhood. Patrols* were appointed to go and break it up the next Sabbath. They were determined that we should not have a Sabbath School in operation. For slaves this was called an incendiary movement.

The Sabbath is not regarded by a large number of the slaves as a day of rest. They have no schools to go to; no moral nor religious instruction at all in many localities where there are hundreds of slaves. Hence they resort to some kind of amusement. Those who make no profession of religion, resort to the woods in large numbers on that day to gamble, fight, get drunk, and break the Sabbath. This is often encouraged by slaveholders. When they wish to have a little sport of that kind, they go among the slaves and give them whiskey, to see them dance, "pat juber," sing and play on the banjo. Then get them to wrestling, fighting, jumping, running foot races, and butting each other like sheep. This is urged on by giving them whiskey; making bets on them; laying chips on one slave's head, and daring another to tip it off with his hand; and if he tipped it off, it would be called an insult, and cause a fight. Before fighting, the parties choose their seconds to stand by them while fighting; a ring or a circle is formed to fight in, and no one is allowed to enter the ring while they are fighting, but their seconds, and the white gentlemen. They are not allowed to fight a duel, nor to use weapons of any kind. The blows are made by kicking, knocking, and butting with their heads; they grab each other by their ears, and jam their heads together like sheep. If they are likely to hurt each other very bad, their masters would rap them with their walking canes, and make them stop. After fighting, they make friends, shake hands, and take a dram together, and there is no more of it.

But this is all principally for want of moral instruction. This is

* Police peculiar to the South.

where they have no Sabbath Schools; no one to read the Bible to them; no one to preach the gospel who is competent to expound the Scriptures, except slaveholders. And the slaves, with but few exceptions, have no confidence at all in their preaching, because they preach a pro-slavery doctrine. They say, "Servants be obedient to your masters;—and he that knoweth his master's will and doeth it not, shall be beaten with many stripes;—means that God will send them to hell, if they disobey their masters. This kind of preaching has driven thousands into infidelity. They view themselves as suffering unjustly under the lash, without friends, without protection of law or gospel, and the green eyed monster tyranny staring them in the face. They know that they are destined to die in that wretched condition, unless they are delivered by the arm of Omnipotence. And they cannot believe or trust in such a religion, as above named.

The poor and loafering class of whites, are about on a par in point of morals with the slaves at the South. They are generally ignorant, intemperate, licentious, and profane. They associate much with the slaves; are often found gambling together on the Sabbath; encouraging slaves to steal from their owners, and sell to them, corn, wheat, sheep, chickens, or any thing of the kind which they can well conceal. For such offences there is no law to reach a slave but lynch law. But if both parties are caught in the act by a white person, the slave is punished with the lash, while the white man is often punished with both lynch and common law. But there is another class of poor white people in the South, who, I think would be glad to see slavery abolished in self defence; they despise the institution because it is impoverishing and degrading to them and their children.

The slave holders are generally rich, aristocratic, overbearing; and they look with utter contempt upon a poor laboring man, who earns his bread by the "sweat of his brow," whether he be moral or immoral, honest or dishonest. No matter whether he is white or black; if he performs manual labor for a livelihood, he is looked upon as being inferior to a slaveholder, and but little better off than the slave, who toils without wages under the lash. It is true, that the slaveholder, and non-slaveholder, are living under the same laws in the same State. But the one is rich, the other is poor; one is educated, the other is uneducated; one has houses, land and influence, the other has none. This being the case, that class of the non-slaveholders would be glad to see slavery abolished, but they dare not speak it aloud.

There is much superstition among the slaves. Many of them believe in what they call "conjuration," tricking, and witchcraft; and some of them pretend to understand the art, and say that by it they can prevent their masters from exercising their will over their slaves. Such are often applied to by others, to give them power to prevent their masters from flogging them. The remedy is most generally some kind of bitter root; they are directed to chew it and spit towards their masters when they are angry with their slaves. At other times they prepare certain kinds of powders, to sprinkle about their masters' dwellings. This is all done for the purpose of defending themselves in some peaceable manner, although I am satisfied that there is no virtue at all in it. I have tried it to perfection when I was a slave at the South. I was then a young man, full of life and vigor, and was very fond of visiting our neighbors slaves, but had no time to visit only Sundays, when I could get a permit to go, or after night, when I could slip off without being seen. If it was found out, the next morning I was called up to give an account of myself for going off without permission; and would very often get a flogging for it.

I got myself into a scrape at a certain time, by going off in this way, and I expected to be severely punished for it. I had a strong notion of running off, to escape being flogged, but was advised by a friend to go to one of those conjurers, who could prevent me from being flogged. I went and informed him of the difficulty. He said if I would pay him a small sum, he would prevent my being flogged. After I had paid him, he mixed up some alum, salt and other stuff into a powder, and said I must sprinkle it about my master, if he should offer to strike me; this would prevent him. He also gave me some kind of bitter root to chew, and spit towards him, which would certainly prevent my being flogged. According to order I used his remedy, and for some cause I was let pass without being flogged that time.

I had then great faith in conjuration and witchcraft. I was led to believe that I could do almost as I pleased, without being flogged. So on the next Sabbath my conjuration was fully tested by my going off, and staying away until Monday morning, without permission. When I returned home, my master declared that he would punish me for going off; but I did not believe that he could do it, while I had this root and dust; and as he approached me, I commenced talking saucy to him. But he soon convinced me that there was no virtue in them. He became so enraged at me for saucing him, that he grasped a handful of switches and punished me severely, in spite of all my roots and powders.

But there was another old slave in that neighborhood, who professed to understand all about conjuration, and I thought I would try his skill. He told me that the first one was only a quack, and if I would only pay him a certain amount in cash, that he would tell me how to prevent any person from striking me. After I had paid him his charge, he told me to go to the cow-pen after night, and get some fresh cow manure, and mix it with red pepper and white people's hair, all to be put into a pot over the fire, and scorched until it could be ground into snuff. I was then to sprinkle it about my master's bedroom, in his hat and boots, and it would prevent him from ever abusing me in any way. After I got it all ready prepared, the smallest pinch of it scattered over a room, was enough to make a horse sneeze from the strength of it; but it did no good. I tried it to my satisfaction. It was my business to make fires in my master's chamber, night and morning. Whenever I could get a chance, I sprinkled a little of this dust about the linen of the bed, where they would breathe it on retiring. This was to act upon them as what is called a kind of love powder, to change their sentiments of anger, to those of love, towards me, but this all proved to be vain imagination. The old man had my money, and I was treated no better for it.

One night when I went in to make a fire, I availed myself of the opportunity of sprinkling a very heavy charge of this powder about my master's bed. Soon after their going to bed, they began to cough and sneeze. Being close around the house, watching and listening, to know what the effect would be, I heard them ask each other what in the world it could be, that made them cough and sneeze so. All the while, I was trembling with fear, expecting every moment I should be called and asked if I knew any thing about it. After this, for fear they might find me out in my dangerous experiments upon them, I had to give them up, for the time being. I was then convinced that running away was the most effectual way by which a slave could escape cruel punishment.

As all the instrumentalities which I as a slave, could bring to bear upon the system, had utterly failed to palliate my sufferings, all hope and consolation fled. I must be a slave for life, and suffer under the lash or die. The influence which this had only tended to make me more unhappy. I resolved that I would be free if running away could make me so. I had heard that Canada was a land of liberty, somewhere in the North; and every wave of trouble that rolled across my breast, caused me to think more and more about Canada, and liberty. But more especially after having been flogged, I have fled to the highest hills of the forest, pressing my way to the North for refuge; but the river Ohio was my limit. To me it was an impassable gulf. I had no rod wherewith to smite the stream, and thereby divide the waters. I had no Moses to go before me and lead the way from bondage to a promised land. Yet I was in a far worse state than Egyptian bondage; for they had houses and land; I had none; they had oxen and sheep; I had none; they had a wise counsel, to tell them what to do, and where to go, and even to go with them; I had none. I was surrounded by opposition on every hand. My friends were few and far between. I have often felt when running away as if I had scarcely a friend on earth.

Sometimes standing on the Ohio River bluff, looking over on a free State, and as far north as my eyes could see, I have eagerly gazed upon the blue sky of the free North, which at times constrained me to cry out from the depths of my soul, Oh! Canada, sweet land of rest—Oh! when shall I get there? Oh, that I had the wings of a dove, that I might soar away to where there is no slavery; no clanking of chains, no captives, no lacerating of backs, no parting of husbands and wives; and where man ceases to be the property of his fellow man. These thoughts have revolved in my mind a thousand times. I have stood upon the lofty banks of the river Ohio, gazing upon the splendid steamboats, wafted with all their magnificence up and down the river, and I thought of the fishes of the water, the fowls of the air, the wild beasts of the forest, all appeared to be free, to go just where they pleased, and I was an unhappy slave!

But my attention was gradually turned in a measure from this subject, by being introduced into the society of young women. This for the time being took my attention from running away, as waiting on the girls appeared to be perfectly congenial to my nature. I wanted to be well thought of by them, and would go to great lengths to gain their affection. I had been taught by the old superstitious slaves, to believe in conjuration, and it was hard for me to give up the notion, for all I had been deceived by them. One of these conjurers, for a small sum agreed to teach me to make any girl love me that I wished. After I had paid him, he told me to get a bull frog, and take a certain bone out of the frog, dry it, and when I got a chance I must step up to any girl whom I wished to make love me, and scratch her somewhere on her naked skin with this bone, and she would be certain to love me, and would follow me in spite of herself; no matter who she might be engaged to, nor who she might be walking with.

So I got me a bone for a certain girl, whom I knew to be under the influence of another young man. I happened to meet her in the company of her lover, one Sunday evening, walking out; so when I got a chance, I fetched her a tremendous rasp across her neck with this bone, which made her jump. But in place of making her love me, it only made her angry with me. She felt more like running after me to retaliate on me for thus abusing her, than she felt like loving me. After I found there was no virtue in the bone of a frog, I thought I would try some other way to carry out my object. I then sought another counsellor among the old superstitious influential slaves; one who professed to be a great friend of mine, told me to get a lock of hair from the head of any girl, and wear it in my shoes: this would cause her to love me above all other persons. As there was another girl whose affections I was anxious to gain, but could not succeed, I thought, without trying the experiment of this hair. I slipped off one night to see the girl, and asked her for a lock of her hair; but she refused to give it. Believing that my success depended greatly upon this bunch of hair, I was bent on having a lock before I left that night let it cost what it might. As it was time for me to start home in order to get any sleep that night, I grasped hold of a lock of her hair, which caused her to screech, but I never let go until I had pulled it out. This of course made the girl mad with me, and I accomplished nothing but gained her displeasure.

Such are the superstitious notions of the great masses of southern slaves. It is given to them by tradition, and can never be erased, while the doors of education are bolted and barred against them. But there is a prohibition by law, of mental and religious instruction. The state of Georgia, by an act of 1770, declared "that it shall not be lawful for any number of free negroes, mulattoes or mestinos, or even slaves in company with white persons, to meet together for the purpose of mental instruction, either before the rising of the sun or after the going down of the same." 2d Brevard's Digest, 254-5. Similar laws exist in most of the slave States, and patrols are sent out after night and on the Sabbath day to enforce them. They go through their respective towns to prevent slaves from meeting for religious worship or mental instruction.

This is the regulation and law of American Slavery, as sanctioned by the Government of the United States, and without which it could not exist. And almost the whole moral, political, and religious power of the nation are in favor of slavery and aggression, and against liberty and justice. I only judge by their actions, which speak louder than words. Slaveholders are put into the highest offices in the gift of the people in both Church and State, thereby making slaveholding popular and reputable.

III

My Courtship and Marriage.—Change of owner.—My first born.—Its sufferings.—My wife abused.—My own anguish.

The circumstances of my courtship and marriage, I consider to be among the most remarkable events of my life while a slave. To think that after I had determined to carry out the great idea which is so universally and practically acknowledged among all the civilized nations of the earth, that I would be free or die, I suffered myself to be turned aside by the fascinating charms of a female, who gradually won my attention from an object so high as that of liberty; and an object which I held paramount to all others.

But when I had arrived at the age of eighteen, which was in the year of 1833, it was my lot to be introduced to the favor of a mulatto slave girl named Malinda, who lived in Oldham County, Kentucky, about four miles from the residence of my owner. Malinda was a medium sized girl, graceful in her walk, of an extraordinary make, and active in business. Her skin was of a smooth texture, red cheeks, with dark and penetrating eyes. She moved in the highest circle* of slaves, and free people of color. She was also one of the best singers I ever heard, and was much esteemed by all who knew her, for her benevolence, talent and industry. In fact, I considered Malinda to be equalled by few, and surpassed by none, for the above qualities, all things considered.

It is truly marvellous to see how sudden a man's mind can be changed by the charms and influence of a female. The first two or three visits that I paid this dear girl, I had no intention of courting or marrying her, for I was aware that such a step would greatly obstruct my way to the land of liberty. I only visited Malinda because I liked her company, as a highly interesting girl. But in spite of myself, before I was aware of it, I was deeply in love; and what made this passion so effectual and almost irresistable, I became satisfied that it was reciprocal. There was a union of feeling, and every visit made the impression stronger and stronger. One or two other young men were paying attention to Malinda, at the same time; one of whom her mother was anxious to have her marry. This of course gave me a fair opportunity of testing Malinda's sincerity. I had just about opposition enough to make the subject interesting. That Malinda loved me above all others on earth, no one could deny. I could read it by the warm reception with which the dear girl always met me, and treated me in her mother's house. I could read it by the warm and affectionate shake of the hand, and gentle smile upon her lovely cheek. I could read it by her always giving me the preference of her company; by her pressing invitations to visit even in opposition to her mother's will. I could read it in the language of her bright and sparkling eye, penciled by the unchangable finger of nature, that spake but could not lie. These strong temptations gradually diverted my attention from my actual condition and from liberty, though not entirely.

But oh! that I had only then been enabled to have seen as I do now, or to have read the following slave code, which is but a stereotyped law of American slavery. It would have saved me I think from having to lament that I was a husband and am the father of slaves who are still left to linger out their days in hopeless bondage. The laws of Kentucky, my native State, with Maryland

* The distinction among slaves is as marked, as the classes of society are in any aristocratic community. Some refusing to associate with others whom they deem beneath them in point of character, color, condition, or the superior importance of their respective masters.

and Virginia, which are said to be the mildest slave States in the Union, noted for their humanity, Christianity and democracy, declare that "Any slave, for rambling in the night, or riding horseback without leave, or running away, may be punished by whipping, cropping and branding in the cheek, or otherwise, not rendering him unfit for labor." "Any slave convicted of petty larceny, murder, or wilfully burning of dwelling houses, may be sentenced to have his right hand cut off; to be hanged in the usual manner, or the head severed from the body, the body divided into four quarters, and head and quarters stuck up in the most public place in the county, where such act was committed."

At the time I joined my wife in holy wedlock, I was ignorant of these ungodly laws; I knew not that I was propagating victims for this kind of torture and cruelty. Malinda's mother was free, and lived in Bedford, about a quarter of a mile from her daughter; and we often met and passed off the time pleasantly. Agreeable to promise, on one Saturday evening, I called to see Malinda, at her mother's residence, with an intention of letting her know my mind upon the subject of marriage. It was a very bright moonlight night; the dear girl was standing in the door, anxiously waiting my arrival. As I approached the door she caught my hand with an affectionate smile, and bid me welcome to her mother's fireside. After having broached the subject of marriage, I informed her of the difficulties which I conceived to be in the way of our marriage; and that I could never engage myself to marry any girl only on certain conditions; near as I can recollect the substance of our conversation upon the subject, it was, that I was religiously inclined; that I intended to try to comply with the requisitions of the gospel, both theoretically and practically through life. Also that I was decided on becoming a free man before I died; and that I expected to get free by running away, and going to Canada, under the British Government. Agreement on those two cardinal questions I made my test for marriage.

I said, "I never will give my heart nor hand to any girl in marriage, until I first know her sentiments upon the all-important subjects of Religion and Liberty. No matter how well I might love her, nor how great the sacrifice in carrying out these God-given principles. And I here pledge myself from this course never to be shaken while a single pulsation of my heart shall continue to throb for Liberty." With this idea Malinda appeared to be well pleased, and with a smile she looked me in the face and said, "I have long entertained the same views, and this has been one of the greatest reasons why I have not felt inclined to enter the married state while a slave; I have always felt a desire to be free; I have long cherished a hope that I should yet be free, either by purchase or running away. In regard to the subject of Religion, I have always felt that it was a good thing, and something that I would seek for at some future period." After I found that Malinda was right upon these all important questions, and that she truly loved me well enough to make me an affectionate wife, I made proposals for marriage. She very modestly declined answering the question then, considering it to be one of a grave character, and upon which our future destiny greatly depended. And notwithstanding she confessed that I had her entire affections, she must have some time to consider the matter. To this I of course consented, and was to meet her on the next Saturday night to decide the question. But for some cause I failed to come, and the next week she sent for me, and on the Sunday evening following I called on her again; she welcomed me with all the kindness of an affectionate lover, and seated me by her side. We soon broached the old subject of marriage, and entered upon a conditional contract of matrimony, viz: that we would marry if our minds should not change within one year; that after marriage we would change our former course and live a pious life; and that we would embrace the earliest opportunity of running away to Canada for our liberty. Clasping each other by the hand, pledging our sacred honor that we would be true, we called on high heaven to witness the rectitude of our purpose. There was nothing that could be more binding upon us as slaves than this; for marriage among American slaves, is disregarded by the laws of this country. It is counted a mere temporary matter; it is a union which may be continued or broken off, with or without the consent of a slaveholder, whether he is a priest or a libertine.

There is no legal marriage among the slaves of the South; I never saw nor heard of such a thing in my life, and I have been through seven of the slave states. A slave marrying according to law, is a thing unknown in the history of American Slavery. And be it known to the disgrace of our country that every slaveholder, who is the keeper of a number of slaves of both sexes, is also the keeper of a house or houses of ill-fame. Licentious white men, can and do, enter at night or day the lodging places of slaves; break up the bonds of affection in families; destroy all their domestic and social union for life; and the laws of the country afford them no protection. Will any man count, if they can be counted, the churches of Maryland, Kentucky, and Virginia, which have slaves connected with them, living in an open state of adultery, never having been married according to the laws of the State, and yet regular members of these various denominations, but more especially the Baptist and Methodist churches? And I hazard nothing in saying, that this state of things exists to a very wide extent in the above states.

I am happy to state that many fugitive slaves, who have been enabled by the aid of an over-ruling providence to escape to the free North with those whom they claim as their wives, notwithstanding all their ignorance and superstition, are not at all disposed to live together like brutes, as they have been compelled to do in slaveholding Churches. But as soon as they get free from slavery they go before some anti-slavery clergyman, and have the solemn ceremony of marriage performed according to the laws of the country. And if they profess religion, and have been baptized by a slaveholding minister, they repudiate it after becoming free, and are rebaptized by a man who is worthy of doing it according to the gospel rule.

The time and place of my marriage, I consider one of the most trying of my life. I was opposed by friends and foes; my mother opposed me because she thought I was too young, and marrying she thought would involve me in trouble and difficulty. My mother-in-law opposed me, because she wanted her daughter to marry a slave who belonged to a very rich man living near by, and who was well known to be the son of his master. She thought no doubt that his master or father might chance to set him free before he died, which would enable him to do a better part by her daughter than I could! And there was no prospect then of my ever being free. But his master has neither died nor yet set his son free, who is now about forty years of age, toiling under the lash, waiting and hoping that his master may die and will him to be free.

The young men are opposed to our marriage for the same reason that Paddy opposed a match when the clergyman was about to pronounce the marriage ceremony of a young couple. He said "if there be any present who have any objections to this couple being joined together in holy wedlock, let them speak now, or hold their peace henceforth." At this time Paddy sprang to his feet and said,

"Sir, I object to this." Every eye was fixed upon him. "What is your objection?" said the clergyman. "Faith," replied Paddy, "Sir I want her myself."

The man to whom I belonged was opposed, because he feared my taking off from his farm some of the fruits of my own labor for Malinda to eat, in the shape of pigs, chickens, or turkeys, and would count it not robbery. So we formed a resolution, that if we were prevented from joining in wedlock, that we would run away, and strike for Canada, let the consequences be what they might. But we had one consolation; Malinda's master was very much in favor of the match, but entirely upon selfish principles. When I went to ask his permission to marry Malinda, his answer was in the affirmative with but one condition, which I consider to be too vulgar to be written in this book. Our marriage took place one night during the Christmas holydays; at which time we had quite a festival given us. All appeared to be wide awake, and we had quite a jolly time at my wedding party. And notwithstanding our marriage was without license or sanction of law, we believed it to be honorable before God, and the bed undefiled. Our Christmas holydays were spent in matrimonial visiting among our friends, while it should have been spent in running away to Canada, for our liberty. But freedom was little thought of by us, for several months after marriage. I often look back to that period even now as one of the most happy seasons of my life; notwithstanding all the contaminating and heart-rending features with which the horrid system of slavery is marked, and must carry with it to its final grave, yet I still look back to that season with sweet remembrance and pleasure, that yet hath power to charm and drive back dull cares which have been accumulated by a thousand painful recollections of slavery. Malinda was to me an affectionate wife. She was with me in the darkest hours of adversity. She was with me in sorrow, and joy, in fasting and feasting, in trial and persecution, in sickness and health, in sunshine and in shade.

Some months after our marriage, the unfeeling master to whom I belonged, sold his farm with the view of moving his slaves to the State of Missouri, regardless of the separation of husbands and wives forever; but for fear of my resuming my old practice of running away, if he should have forced me to leave my wife, by my repeated requests, he was constrained to sell me to his brother, who lived within seven miles of Wm. Gatewood, who then held Malinda as his property. I was permitted to visit her only on Saturday nights, after my work was done, and I had to be at home before sunrise on Monday mornings or take a flogging. He proved to be so oppressive, and so unreasonable in punishing his victims, that I soon found that I should have to run away in self-defence. But he soon began to take the hint, and sold me to Wm. Gatewood the owner of Malinda. With my new residence I confess that I was much dissatisfied. Not that Gatewood was a more cruel master than my former owner—not that I was opposed to living with Malinda, who was then the centre and object of my affections—but to live where I must be eye witness to her insults, scourgings and abuses, such as are common to be inflicted upon slaves, was more than I could bear. If my wife must be exposed to the insults and licentious passions of wicked slavedrivers and overseers; if she must bear the stripes of the lash laid on by an unmerciful tyrant; if this is to be done with impunity, which is frequently done by slaveholders and their abettors, Heaven forbid that I should be compelled to witness the sight.

Not many months after I took up my residence on Wm. Gatewood's plantation, Malinda made me a father. The dear little daughter was called Mary Frances. She was nurtured and caressed by her mother and father, until she was large enough to creep over the floor after her parents, and climb up by a chair before I felt it to be my duty to leave my family and go into a foreign country for a season. Malinda's business was to labor out in the field the greater part of her time, and there was no one to take care of poor little Frances, while her mother was toiling in the field. She was left at the house to creep under the feet of an unmerciful old mistress, whom I have known to slap with her hand the face of little Frances, for crying after her mother, until her little face was left black and blue. I recollect that Malinda and myself came from the field one summer's day at noon, and poor little Frances came creeping to her mother smiling, but with large tear drops standing in her dear little eyes, sobbing and trying to tell her mother that she had been abused, but was not able to utter a word. Her little face was bruised black with the whole print of Mrs. Gatewood's hand. This print was plainly to be seen for eight days after it was done. But oh! this darling child was a slave; born of a slave mother. Who can imagine what could be the feelings of a father and mother, when looking upon their infant child whipped and tortured with impunity, and they placed in a situation where they could afford it no protection. But we were all claimed and held as property; the father and mother were slaves!

On this same plantation I was compelled to stand and see my wife shamefully scourged and abused by her master; and the manner in which this was done, was so violently and inhumanly committed upon the person of a female, that I despair in finding decent language to describe the bloody act of cruelty. My happiness or pleasure was then all blasted; for it was sometimes a pleasure to be with my little family even in slavery. I loved them as my wife and child. Little Frances was a pretty child; she was quiet, playful, bright, and interesting. She had a keen black eye, and the very image of her mother was stamped upon her cheek; but I could never look upon the dear child without being filled with sorrow and fearful apprehensions, of being separated by slaveholders, because she was a slave, regarded as property. And unfortunately for me, I am the father of a slave, a word too obnoxious to be spoken by a fugitive slave. It calls fresh to my mind the separation of husband and wife; of stripping, tying up and flogging; of tearing children from their parents, and selling them on the auction block. It calls to mind female virtue trampled under foot with impunity. But oh! when I remember that my daughter, my only child, is still there, destined to share the fate of all these calamities, it is too much to bear. If ever there was any one act of my life while a slave, that I have to lament over, it is that of being a father and a husband of slaves. I have the satisfaction of knowing that I am only the father of one slave. She is bone of my bone, and flesh of my flesh; poor unfortunate child. She was the first and shall be the last slave that ever I will father, for chains and slavery on this earth.

IV

My first adventure for liberty.—Parting Scene.—Journey up the river.—Safe arrival in Cincinnati.—Journey to Canada. —Suffering from cold and hunger.—Denied food and shelter by some.—One noble exception.—Subsequent success.—Arrival at Perrysburgh.—I obtained employment through the winter.—My return to Kentucky to get my family.

In the fall or winter of 1837 I formed a resolution that I would escape, if possible, to Canada, for my Liberty. I commenced from that hour making preparations for the dangerous experiment of breaking the chains that bound me as a slave. My preparation for this voyage consisted in the accumulation of a little money, perhaps not exceeding two dollars and fifty cents, and a suit which I had never been seen or known to wear before; this last was to avoid detection.

On the twenty-fifth of December, 1837, my long anticipated time had arrived when I was to put into operation my former resolution, which was to bolt for Liberty or consent to die a Slave. I acted upon the former, although I confess it to be one of the most self-denying acts of my whole life, to take leave of an affectionate wife, who stood before me on my departure, with dear little Frances in her arms, and with tears of sorrow in her eyes as she bid me a long farewell. It required all the moral courage that I was master of to suppress my feelings while taking leave of my little family.

Had Malinda known my intention at that time, it would not have been possible for me to have got away, and I might have to this day been a slave. Notwithstanding every inducement which was held out to me to run away if I would be free, and the voice of liberty was thundering in my very soul, "Be free, oh, man! be free," I was struggling against a thousand obstacles which had clustered around my mind to bind my wounded spirit still in the dark prison of mental degradation. My strong attachments to friends and relatives, with all the love of home and birth-place which is so natural among the human family, twined about my heart and were hard to break away from. And withal, the fear of being pursued with guns and blood-hounds, and of being killed, or captured and taken to the extreme South, to linger out my days in hopeless bondage on some cotton or sugar plantation, all combined to deter me. But I had counted the cost, and was fully prepared to make the sacrifice. The time for fulfilling my pledge was then at hand. I must forsake friends and neighbors, wife and child, or consent to live and die a slave.

By the permission of my keeper, I started out to work for myself on Christmas. I went to the Ohio River, which was but a short distance from Bedford. My excuse for wanting to go there was to get work. High wages were offered for hands to work in a slaughter-house. But in place of my going to work there, according to promise, when I arrived at the river I managed to find a conveyance to cross over into a free state. I was landed in the village of Madison, Indiana, where steamboats were landing every day and night, passing up and down the river, which afforded me a good opportunity of getting a boat passage to Cincinnati. My anticipation being worked up to the highest pitch, no sooner was the curtain of night dropped over the village, than I secreted myself where no one could see me, and changed my suit ready for the passage. Soon I heard the welcome sound of a Steamboat coming up the river Ohio, which was soon to waft me beyond the limits of the human slave markets of Kentucky. When the boat had landed at Madison, notwithstanding my strong desire to get off, my heart trembled within me in view of the great danger to which I was exposed in taking passage on board of a Southern steamboat; hence before I took passage, I kneeled down before the Great I Am, and prayed for his aid and protection, which He bountifully bestowed even beyond my expectation; for I felt myself to be unworthy. I then stept boldly on the deck of this splendid swift-running Steamer, bound for the city of Cincinnati. This being the first voyage that I had ever taken on board of a Steamboat, I was filled with fear and excitement, knowing that I was surrounded by the vilest enemies of God and man, liable to be seized and bound hand and foot, by any white man, and taken back into captivity. But I crowded myself back from the light among the deck passengers, where it would be difficult to distinguish me from a white man. Every time during the night that the mate came round with a light after the hands, I was afraid he would see I was a colored man, and take me up; hence I kept from the light as much as possible. Some men love darkness rather than light, because their deeds are evil; but this was not the case with myself; it was to avoid detection in doing right. This was one of the instances of my adventures that my affinity with the Anglo-Saxon race, and even slaveholders, worked well for my escape. But no thanks to them for it. While in their midst they have not only robbed me of my labor and liberty, but they have almost entirely robbed me of my dark complexion. Being so near the color of a slaveholder, they could not, or did not find me out that night among the white passengers. There was one of the deck hands on board called out on his watch, whose hammock was swinging up near by me. I asked him if he would let me lie in it. He said if I would pay him twenty-five cents that I might lie in it until day. I readily paid him the price and got into the hammock. No one could see my face to know whether I was white or colored, while I was in the hammock; but I never closed my eyes for sleep that night. I had often heard of explosions on board of Steamboats; and every time the boat landed, and blowed off steam, I was afraid the boilers had bursted and we should all be killed; but I lived through the night amid the many dangers to which I was exposed. I still maintained my position in the hammock, until the next morning about 8 o'clock, when I heard the passengers saying the boat was near Cincinnati; and by this time I supposed that the attention of the people would be turned to the city, and I might pass off unnoticed.

There were no questions asked me while on board the boat. The boat landed about 9 o'clock in the morning in Cincinnati, and I waited until after most of the passengers had gone off of the boat; I then walked as gracefully up street as if I was not running away, until I had got pretty well up Broadway. My object was to go to Canada, but having no knowledge of the road, it was necessary for me to make some inquiry before I left the city. I was afraid to ask a white person, and I could see no colored person to ask. But fortunately for me I found a company of little boys at play in the street, and through these little boys, by asking them indirect questions, I found the residence of a colored man.

"Boys, can you tell me where that old colored man lives who saws wood, and works at jobs around the streets?"

"What is his name?" said one of the boys.

"I forget."

"Is it old Job Dundy?"

"Is Dundy a colored man?"

"Yes, sir."

"That is the very man I am looking for; will you show me where he lives?"

"Yes," said the little boy, and pointed me out the house.

Mr. D. invited me in, and I found him to be a true friend. He asked me if I was a slave from Kentucky, and if I ever intended to go back into slavery? Not knowing yet whether he was truly in favor of slaves running away, I told him I had just come over to spend my Christmas Holydays, and that I was going back. His reply was, "my son, I would never go back if I was in your place; you have a right to your liberty." I then asked him how I should get my freedom? He referred me to Canada, over which waved freedom's flag, defended by the British Government, upon whose soil there cannot be the foot print of a slave.

He then commenced telling me of the facilities for my escape to Canada; of the Abolitionists; of the Abolition Societies, and of their fidelity to the cause of suffering humanity. This was the first time in my life that ever I had heard of such people being in existence as the Abolitionists. I supposed that they were a different race of people. He conducted me to the house of one of these warm-hearted friends of God and the slave. I found him willing to aid a poor fugitive on his way to Canada, even to the dividing of the last cent, or morsel of bread if necessary.

These kind friends gave me something to eat, and started me on my way to Canada, with a recommendation to a friend on my way. This was the commencement of what was called the under ground rail road to Canada. I walked with bold courage, trusting in the arm of Omnipotence; guided by the unchangeable North Star by night, and inspired by an elevated thought that I was fleeing from a land of slavery and oppression, bidding farewell to handcuffs, whips, thumb-screws and chains.

I travelled on until I had arrived at the place where I was directed to call on an Abolitionist, but I made no stop: so great were my fears of being pursued by the pro-slavery hunting dogs of the South. I prosecuted my journey vigorously for nearly forty-eight hours without food or rest, struggling against external difficulties such as no one can imagine who has never experienced the same: not knowing what moment I might be captured while travelling among strangers, through cold and fear, breasting the north winds, being thinly clad, pelted by the snow storms through the dark hours of the night, and not a house in which I could enter to shelter me from the storm.

The second night from Cincinnati, about midnight, I thought that I should freeze; my shoes were worn through, and my feet were exposed to the bare ground. I approached a house on the roadside, knocked at the door, and asked admission to their fire, but was refused. I went to the next house, and was refused the privilege of their fire-side, to prevent my freezing. This I thought was hard treatment among the human family. But—

> "Behind a frowning Providence there was a smiling face,"

which soon shed beams of light upon unworthy me.

The next morning I was still found struggling on my way, faint, hungry, lame, and rest-broken. I could see people taking breakfast from the roadside, but I did not dare to enter their houses to get my breakfast, for neither love nor money. In passing a low cottage, I saw the breakfast table spread with all its bounties, and I could see no male person about the house; the temptation for food was greater than I could resist.

I saw a lady about the table, and I thought that if she was ever so much disposed to take me up, that she would have to catch and hold me, and that would have been impossible. I stepped up to the door with my hat off, and asked her if she would be good enough to sell me a sixpence worth of bread and meat. She cut off a piece and brought it to me; I thanked her for it, and handed her the pay, but instead of receiving it, she burst into tears, and said "never mind the money," but gently turned away bidding me go on my journey. This was altogether unexpected to me: I had found a friend in the time of need among strangers, and nothing could be more cheering in the day of trouble than this. When I left that place I started with bolder courage. The next night I put up at a tavern, and continued stopping at public houses until my means were about gone. When I got to the Black Swamp in the county of Wood, Ohio, I stopped one night at a hotel, after travelling all day through mud and snow; but I soon found that I should not be able to pay my bill. This was about the time that the "wild-cat banks" were in a flourishing state, and "shin plasters"* in abundance; they would charge a dollar for one night's lodging.

After I had found out this, I slipped out of the bar room into the kitchen where the landlady was getting supper; as she had quite a number of travellers to cook for that night, I told her if she would accept my services, I would assist her in getting supper; that I was a cook. She very readily accepted the offer, and I went to work.

* Nickname for temporary paper money.

She was very much pleased with my work, and the next morning I helped her to get breakfast. She then wanted to hire me for all winter, but I refused for fear I might be pursued. My excuse to her was that I had a brother living in Detroit, whom I was going to see on some important business, and after I got that business attended to, I would come back and work for them all winter.

When I started the second morning they paid me fifty cents beside my board, with the understanding that I was to return; but I have not gone back yet.

I arrived the next morning in the village of Perrysburgh, where I found quite a settlement of colored people, many of whom were fugitive slaves. I made my case known to them and they sympathized with me. I was a stranger, and they took me in and persuaded me to spend the winter in Perrysburgh, where I could get employment and go to Canada the next spring, in a steamboat which ran from Perrysburgh, if I thought it proper so to do.

I got a job of chopping wood during that winter which enabled me to purchase myself a suit, and after paying my board the next spring, I had saved fifteen dollars in cash. My intention was to go back to Kentucky after my wife.

When I got ready to start, which was about the first of May, my friends all persuaded me not to go, but to get some other person to go, for fear I might be caught and sold off from my family into slavery forever. But I could not refrain from going back myself, believing that I could accomplish it better than a stranger.

The money that I had would not pass in the South, and for the purpose of getting it off to a good advantage, I took a steamboat passage to Detroit, Michigan, and there I spent all my money for dry goods, to peddle out on my way back through the State of Ohio. I also purchased myself a pair of false whiskers to put on when I got back to Kentucky, to prevent any one from knowing me after night, should they see me. I then started back after my little family.

V

My safe arrival at Kentucky.—Surprise and delight to find my family.—Plan for their escape projected.—Return to Cin-

cinnati.—My betrayal by traitors.—Imprisonment in Covington, Kentucky.—Return to slavery.—Infamous proposal of the slave catchers.—My reply.

I succeeded very well in selling out my goods, and when I arrived in Cincinnati, I called on some of my friends who had aided me on my first escape. They also opposed me in going back only for my own good. But it has ever been characteristic of me to persevere in what I undertake.

I took a Steamboat passage which would bring me to where I should want to land about dark, so as to give me a chance to find my family during the night if possible. The boat landed me at the proper place, and at the proper time accordingly. This landing was about six miles from Bedford, where my mother and wife lived, but with different families. My mother was the cook at a tavern, in Bedford. When I approached the house where mother was living, I remembered where she slept in the kitchen; her bed was near the window.

It was a bright moonlight night, and in looking through the kitchen window, I saw a person lying in bed about where my mother had formerly slept. I rapped on the glass which awakened the person in whom I recognized my dear mother, but she knew me not, as I was dressed in disguise with my false whiskers on; but she came to the window and asked who I was and what I wanted. But when I took off my false whiskers, and spoke to her, she knew my voice, and quickly sprang to the door, clasping my hand, exclaiming, "Oh! is this my son," drawing me into the room; where I was so fortunate as to find Malinda, and little Frances, my wife and child, whom I had left to find the fair climes of liberty, and whom I was then seeking to rescue from perpetual slavery.

They never expected to see me again in this life. I am entirely unable to describe what my feelings were at that time. It was almost like the return of the prodigal son. There was weeping and rejoicing. They were filled with surprise and fear; with sadness and joy. The senation of joy at that moment flashed like lightning over my afflicted mind, mingled with a thousand dreadful apprehensions, that none but a heart-wounded slave father and husband like myself can possibly imagine. After talking the matter over, we decided it was not best to start with my family that night, as it was very uncertain whether we should get a boat passage immediately.

And in case of failure, if Malinda should get back even before daylight the next morning, it would have excited suspicion against her, as it was not customary for slaves to leave home at that stage of the week without permission. Hence we thought it would be the most effectual way for her to escape, to start on Saturday night; this being a night on which the slaves of Kentucky are permitted to visit around among their friends, and are often allowed to stay until the afternoon on Sabbath day.

I gave Malinda money to pay her passage on board of a Steamboat to Cincinnati, as it was not safe for me to wait for her until Saturday night; but she was to meet me in Cincinnati, if possible, the next Sunday. Her father was to go with her to the Ohio River on Saturday night, and if a boat passed up during the night she was to get on board at Madison, and come to Cincinnati. If she should fail in getting off that night, she was to try it the next Saturday night. This was the understanding when we separated. This we thought was the best plan for her escape, as there had been so much excitement caused by my running away.

The owners of my wife were very much afraid that she would follow me; and to prevent her they had told her and other slaves that I had been persuaded off by the Abolitionists, who had promised to set me free, but had sold me off to New Orleans. They told the slaves to beware of the abolitionists, that their object was to decoy off slaves and then sell them off in New Orleans. Some of them believed this, and others believed it not; and the owners of my wife were more watchful over her than they had ever been before as she was unbelieving.

This was in the month of June, 1838. I left Malinda on a bright but lonesome Wednesday night. When I arrived at the river Ohio, I found a small craft chained to a tree, in which I ferried myself across the stream.

I succeeded in getting a Steamboat passage back to Cincinnati, where I put up with one of my abolition friends who knew that I had gone after my family, and who appeared to be much surprised to see me again. I was soon visited by several friends who knew of my having gone back after my family. They wished to know why I had not brought back my family with me; but after they understood the plan, and that my family was expected to be in Cincinnati within a few days, they thought it the best and safest plan for us to take a stage passage out to Lake Erie. But being short of money, I was not able to pay my passage in the stage, even if it would have prevented me from being caught by the slave hunters of Cincinnati, or save me from being taken back into bondage for life.

These friends proposed helping me by subscription; I accepted their kind offer, but in going among friends to solicit aid for me, they happened to get among traitors, and kidnappers, both white and colored men, who made their living by that kind of business. Several persons called on me and made me small donations, and among them two white men came in professing to be my friends. They told me not to be afraid of them, they were abolitionists. They asked me a great many questions. They wanted to know if I needed any help? and they wanted to know if it could be possible that a man so near white as myself could be a slave? Could it be possible that men would make slaves of their own children? They expressed great sympathy for me, and gave me fifty cents each; by this they gained my confidence. They asked my master's name; where he lived, &c. After which they left the room, bidding me God speed. These traitors, or land pirates, took passage on board of the first Steamboat down the river, in search of my owners. When they found them, they got a reward of three hundred dollars offered for the re-capture of this "stray" which they had so long and faithfully been hunting, by day and by night, by land and by water, with dogs and with guns, but all without success. This being the last and only chance for dragging me back into hopeless bondage, time and money was no object when they saw a prospect of my being re-taken.

Mr. Gatewood got two of his slaveholding neighbors to go with him to Cincinnati, for the purpose of swearing to anything which might be necessary to change me back into property. They came on to Cincinnati, and with but little effort they soon rallied a mob of ruffians who were willing to become the watch-dogs of slaveholders, for a dram, in connection with a few slavehunting petty constables.

While I was waiting the arrival of my family, I got a job of digging a cellar for the good lady where I was stopping, and while I was digging under the house, all at once I heard a man enter the house; another stept up to the cellar door to where I was at work; he looked in and saw me with my coat off at work. He then rapped over the cellar door on the house side, to notify the one who had entered the house to look for me that I was in the cellar. This strange conduct soon excited suspicion so strong in me, that I could not stay in the cellar and started to come out, but the man who stood by the door, rapped again on the house side, for the other to come to his aid, and told me to stop. I attempted to pass out by him, and he caught hold of me, and drew a pistol, swearing if I did not stop he would shoot me down. By this time I knew I was betrayed.

I asked him what crime I had committed that I should be murdered.

"I will let you know, very soon," said he.

By this time there were others coming to his aid, and I could see no way by which I could possibly escape the jaws of that hell upon earth.

All my flattering prospects of enjoying my own fire-side, with my little family, were then blasted and gone; and I must bid farewell to friends and freedom forever.

In vain did I look to the infamous laws of the Commonwealth of Ohio, for that protection against violence and outrage, that even the vilest criminal with a white skin might enjoy. But oh! the dreadful thought, that after all my sacrifice and struggling to rescue my family from the hands of the oppressor; that I should be dragged back into cruel bondage to suffer the penalty of a tyrant's law, to endure stripes and imprisonment, and to be shut out from all moral as well as intellectual improvement, and linger out almost a living death.

When I saw a crowd of blood-thirsty, unprincipled slave hunters rushing upon me armed with weapons of death, it was no use for me to undertake to fight my way through against such fearful odds.

But I broke away from the man who stood by with his pistol drawn to shoot me if I should resist, and reached the fence and attempted to jump over it before I was overtaken; but the fence being very high I was caught by my legs before I got over.

I kicked and struggled with all my might to get away, but without success. I kicked a new cloth coat off of his back, while he was holding on to my leg. I kicked another in his eye; but they never let me go until they got more help. By this time, there was a crowd on the out side of the fence with clubs to beat me back. Finally, they succeeded in dragging me from the fence and overpowered me by numbers and choked me almost to death.

These ruffians dragged me through the streets of Cincinnati, to what was called a justice office. But it was more like an office of injustice.

When I entered the room I was introduced to three slaveholders, one of whom was a son of Wm. Gatewood, who claimed me as his property. They pretended to be very glad to see me.

They asked me if I did not want to see my wife and child; but I made no reply to any thing that was said until I was delivered up as a slave. After they were asked a few questions by the court, the old pro-slavery squire very gravely pronounced me to be the property of Mr. Gatewood.

The office being crowded with spectators, many of whom were colored persons, Mr. G. was afraid to keep me in Cincinnati, two or three hours even, until a steamboat got ready to leave for the South. So they took me across the river, and locked me up in Covington jail, for safe keeping. This was the first time in my life that I had been put into a jail. It was truly distressing to my feelings to be locked up in a cold dungeon for no crime. The jailor not being at home, his wife had to act in his place. After my owners had gone back to Cincinnati, the jailor's wife, in company with another female, came into the jail and talked with me very friendly.

I told them all about my situation, and these ladies said they hoped that I might get away again, and went so far as to tell me if I should be kept in the jail that night, there was a hole under the wall of the jail where a prisoner had got out. It was only filled up with loose dirt, they said, and I might scratch it out and clear myself.

This I thought was a kind word from an unexpected friend: I had power to have taken the key from those ladies, in spite of them, and have cleared myself; but knowing that they would have to suffer perhaps for letting me get away, I thought I would wait until after dark, at which time I should try to make my escape, if they should not take me out before that time. But within two or three hours, they came after me, and conducted me on board of a boat, on which we all took passage down to Louisville. I was not confined in any way, but was well guarded by five men, three of whom were slaveholders, and the two young men from Cincinnati, who had betrayed me.

After the boat had got fairly under way, with these vile men standing around me on the upper deck of the boat, and she under full speed carrying me back into a land of torment, I could see no possible way of escape. Yet, while I was permitted to gaze on the beauties of nature, on free soil, as I passed down the river, things looked to me uncommonly pleasant: The green trees and wild flowers of the forest; the ripening harvest fields waving with the gentle breezes of Heaven; and the honest farmers tilling their soil and living by their own toil. These things seem to light upon my vision with a peculiar charm. I was conscious of what must be my fate; a wretched victim for Slavery without limit; to be sold like an ox, into hopeless bondage, and to be worked under the flesh-devouring lash during life, without wages.

This was to me an awful thought; every time the boat ran near the shore, I was tempted to leap from the deck down into the water, with a hope of making my escape. Such was then my feeling.

But on a moment's reflection, reason with her warning voice overcame this passion by pointing out the dreadful consequences of one's committing suicide. And this I thought would have a very striking resemblance to the act, and I declined putting into practice this dangerous experiment, though the temptation was great.

These kidnapping gentlemen, seeing that I was much dissatisfied, commenced talking to me, by saying that I must not be cast down; they were going to take me back home to live with my family, if I would promise not to run away again.

To this I agreed, and told them that this was all that I could ask, and more than I had expected.

But they were not satisfied with having recaptured me, because they had lost other slaves and supposed that I knew their whereabouts; and truly I did. They wanted me to tell them; but before telling I wanted them to tell who it was that had betrayed me into their hands. They said that I was betrayed by two colored men in Cincinnati, whose names they were backward in telling, because their business in connection with themselves was to betray and catch fugitive slaves for the reward offered. They undertook to justify the act by saying if they had not betrayed me, that somebody else would, and if I would tell them where they could catch a number of other runaway slaves, they would pay for me and set me free, and would then take me in as one of the Club. They said I would soon make money enough to buy my wife and child out of slavery.

But I replied, "No, gentlemen, I cannot commit or do an act of that kind, even if it were in my power so to do. I know that I am now in the power of a master who can sell me from my family for life, or punish me for the crime of running away, just as he pleases: I know that I am a prisoner for life, and have no way of extricating myself; and I also know that I have been deceived and betrayed by men who professed to be my best friends; but can all this justify me in becoming a traitor to others? Can I do that which I complain of others for doing unto me? Never, I trust, while a single pulsation of my heart continues to beat, can I consent to betray a fellow man like myself back into bondage, who has escaped. Dear as I love my wife and little child, and as much as I should like to enjoy freedom and happiness with them, I am unwilling to bring this about by betraying and destroying the liberty and happiness of others who have never offended me!"

I then asked them again if they would do me the kindness to tell me who it was betrayed me into their hands at Cincinnati? They agreed to tell me with the understanding that I was to tell where there was living, a family of slaves at the North, who had run away from Mr. King of Kentucky. I should not have agreed to this, but I knew the slaves were in Canada, where it was not possible for them to be captured. After they had told me the names of the persons who betrayed me, and how it was done, then I told them their slaves were in Canada, doing well. The two white men were Constables, who claimed the right of taking up any strange colored person as a slave; while the two colored kidnappers, under the pretext of being abolitionists, would find out all the fugitives they could, and inform these Constables for which they got a part of the reward, after they had found out where the slaves were from, the name of his master, &c. By the agency of these colored men, they were seized by a band of white ruffians, locked up in jail, and their master sent for. These colored kidnappers, with the Constables, were getting rich by betraying fugitive slaves. This was told to me by one of the Constables, while they were all standing around trying to induce me to engage in the same business for the sake of regaining my own liberty, and that of my wife and child. But my answer even there, under the most trying circumstances, surrounded by the strongest enemies of God and man, was most emphatically in the negative. "Let my punishment be what it may, either with the lash or by selling me away from my friends and home; let my destiny be what you please, I can never engage in this business for the sake of getting free."

They said I should not be sold nor punished with the lash for what I had done, but I should be carried back to Bedford, to live with my wife. Yet when the boat got to where we should have landed, she wafted by without making any stop. I felt awful in view of never seeing my family again; they asked what was the matter? what made me look so cast down? I informed them that I knew I was to be sold in the Louisville slave market, or in New Orleans, and I never expected to see my family again. But they tried to pacify me by promising not to sell me to a slave trader who would take me off to New Orleans; cautioning me at the same time not to let it be known that I had been a runaway. This would very much lessen the value of me in market. They would not punish me by putting irons on my limbs, but would give me a good name, and sell me to some gentleman in Louisville for a house servant. They thought I would soon make money enough to buy myself, and would not part with me if they could get along without. But I had cost them so much in advertising and looking for me, that they were involved by it. In the first place they paid eight hundred and fifty dollars for me; and when I first run away, they paid one hundred for advertising and looking after me; and now they had to pay about forty dollars, expenses travelling to and from Cincinnati, in addition to the three hundred dollars reward; and they were not able to pay the reward without selling me.

I knew then the only alternative left for me to extricate myself was to use deception, which is the most effective defence a slave can use. I pretended to be satisfied for the purpose of getting an opportunity of giving them the slip.

But oh, the distress of mind, the lamentable thought that I should never again see the face nor hear the gentle voice of my nearest and dearest friends in this life. I could imagine what must be my fate from my peculiar situation. To be sold to the highest bidder, and then wear the chains of slavery down to the grave. The day star of liberty which had once cheered and gladdened my heart in freedom's land, had then hidden itself from my vision, and the dark and dismal frown of slavery had obscured the sunshine of freedom from me, as they supposed for all time to come.

But the understanding between us was, I was not to be tied, chained, nor flogged; for if they should take me into the city handcuffed and guarded by five men the question might be asked what crime I had committed? And if it should be known that I had been a runaway to Canada, it would lessen the value of me at least one hundred dollars.

VI

Arrival at Louisville, Ky.—Efforts to sell me.—Fortunate escape from the man-stealers in the public street.—I return to Bedford, Ky.—The rescue of my family again attempted.—I started alone expecting them to follow.—After waiting some months I resolve to go back again to Kentucky.

When the boat arrived at Louisville, the day being too far spent for them to dispose of me, they had to put up at a Hotel. When we left the boat, they were afraid of my bolting from them in the street, and to prevent this they took hold of my arms, one on each side of me, gallanting me up to the hotel with as much propriety as if I had been a white lady. This was to deceive the people, and prevent my getting away from them.

They called for a bed-room to which I was conducted and locked within. That night three of them lodged in the same room to guard me. They locked the door and put the key under the head of their bed. I could see no possible way for my escape without jumping out of a three-story house window.

It was almost impossible for me to sleep that night in my peculiar situation. I passed the night in prayer to our Heavenly Father, asking that He would open to me even the smallest chance for escape.

The next morning after they had taken breakfast, four of them left me in the care of Dan Lane. He was what might be called one of the watch dogs of Kentucky. There was nothing too mean for him to do. He never blushed to rob a slave mother of her children, no matter how young or small. He was also celebrated for slave selling, kidnapping, and negro hunting. He was well known in that region by the slaves as well as the slaveholders, to have all the qualifications necessary for his business. He was a drunkard, a gambler, a profligate, and a slaveholder.

While the other four were looking around through the city for a purchaser, Dan was guarding me with his bowie knife and pistols. After a while the others came in with two persons to buy me, but on seeing me they remarked that they thought I would run away, and asked me if I had ever run away. Dan sprang to his feet and answered the question for me, by telling one of the most palpable falsehoods that ever came from the lips of a slaveholder. He declared that I had never run away in my life!

Fortunately for me, Dan, while the others were away, became unwell; and from taking salts, or from some other cause, was compelled to leave his room. Off he started to the horse stable which was located on one of the most public streets of Louisville, and of course I had to accompany him. He gallanted me into the stable by the arm, and placed himself back in one of the horses stalls and ordered me to stand by until he was ready to come out.

At this time a thousand thoughts were flashing through my mind with regard to the propriety of trying the springs of my heels, which nature had so well adapted for taking the body out of danger, even in the most extraordinary emergencies. I thought in the attempt to get away by running, if I should not succeed, it could make my condition no worse, for they could but sell me and this they were then trying to do. These thoughts impelled me to keep edging towards the door, though very cautiously. Dan kept looking around after me as if he was not satisfied at my getting so near to the door. But the last I saw of him in the stable was just as he turned his eyes from me; I nerved myself with all the moral courage I could command and bolted for the door, perhaps with the fleetness of a much frightened deer, who never looks behind in time of peril. Dan was left in the stable to make ready for the race, or jump out into the street half dressed, and thereby disgrace himself before the public eye.

It would be impossible for me to set forth the speed with which I ran to avoid my adversary; I succeeded in turning a corner before Dan got sight of me, and by fast running, turning corners, and jumping high fences, I was enabled to effect my escape.

In running so swiftly through the public streets, I thought it would be a safer course to leave the public way, and as quick as thought I spied a high board fence by the way and attempted to leap over it. The top board broke and down I came into a hen-coop which stood by the fence. The dogs barked, and the hens flew and cackled so, that I feared it would lead to my detection before I could get out of the yard.

The reader can only imagine how great must have been the excited state of my mind while exposed to such extraordinary peril and danger on every side. In danger of being seized by a savage dog, which sprang at me when I fell into the hen-coop; in danger of being apprehended by the tenants of the lot; in danger of being shot or wounded by any one who might have attempted to stop me, a runaway slave; and in danger on the other hand of being overtaken and getting in conflict with my adversary. With these fearful apprehensions, caution dictated me not to proceed far by day-light in this slaveholding city.

At this moment every nerve and muscle of my whole system was in full stretch; and every facility of the mind brought into action striving to save myself from being re-captured. I dared not go to the forest, knowing that I might be tracked by bloodhounds, and overtaken. I was so fortunate as to find a hiding place in the city which seemed to be pointed out by the finger of Providence. After running across lots, turning corners, and shunning my fellow men, as if they were wild ferocious beasts, I found a hiding place in a pile of boards or scantling, where I kept concealed during that day.

No tongue nor pen can describe the dreadful apprehensions under which I labored for the space of ten or twelve hours. My hiding place happened to be between two workshops, where there were men at work within six or eight feet of me. I could imagine that I heard them talking about me, and at other times thought I heard the footsteps of Daniel Lane in close pursuit. But I retained my position there until 9 or 10 o'clock at night, without being discovered; after which I attempted to find my way out, which was exceedingly difficult. The night being very dark, in a strange city, among slaveholders and slave hunters, to me it was like a person entering a wilderness among wolves and vipers, blindfolded. I was compelled from necessity to enter this place for refuge under the most extraordinary state of excitement, without regard to its geographical position. I found myself surrounded with a large block of buildings, which comprised a whole square, built up mostly on three sides, so that I could see no way to pass out without exposing myself perhaps to the gaze of patrols, or slave catchers.

In wandering around through the dark, I happened to find a calf in a back yard, which was bawling after the cow; the cow was also lowing in another direction, as if they were trying to find each other. A thought struck me that there must be an outlet somewhere about, where the cow and calf were trying to meet. I started in the direction where I heard the lowing of the cow, and I found an arch or tunnel extending between two large brick buildings, where I could see nothing of the cow but her eyes, shining like balls of fire through the dark tunnel, between the walls, through which I passed to where she stood. When I entered the streets I found them well lighted up. My heart was gladdened to know there was another chance for my escape. No bird ever let out of a cage felt more like flying, than I felt like running.

Before I left the city, I chanced to find by the way, an old man of color. Supposing him to be a friend, I ventured to make known my situation, and asked him if he would get me a bite to eat. The old man most cheerfully complied with my request. I was then about forty miles from the residence of Wm. Gatewood, where my wife, whom I sought to rescue from slavery, was living. This was also in the direction it was necessary for me to travel in order to get back to the free North. Knowing that the slave catchers would most likely be watching the public highway for me, to avoid them I made my way over the rocky hills, woods and plantations, back to Bedford.

I travelled all that night, guided on my way by the shining stars of heaven alone. The next morning just before the break of day, I came right to a large plantation, about which I secreted myself, until the darkness of the next night began to disappear. The morning larks commenced to chirp and sing merrily—pretty soon I heard the whip crack, and the voice of the ploughman driving in the corn field. About breakfast time, I heard the sound of a horn; saw a number of slaves in the field with a white man, who I supposed to be their overseer. He started to the house before the slaves, which gave me an opportunity to get the attention of one of the slaves, whom I met at the fence, before he started to his breakfast, and made known to him my wants and distresses. I also requested him to bring me a piece of bread if he could when he came back to the field.

The hospitable slave complied with my request. He came back to the field before his fellow laborers, and brought me something to eat, and as an equivalent for his kindness, I instructed him with regard to liberty, Canada, the way of escape, and the facilities by the way. He pledged his word that himself and others would be in Canada, in less than six months from that day. This closed our interview, and we separated. I concealed myself in the forest until about sunset, before I pursued my journey; and the second night from Louisville, I arrived again in the neighborhood of Bedford, where my little family were held in bondage, whom I so earnestly strove to rescue.

I concealed myself by the aid of a friend in that neighborhood, intending again to make my escape with my family. This confidential friend then carried a message to Malinda, requesting her to meet me on one side of the village.

We met under the most fearful apprehensions, for my pursuers had returned from Louisville, with the lamentable story that I was gone, and yet they were compelled to pay three hundred dollars to the Cincinnati slave catchers for re-capturing me there.

Daniel Lane's account of my escape from him, looked so unreasonable to slaveholders, that many of them charged him with selling me and keeping the money; while others believed that I had got away from him, and was then in the neighborhood, trying to take off my wife and child, which was true. Lane declared that in less than five minutes after I ran out of the stable in Louisville, he had over twenty men running and looking in every direction after me; but all without success. They could hear nothing of me. They had turned over several tons of hay in a large loft, in search, and I was not to be found there. Dan imputed my escape to my godliness! He said that I must have gone up in a chariot of fire, for I went off by flying; and that he should never again have any thing to do with a praying negro.

Great excitement prevailed in Bedford, and many were out watching for me at the time Malinda was relating to me these facts. The excitement was then so great among the slaveholders—who were anxious to have me re-captured as a means of discouraging other slaves from running away—that time and money were no object while there was the least prospect of their success. I therefore declined making an effort just at that time to escape with my little family. Malinda managed to get me into the house of a friend that night, in the village, where I kept concealed several days seeking an opportunity to escape with Malinda and Frances to Canada.

But for some time Malinda was watched so very closely by white and by colored persons, both day and night, that it was not possible for us to escape together. They well knew that my little family was the only object of attraction that ever had or ever would induce me to come back and risk my liberty over the threshold of slavery—therefore this point was well guarded by the watch dogs of slavery, and I was compelled again to forsake my wife for a season, or surrender, which was suicidal to the cause of freedom, in my judgment.

The next day after my arrival in Bedford, Daniel Lane came to the very house wherein I was concealed and talked in my hearing to the family about my escape from him out of the stable in Louisville. He was near enough for me to have laid my hands on his head while in that house—and the intimidation which this produced on me was more than I could bear. I was also aware of the great temptation of the reward offered to white or colored persons for my apprehension; I was exposed to other calamities which rendered it altogether unsafe for me to stay longer under that roof.

One morning about 2 o'clock, I took leave of my little family and started for Canada. This was almost like tearing off the limbs from my body. When we were about to separate, Malinda clasped my hand exclaiming, "oh my soul! my heart is almost broken at the thought of this dangerous separation. This may be the last time we shall ever see each other's faces in this life, which will destroy all my future prospects of life and happiness forever." At this time the poor unhappy woman burst into tears and wept loudly; and my eyes were not dry. We separated with the understanding that she was to wait until the excitement was all over; after which she was to meet me at a certain place in the State of Ohio; which would not be longer than two months from that time.

I succeeded that night in getting a steamboat conveyance back to Cincinnati, or within ten miles of the city. I was apprehensive that there were slave-hunters in Cincinnati, watching the arrival of every boat up the river, expecting to catch me; and the boat landing to take in wood ten miles below the city, I got off and walked into Cincinnati, to avoid detection.

On my arrival at the house of a friend, I heard that the two young men who betrayed me for the three hundred dollars had returned and were watching for me. One of my friends in whom they had great confidence, called on the traitors, after he had talked with me, and asked them what they had done with me. Their reply was that I had given them the slip, and that they were glad of it, because they believed that I was a good man, and if they could see me on my way to Canada, they would give me money to aid me on my escape. My friend assured them that if they would give any thing to aid me on my way, much or little, if they would put the same into his hands, he would give it to me that night, or return it to them the next morning.

They then wanted to know where I was and whether I was in the city; but he would not tell them, but one of them gave him one dollar for me, promising that if I was in the city, and he would let him know the next morning, he would give me ten dollars.

But I never waited for the ten dollars. I received one dollar of the amount which they got for betraying me, and started that night for the north. Their excuse for betraying me, was, that catching runaways was their business, and if they had not done it somebody else would, but since they had got the reward they were glad that I had made my escape.

Having travelled the road several times from Cincinnati to Lake Erie, I travelled through without much fear or difficulty. My friends in Perrysburgh, who knew that I had gone back into the very jaws of slavery after my family, were much surprised at my return, for they had heard that I was re-captured.

After I had waited three months for the arrival of Malinda and she came not, it caused me to be one of the most unhappy fugitives that ever left the South. I had waited eight or nine months without hearing from my family. I felt it to be my duty, as a husband and father, to make one more effort. I felt as if I could not give them up to be sacrificed on the "bloody altar of slavery." I felt as if love, duty, humanity and justice, required that I should go back, putting my trust in the God of Liberty for success.

VII

My safe return to Kentucky.—The perils I encountered there. —Again betrayed, and taken by a mob; ironed and imprisoned.—Narrow escape from death.—Life in a slave prison.

I prepared myself for the journey before named, and started back in the month of July, 1839.

My intention was, to let no person know my business until I returned back to the North. I went to Cincinnati, and got a passage down on board of a boat just as I did the first time, without any misfortune or delay. I called on my mother, and the raising of a dead body from the grave could not have been more surprising to any one than my arrival was to her, on that sad summer's night. She was not able to suppress her feelings. When I entered the room, there was but one other person in the house with my mother, and this was a little slave girl who was asleep when I entered. The impulsive feeling which is ever ready to act itself out at the return of a long absent friend, was more than my bereaved mother could suppress. And unfortunately for me, the loud shouts of joy at that late hour of the night, awakened the little slave girl, who afterwards betrayed me. She kept perfectly still, and never let either of us know that she was awake, in order that she might hear our conversation and report it. Mother informed me where my family was living, and that she would see them the next day, and would make arrangements for us to meet the next night at that house after the people in the village had gone to bed. I then went off and concealed myself during the next day, and according to promise came back the next night about eleven o'clock.

When I got near the house, moving very cautiously, filled with fearful apprehensions, I saw several men walking around the house as if they were looking for some person. I went back and waited about one hour, before I returned, and the number of men had increased. They were still to be seen lurking about this house, with dogs following them. This strange movement frightened me off again, and I never returned until after midnight, at which time I slipped up to the window, and rapped for my mother, who sprang to it and informed me that I was betrayed by the girl who overheard our conversation the night before. She thought that if I could keep out of the way for a few days, the white people would think that this girl was mistaken, or had lied. She had told her old mistress that I was there that night, and had made a plot with my mother to get my wife and child there the next night, and that I was going to take them off to Canada.

I went off to a friend of mine, who rendered me all the aid that one slave could render another, under the circumstances. Thank God he is now free from slavery, and is doing well. He was a messenger for me to my wife and mother, until at the suggestion of my mother, I changed an old friend for a new one, who betrayed me for the sum of five dollars.

We had set the time when we were to start for Canada, which was to be on the next Saturday night. My mother had an old friend whom she thought was true, and she got him to conceal me in a barn, not over two miles from the village. This man brought provisions to me, sent by my mother, and would tell me the news which was in circulation about me, among the citizens. But the poor fellow was not able to withstand the temptation of money.

My owners had about give me up, and thought the report of the slave girl was false; but they had offered a little reward among the slaves for my apprehension. The night before I was betrayed, I met with my mother and wife, and we had set up nearly all night plotting to start on the next Saturday night. I hid myself away in the flax in the barn, and being much rest broken I slept until the next morning about 9 o'clock. Then I was awakened by a mob of blood thirsty slaveholders, who had come armed with all the implements of death, with a determination to reduce me again to a life of slavery, or murder me on the spot.

When I looked up and saw that I was surrounded, they were exclaiming at the top of their voices, "shoot him down! shoot him down!" "If he offers to run, or to resist, kill him!"

I saw it was no use then for me to make any resistance, as I should be murdered. I felt confident that I had been betrayed by a slave, and all my flattering prospects of rescuing my family were gone for ever, and the grim monster slavery with all its horrors was staring me in the face.

I surrendered myself to this hostile mob at once. The first thing done, after they had laid violent hands on me, was to bind my hands behind me with a cord, and rob me of all I possessed.

In searching my pockets, they found my certificate from the Methodist E. Church, which had been given me by my classleader, testifying to my worthiness as a member of that church. And what made the matter look more disgraceful to me, many of this mob were members of the M. E. Church, and they were the persons who took away my church ticket, and then robbed me also of fourteen dollars in cash, a silver watch for which I paid ten dollars, a pocket knife for which I paid seventy-five cents, and a Bible for which I paid sixty-two and one half cents. All this they tyrannically robbed me of, and yet my owner, Wm. Gatewood, was a regular member of the same church to which I belonged.

He then had me taken to a blacksmith's shop, and most wickedly had my limbs bound with heavy irons, and then had my body locked within the cold dungeon walls of the Bedford jail, to be sold to a Southern slave trader.

My heart was filled with grief—my eyes were filled with tears. I could see no way of escape. I could hear no voice of consolation. Slaveholders were coming to the dungeon window in great numbers to ask me questions. Some were rejoicing—some swearing, and others saying that I ought to be hung; while others were in favor of sending both me and my wife to New Orleans. They supposed that I had informed her all about the facilities for slaves to escape to Canada, and that she would tell other slaves after I was gone; hence we must all be sent off to where we could neither escape ourselves, nor instruct others the way.

In the afternoon of the same day Malinda was permitted to visit the prison wherein I was locked, but was not permitted to enter the door. When she looked through the dungeon grates and saw my sad situation, which was caused by my repeated adventures to rescue her and my little daughter from the grasp of slavery, it was more than she could bear without bursting in tears. She plead for admission into the cold dungeon where I was confined, but without success. With manacled limbs; with wounded spirit; with sympathising tears and with bleeding heart, I entreated Malinda to weep not for me, for it only added to my grief, which was greater than I could bear.

I have often suffered from the sting of the cruel slave driver's lash on my quivering flesh—I have suffered from corporeal punishment in its various forms—I have mingled my sorrows with those that were bereaved by the ungodly soul drivers—and I also know what it is to shed the sympathetic tear at the grave of a departed friend; but all this is but a mere trifle compared with my sufferings from then to the end of six months subsequent.

The second night while I was in jail, two slaves came to the dungeon grates about the dead hour of night, and called me to the grates to have some conversation about Canada, and the facilities for getting there. They knew that I had travelled over the road, and they were determined to run away and go where they could be free. I of course took great pleasure in giving them directions how and where to go, and they started in less than a week from that time and got clear to Canada. I have seen them both since I came back to the north myself. They were known by the names of King and Jack.

The third day I was brought out of the prison to be carried off with my little family to the Louisville slave market. My hands were fastened together with heavy irons, and two men to guard me with loaded rifles, one of whom led the horse upon which I rode. My wife and child were set upon another nag. After we were all ready to start my old master thought I was not quite safe enough, and ordered one of the boys to bring him a bed cord from the store. He then tied my feet together under the horse, declaring that if I flew off this time, I should fly off with the horse.

Many tears were shed on that occasion by our friends and relatives, who saw us dragged off in irons to be sold in the human flesh market. No tongue could express the deep anguish of my soul when I saw the silent tear drops streaming down the sable cheeks of an aged slave mother, at my departure; and that too, caused by a black hearted traitor who was himself a slave:

I love the man with a feeling soul,
Whose passions are deep and strong;
Whose cords, when touched with a kindred power,
Will vibrate loud and long:

The man whose word is bond and law—
Who ne'er for gold or power,
Would kiss the hand that would stab the heart
In adversity's trying hour.

I love the man who delights to help
The panting, struggling poor:
The man that will open his heart,
Nor close against the fugitive at his door.

Oh give me a heart that will firmly stand,
When the storm of affliction shall lower—
A hand that will never shrink, if grasped,
In misfortune's darkest hour.

As we approached the city of Louisville, we attracted much attention, my being tied and handcuffed, and a person leading the horse upon which I rode. The horse appeared to be much frightened at the appearance of things in the city, being young and skittish. A carriage passing by jammed against the nag, which caused him to break from the man who was leading him, and in his fright throw me off backwards. My hands being confined with irons, and my feet tied under the horse with a rope, I had no power to help myself. I fell back off of the horse and could not extricate myself from this dreadful condition; the horse kicked with all his might while I was tied so close to his rump that he could only strike me with his legs by kicking.

The breath was kicked out of my body, but my bones were not broken. No one who saw my situation would have given five dollars for me. It was thought by all that I was dead and would never come to life again. When the horse was caught the cords were cut from my limbs, and I was rubbed with whiskey, camphor, &c., which brought me to life again.

Many bystanders expressed sympathy for me in my deplorable condition, and contempt for the tyrant who tied me to the young horse.

I was then driven through the streets of the city with my little family on foot, to jail, wherein I was locked with handcuffs yet on. A physician was then sent for, who doctored me several days before I was well enough to be sold in market.

The jail was one of the most disagreeable places I ever was confined in. It was not only disagreeable on account of the filth and dirt of the most disagreeable kind; but there were bed-bugs, fleas, lice and mosquitoes in abundance, to contend with. At night we had to lie down on the floor in this filth. Our food was very scanty, and of the most inferior quality. No gentleman's dog would eat what we were compelled to eat or starve.

I had not been in this prison many days before Madison Garrison, the soul driver, bought me and my family to sell again in the New Orleans slave market. He was buying up slaves to take to New Orleans. So he took me and my little family to the work-house, to be kept under lock and key at work until he had bought up as many as he wished to take off to the South.

The work-house of Louisville was a very large brick building, built on the plan of a jail or State's prison, with many apartments to it, divided off into cells wherein prisoners were locked up after night. The upper apartments were occupied by females, principally. This prison was enclosed by a high stone wall, upon which stood watchmen with loaded guns to guard the prisoners from breaking out, and on either side there were large iron gates.

When Garrison conducted me with my family to the prison in which we were to be confined until he was ready to take us to New Orleans, I was shocked at the horrid sight of the prisoners on entering the yard. When the large iron gate or door was thrown open to receive us, it was astonishing to see so many whites as well as colored men loaded down with irons, at hard labor; under the supervision of overseers.

Some were sawing stone, some cutting stone, and others breaking stone. The first impression which was made on my mind when I entered this place of punishment, made me think of hell, with all its terrors of torment; such as "weeping, wailing, and gnashing of teeth," which was then the idea that I had of the infernal regions from oral instruction. And I doubt whether there can be a better picture of it drawn, than may be sketched from an American slave prison.

In this prison almost every prisoner had a heavy log chain riveted about his leg. It would indeed be astonishing to a Christian man to stand in that prison one half hour and hear and see the contaminating influence of Southern slavery on the body and mind of man—you may there find almost every variety of character to look on. Some singing, some crying, some praying, and others swearing. The people of color who were in there were slaves, there without crime, but for safe keeping, while the whites were some of the most abandoned characters living. The keeper took me up to the anvil block and fastened a chain about my leg, which I had to drag after me both day and night during three months. My labor was sawing stone; my food was coarse corn bread and beef shanks and cows heads with pot liquor, and a very scanty allowance of that.

I have often seen the meat spoiled when brought to us, covered with flies and fly blows, and even worms crawling over when we were compelled to eat it, or go without any at all. It was all spread out on a long table in separate plates; and at the sound of a bell, every one would take his plate, asking no questions. After hastily eating, we were hurried back to our work, each man dragging a heavy log chain after him to his work.

About a half hour before night they were commanded to stop work, take a bite to eat, and then be locked up in a small cell until the next morning after sunrise. The prisoners were locked in, two together. My bed was a cold stone floor with but little bedding! My visitors were bed-bugs and mosquitoes.

VIII

Character of my prison companions.—Jail breaking contemplated.—Defeat of our plan.—My wife and child removed. —Disgraceful proposal to her, and cruel punishment.—Our departure in a coffle for New Orleans.—Events of our journey.

Most of the inmates of this prison I have described, were white men who had been sentenced there by the law, for depredations committed by them. There was in that prison, gamblers, and even murders. There were also in the female department, harlots, pick-pockets, and adulteresses. In such company, and under such influences, where there was constant swearing, lying, cheating, and stealing, it was almost impossible for a virtuous person to avoid pollution, or to maintain their virtue. No place or places in this country can be better calculated to inculcate vice of every kind than a Southern work house or house of correction.

After a profligate, thief, or a robber, has learned all that they can out of prison, they might go in one of those prisons and learn something more—they might properly be called robber colleges;

and if slaveholders understood this they would never let their slaves enter them. No man would give much for a slave who had been kept long in one of these prisons.

I have often heard them telling each other how they robbed houses, and persons on the high way, by knocking them down, and would rob them, pick their pockets, and leave them half dead. Others would tell of stealing horses, cattle, sheep, and slaves; and when they would be sometimes apprehended, by the aid of their friends, they would break jail. But they could most generally find enough to swear them clear of any kind of villany. They seemed to take great delight in telling of their exploits in robbery. There was a regular combination of them who had determined to resist law, wherever they went, to carry out their purposes.

In conversing with myself, they learned that I was notorious for running away, and professed sympathy for me. They thought that I might yet get to Canada, and be free, and suggested a plan by which I might accomplish it; and one way was, to learn to read and write, so that I might write myself a pass ticket, to go just where I pleased, when I was taken out of the prison; and they taught me secretly all they could while in the prison.

But there was another plan which they suggested to me to get away from slavery; that was to break out of the prison and leave my family. I consented to engage in this plot, but not to leave my family.

By my conduct in the prison, after having been there several weeks, I had gained the confidence of the keeper, and the turnkey. So much so, that when I wanted water or anything of the kind, they would open my door and hand it in to me. One of the turnkeys was an old colored man, who swept and cleaned up the cells, supplied the prisoners with water, &c.

On Sundays in the afternoon, the watchmen of the prison were most generally off, and this old slave, whose name was Stephen, had the prisoners to attend to. The white prisoners formed a plot to break out on Sunday in the afternoon, by making me the agent to get the prison keys from old Stephen.

I was to prepare a stone that would weigh about one pound, tie it up in a rag, and keep it in my pocket to strike poor old Stephen with, when he should open my cell door. But this I would not consent to do, without he should undertake to betray me.

I gave old Stephen one shilling to buy me a water melon, which he was to bring to me in the afternoon. All the prisoners were to be ready to strike, just as soon as I opened their doors. When Stephen opened my door to hand me the melon, I was to grasp him by the collar, raise the stone over his head, and say to him, that if he made any alarm that I should knock him down with the stone. But if he would be quiet he should not be hurt. I was then to take all the keys from him, lock him up in the cell—take a chisel and cut the chain from my own leg, then unlock all the cells below, and let out the other prisoners, who were all to cut off their chains. We were then to go and let out old Stephen, and make him go off with us. We were to form a line and march to the front gate of the prison with a sledge hammer, and break it open, and if we should be discovered, and there should be any out-cry, we were all to run and raise the alarm of fire, so as to avoid detection. But while we were all listening for Stephen to open the door with the melon, he came and reported that he could not get one, and handed me back the money through the window. All were disappointed, and nothing done. I looked upon it as being a fortunate thing for me, for it was certainly a very dangerous experiment for a slave, and they could never get me to consent to be the leader in that matter again.

A few days after, another plot was concocted to break prison, but it was betrayed by one of the party, which resulted in the most cruel punishment to the prisoners concerned in it; and I felt thankful that my name was not connected with it. They were not only flogged, but they were kept on bread and water alone, for many days. A few days after we were put in this prison, Garrison came and took my wife and child out, I knew not for what purpose, nor to what place, but after the absence of several days I supposed that he had sold them. But one morning, the outside door was thrown open, and Malinda thrust in by the ruthless hand of Garrison, whose voice was pouring forth the most bitter oaths and abusive language that could be dealt out to a female; while her heart-rending shrieks and sobbing, was truly melting to the soul of a father and husband.

The language of Malinda was, "Oh! my dear little child is gone? What shall I do? my child is gone." This most distressing sound struck a sympathetic chord through all the prison among the prisoners. I was not permitted to go to my wife and inquire what had become of little Frances. I never expected to see her again, for I supposed that she was sold.

That night, however, I had a short interview with my much abused wife, who told me the secret. She said that Garrison had taken her to a private house where he kept female slaves for the basest purposes. It was a resort for slave trading profligates and soul drivers, who were interested in the same business.

Soon after she arrived at this place, Garrison gave her to understand what he brought her there for, and made a most disgraceful assault on her virtue, which she promptly repeled; and for which Garrison punished her with the lash, threatening her that if she did not submit that he would sell her child. The next day he made the same attempt, which she resisted, declaring that she would not submit to it; and again he tied her up and flogged her until her garments were stained with blood.

He then sent our child off to another part of the city, and said he meant to sell it and that she should never see it again. He then drove Malinda before him to the work-house, swearing by his Maker that she should submit to him or die. I have already described her entrance in the prison.

Two days after this he came again and took Malinda out of the prison. It was several weeks before I saw her again, and learned that he had not sold her or the child. At the same time he was buying up other slaves to take to New Orleans. At the expiration of three months he was ready to start with us for the New Orleans slave market, but we never knew when we were to go, until the hour had arrived for our departure.

One Sabbath morning Garrison entered the prison and commanded that our limbs should be made ready for the coffles. They called us up to an anvil block, and the heavy log chains which we had been wearing on our legs during three months, were cut off. I had been in the prison over three months; but he had other slaves who had not been there so long. The hand-cuffs were then put on to our wrists. We were coupled together two and two—the right hand of one to the left hand of another, and a long chain to connect us together.

The other prisoners appeared to be sorry to see us start off in this way. We marched off to the river Ohio, to take passage on board of the steamboat Water Witch. But this was at a very low time of water, in the fall of 1839. The boat got aground, and did not get off that night; and Garrison had to watch us all night to keep any from getting away. He also had a very large savage dog, which was trained up to catch runaway slaves.

We were more than six weeks getting to the city of New Orleans, in consequence of low water. We were shifted on to several boats before we arrived at the mouth of the river Ohio. But we got but very little rest at night. As all were chained together night and day, it was impossible to sleep, being annoyed by the bustle and crowd of the passengers on board; by the terrible thought that we were destined to be sold in market as sheep or oxen; and annoyed by the galling chains that cramped our wearied limbs, on the tedious voyage. But I had several opportunities to have run away from Garrison before we got to the mouth of the Ohio river. While they were shifting us from one boat to another, my hands were some times loosed, until they got us all on board—and I know that I should have broke away had it not been for the sake of my wife and child who was with me. I could see no chance to get them off, and I could not leave them in that condition—and Garrison was not so much afraid of my running away from him while he held on to my family, for he knew from the great sacrifices which I had made to rescue them from slavery, that my attachment was too strong to run off and leave them in his hands, while there was the least hope of ever getting them away with me.

IX

Our arrival and examination at Vicksburg.—An account of slave sales.—Cruel punishment with the paddle.—Attempts to sell myself by Garrison's direction.—Amusing interview with a slave buyer.—Deacon Whitfield's examination.—He purchases the family.—Character of the Deacon.

When we arrived at the city of Vicksburg, he intended to sell a portion of his slaves there, and stopped for three weeks trying to sell. But he met with very poor success.

We had there to pass through an examination or inspection by a city officer, whose business it was to inspect slave property that was brought to that market for sale. He examined our backs to see if we had been much scarred by the lash. He examined our limbs, to see whether we were inferior.

As it is hard to tell the ages of slaves, they look in their mouths at their teeth, and prick up the skin on the back of their hands, and if the person is very far advanced in life, when the skin is pricked up, the pucker will stand so many seconds on the back of the hand.

But the most rigorous examinations of slaves by those slave inspectors, is on the mental capacity. If they are found to be very intelligent, this is pronounced the most objectionable of all other qualities connected with the life of a slave. In fact, it undermines the whole fabric of his chattelhood; it prepares for what slaveholders are pleased to pronounce the unpardonable sin when committed by a slave. It lays the foundation for running away, and going to Canada. They also see in it a love for freedom, patriotism, insurrection, bloodshed, and exterminating war against American slavery.

Hence they are very careful to inquire whether a slave who is for sale can read or write. This question has been asked me often by slave traders, and cotton planters, while I was there for market. After conversing with me, they have sworn by their Maker, that they would not have me among their negroes; and that they saw the devil in my eye; I would run away, &c.

I have frequently been asked also, if I had ever run away; but Garrison would generally answer this question for me in the negative. He could have sold my little family without any trouble, for the sum of one thousand dollars. But for fear he might not get me off at so great an advantage, as the people did not like my appearance, he could do better by selling us all together. They all wanted my wife, while but very few wanted me. He asked for me and my family twenty-five hundred dollars, but was not able to get us off at that price.

He tried to speculate on my Christian character. He tried to make it appear that I was so pious and honest that I would not run away for ill treatment; which was a gross mistake, for I never had religion enough to keep me from running away from slavery in my life.

But we were taken from Vicksburg, to the city of New Orleans, where we were to be sold at any rate. We were taken to a trader's yard or a slave prison on the corner of St. Joseph street. This was a common resort for slave traders, and planters who wanted to buy slaves; and all classes of slaves were kept there for sale, to be sold in private or public—young or old, males or females, children or parents, husbands or wives.

Every day at 10 o'clock they were exposed for sale. They had to be in trim for showing themselves to the public for sale. Every one's head had to be combed, and their faces washed, and those who were inclined to look dark and rough, were compelled to wash in greasy dish water, in order to make them look slick and lively.

When spectators would come in the yard, the slaves were ordered out to form a line. They were made to stand up straight, and look as sprightly as they could; and when they were asked a question, they had to answer it as promptly as they could, and try to induce the spectators to buy them. If they failed to do this, they were severely paddled after the spectators were gone. The object for using the paddle in the place of a lash was, to conceal the marks which would be made by the flogging. And the object for flogging under such circumstances, is to make the slaves anxious to be sold.

The paddle is made of a piece of hickory timber, about one inch thick, three inches in width, and about eighteen inches in length. The part which is applied to the flesh is bored full of quarter inch auger holes, and every time this is applied to the flesh of the victim, the blood gushes through the holes of the paddle, or a blister makes its appearance. The persons who are thus flogged, are always stripped naked, and their hands tied together. They are then bent over double, their knees are forced between their elbows, and a stick is put through between the elbows and the bend of the legs, in order to hold the victim in that position, while the paddle is applied to those parts of the body which would not be so likely to be seen by those who wanted to buy slaves.

I was kept in this prison for several months, and no one would buy me for fear I would run away. One day while I was in this prison, Garrison got mad with my wife, and took her off in one of the rooms, with his paddle in hand, swearing that he would paddle her; and I could afford her no protection at all, while the strong arm of the law, public opinion and custom, were all against me. I have often heard Garrison say, that he had rather paddle a female, than eat when he was hungry—that it was music for him to hear them scream, and to see their blood run.

After the lapse of several months, he found that he could not dispose of my person to a good advantage, while he kept me in that prison confined among the other slaves. I do not speak with vanity when I say the contrast was so great between myself and ordinary slaves, from the fact that I had enjoyed superior advantages, to which I have already referred. They have their slaves classed off and numbered.

Garrison came to me one day and informed me that I might go out through the city and find myself a master. I was to go to the Hotels, boarding houses, &c.—tell them that my wife was a good cook, wash-woman, &c.,—and that I was a good dining room servant, carriage driver, or porter—and in this way I might find some gentleman who would buy us both; and that this was the only hope of our being sold together.

But before starting me out, he dressed me up in a suit of his old clothes, so as to make me look respectable, and I was so much better dressed than usual that I felt quite gay. He would not allow my wife to go out with me however, for fear we might get away. I was out every day for several weeks, three or four hours in each day, trying to find a new master, but without success.

Many of the old French inhabitants have taken slaves for their wives, in this city, and their own children for their servants. Such commonly are called Creoles. They are better treated than other slaves, and I resembled this class in appearance so much that the French did not want me. Many of them set their mulatto children free, and make slaveholders of them.

At length one day I heard that there was a gentleman in the city from the State of Tennessee, to buy slaves. He had brought down two rafts of lumber for market, and I thought if I could get him to buy me with my family, and take us to Tennessee, from there, I would stand a better opportunity to run away again and get to Canada, than I would from the extreme South.

So I brushed up myself and walked down to the river's bank, where the man was pointed out to me standing on board of his raft, I approached him, and after passing the usual compliments I said:

"Sir, I understand that you wish to purchase a lot of servants and I have called to know if it is so."

He smiled and appeared to be much pleased at my visit on such laudable business, supposing me to be a slave trader. He commenced rubbing his hands together, and replied by saying: "Yes sir, I am glad to see you. It is a part of my business here to buy slaves, and if I could get you to take my lumber in part pay I should like to buy four or five of your slaves at any rate. What kind of slaves have you, sir?"

After I found that he took me to be a slave trader I knew that it would be of no use for me to tell him that I was myself a slave looking for a master, for he would have doubtless brought up the same objection that others had brought up,—that I was too white; and that they were afraid that I could read and write; and would never serve as a slave, but run away. My reply to the question respecting the quality of my slaves was, that I did not think his lumber would suit me—that I must have the cash for my negroes, and turned on my heel and left him!

I returned to the prison and informed my wife of the fact that I had been taken to be a slaveholder. She thought that in addition to my light complexion my being dressed up in Garrison's old slave trading clothes might have caused the man to think that I was a slave trader, and she was afraid that we should yet be separated if I should not succeed in finding some body to buy us.

Every day to us was a day of trouble, and every night brought new and fearful apprehensions that the golden link which binds together husband and wife might be broken by the heartless tyrant before the light of another day.

Deep has been the anguish of my soul when looking over my little family during the silent hours of the night, knowing the great danger of our being sold off at auction the next day and parted forever. That this might not come to pass, many have been the tears and prayers which I have offered up to the God of Israel that we might be preserved.

While waiting here to be disposed of, I heard of one Francis Whitfield, a cotton planter, who wanted to buy slaves. He was represented to be a very pious soul, being a deacon of a Baptist church. As the regulations, as well as public opinion generally, were against slaves meeting for religious worship, I thought it would give me a better opportunity to attend to my religious duties should I fall into the hands of this deacon.

So I called on him and tried to show to the best advantage, for the purpose of inducing him to buy me and my family. When I approached him, I felt much pleased at his external appearance—I addressed him in the following words as well as I can remember:

"Sir, I understand you are desirous of purchasing slaves?"

With a very pleasant smile, he replied, "Yes, I do want to buy some, are you for sale?"

"Yes sir, with my wife and one child."

Garrison had given me a note to show wherever I went, that I was for sale, speaking of my wife and child, giving us a very good character of course—and I handed him the note.

After reading it over he remarked, "I have a few questions to ask you, and if you will tell me the truth like a good boy, perhaps I may buy you with your family. In the first place, my boy, you are a little too near white. I want you to tell me now whether you can read or write?"

My reply was in the negative.

"Now I want you to tell me whether you have run away? Don't tell me no stories now, like a good fellow, and perhaps I may buy you."

But as I was not under oath to tell him the whole truth, I only gave him a part of it, by telling him that I had run away once.

He appeared to be pleased at that, but cautioned me to tell him the truth, and asked me how long I stayed away, when I ran off?

I told him that I was gone a month.

He assented to this by a bow of his head, and making a long grunt saying, "That's right, tell me the truth like a good boy."

The whole truth was that I had been off in the state of Ohio, and other free states, and even to Canada; besides this I was notorious for running away, from my boyhood.

I never told him that I had been a runaway longer than one month—neither did I tell him that I had not run away more than once in my life; for these questions he never asked me.

I afterwards found him to be one of the basest hypocrites that I ever saw. He looked like a saint—talked like the best of slave holding Christians, and acted at home like the devil.

When he saw my wife and child, he concluded to buy us. He paid for me twelve hundred dollars, and one thousand for my wife and child. He also bought several other slaves at the same time, and took home with him. His residence was in the parish of Claiborn, fifty miles up from the mouth of Red River.

When we arrived there, we found his slaves poor, ragged, stupid, and half-starved. The food he allowed them per week, was one peck of corn for each grown person, one pound of pork, and sometimes a quart of molasses. This was all that they were allowed, and if they got more they stole it.

He had one of the most cruel overseers to be found in that section of the country. He weighed and measured out to them, their week's allowance of food every Sabbath morning. The overseer's horn was sounded two hours before daylight for them in the morning, in order that they should be ready for work before daylight. They were worked from daylight until after dark, without stopping but one half hour to eat or rest, which was at noon. And at the busy season of the year, they were compelled to work just as hard on the Sabbath, as on any other day.

X

Cruel treatment on Whitfield's farm.—Exposure of the children.—Mode of extorting extra labor.—Neglect of the sick.—Strange medicine used.—Death of our second child.

My first impressions when I arrived on the Deacon's farm, were that he was far more like what the people call the devil, than he was like a deacon. Not many days after my arrival there, I heard the Deacon tell one of the slave girls, that he had bought her for a wife for his boy Stephen, which office he compelled her fully to perform against her will. This he enforced by a threat. At first the poor girl neglected to do this, having no sort of affection for the man—but she was finally forced to it by an application of the driver's lash, as threatened by the Deacon.

The next thing I observed was that he made the slave driver strip his own wife, and flog her for not doing just as her master had ordered. He had a white overseer, and a colored man for a driver, whose business it was to watch and drive the slaves in the field, and do the flogging according to the orders of the overseer.

Next a mulatto girl who waited about the house, on her mistress, displeased her, for which the Deacon stripped and tied her up. He then handed me the lash and ordered me to put it on—but I told him I never had done the like, and hoped he would not compel me to do it. He then informed me that I was to be his overseer, and that he had bought me for that purpose. He was paying a man eight hundred dollars a year to oversee, and he believed I was competent to do the same business, and if I would do it up right he would put nothing harder on me to do; and if I knew not how to flog a slave, he would set me an example by which I might be governed. He then commenced on this poor girl, and gave her two hundred lashes before he had her untied.

After giving her fifty lashes, he stopped and lectured her a while, asking her if she thought that she could obey her mistress, &c. She promised to do all in her power to please him and her mistress, if he would have mercy on her. But this plea was all vain. He commenced on her again; and this flogging was carried on in the most inhuman manner until she had received two hundred stripes on her naked quivering flesh, tied up and exposed to the public gaze of all. And this was the example that I was to copy after.

He then compelled me to wash her back off with strong salt brine, before she was untied, which was so revolting to my feelings, that I could not refrain from shedding tears.

For some cause he never called on me again to flog a slave. I presume he saw that I was not savage enough. The above was about the first items of the Deacon's conduct which struck me with peculiar disgust.

After having enjoyed the blessings of civil and religious liberty for a season, to be dragged into that horrible place with my family, to linger out my existence without the aid of religious societies, or the light of revelation, was more than I could endure. I really felt as if I had got into one of the darkest corners of the earth. I thought I was almost out of humanity's reach, and should never again have the pleasure of hearing the gospel sound, as I could see no way by which I could extricate myself; yet I never omitted to pray for deliverance. I had faith to believe that the Lord could see our wrongs and hear our cries.

I was not used quite as bad as the regular field hands, as the greater part of my time was spent working about the house; and my wife was the cook.

This country was full of pine timber, and every slave had to prepare a light wood torch, over night, made of pine knots, to meet the overseer with, before daylight in the morning. Each person had to have his torch lit, and come with it in his hand to the gin house, before the overseer and driver, so as to be ready to go to the cotton field by the time they could see to pick out cotton. These lights looked beautiful at a distance.

The object of blowing the horn for them two hours before day, was, that they should get their bite to eat, before they went to the field, that they need not stop to eat but once during the day. Another object was, to do up their flogging which had been omitted over night. I have often heard the sound of the slave driver's lash on the backs of the slaves, and their heart-rending shrieks, which were enough to melt the heart of humanity, even among the most barbarous nations of the earth.

But the Deacon would keep no overseer on his plantation, who neglected to perform this every morning. I have heard him say that he was no better pleased than when he could hear the overseer's loud complaining voice, long before daylight in the morning, and the sound of the driver's lash among the toiling slaves.

This was a very warm climate, abounding with mosquitoes, galinippers and other insects which were exceedingly annoying to the poor slaves by night and day, at their quarters and in the field. But more especially to their helpless little children, which they had to carry with them to the cotton fields, where they had to set on the damp ground alone from morning till night, exposed to the scorching rays of the sun, liable to be bitten by poisonous rattle snakes which are plenty in that section of the country, or to be devoured by large alligators, which are often seen creeping through the cotton fields going from swamp to swamp seeking their prey.

The cotton planters generally, never allow a slave mother time to go to the house, or quarter during the day to nurse her child; hence they have to carry them to the cotton fields and tie them in the shade of a tree, or in clusters of high weeds about in the fields, where they can go to them at noon, when they are allowed to stop work for one half hour. This is the reason why so very few slave children are raised on these cotton plantations, the mothers have no time to take care of them—and they are often found dead in the field and in the quarter for want of the care of their mothers. But I never was eye witness to a case of this kind, but have heard many narrated by my slave brothers and sisters, some of which occurred on the Deacon's plantation.

Their plan of getting large quantities of cotton picked is not only to extort it from them by the lash, but hold out an inducement and deceive them by giving small prizes. For example; the overseer will offer something worth one or two dollars to any slave who will pick out the most cotton in one day; dividing the hands off in three classes and offering a prize to the one who will pick out the most cotton in each of the classes. By this means they are all interested in trying to get the prize.

After making them try it over several times and weighing what cotton they pick every night, the overseer can tell just how much every hand can pick. He then gives the present to those that pick the most cotton, and then if they do not pick just as much afterward they are flogged.

I have known the slaves to be so much fatigued from labor that they could scarcely get to their lodging places from the field at night. And then they would have to prepare something to eat before they could lie down to rest. Their corn they had to grind on a hand mill for bread stuff, or pound it in a mortar; and by the time they would get their suppers it would be midnight; then they would herd down all together and take but two or three hours rest, before the overseer's horn called them up again to prepare for the field.

At the time of sickness among slaves they had but very little attention. The master was to be the judge of their sickness, but never had studied the medical profession. He always pronounced a slave who said he was sick, a liar and a hypocrite; said there was nothing the matter, and he only wanted to keep from work.

His remedy was most generally strong red pepper tea, boiled till it was red. He would make them drink a pint cup full of it at one dose. If he should not get better very soon after it, the dose was repeated. If that should not accomplish the object for which it was given, or have the desired effect, a pot or kettle was then put over the fire with a large quantity of chimney soot, which was boiled down until it was as strong as the juice of tobacco, and the poor sick slave was compelled to drink a quart of it.

This would operate on the system like salts, or castor oil. But if the slave should not be very ill, he would rather work as long as he could stand up, than to take this dreadful medicine.

If it should be a very valuable slave, sometimes a physician was sent for and something done to save him. But no special aid is afforded the suffering slave even in the last trying hour, when he is called to grapple with the grim monster death. He has no Bible, no family altar, no minister to address to him the consolations of the gospel, before he launches into the spirit world. As to the burial of slaves, but very little more care is taken of their dead bodies than if they were dumb beasts.

My wife was very sick while we were both living with the Deacon. We expected every day would be her last. While she was sick, we lost our second child, and I was compelled to dig my own child's grave and bury it myself without even a box to put it in.

XI

I attend a prayer meeting.—Punishment therefor threatened.—I attempt to escape alone.—My return to take my family.—Our sufferings.—Dreadful attack of wolves.—Our recapture.

Some months after Malinda had recovered from her sickness, I got permission from the Deacon, on one Sabbath day, to attend a prayer meeting, on a neighboring plantation, with a few old superannuated slaves, although this was contrary to the custom of the country—for slaves were not allowed to assemble for religious worship. Being more numerous than the whites there was fear of rebellion, and the overpowering of their oppressors in order to obtain freedom.

But this gentleman on whose plantation I attended the meeting was not a Deacon nor a professor of religion. He was not afraid of a few old Christian slaves rising up to kill their master because he allowed them to worship God on the Sabbath day.

We had a very good meeting, although our exercises were not conducted in accordance with an enlightened Christianity; for we had no Bible—no intelligent leader—but a conscience, prompted by our own reason, constrained us to worship God the Creator of all things.

When I returned home from meeting I told the other slaves what a good time we had at our meeting, and requested them to go with me to meeting there on the next Sabbath. As no slave was allowed to go from the plantation on a visit without a written pass from his master, on the next Sabbath several of us went to the Deacon, to get permission to attend that prayer meeting; but he refused to let any go. I thought I would slip off and attend the meeting and get back before he would miss me, and would not know that I had been to the meeting.

When I returned home from the meeting as I approached the house I saw Malinda, standing out at the fence looking in the direction in which I was expected to return. She hailed my approach, not with joy, but with grief. She was weeping under great distress of mind, but it was hard for me to extort from her the reason why she wept. She finally informed me that her master had found out that I had violated his law, and I should suffer the penalty, which was five hundred lashes, on my naked back.

I asked her how he knew that I had gone?

She said I had not long been gone before he called for me and I was not to be found. He then sent the overseer on horseback to the place where we were to meet to see if I was there. But when the overseer got to the place, the meeting was over and I had gone back home, but had gone a nearer route through the woods and the overseer happened not to meet me. He heard that I had been there and hurried back home before me and told the Deacon, who ordered him to take me on the next morning, strip off my clothes, drive down four stakes in the ground and fasten my limbs to them; then strike me five hundred lashes for going to the prayer meeting. This was what distressed my poor companion. She thought it was more than I could bear, and that it would be the death of me. I concluded then to run away—but she thought they would catch me with the blood hounds by their taking my track. But to avoid them I thought I would ride off on one of the Deacon's mules. She thought if I did, they would sell me.

"No matter, I will try it," said I, "let the consequences be what they may. The matter can be no worse than it now is." So I tackled up the Deacon's best mule with his saddle, &c., and started that night and went off eight or ten miles from home. But I found the mule to be rather troublesome, and was like to betray me by braying, especially when he would see cattle, horses, or any thing of the kind in the woods.

The second night from home I camped in a cane break down in the Red River swamp not a great way off from the road, perhaps not twenty rods, exposed to wild ferocious beasts which were numerous in that section of country. On that night about the middle of the night the mule heard the sound of horses feet on the road, and he commenced stamping and trying to break away. As the horses seemed to come nearer, the mule commenced trying to bray, and it was all that I could do to prevent him from making a loud bray there in the woods, which would have betrayed me.

I supposed that it was the overseer out with the dogs looking for me, and I found afterwards that I was not mistaken. As soon as the people had passed by, I mounted the mule and took him home to prevent his betraying me. When I got near by home I stripped off the tackling and turned the mule loose. I then slipt up to the cabin wherein my wife laid and found her awake, much distressed about me. She informed me that they were then out looking for me, and that the Deacon was bent on flogging me nearly to death, and then selling me off from my family. This was truly heart-rending to my poor wife; the thought of our being torn apart in a strange land after having been sold away from all her friends and relations, was more than she could bear.

The Deacon had declared that I should not only suffer for the crime of attending a prayer meeting without his permission, and for running away, but for the awful crime of stealing a jackass, which was death by the law when committed by a negro.

But I well knew that I was regarded as property, and so was the ass; and I thought if one piece of property took off another, there could be no law violated in the act; no more sin committed in this than if one jackass had rode off another.

But after consultation with my wife I concluded to take her and my little daughter with me and they would be guilty of the same crime that I was, so far as running away was concerned; and if the Deacon sold one he might sell us all, and perhaps to the same person.

So we started off with our child that night, and made our way down to the Red River swamps among the buzzing insects and wild beasts of the forest. We wandered about in the wilderness for eight or ten days before we were apprehended, striving to make our way from slavery; but it was all in vain. Our food was parched corn, with wild fruit such as pawpaws, percimmons, grapes, &c. We did at one time chance to find a sweet potato patch where we got a few potatoes; but most of the time, while we were out, we were lost. We wanted to cross the Red River but could find no conveyance to cross in.

I recollect one day of finding a crooked tree which bent over the river or over one fork of the river, where it was divided by an island. I should think that the tree was at least twenty feet from the surface of the water. I picked up my little child, and my wife followed me, saying, "if we perish let us all perish together in the stream." We succeeded in crossing over. I often look back to that dangerous event even now with astonishment, and wonder how I could have run such a risk. What would induce me to run the same risk now? What could induce me now to leave home and friends and go to the wild forest and lay out on the cold ground night after night without covering, and live on parched corn?

What would induce me to take my family and go into the Red River swamps of Louisiana among the snakes and alligators, with all the liabilities of being destroyed by them, hunted down with blood hounds, or lay myself liable to be shot down like the wild beasts of the forest? Nothing I say, nothing but the strongest love of liberty, humanity, and justice to myself and family, would induce me to run such a risk again.

When we crossed over on the tree we supposed that we had crossed over the main body of the river, but we had not proceeded far on our journey before we found that we were on an Island surrounded by water on either side. We made our bed that night in a pile of dry leaves which had fallen from off the trees. We were much rest-broken, wearied from hunger and travelling through briers, swamps and cane brakes—consequently we soon fell asleep after lying down. About the dead hour of the night I was aroused by the awful howling of a gang of blood-thirsty wolves, which had found us out and surrounded us as their prey, there in the dark wilderness many miles from any house or settlement.

My dear little child was so dreadfully alarmed that she screamed loudly with fear—my wife trembling like a leaf on a tree, at the thought of being devoured there in the wilderness by ferocious wolves.

The wolves kept howling, and were near enough for us to see their glaring eyes, and hear their chattering teeth. I then thought that the hour of death for us was at hand; that we should not live to see the light of another day; for there was no way for our escape. My little family were looking up to me for protection, but I could afford them none. And while I was offering up my prayers to that God who never forsakes those in the hour of danger who trust in him, I thought of Deacon Whitfield; I thought of his profession, and doubted his piety. I thought of his hand-cuffs, of his whips, of his chains, of his stocks, of his thumb-screws, of his slave driver and overseer, and of his religion; I also thought of his opposition to prayer meetings, and of his five hundred lashes promised me for attending a prayer meeting. I thought of God, I thought of the devil, I thought of hell; and I thought of heaven, and wondered whether I should ever see the Deacon there. And I calculated that if heaven was made up of such Deacons, or such persons, it could not be filled with love to all mankind, and with glory and eternal happiness, as we know it is from the truth of the Bible.

The reader may perhaps think me tedious on this topic, but indeed it is one of so much interest to me, that I find myself entirely unable to describe what my own feelings were at that time. I was so much excited by the fierce howling of the savage wolves, and the frightful screams of my little family, that I thought of the future; I thought of the past; I thought the time of my departure had come at last.

My impression is, that all these thoughts and thousands of others, flashed through my mind, while I was surrounded by those wolves. But it seemed to be the will of a merciful providence, that our lives should be spared, and that we should not be destroyed by them.

I had no weapon of defence but a long bowie knife which I had slipped from the Deacon. It was a very splendid blade, about two feet in length, and about two inches in width. This used to be a part of his armor of defence while walking about the plantation among his slaves.

The plan which I took to expel the wolves was a very dangerous one, but it proved effectual. While they were advancing to me, prancing and accumulating in number, apparently of all sizes and grades, who had come to the feast, I thought just at this time, that there was no alternative left but for me to make a charge with my bowie knife. I well knew from the action of the wolves, that if I made no farther resistance, they would soon destroy us, and if I made a break at them, the matter could be no worse. I thought if I must die, I would die striving to protect my little family from destruction, die striving to escape from slavery. My wife took a club in one hand, and her child in the other, while I rushed forth with my bowie knife in hand, to fight off the savage wolves. I made one desperate charge at them, and at the same time making a loud yell at the top of my voice, that caused them to retreat and scatter, which was equivalent to a victory on our part. Our prayers were answered, and our lives spared through the night. We slept no more that night, and the next morning there were no wolves to be seen or heard, and we resolved not to stay on that island another night.

We travelled up and down the river side trying to find a place where we could cross. Finally we found a lot of drift wood clogged together, extending across the stream at a narrow place in the river, upon which we crossed over. But we had not yet surmounted our greatest difficulty. We had to meet one which was far more formidable than the first. Not many days after I had to face the Deacon.

We had been wandering about through the cane brakes, bushes, and briers, for several days, when we heard the yelping of blood hounds, a great way off, but they seemed to come nearer and nearer to us. We thought after awhile that they must be on our track; we listened attentively at the approach. We knew it was no use for us to undertake to escape from them, and as they drew nigh, we heard the voice of a man hissing on the dogs.

After awhile we saw the hounds coming in full speed on our track, and the soul drivers close after them on horse back, yelling like tigers, as they came in sight. The shrill yelling of the savage blood hounds as they drew nigh made the woods echo.

The first impulse was to run to escape the approaching danger of ferocious dogs, and blood-thirsty slave hunters, who were so rapidly approaching me with loaded muskets and bowie knives, with a determination to kill or capture me and my family. I started to run with my little daughter in my arms, but stumbled and fell down and scratched the arm of little Frances with a brier, so that it bled very much; but the dear child never cried, for she seemed to know the danger to which we were exposed.

But we soon found that it was no use for us to run. The dogs were soon at our heels, and we were compelled to stop, or be torn to pieces by them. By this time, the soul drivers came charging up on their horses, commanding us to stand still or they would shoot us down.

Of course I surrendered up for the sake of my family. The most abusive terms to be found in the English language were poured forth on us with bitter oaths. They tied my hands behind me, and drove us home before them, to suffer the penalty of a slaveholder's broken law.

As we drew nigh the plantation my heart grew faint. I was aware that we should have to suffer almost death for running off. I was filled with dreadful apprehensions at the thought of meeting a professed follower of Christ, whom I knew to be a hypocrite! No tongue, no pen can ever describe what my feelings were at that time.

XII

My sad condition before Whitfield.—My terrible punishment. —Incidents of a former attempt to escape.—Jack at a farm house.—Six pigs and a turkey.—Our surprise and arrest.

The reader may perhaps imagine what must have been my feelings when I found myself surrounded on the island with my little family, at midnight, by a gang of savage wolves. This was one of those trying emergencies in my life when there was apparently but one step between us and the grave. But I had no cords wrapped about my limbs to prevent my struggling against the impending danger to which I was then exposed. I was not denied the consolation of resisting in self defence, as was now the case. There was no Deacon standing before me, with a loaded rifle, swearing that I should submit to the torturing lash, or be shot down like a dumb beast.

I felt that my chance was by far better among the howling wolves in the Red River Swamp, than before Deacon Whitfield, on the cotton plantation. I was brought before him as a criminal before a bar, without counsel, to be tried and condemned by a tyrant's law. My arms were bound with a cord, my spirit broken, and my little family standing by weeping. I was not allowed to plead my own cause, and there was no one to utter a word in my behalf.

He ordered that the field hands should be called together to witness my punishment, that it might serve as a caution to them never to attend a prayer meeting, or run away as I had, lest they should receive the same punishment.

At the sound of the overseer's horn, all the slaves came forward and witnessed my punishment. My clothing was stripped off and I was compelled to lie down on the ground with my face to the earth. Four stakes were driven in the ground, to which my hands and feet were tied. Then the overseer stood over me with the lash and laid it on according to the Deacon's order. Fifty lashes were laid on before stopping. I was then lectured with reference to my going to prayer meeting without his orders, and running away to escape flogging.

While I suffered under this dreadful torture, I prayed, and wept, and implored mercy at the hand of slavery, but found none. After I was marked from my neck to my heels, the Deacon took the gory lash, and said he thought there was a spot on my back yet where he could put in a few more. He wanted to give me something to remember him by, he said.

After I was flogged almost to death in this way, a paddle was brought forward and eight or ten blows given me with it, which was by far worse than the lash. My wounds were then washed with salt brine, after which I was let up. A description of such paddles I have already given in another page. I was so badly punished that I was not able to work for several days. After being flogged as described, they took me off several miles to a shop and had a heavy iron collar riveted on my neck with prongs extending above my head, on the end of which there was a small bell. I was not able to reach the bell with my hand. This heavy load of iron I was compelled to wear for six weeks. I never was allowed to lie in the same house with my family again while I was a slave of Whitfield. I either had to sleep with my feet in the stocks, or be chained with a large log chain to a log over night, with no bed or bedding to rest my wearied limbs on, after toiling all day in the cotton field. I suffered almost death while kept in this confinement; and he had ordered the overseer never to let me loose again; saying that I thought of getting free by running off, but no negro should ever get away from him alive.

I have omitted to state that this was the second time I had run away from him; while I was gone the first time, he extorted from my wife the fact that I had been in the habit of running away, before we left Kentucky; that I had been to Canada, and that I was trying to learn the art of reading and writing. All this was against me.

It is true that I was striving to learn myself to write. I was a kind of a house servant and was frequently sent off on errands, but never without a written pass; and on Sundays I have sometimes got permission to visit our neighbor's slaves, and I have often tried to write myself a pass.

Whenever I got hold of an old letter that had been thrown away, or a piece of white paper, I would save it to write on. I have often gone off in the woods and spent the greater part of the day alone, trying to learn to write myself a pass, by writing on the backs of old letters; copying after the pass that had been written by Whitfield; by so doing I got the use of the pen and could form letters as well as I can now, but knew not what they were.

The Deacon had an old slave by the name of Jack whom he bought about the time that he bought me. Jack was born in the State of Virginia. He had some idea of freedom; had often run away, but was very ignorant; knew not where to go for refuge; but understood all about providing something to eat when unjustly deprived of it.

So for ill treatment, we concluded to take a tramp together. I was to be the pilot, while Jack was to carry the baggage and keep us in provisions. Before we started, I managed to get hold of a suit of clothes the Deacon possessed, with his gun, ammunition and bowie knife. We also procured a blanket, a joint of meat, and some bread.

We started in a northern direction, being bound for the city of Little Rock, State of Arkansas. We travelled by night and laid by in the day, being guided by the unchangeable North Star; but at length, our provisions gave out, and it was Jack's place to get more. We came in sight of a large plantation one morning, where we saw people of color, and Jack said he could get something there, among the slaves, that night, for us to eat. So we concealed ourselves, in sight of this plantation until about bed time, when we saw the lights extinguished.

During the day we saw a female slave passing from the dwelling house to the kitchen as if she was the cook; the house being about three rods from the landlord's dwelling. After we supposed the whites were all asleep, Jack slipped up softly to the kitchen to try his luck with the cook, to see if he could get any thing from her to eat.

I would remark that the domestic slaves are often found to be traitors to their own people, for the purpose of gaining favor with their masters; and they are encouraged and trained up by them to report every plot they know of being formed about stealing any thing, or running away, or any thing of the kind; and for which they are paid. This is one of the principal causes of the slaves being divided among themselves, and without which they could not be held in bondage one year, and perhaps not half that time.

I now proceed to describe the unsuccessful attempt of poor Jack to obtain something from the female slave to satisfy hunger. The planter's house was situated on an elevated spot on the side of a hill. The fencing about the house and garden was very crookedly laid up with rails. The night was rather dark and rainy, and Jack left me with the understanding that I was to stay at a certain place until he returned. I cautioned him before he left me to be very careful—and after he started, I left the place where he was to find me when he returned, for fear something might happen which might lead to my detection, should I remain at that spot. So I left it and went off where I could see the house, and that place too.

Jack had not long been gone, before I heard a great noise; a man, crying out with a loud voice, "Catch him! Catch him!" and hissing the dogs on, and they were close after Jack. The next thing I saw, was Jack running for life, and an old white man after him, with a gun, and his dogs. The fence being on sidling ground, and wet with the rain, when Jack ran against it he knocked down several pannels of it and fell, tumbling over and over to the foot of the hill; but soon recovered and ran to where he had left me; but I was gone. The dogs were still after him.

There happened to be quite a thicket of small oak shrubs and bushes in the direction he ran. I think he might have been heard running and straddling bushes a quarter of a mile! the poor fellow hurt himself considerably in straddling over bushes in that way, in making his escape.

Finally the dogs relaxed their chase and poor Jack and myself again met in the thick forest. He said when he rapped on the cook-house door, the colored woman came to the door. He asked her if she would let him have a bite of bread if she had it, that he was a poor hungry absconding slave. But she made no reply to what he said but immediately sounded the alarm by calling loudly after her master, saying, "here is a runaway negro!" Jack said that he was going to knock her down but her master was out within one moment, and he had to run for his life.

As soon as we got our eyes fixed on the North Star again, we started on our way. We travelled on a few miles and came to another large plantation, where Jack was determined to get something to eat. He left me at a certain place while he went up to the house to find something if possible.

He was gone some time before he returned, but when I saw him coming, he appeared to be very heavy loaded with a bag of something. We walked off pretty fast until we got some distance in the woods. Jack then stopped and opened his bag in which he had six small pigs. I asked him how he got them without making any noise; and he said that he found a bed of hogs, in which there were the pigs with their mother. While the pigs were sucking he crawled up to them without being discovered by the sow, and took them by their necks one after another, and choked them to death, and slipped them into his bag!

We intended to travel on all that night and lay by the next day in the forest and cook up our pigs. We fell into a large road leading on the direction which we were travelling, and had not proceeded over three miles before I found a white hat lying in the road before me. Jack being a little behind me I stopped until he came up, and showed it to him. He picked it up. We looked a few steps farther and saw a man lying by the way, either asleep or intoxicated, as we supposed.

I told Jack not to take the hat, but he would not obey me. He had only a piece of a hat himself, which he left in exchange for the other. We travelled on about five miles farther, and in passing a house discovered a large turkey sitting on the fence, which temptation was greater than Jack could resist. Notwithstanding he had six very nice fat little pigs on his back, he stepped up and took the turkey off the fence.

By this time it was getting near day-light and we left the road and went off a mile or so among the hills of the forest, where we struck camp for the day. We then picked our turkey, dressed our pigs, and cooked two of them. We got the hair off by singeing them over the fire, and after we had eaten all we wanted, one of us slept while the other watched. We had flint, punk, and powder to strike fire with. A little after dark the next night, we started on our way.

But about ten o'clock that night just as we were passing through a thick skirt of woods, five men sprang out before us with fire-arms, swearing if we moved another step, they would shoot us down; and each man having his gun drawn up for shooting we had no chance to make any defence, and surrendered sooner than run the risk of being killed.

They had been lying in wait for us there, for several hours. They had seen a reward out, for notices were put up in the most public places, that fifty dollars would be paid for me, dead or alive, if I should not return home within so many days. And the reader will remember that neither Jack nor myself was able to read the advertisement. It was of very little consequence with the slave catchers, whether they killed us or took us alive, for the reward was the same to them.

After we were taken and tied, one of the men declared to me that he would have shot me dead just as sure as he lived, if I had moved one step after they commanded us to stop. He had his gun leveled at my breast, already cocked, and his finger on the trigger. The way they came to find us out was from the circumstance of Jack's taking the man's hat in connection with the advertisement. The man whose hat was taken was drunk; and the next morning when he came to look for his hat it was gone and Jack's old hat lying in the place of it; and in looking round he saw the tracks of two persons in the dust, who had passed during the night, and one of them having but three toes on one foot. He followed these tracks until they came to a large mud pond, in a lane on one side of which a person might pass dry shod; but the man with three toes on one foot had plunged through the mud. This led the man to think there must be runaway slaves, and from out of that neighborhood; for all persons in that settlement knew which side of that mud hole to go. He then got others to go with him, and they followed us until our track left the road. They supposed that we had gone off in the woods to lay by until night, after which we should pursue our course.

After we were captured they took us off several miles to where one of them lived, and kept us over night. One of our pigs was cooked for us to eat that night; and the turkey the next morning. But we were both tied that night with our hands behind us, and our feet were also tied. The doors were locked, and a bedstead was set against the front door, and two men slept in it to prevent our getting out in the night. They said that they knew how to catch runaway negroes, and how to keep them after they were caught.

They remarked that after they found we had stopped to lay by until night, and they saw from our tracks what direction we were travelling, they went about ten miles on that direction, and hid by the road side until we came up that night. That night after all had got fast to sleep, I thought I would try to get out, and I should have succeeded, if I could have moved the bed from the door. I managed to untie myself and crawled under the bed which was placed at the door, and strove to remove it, but in so doing I awakened the men and they got up and confined me again, and watched me until day light, each with a gun in hand.

The next morning they started with us back to Deacon Whitfield's plantation; but when they got within ten miles of where he lived they stopped at a public house to stay over night; and who should we meet there but the Deacon, who was then out looking for me.

The reader may well imagine how I felt to meet him. I had almost as soon come in contact with Satan himself. He had two long poles or sticks of wood brought in to confine us to. I was compelled to lie on my back across one of those sticks with my arms out, and have them lashed fast to the log with a cord. My feet were also tied to the other, and there I had to lie all that night with my back across this stick of wood, and my feet and hands tied. I suffered that night under the most excruciating pain. From the tight binding of the cord the circulation of the blood in my arms and feet was almost entirely stopped. If the night had been much longer I must have died in that confinement.

The next morning we were taken back to the Deacon's farm, and both flogged for going off, and set to work. But there was some allowance made for me on account of my being young. They said that they knew old Jack had pursuaded me off, or I never would have gone. And the Deacon's wife begged that I might be favored some, for that time, as Jack had influenced me, so as to bring up my old habits of running away that I had entirely given up.

XIII

I am sold to gamblers.—They try to purchase my family. —Our parting scene.—My good usage.—I am sold to an Indian.—His confidence in my integrity manifested.

The reader will remember that this brings me back to the time the Deacon had ordered me to be kept in confinement until he got a chance to sell me, and that no negro should ever get away from him and live. Some days after this we were all out at the gin house ginning cotton, which was situated on the road side, and there came along a company of men, fifteen or twenty in number, who were Southern sportsmen. Their attention was attracted by the load of iron which was fastened about my neck with a bell attached. They stopped and asked the Deacon what that bell was put on my neck for? and he said it was to keep me from running away, &c.

They remarked that I looked as if I might be a smart negro, and asked if he wanted to sell me. The reply was, yes. They then got off their horses and struck a bargain with him for me. They bought me at a reduced price for speculation.

After they had purchased me, I asked the privilege of going to the house to take leave of my family before I left, which was granted by the sportsmen. But the Deacon said I should never again step my foot inside of his yard; and advised the sportsmen not to take the irons from my neck until they had sold me; that if they gave me the least chance I would run away from them, as I did from him. So I was compelled to mount a horse and go off with them as I supposed, never again to meet my family in this life.

We had not proceeded far before they informed me that they had bought me to sell again, and if they kept the irons on me it would be detrimental to the sale, and that they would therefore take off the irons and dress me up like a man and throw away the old rubbish which I then had on; and they would sell me to some one who would treat me better than Deacon Whitfield. After they had cut off the irons and dressed me up, they crossed over Red River into Texas, where they spent some time horse racing and gambling; and although they were wicked black legs of the basest character, it is but due to them to say, that they used me far better than ever the Deacon did. They gave me plenty to eat and put nothing hard on me to do. They expressed much sympathy for me in my bereavement; and almost every day they gave me money more or less, and by my activity in waiting on them, and upright conduct, I got into the good graces of them all, but they could not get any person to buy me on account of the amount of intelligence which they supposed me to have; for many of them thought that I could read and write. When they left Texas, they intended to go to the Indian Territory west of the Mississippi, to attend a great horse race which was to take place. Not being much out of their way to go past Deacon Whitfield's again, I prevailed on them to call on him for the purpose of trying to purchase my wife and child; and I promised them that if they would buy my wife and child, I would get some person to purchase us from them. So they tried to grant my request by calling on the Deacon, and trying to make the purchase. As we approached the Deacon's plantation, my heart was filled with a thousand painful and fearful apprehensions. I had the fullest confidence in the blacklegs with whom I travelled, believing that they would do according to promise, and go to the fullest extent of their ability to restore peace and consolation to a bereaved family—to re-unite husband and wife, parent and child, who had long been severed by slavery through the agency of Deacon Whitfield. But I knew his determination in relation to myself, and I feared his wicked opposition to a restoration of myself and little family, which he had divided, and soon found that my fears were not without foundation.

When we rode up and walked into his yard, the Deacon came out and spoke to all but myself; and not finding me in tattered rags as a substitute for clothes, nor having an iron collar or bell about my neck, as was the case when he sold me, he appeared to be much displeased.

"What did you bring that negro back here for?" said he.

"We have come to try to buy his wife and child; for we can find no one who is willing to buy him alone; and we will either buy or sell so that the family may be together," said they.

While this conversation was going on, my poor bereaved wife, who never expected to see me again in this life, spied me and came rushing to me through the crowd, throwing her arms about my neck exclaiming in the most sympathetic tones, "Oh! my dear husband! I never expected to see you again!" The poor woman was bathed with tears of sorrow and grief. But no sooner had she reached me, than the Deacon peremptorily commanded her to go to her work. This she did not obey, but prayed that her master would not separate us again, as she was there alone, far from friends and relations whom she should never meet again. And now to take away her husband, her last and only true friend, would be like taking her life!

But such appeals made no impression on the unfeeling Deacon's heart. While he was storming with abusive language, and even using the gory lash with hellish vengeance to separate husband and wife, I could see the sympathetic tear-drop, stealing its way down the cheek of the profligate and black-leg, whose object it now was to bind up the broken heart of a wife, and restore to the arms of a bereaved husband, his companion.

They were disgusted at the conduct of Whitfield and cried out shame, even in his presence. They told him that they would give a thousand dollars for my wife and child, or any thing in reason. But no! he would sooner see me to the devil than indulge or gratify me after my having run away from him; and if they did not remove me from his presence very soon, he said he should make them suffer for it.

But all this, and even the gory lash had yet failed to break the grasp of poor Malinda, whose prospect of connubial, social, and future happiness was all at stake. When the dear woman saw there was no help for us, and that we should soon be separated forever, in the name of Deacon Whitfield, and American slavery to meet no more as husband and wife, parent and child—the last and loudest appeal was made on our knees. We appealed to the God of justice and to the sacred ties of humanity; but this was all in vain. The louder we prayed the harder he whipped, amid the most heart-rending shrieks from the poor slave mother and child, as little Frances stood by, sobbing at the abuse inflicted on her mother.

"Oh! how shall I give my husband the parting hand never to meet again? This will surely break my heart," were her parting words.

I can never describe to the reader the awful reality of that separation—for it was enough to chill the blood and stir up the deepest feeling of revenge in the hearts of slaveholding black-legs, who as they stood by, were threatening, some weeping, some swearing and others declaring vengeance against such treatment being inflicted on a human being. As we left the plantation, as far as we could see and hear, the Deacon was still laying on the gory lash, trying to prevent poor Malinda from weeping over the loss of her departed husband, who was then, by the hellish laws of slavery, to her, theoretically and practically dead. One of the black-legs exclaimed that hell was full of just such deacons as Whitfield. This occurred in December, 1840. I have never seen Malinda, since that period. I never expect to see her again.

The sportsmen to whom I was sold, showed their sympathy for me not only by word but by deeds. They said that they had made the most liberal offer to Whitfield, to buy or sell for the sole purpose of reuniting husband and wife. But he stood out against it—they felt sorry for me. They said they had bought me to speculate on, and were not able to lose what they had paid for me. But they would make a bargain with me, if I was willing, and would lay a plan, by which I might yet get free. If I would use my influence so as to get some person to buy me while traveling about with them, they would give me a portion of the money for which they sold me, and they would also give me directions by which I might yet run away and go to Canada.

This offer I accepted, and the plot was made. They advised me to act very stupid in language and thought, but in business I must be spry; and that I must persuade men to buy me, and promise them that I would be smart.

We passed through the State of Arkansas and stopped at many places, horse-racing and gambling. My business was to drive a wagon in which they carried their gambling apparatus, clothing, &c. I had also to black boots and attend to horses. We stopped at Fayetteville, where they almost lost me, betting on a horse race.

They went from thence to the Indian Territory, among the Cherokee Indians, to attend the great races which were to take place there. During the races there was a very wealthy half Indian of that tribe, who became much attached to me, and had some notion of buying me, after hearing that I was for sale, being a slaveholder. The idea struck me rather favorable, for several reasons. First, I thought I should stand a better chance to get away from an Indian than from a white man. Second, he wanted me only for a kind of body servant to wait on him—and in this case I knew that I should fare better than I should in the field. And my owners also told me that it would be an easy place to get away from. I took their advice for fear I might not get another chance so good as that, and prevailed on the man to buy me. He paid them nine hundred dollars, in gold and silver, for me. I saw the money counted out.

After the purchase was made, the sportsmen got me off to one side, and according to promise they gave me a part of the money, and directions how to get from there to Canada. They also advised me how to act until I got a good chance to run away. I was to embrace the earliest opportunity of getting away, before they should become acquainted with me. I was never to let it be known where I was from, nor where I was born. I was to act quite stupid and ignorant. And when I started I was to go up the boundary line, between the Indian Territory and the States of Arkansas and Missouri, and this would fetch me out on the Missouri River, near Jefferson City, the capital of Missouri. I was to travel at first by night, and to lay by in daylight, until I got out of danger.

The same afternoon that the Indian bought me, he started with me to his residence, which was fifty or sixty miles distant. And so great was his confidence in me, that he entrusted me to carry his money. The amount must have been at least five hundred dollars, which was all in gold and silver; and when we stopped over night the money and horses were all left in my charge.

It would have been a very easy matter for me to have taken one of the best horses, with the money, and run off. And the temptation was truly great to a man like myself, who was watching for the earliest opportunity to escape; and I felt confident that I should never have a better opportunity to escape full handed than then.

XIV

Character of my Indian Master.—Slavery among the Indians less cruel.—Indian carousal.—Enfeebled health of my Indian Master.—His death.—My escape.—Adventure in a wigwam.—Successful progress toward liberty.

The next morning I went home with my new master; and by the way it is only doing justice to the dead to say, that he was the most reasonable, and humane slaveholder that I have ever belonged to. He was the last man that pretended to claim property in my person; and although I have freely given the names and residences of all others who have held me as a slave, for prudential reasons I shall omit giving the name of this individual.

He was the owner of a large plantation and quite a number of slaves. He raised corn and wheat for his own consumption only. There was no cotton, tobacco, or anything of the kind produced among them for market. And I found this difference between negro slavery among the Indians, and the same thing among the white slaveholders of the South. The Indians allow their slaves enough to eat and wear. They have no overseers to whip nor drive them. If a slave offends his master, he sometimes, in the heat of passion, undertakes to chastise him; but it is as often the case as otherwise, that the slave gets the better of the fight, and even flogs his master;* for which there is no law to punish him; but when the fight is over that is the last of it. So far as religious instruction is concerned, they have it on terms of equality, the bond and the free; they have no respect of persons, they have neither slave laws nor negro pews. Neither do they separate husbands and wives, nor parents and children. All things considered, if I must be a slave, I had by far, rather be a slave to an Indian, than to a white man, from the experience I have had with both.

A majority of the Indians were uneducated, and still followed up their old heathen traditional notions. They made it a rule to have an Indian dance or frolic, about once a fortnight; and they would come together far and near to attend these dances. They would most generally commence about the middle of the afternoon; and would give notice by the blowing of horns. One would commence blowing and another would answer, and so it would go all round the neighborhood. When a number had got together, they would strike a circle about twenty rods in circumference, and kindle up fires about twenty feet apart, all around, in this circle. In the centre they would have a large fire to dance around, and at each one of the small fires there would be a squaw to keep up the fire, which looked delightful off at a distance.

* This singular fact is corroborated in a letter read by the publisher, from an acquaintance while passing through this country in 1849.

But the most degrading practice of all, was the use of intoxicating drinks, which were used to a great excess by all that attended these stump dances. At almost all of these fires there was some one with rum to sell. There would be some dancing, some singing, some gambling, some fighting, and some yelling; and this was kept up often for two days and nights together.

Their dress for the dance was most generally a great bunch of bird feathers, coon tails, or something of the kind stuck in their heads, and a great many shells tied about their legs to rattle while dancing. Their manner of dancing is taking hold of each others hands and forming a ring around the large fire in the centre, and go stomping around it until they would get drunk or their heads would get to swimming, and they they would go off and drink, and another set come on. Such were some of the practises indulged in by these Indian slaveholders.

My last owner was in a declining state of health when he bought me; and not long after he bought me he went off forty or fifty miles from home to be doctored by an Indian doctor, accompanied by his wife. I was taken along also to drive the carriage and to wait upon him during his sickness. But he was then so feeble, that his life was of but short duration after the doctor commenced on him.

While he lived, I waited on him according to the best of my ability. I watched over him night and day until he died, and even prepared his body for the tomb, before I left him. He died about midnight and I understood from his friends that he was not to be buried until the second day after his death. I pretended to be taking on at a great rate about his death, but I was more excited about running away, than I was about that, and before daylight the next morning I proved it, for I was on my way to Canada.

I never expected a better opportunity would present itself for my escape. I slipped out of the room as if I had gone off to weep for the deceased, knowing that they would not feel alarmed about me until after my master was buried and they had returned back to his residence. And even then, they would think that I was somewhere on my way home; and it would be at least four or five days before they would make any stir in looking after me. By that time, if I had no bad luck, I should be out of much danger.

After the first day, I laid by in the day and traveled by night for several days and nights, passing in this way through several tribes of Indians. I kept pretty near the boundary line. I recollect getting lost one dark rainy night. Not being able to find the road I came into an Indian settlement at the dead hour of the night. I was wet, wearied, cold and hungry; and yet I felt afraid to enter any of their houses or wigwams, not knowing whether they would be friendly or not. But I knew the Indians were generally drunkards, and that occasionally a drunken white man was found straggling among them, and that such an one would be more likely to find friends from sympathy than an upright man.

So I passed myself off that night as a drunkard among them. I walked up to the door of one of their houses, and fell up against it, making a great noise like a drunken man; but no one came to the door. I opened it and staggered in, falling about, and making a great noise. But finally an old woman got up and gave me a blanket to lie down on.

There was quite a number of them lying about on the dirt floor, but not one could talk or understand a word of the English language. I made signs so as to let them know that I wanted something to eat, but they had nothing, so I had to go without that night. I laid down and pretended to be asleep, but I slept none that night, for I was afraid that they would kill me if I went to sleep. About one hour before day, the next morning, three of the females got up and put into a tin kettle a lot of ashes with water, to boil, and then poured into it about one quart of corn. After letting it stand a few moments, they poured it into a trough, and pounded it into thin hominy. They washed it out, and boiled it down, and called me up to eat my breakfast of it.

After eating, I offered them six cents, but they refused to accept it. I then found my way to the main road, and traveled all that day on my journey, and just at night arrived at a public house kept by an Indian, who also kept a store. I walked in and asked if I could get lodging, which was granted; but I had not been there long before three men came riding up about dusk, or between sunset and dark. They were white men, and I supposed slaveholders. At any rate when they asked if they could have lodging, I trembled for fear they might be in pursuit of me. But the landlord told them that he could not lodge them, but they could get lodging about two miles off, with a white man, and they turned their horses and started.

The landlord asked me where I was traveling to, and where I was from. I told him that I had been out looking at the country;

that I had thought of buying land, and that I lived in the State of Ohio, in the village of Perrysburgh. He then said that he had lived there himself, and that he had acted as an interpreter there among the Maumee tribe of Indians for several years. He then asked who I was acquainted with there? I informed him that I knew Judge Hollister, Francis Hollister, J. W. Smith, and others. At this he was so much pleased that he came up and took me by the hand, and received me joyfully, after seeing that I was acquainted with those of his old friends.

I could converse with him understandingly from personal acquaintance, for I had lived there when I first ran away from Kentucky. But I felt it to be my duty to start off the next morning before breakfast, or sunrise. I bought a dozen of eggs, and had them boiled to carry with me to eat on the way. I did not like the looks of those three men, and thought I would get on as fast as possible for fear I might be pursued by them.

I was then about to enter the territory of another slave State, Missouri. I had passed through the fiery ordeal of Sibley, Gatewood, and Garrison, and had even slipped through the fingers of Deacon Whitfield. I had doubtless gone through great peril in crossing the Indian territory, in passing through the various half civilized tribes, who seemed to look upon me with astonishment as I passed along. Their hands were almost invariably filled with bows and arrows, tomahawks, guns, butcher knives, and all the various implements of death which are used by them. And what made them look still more frightful, their faces were often painted red, and their heads muffled with birds feathers, bushes, coons tails and owls heads. But all this I had passed through, and my long enslaved limbs and spirit were then in full stretch for emancipation. I felt as if one more short struggle would set me free.

XV

Adventure on the Prairie.—I borrow a horse without leave. —Rapid traveling one whole night.—Apology for using other men's horses.—My manner of living on the road.

Early in the morning I left the Indian territory as I have already said, for fear I might be pursued by the three white men whom I had seen there over night; but I had not proceeded far before my fears were magnified a hundred fold.

I always dreaded to pass through a prairie, and on coming to one which was about six miles in width, I was careful to look in every direction to see whether there was any person in sight before I entered it; but I could see no one. So I started across with a hope of crossing without coming in contact with any one on the prairie. I walked as fast as I could, but when I got about midway of the prairie, I came to a high spot where the road forked, and three men came up from a low spot as if they had been there concealed. They were all on horse back, and I supposed them to be the same men that had tried to get lodging where I stopped over night. Had this been in timbered land, I might have stood some chance to have dodged them, but there I was, out in the open prairie, where I could see no possible way by which I could escape.

They came along slowly up behind me, and finally passed, and spoke or bowed their heads on passing, but they traveled in a slow walk and kept but a very few steps before me, until we got nearly across the prairie. When we were coming near a plantation a piece off from the road on the skirt of the timbered land, they whipped up their horses and left the road as if they were going across to this plantation. They soon got out of my sight by going down into a valley which lay between us and the plantation. Not seeing them rise the hill to go up to the farm, excited greater suspicion in my mind, so I stepped over on the brow of the hill, where I could see what they were doing, and to my surprise I saw them going right back in the direction they had just came, and they were going very fast. I was then satisfied that they were after me and that they were only going back to get more help to assist them in taking me, for fear that I might kill some of them if they undertook it. The first impression was that I had better leave the road immediately; so I bolted from the road and ran as fast as I could for some distance in the thick forest, and concealed myself for about fifteen or twenty minutes, which were spent in prayer to God for his protecting care and guidance.

My impression was that when they should start in pursuit of me again, they would follow on in the direction which I was going when they left me; and not finding or hearing of me on the road, they would come back and hunt through the woods around, and if they could find no track they might go and get dogs to trace me out.

I thought my chance of escape would be better, if I went back to the same side of the road that they first went, for the purpose of deceiving them; as I supposed that they would not suspect my going in the same direction that they went, for the purpose of escaping from them.

So I traveled all that day square off from the road through the wild forest without any knowledge of the country whatever for I had nothing to travel by but the sun by day, and the moon and stars by night. Just before night I came in sight of a large plantation, where I saw quite a number of horses running at large in a field, and knowing that my success in escaping depended upon my getting out of that settlement within twenty-four hours, to save myself from everlasting slavery, I thought I should be justified in riding one of those horses, that night, if I could catch one. I cut a grape vine with my knife, and made it into a bridle; and shortly after dark I went into the field and tried to catch one of the horses. I got a bunch of dry blades of fodder and walked up softly towards the horses, calling to them "cope," "cope," "cope;" but there was only one out of the number that I was able to get my hand on, and that was an old mare, which I supposed to be the mother of all the rest; and I knew that I could walk faster than she could travel. She had a bell on and was very thin in flesh; she looked gentle and walked on three legs only. The young horses pranced and galloped off. I was not able to get near them, and the old mare being of no use to me, I left them all. After fixing my eyes on the north star I pursued my journey, holding on to my bridle with a hope of finding a horse upon which I might ride that night.

I found a road leading pretty nearly in the direction which I wanted travel, and I kept it. After traveling several miles I found another large plantation where there was a prospect of finding a horse. I stepped up to the barn-yard, wherein I found several horses. There was a little barn standing with the door open, and I found it quite an easy task to get the horses into the barn, and select out the best looking one of them. I pulled down the fence, led the noble beast out and mounted him, taking a northern direction, being able to find a road which led that way. But I had not gone over three or four miles before I came to a large stream of water which was past fording; yet I could see that it had been forded by the road track, but from high water it was then impassable. As the horse seemed willing to go in I put him through; but before he got in far, he was in water up to his sides and finally the water came over his back and he swam over. I got as wet as could be, but the horse carried me safely across at the proper place. After I got out a mile or so from the river, I came into a large prairie, which I think must have been twenty or thirty miles in width, and the road ran across it about in the direction that I wanted to go. I laid whip to the horse, and I think he must have carried me not less than forty miles that night, or before sun rise the next morning. I then stopped him in a spot of high grass in an old field, and took off the bridle. I thanked God, and thanked the horse for what he had done for me, and wished him a safe journey back home.

I know the poor horse must have felt stiff, and tired from his speedy jaunt, and I felt very bad myself, riding at that rate all night without a saddle; but I felt as if I had too much at stake to favor either horse flesh or man flesh. I could indeed afford to crucify my own flesh for the sake of redeeming myself from perpetual slavery.

Some may be disposed to find fault with my taking the horse as I did; but I did nothing more than nine out of ten would do if they were placed in the same circumstances. I had no disposition to steal a horse from any man. But I ask, if a white man had been captured by the Cherokee Indians and carried away from his family for life into slavery, and could see a chance to escape and get back to his family; should the Indians pursue him with a determination to take him back or take his life, would it be a crime for the poor fugitive, whose life, liberty and future happiness were all at stake, to mount any man's horse by the way side, and ride him without asking any questions, to effect his escape? Or who would not do the same thing to rescue a wife, child, father, or mother? Such an act committed by a white man under the same circumstances would not only be pronounced proper, but praiseworthy; and if he neglected to avail himself of such a means of escape he would be pronounced a fool. Therefore from this act I have nothing to regret, for I have done nothing more than any other reasonable person would have done under the same circumstances. But I had good luck from the morning I left the horse until I got back into the

State of Ohio. About two miles from where I left the horse, I found a public house on the road, where I stopped and took breakfast. Being asked where I was traveling, I replied that I was going home to Perrysburgh, Ohio, and that I had been out to look at the land in Missouri, with a view of buying. They supposed me to be a native of Ohio, from the fact of my being so well acquainted with its location, its principal cities, inhabitants, &c.

The next night I put up at one of the best hotels in the village where I stopped, and acted wth as much independence as if I was worth a million of dollars; talked about buying land, stock and village property, and contrasting it with the same kind of property in the State of Ohio. In this kind of talk they were most generally interested, and I was treated just like other travelers. I made it a point to travel about thirty miles each day on my way to Jefferson City. On several occasions I have asked the landlords where I have stopped over night, if they could tell me who kept the best house where I would stop the next night, which was most generally in a small village. But for fear I might forget, I would get them to give me the name on a piece of paper as a kind of recommend. This would serve as an introduction through which I have always been well received from one landlord to another, and I have always stopped at the best houses, eaten at the first tables, and slept in the best beds. No man ever asked me whether I was bond or free, black or white, rich or poor; but I always presented a bold front and showed the best side out, which was all the pass I had. But when I got within about one hundred miles of Jefferson City, where I expected to take a steamboat passage to St. Louis, I stopped over night at a hotel, where I met with a young white man who was traveling on to Jefferson City on horse back, and was also leading a horse with a saddle and bridle on.

I asked him if he would let me ride the horse which he was leading, as I was going to the same city? He said that it was a hired horse, that he was paying at the rate of fifty cents per day for it, but if I would pay the same I could ride him. I accepted the offer and we rode together to the city. We were on the road together two or three days; stopped and ate and slept together at the same hotels.

XVI

Stratagem to get on board the steamer.—My Irish friends. —My success in reaching Cincinnati.—Reflections on again seeing Kentucky.—I get employment in a hotel.—My fright at seeing the gambler who sold me.—I leave Ohio with Mr. Smith.—His letter.—My education.

The greatest of my adventures came off when I arrived at Jefferson City. There I expected to meet an advertisement for my person; it was there I must cross the river or take a steamboat down; it was there I expected to be interrogated and required to prove whether I was actually a free man or a slave. If I was free, I should have to show my free papers; and if I was a slave I should be required to tell who my master was.

I stopped at a hotel, however, and ascertained that there was a steamboat expected down the river that day for St. Louis. I also found out that there were several passengers at that house who were going down on board of the first boat. I knew that the captain of a steamboat could not take a colored passenger on board of his boat from a slave state without first ascertaining whether such person was bond or free; I knew that this was more than he would dare to do by the laws of the slave states—and now to surmount this difficulty it brought into exercise all the powers of my mind. I would have got myself boxed up as freight, and have been forwarded to St. Louis, but I had no friend that I could trust to do it for me. This plan has since been adopted by some with success. But finally I thought I might possibly pass myself off as a body servant to the passengers going from the hotel down.

So I went to a store and bought myself a large trunk, and took it to the hotel. Soon, a boat came in which was bound to St. Louis, and the passengers started down to get on board. I took up my large trunk, and started along after them as if I was their servant. My heart trembled in view of the dangerous experiment which I was then about to try. It required all the moral courage that I was master of to bear me up in view of my critical condition. The white people that I was following walked on board and I after them. I acted as if the trunk was full of clothes, but I had not a stitch of clothes in it. The passengers went up into the cabin and I followed them with the trunk. I suppose this made the captain think that I was their slave.

I not only took the trunk in the cabin but stood by it until after the boat had started as if it belonged to my owners; and I was taking care of it for them; but as soon as the boat got fairly under way, I knew that some account would have to be given of me; so I then took my trunk down on the deck among the deck passengers to prepare myself to meet the clerk of the boat, when he should come to collect fare from the deck passengers.

Fortunately for me there was quite a number of deck passengers on board, among whom there were many Irish. I insinuated myself among them so as to get into their good graces, believing that if I should get into a difficulty they would stand by me. I saw several of these persons going up to the saloon buying whiskey, and I thought this might be the most effectual way by which I could gain speedily their respect and sympathy. So I participated with them pretty freely for awhile, or at least until after I got my fare settled. I placed myself in a little crowd of them, and invited them all up to the bar with me, stating that it was my treat. This was responded to, and they walked up and drank and I footed the bill. This, of course, brought us into a kind of union. We sat together and laughed and talked freely. Within ten or fifteen minutes I remarked that I was getting dry again, and invited them up and treated again. By this time I was thought to be one of the most liberal and gentlemanly men on board, by these deck passengers; they were ready to do any thing for me—they got to singing songs, and telling long yarns in which I took quite an active part; but it was all for effect.

By this time the porter came around ringing his bell for all passengers who had not paid their fare, to walk up to the captain's office and settle it. Some of my Irish friends had not yet settled, and I asked one of them if he would be good enough to take my money and get me a ticket when he was getting one for himself, and he quickly replied, "yes, sir, I will get you a ticket." So he relieved me of my greatest trouble. When they came round to gather the tickets before we got to St. Louis, my ticket was taken with the rest, and no questions were asked me.

The next day the boat arrived at St. Louis; my object was to take passage on board of the first boat which was destined for Cincinnati, Ohio; and as there was a boat going out that day for Pittsburgh, I went on board to make some inquiry about the fare &c., and found the steward to be a colored man with whom I was acquainted. He lived in Cincinnati, and had rendered me some assistance in making my escape to Canada, in the summer of 1838, and he also very kindly aided me then in getting back into a land of freedom. The swift running steamer started that afternoon on her voyage, which soon wafted my body beyond the tryannical limits of chattel slavery. When the boat struck the mouth of the river Ohio, and I had once more the pleasure of looking on that lovely stream, my heart leaped up for joy at the glorious prospect that I should again be free. Every revolution of the mighty steam-engine seemed to bring me nearer and nearer the "promised land." Only a few days had elapsed, before I was permitted by the smiles of a good providence, once more to gaze on the green hill-tops and valleys of old Kentucky, the State of my nativity. And notwithstanding I was deeply interested while standing on the deck of the steamer looking at the beauties of nature on either side of the river, as she pressed her way up the stream, my very soul was pained to look upon the slaves in the fields of Kentucky, still toiling under their task-masters without pay. It was on this soil I first breathed the free air of Heaven, and felt the bitter pangs of slavery—it was here that I first learned to abhor it. It was here I received the first impulse of human rights—it was here that I first entered my protest against the bloody institution of slavery, by running away from it, and declared that I would no longer work for any man as I had done, without wages.

When the steamboat arrived at Portsmouth, Ohio, I took off my trunk with the intention of going to Canada. But my funds were almost exhausted, so I had to stop and go to work to get money to travel on. I hired myself at the American Hotel to a Mr. McCoy to do the work of a porter, to black boots, &c., for which he was to pay me $12 per month. I soon found the landlord to be bad pay, and not only that, but he would not allow me to charge for blacking boots, although I had to black them after everybody had gone to bed at night, and set them in the bar-room, where the gentlemen could come and get them in the morning while I was at other work. I had nothing extra for this, neither would he pay me my regular wages; so I thought this was a little too much like slavery, and devised a plan by which I got some pay for my work.

I made it a point never to blacken all the boots and shoes overnight, neither would I put any of them in the bar-room, but lock them up in a room where no one could get them without calling for me. I got a piece of broken vessel, placed it in the room just before the boots, and put into it several pieces of small change, as if it had been given me for boot blacking; and almost every one that came in after their boots, would throw some small trifle into my contribution box, while I was there blacking away. In this way, I made more than my landlord paid me, and I soon got a good stock of cash again. One morning I blacked a gentleman's boots who came in during the night by a steamboat. After he had put on his boots, I was called into the bar-room to button his straps; and while I was performing this service, not thinking to see anybody that knew me, I happened to look up at the man's face and who should it be but one of the very gamblers who had recently sold me. I dropped his foot and bolted from the room as if I had been struck by an electric shock. The man happened not to recognize me, but this strange conduct on my part excited the landlord, who followed me out to see what was the matter. He found me with my hand to my breast, groaning at a great rate. He asked me what was the matter; but I was not able to inform him correctly, but said that I felt very bad indeed. He of course thought I was sick with the colic and ran in the house and got some hot stuff for me, with spice, ginger, &c. But I never got able to go into the bar-room until long after breakfast time, when I knew this man was gone; then I got well.

And yet I have no idea that the man would have hurt a hair of my head; but my first thought was that he was after me. I then made up my mind to leave Portsmouth; its location being right on the border of a slave State.

A short time after this a gentleman put up there over night named Smith, from Perrysburgh, with whom I was acquainted in the North. He was on his way to Kentucky to buy up a drove of fine horses, and he wanted me to go and help him to drive his horses out to Perrysburgh, and said he would pay all my expenses if I would go. So I made a contract to go and agreed to meet him the next week, on a set day, in Washington, Ky., to start with his drove to the north. Accordingly at the time I took a steamboat passage down to Maysville, near where I was to meet Mr. Smith with my trunk. When I arrived at Maysville, I found that Washington was still six miles back from the river. I stopped at a hotel and took my breakfast, and who should I see there but a captain of a boat, who saw me but two years previous going down the river Ohio with handcuffs on, in a chain gang; but he happened not to know me. I left my trunk at the hotel and went out to Washington, where I found Mr. Smith, and learned that he was not going to start off with his drove until the next day.

The following letter which was addressed to the committee to investigate the truth of my narrative, will explain this part of it to the reader and corroborate my statements:

MAUMEE CITY, April 5, 1845.

CHAS. H. STEWART, ESQ.

DEAR SIR:—Your favor of 13th February, addressed to me at Perrysburgh, was not received until yesterday; having removed to this place, the letter was not forwarded as it should have been. In reply to your inquiry respecting Henry Bibb, I can only say that about the year 1838 I became acquainted with him at Perrysburgh —employed him to do some work by the job which he performed well, and from his apparent honesty and candor, I became much interested in him. About that time he went South for the purpose, as was said, of getting his wife, who was there in slavery. In the spring of 1841, I found him at Portsmouth on the Ohio River, and after much persuasion, employed him to assist my man to drive home some horses and cattle which I was about purchasing near Maysville, Ky. My confidence in him was such that when about half way home I separated the horses from the cattle, and left him with the latter, with money and instructions to hire what help he wanted to get to Perrysburgh. This he accomplished to my entire satisfaction. He worked for me during the summer, and I was unwilling to part with him, but his desire to go to school and mature plans for the liberation of his wife, were so strong that he left for Detroit, where he could enjoy the society of his colored brethren. I have heard his story and must say that I have not the least reason to suspect it being otherwise than true, and furthermore, I firmly believe, and have for a long time, that he has the foundation to make himself useful. I shall always afford him all the facilities in my power to assist him, until I hear of something in relation to him to alter my mind.

Yours in the cause of truth.

J. W. SMITH

When I arrived at Perrysburgh, I went to work for Mr. Smith for several months. This family I found to be one of the most kind-hearted, and unprejudiced that I ever lived with. Mr. and Mrs. Smith lived up to their profession.

I resolved to go to Detroit, that winter, and go to school, in January 1842. But when I arrived at Detroit I soon found that I was not able to give myself a very thorough education. I was among strangers, who were not disposed to show me any great favors. I had every thing to pay for, and clothing to buy, so I graduated within three weeks! And this was all the schooling that I have ever had in my life.

W. C. Monroe was my teacher; to him I went about two weeks only. My occupation varied according to circumstances, as I was not settled in mind about the condition of my bereaved family for several years, and could not settle myself down at any permanent business. I saw occasionally, fugitives from Kentucky, some of whom I knew, but none of them were my relatives; none could give me the information which I desired most.

XVII

Letter from W. H. Gatewood.—My reply.—My efforts as a public lecturer.—Singular incident in Steubenville.—Meeting with a friend of Whitfield in Michigan.—Outrage on a canal packet.—Fruitless efforts to find my wife.

The first direct information that I received concerning any of my relations, after my last escape from slavery, was communicated in a letter from Wm. H. Gatewood, my former owner, which I here insert word for word, without any correction:

Bedford, Trimble County, Ky.

Mr. H. Bibb,

Dear Sir:—After my respects to you and yours &c., I received a small book which you sent to me that I peroseed and found it was sent by H. Bibb I am a stranger in Detroit and know no man there without it is Walton H. Bibb if this be the man please to write to me and tell me all about that place and the people I will tell you the news here as well as I can your mother is still living here and she is well the people are generally well in this cuntry times are dull and produce low give my compliments to King, Jack, and all my friends in that cuntry I read that book you sent me and think it will do very well—George is sold, I do not know any thing about him I have nothing more at present, but remain yours &c

W. H. Gatewood

February 9th, 1844.

P. S. You will please to answer this letter.

Never was I more surprised than at the reception of this letter, it came so unexpected to me. There had just been a State Convention held in Detroit, by the free people of color, the proceedings of which were published in pamphlet form. I forwarded several of them to distinguished slaveholders in Kentucky—one among others was Mr. Gatewood, and gave him to understand who sent it. After showing this letter to several of my anti-slavery friends, and asking their opinions about the propriety of my answering it, I was advised to do it, as Mr. Gatewood had no claim on me as a slave, for he had sold and got the money for me and my family. So I wrote him an answer, as near as I can recollect, in the following language:

Dear Sir:—I am happy to inform you that you are not mistaken in the man whom you sold as property, and received pay for as such. But I thank God that I am not property now, but am regarded as a man like yourself, and although I live far north, I am enjoying a comfortable living by my own industry. If you should ever chance to be traveling this way, and will call on me, I will use you better than you did me while you held me as a slave. Think not that I have any malice against you, for the cruel treatment which you inflicted on me while I was in your power. As it was the custom of your country, to treat your fellow men as you did me and my little family, I can freely forgive you.

I wish to be remembered in love to my aged mother, and friends; please tell her that if we should never meet again in this life, my prayer shall be to God that we may meet in Heaven, where parting shall be no more.

You wish to be remembered to King and Jack. I am pleased, sir, to inform you that they are both here, well, and doing well. They are both living in Canada West. They are now the owners of better farms than the men are who once owned them.

You may perhaps think hard of us for running away from slavery, but as to myself, I have but one apology to make for it, which is this: I have only to regret that I did not start at an earlier period. I might have been free long before I was. But you had it in your power to have kept me there much longer than you did. I think it is very probable that I should have been a toiling slave on your plantation to-day, if you had treated me differently.

To be compelled to stand by and see you whip and slash my wife without mercy, when I could afford her no protection, not even by offering myself to suffer the lash in her place, was more than I felt it to be the duty of a slave husband to endure, while the way was open to Canada. My infant child was also frequently flogged by Mrs. Gatewood, for crying, until its skin was bruised literally purple. This kind of treatment was what drove me from home and family, to seek a better home for them. But I am willing to forget the past. I should be pleased to hear from you again, on the reception of this, and should also be very happy to correspond with you often, if it should be agreeable to yourself. I subscribe myself a friend to the oppressed, and Liberty forever.

Henry Bibb.

William Gatewood.
Detroit, March 23d, 1844.

The first time that I ever spoke before a public audience, was to give a narration of my own sufferings and adventures, connected with slavery. I commenced in the village of Adrian, State of Michigan, May, 1844. From that up to the present period, the principle part of my time has been faithfully devoted to the cause of freedom—nerved up and encouraged by the sympathy of anti-slavery friends on the one hand, and prompted by a sense of duty to my enslaved countrymen on the other, especially, when I remembered that slavery had robbed me of my freedom—deprived me of education—banished me from my native State, and robbed me of my family.

I went from Michigan to the State of Ohio, where I traveled over some of the Southern counties of that State, in company with Samuel Brooks, and Amos Dresser, lecturing upon the subject of American Slavery. The prejudice of the people at that time was very strong against the abolitionists; so much so that they were frequently mobbed for discussing the subject.

We appointed a series of meetings along on the Ohio River, in sight of the State of Virginia; and in several places we had Virginians over to hear us upon the subject. I recollect our having appointed a meeting in the city of Steubenville, which is situated on the bank of the river Ohio. There was but one known abolitionist living in that city, named George Ore. On the day of our meeting, when we arrived in this splendid city there was not a church, school house, nor hall, that we could get for love or money, to hold our meeting in. Finally, I believe that the Whigs consented to let us have the use of their club room, to hold the meeting in; but before the hour had arrived for us to commence, they re-considered the matter, and informed us that we could not have the use of their house for an abolition meeting.

We then got permission to hold forth in the public market house, and even then so great was the hostility of the rabble, that they tried to bluff us off, by threats and epithets. Our meeting was advertised to take place at nine o'clock, A.M. The pro-slavery parties hired a colored man to take a large auction bell, and go all over the city ringing it, and crying, "ho ye! ho ye! Negro auction to take place in the market house, at nine o'clock, by George Ore!" This cry was sounded all over the city, which called out many who would not otherwise have been present. They came to see if it was really the case. The object of the rabble in having the bell rung was, to prevent us from attempting to speak. But at the appointed hour, Bro. Dresser opened the meeting with prayer, and Samuel Brooks mounted the block and spoke for fifteen or twenty minutes, after which Mr. Dresser took the block and talked about one hour upon the wickedness of slaveholding. There were not yet many persons present. They were standing off I suppose to see if I was to be offered for sale. Many windows were hoisted and store doors open, and they were looking and listening to what was said. After Mr. Dresser was through, I was called to take the stand. Just at this moment there was no small stir in rushing forward; so much indeed, that I thought they were coming up to mob me. I should think that in less than fifteen minutes there were about one thousand persons standing around, listening. I saw many of them shedding tears while I related the sad story of my wrongs. At twelve o'clock we adjourned the meeting, to meet again at the same place at two P.M. Our afternoon meeting was well attended until nearly sunset, at which time, we saw some signs of a mob and adjourned. The mob followed us that night to the house of Mr. Ore, and they were yelling like tigers, until late that night, around the house, as if they wanted to tear it down.

In the fall of 1844, S. B. Treadwell, of Jackson, and myself, spent two or three months in lecturing through the State of Michigan, upon the abolition of slavery, in a section of country where abolitionists were few and far between. Our meetings were generally appointed in small log cabins, school houses, among the farmers, which were some times crowded full; and where they had no horse teams, it was often the case that there would be four or five ox teams come, loaded down with men, women and children, to attend our meetings.

But the people were generally poor, and in many places not able to give us a decent night's lodging. We most generally carried with us a few pounds of candles to light up the houses wherein we held our meetings after night; for in many places, they had neither candles nor candlesticks. After meeting was out, we have frequently gone from three to eight miles to get lodging, through the dark forest, where there was scarcely any road for a wagon to run on.

I have traveled for miles over swamps, where the roads were covered with logs, without any dirt over them, which has sometimes shook and jostled the wagon to pieces, where we could find no shop or any place to mend it. We would have to tie it up with bark, or take the lines to tie it with, and lead the horse by the bridle. At other times we were in mud up to the hubs of the wheels. I recollect one evening, we lectured in a little village where there happened to be a Southerner present, who was a personal friend of Deacon Whitfield, who became much offended at what I said about his "Bro. Whitfield," and complained about it after the meeting was out.

He told the people not to believe a word that I said, that it was all a humbug. They asked him how he knew? "Ah!" said he, "he has slandered Bro. Whitfield. I am well acquainted with him, we both belonged to one church; and Whitfield is one of the most respectable men in all that region of country." They asked if he (Whitfield) was a slaveholder?

The reply was, "Yes, but he treated his slaves well."

"Well," said one, "that only proves that he has told us the truth; for all we wish to know, is that there is such a man as Whitfield, as represented by Bibb, and that he is a slaveholder."

On the 2d Sept., 1847, I started from Toledo on board the canal packet Erie, for Cincinnati, Ohio. But before going on board, I was waited on by one of the boat's crew, who gave me a card of the boat, upon which was printed, that no pains would be spared to render all passengers comfortable who might favor them with their patronage to Cincinnati. This card I slipped into my pocket, supposing it might be of some use to me. There were several drunken loafers on board going through as passengers, one of whom used the most vulgar language in the cabin, where there were ladies, and even vomited! But he was called a white man, and a Southerner, which made it all right. I of course took my place in the cabin with the rest, and there was nothing said against it that night. When the passengers went forward to settle their fare I paid as much as any other man, which entitled me to the same privileges. The next morning at the ringing of the breakfast bell, the proprietor of the packet line, Mr. Samuel Doyle, being on board, invited the passengers to sit up to breakfast. He also invited me personally to sit up to the table. But after we were all seated, and some had begun to eat, he came and ordered me up from the table, and said I must wait until the rest were done.

I left the table without making any reply, and walked out on the deck of the boat. After breakfast the passengers came up, and the cabin boy was sent after me to come to breakfast, but I refused. Shortly after, this man who had ordered me from the table, came up with the ladies. I stepped up and asked him if he was the captain of the boat. His answer was no, that he was one of the proprietors. I then informed him that I was going to leave his boat at the first stopping place, but before leaving I wanted to ask him a few questions: "Have I misbehaved to any one on board of this boat? Have I disobeyed any law of this boat?"

"No," said he.

"Have I not paid you as much as any other passenger through to Cincinnati?"

"Yes," said he.

"Then I am sure that I have been insulted and imposed upon, on board of this boat, without any just cause whatever."

"No one has misused you, for you ought to have known better than to have come to the table where there were white people."

"Sir, did you not ask me to come to the table?"

"Yes, but I did not know that you was a colored man, when I asked you; and then it was better to insult one man than all the passengers on board of the boat."

"Sir, I do not believe that there is a gentleman or lady on board of this boat who would have considered it an insult for me to have taken my breakfast, and you have imposed upon me by taking my money and promising to use me well, and then to insult me as you have."

"I don't want any of your jaw," said he.

"Sir, with all due respect to your elevated station, you have imposed upon me in a way which is unbecoming a gentleman. I have paid my money, and behaved myself as well as any other man, and I am determined that no man shall impose on me as you have, by deceiving me, without my letting the world know it. I would rather a man should rob me of my money at midnight, than to take it in that way."

I left this boat at the first stopping place, and took the next boat to Cincinnati. On the last boat I had no cause to complain of my treatment. When I arrived at Cincinnati, I published a statement of this affair in the *Daily Herald.*

The next day Mr. Doyle called on the editor in a great passion. "Here," said he, "what does this mean."

"What, sir?" said the editor quietly.

"Why, the stuff here, read it and see."

"Read it yourself," answered the editor.

"Well, I want to know if you sympathize with this nigger here."

"Who, Mr. Bibb? Why yes, I think he is a gentleman, and should be used as such."

"Why this is all wrong—all of it."

"Put your finger on the place, and I will right it."

"Well, he says that we took his money, when we paid part back. And if you take his part, why I'll have nothing to do with your paper."

So ended his wrath.

In 1845, the anti-slavery friends of Michigan employed me to take the field as an anti-slavery Lecturer, in that State, during the Spring, Summer, and Fall, pledging themselves to restore to me my wife and child, if they were living, and could be reached by human agency, which may be seen by the following circular from the *Signal of Liberty:*

> To Liberty Friends:—In the *Signal* of the 28th inst. is a report from the undersigned respecting Henry Bibb. His narrative always

excites deep sympathy for himself and favorable bias for the cause, which seeks to abolish the evils he so powerfully portrays. Friends and foes attest his efficiency.

Mr. Bibb has labored much in lecturing, yet has collected but a bare pittance. He has received from Ohio lucrative offers, but we have prevailed on him to remain in this State.

We think that a strong obligation rests on the friends in this state to sustain Mr. Bibb, and restore to him his wife and child. Under the expectation that Michigan will yield to these claims; will support their laborer, and re-unite the long severed ties of husband and wife, parent and child, Mr. Bibb will lecture through the whole State.

Our object is to prepare friends for the visit of Mr. Bibb, and to suggest an effective mode of operations for the whole State.

Let friends in each vicinity appoint a collector—pay to him all contributions for the freedom of Mrs. Bibb and child; then transmit them to us. We will acknowledge them in the *Signal*, and be responsible for them. We will see that the proper measures for the freedom of Mrs. Bibb and child are taken, and if it be within our means we will accomplish it—nay we will accomplish it, if the objects be living and the friends sustain us. But should we fail, the contributions will be held subject to the order of the donors, less however, by a proportionate deduction of expenses from each.

The hope of this re-union will nerve the heart and body of Mr. Bibb to re-doubled effort in a cause otherwise dear to him. And as he will devote his whole time systematically to the anti-slavery cause, he must also depend on friends for the means of livelihood. We bespeak for him your hospitality, and such pecuniary contributions as you can afford, trusting that the latter may be sufficient to enable him to keep the field.

A. L. PORTER,
C. H. STEWART,
SILAS M. HOLMES

DETROIT, APRIL 22, 1845.

I have every reason to believe that they acted faithfully in the matter, but without success. They wrote letters in every quarter where they would be likely to gain any information respecting her. There were also two men sent from Michigan in the summer of 1845, down South, to find her if possible, and report—and whether they found out her condition, and refused to report, I am not able to say—but suffice it to say that they never have reported. They were respectable men and true friends of the cause, one of whom was a Methodist minister, and the other a cabinet maker, and both white men.

The small spark of hope which had still lingered about my heart had almost become extinct.

XVIII

My last effort to recover my family.—Sad tidings of my wife.—Her degradation.—I am compelled to regard our relation as dissolved forever.

In view of the failure to hear any thing of my wife, many of my best friends advised me to get married again, if I could find a suitable person. They regarded my former wife as dead to me, and all had been done that could be.

But I was not yet satisfied myself, to give up. I wanted to know certainly what had become of her. So in the winter of 1845, I resolved to go back to Kentucky, my native State, to see if I could hear anything from my family. And against the advice of all my friends, I went back to Cincinnati, where I took passage on board of a Southern steamboat to Madison, in the State of Indiana, which was only ten miles from where Wm. Gatewood lived, who was my former owner. No sooner had I landed in Madison, than I learned, on inquiry, and from good authority, that my wife was living in a state of adultery with her master, and had been for the last three years. This message she sent back to Kentucky, to her mother and friends. She also spoke of the time and manner of our separation by Deacon Whitfield, my being taken off by the Southern blacklegs, to where she knew not; and that she had finally given me up. The child she said was still with her. Whitfield had sold her to this man for the above purposes at a high price, and she was better used than ordinary slaves. This was a death blow to all my hopes and pleasant plans. While I was in Madison I hired a white man to go over to Bedford, in Kentucky, where my mother was then living, and bring her over into a free State to see me. I hailed her approach with unspeakable joy. She informed me too, on inquiring whether my family had ever been heard from, that the report which I had just heard in relation to Malinda was substantially true, for it was the same message that she had sent to her mother and friends. And my mother thought it was no use for me to run any more risks, or to grieve myself any more about her.

From that time I gave her up into the hands of an all-wise Providence. As she was then living with another man, I could no longer regard her as my wife. After all the sacrifices, sufferings, and risks which I had run, striving to rescue her from the grasp of slavery; every prospect and hope was cut off. She has ever since been regarded as theoretically and practically dead to me as a wife, for she was living in a state of adultery, according to the law of God and man.

Poor unfortunate woman, I bring no charge of guilt against her, for I know not all the circumstances connected with the case. It is consistent with slavery, however, to suppose that she became reconciled to it, from the fact of her sending word back to her friends and relatives that she was much better treated than she had ever been before, and that she had also given me up. It is also reasonable to suppose that there might have been some kind of attachment formed by living together in this way for years; and it is quite probable that they have other children according to the law of nature, which would have a tendency to unite them stronger together.

In view of all the facts and circumstances connected with this matter, I deem further comments and explanations unnecessary on my part. Finding myself thus isolated in this peculiarly unnatural state, I resolved, in 1846, to spend my days in traveling, to advance the anti-slavery cause. I spent the summer in Michigan, but in the subsequent fall I took a trip to New England, where I spent the winter. And there I found a kind reception wherever I traveled among the friends of freedom.

While traveling about in this way among strangers, I was sometimes sick, with no permanent home, or bosom friend to sympathise or take that care of me which an affectionate wife would. So I conceived the idea that it would be better for me to change my position, provided I should find a suitable person.

In the month of May, 1847, I attended the anti-slavery anniversary in the city of New York, where I had the good fortune to be introduced to the favor of a Miss Mary E. Miles, of Boston; a lady whom I had frequently heard very highly spoken of, for her activity and devotion to the anti-slavery cause, as well as her talents and learning, and benevolence in the cause of reforms, generally. I was very much impressed with the personal appearance of Miss Miles, and was deeply interested in our first interview, because I found that her principles and my own were nearly one and the same. I soon found by a few visits, as well as by letters, that she possessed moral principle, and frankness of disposition, which is often sought for but seldom found. These, in connection with other amiable qualities, soon won my entire confidence and affection. But this secret I kept to myself until I was fully satisfied that this feeling was reciprocal; that there was indeed a congeniality of principles and feeling, which time nor eternity could never change.

When I offered myself for matrimony, we mutually engaged ourselves to each other, to marry in one year, with this condition, viz: that if either party should see any reason to change their mind within that time, the contract should not be considered binding. We kept up a regular correspondence during the time, and in June, 1848, we had the happiness to be joined in holy wedlock. Not in slaveholding style, which is a mere farce, without the sanction of law or gospel; but in accordance with the laws of God and our country. My beloved wife is a bosom friend, a help-meet, a loving companion in all the social, moral, and religious relations of life. She is to me what a poor slave's wife can never be to her husband while in the condition of a slave; for she can not be true to her husband contrary to the will of her master. She can neither be pure nor virtuous, contrary to the will of her master. She dare not refuse to be reduced to a state of adultery at the will of her master; from the fact that the slaveholding law, customs and teachings are all against the poor slaves.

I presume there are no class of people in the United States who so highly appreciate the legality of marriage as those persons who have been held and treated as property. Yes, it is that fugitive who knows from sad experience, what it is to have his wife tyrannically snatched from his bosom by a slaveholding professor of religion, and finally reduced to a state of adultery, that knows how to appreciate the law that repels such high-handed villainy. Such as that to which the writer has been exposed. But thanks be to God, I am now free from the hand of the cruel oppressor, no more to be plundered of my dearest rights; the wife of my bosom, and my poor unoffending offspring. Of Malinda I will only add a word in conclusion. The relation once subsisting between us, to which I clung, hoping against hope, for years, after we were torn assunder, not having been sanctioned by any loyal power, cannot be cancelled by a legal process. Voluntarily assumed without law mutually, it was by her relinquished years ago without my knowledge, as before named; during which time I was making every effort to secure her restoration. And it was not until after living alone in the world for more than eight years without a companion known in law or morals, that I changed my condition.

XIX

Comments on S. Gatewood's letter about slaves stealing. —Their conduct vindicated.—Comments on W. Gatewood's letter.

But it seems that I am not now beyond the reach of the foul slander of slaveholders. They are not satisfied with selling and banishing me from my native State. As soon as they got news of my being in the Free North, exposing their peculiar Institution, a libelous letter was written by Silas Gatewood of Kentucky, a son of one of my former owners, to a Northern Committee, for publication, which he thought would destroy my influence and character.

He has charged me with the awful crime of taking from my keeper and oppressor, some of the fruits of my own labor for the benefit of myself and family.

But while writing this letter he seems to have overlooked the disgraceful fact that he was guilty himself of what would here be regarded highway robbery, in his conduct to me as narrated [earlier in] this narrative.

A word in reply to Silas Gatewood's letter. I am willing to admit all that is true, but shall deny that which is so basely false. In the first place, he puts words in my mouth that I never used. He says that I represented that "my mother belonged to James Bibb." I deny ever having said so in private or public. He says that I stated that Bibb's daughter married a Sibley. I deny it. He also says that the first time that I left Kentucky for my liberty, I was gone about two years, before I went back to rescue my family. I deny it. I was gone from Dec. 25th, 1837, to May, or June, 1838. He says that I went back the second time for the purpose of taking off my family, and eight or ten more slaves to Canada. This I will not pretend to deny. He says I was guilty of disposing of articles from the farm for my own use, and pocketing the money, and that his father caught me stealing a sack full of wheat. I admit the fact. I acknowledge the wheat.

And who had a better right to eat of the fruits of my own hard earnings than myself? Many a long summer's day have I toiled with my wife and other slaves, cultivating his father's fields, and gathering in his harvest, under the scorching rays of the sun, without half enough to eat, or clothes to wear, and at the same time his meat-house was filled with bacon and bread stuff; his dairy with butter and cheese; his barn with grain, husbanded by the unrequited toil of the slaves. And yet if a slave presumed to take a little from the abundance which he had made by his own sweat and toil, to supply the demands of nature, to quiet the craving appetite which is sometimes almost irresistible, it is called stealing by slaveholders.

But I did not regard it as stealing then, I do not regard it as such now. I hold that a slave has a moral right to eat drink and wear all that he needs, and that it would be a sin on his part to suffer and starve in a country where there is a plenty to eat and wear within his reach. I consider that I had a just right to what I took, because it was the labor of my own hands. Should I take from a neighbor as a freeman, in a free country, I should consider myself guilty of doing wrong before God and man. But was I the slave of Wm. Gatewood to-day, or any other slaveholder, working without wages, and suffering with hunger or for clothing, I should not stop to inquire whether my master would approve of my helping myself to what I needed to eat or wear. For while the slave is regarded as property, how can he steal from his master? It is contrary to the very nature of the relation existing between master and slave, from the fact that there is no law to punish a slave for theft, but lynch law; and the way they avoid that is to hide well. For illustration, a slave from the State of Virginia, for cruel treatment left the State between daylight and dark, being borne off by one of his master's finest horses, and finally landed in Canada, where the British laws recognise no such thing as property in a human being. He was pursued by his owners, who expected to take advantage of the British law by claiming him as a fugitive from justice, and as such he was arrested and brought before the court of Queen's Bench. They swore that he was, at a certain time, the slave of Mr. A., and that he ran away at such a time and stole and brought off a horse. They enquired who the horse belonged to, and it was ascertained that the slave and horse both belonged to the same person. The court therefore decided that the horse and the man were both recognised, in the State of Virginia, alike, as articles of property, belonging to the same person—therefore, if there was theft committed on either side, the former must have stolen off the latter—the horse brought away the man, and not the man the horse. So the man was discharged and pronounced free according to the laws of Canada. There are several other letters published in this work upon the same subject, from slaveholders, which it is hardly necessary for me to notice. However, I feel thankful to the writers for the endorsement and confirmation which they have given to my story. No matter what their motives were, they have done me and the anti-slavery cause good service in writing those letters—but more especially the Gatewood's. Silas Gatewood has done more for me than all the rest. He has labored so hard in his long communication in trying to expose me, that he has proved every thing that I could have asked of him; and for which I intend to reward him by forwarding him one of my books, hoping that it may be the means of converting him from a slaveholder to an honest man, and an advocate of liberty for all mankind.

The reader will see in the introduction that Wm. Gatewood writes a more cautious letter upon the subject than his son Silas. "It is not a very easy matter to catch old birds with chaff," and I presume if Silas had the writing of his letter over again, he would not be so free in telling all he knew, and even more, for the sake of making out a strong case. The object of his writing such a letter will doubtless be understood by the reader. It was to destroy public confidence in the victims of slavery, that the system might not be exposed—it was to gag a poor fugitive who had undertaken to plead his own cause and that of his enslaved brethren. It was a feeble attempt to suppress the voice of universal freedom which is now thundering on every gale. But thank God it is too late in the day.

Go stop the mighty thunder's roar,
Go hush the ocean's sound,
Or upward like the eagle soar
To skies' remotest bound.

And when thou hast the thunder stopped,
And hushed the ocean's waves,
Then, freedom's spirit bind in chains,
And ever hold us slaves.

And when the eagle's boldest feat,
Thou canst perform with skill,
Then, think to stop proud freedom's march,
And hold the bondman still.

XX

Review of my narrative.—Licentiousness a prop of slavery. —A case of mild slavery given.—Its revolting features.— Times of my purchase and sale by professed Christians.— Concluding remarks.

I now conclude my narrative, by reviewing briefly what I have written. This little work has been written without any personal aid or a knowledge of the English grammar, which must in part be my apology for many of its imperfections.

I find in several places, where I have spoken out the deep feelings of my soul, in trying to describe the horrid treatment which I have so often received at the hands of slaveholding professors of religion, that I might possibly make a wrong impression on the minds of some northern freemen, who are unacquainted theoretically or practically with the customs and treatment of American slaveholders to their slaves. I hope that it may not be supposed by any, that I have exaggerated in the least, for the purpose of making out the system of slavery worse than it really is, for, to exaggerate upon the cruelties of this system, would be almost impossible; and to write herein the most horrid features of it would not be in good taste for my book.

I have long thought from what has fallen under my own observation while a slave, that the strongest reason why southerners stick with such tenacity to their "peculiar institution," is because licentious white men could not carry out their wicked purposes among the defenceless colored population as they now do, without being exposed and punished by law, if slavery was abolished. Female virtue could not be trampled under foot with impunity, and marriage among the people of color kept in utter obscurity.

On the other hand, lest it should be said by slaveholders and their apologists, that I have not done them the justice to give a sketch of the best side of slavery, if there can be any best side to it; therefore in conclusion, they may have the benefit of the following case, that fell under the observation of the writer. And I challenge America to show a milder state of slavery than this. I once knew a Methodist in the state of Ky., by the name of Young, who was the owner of a large number of slaves, many of whom belonged to the same church with their master. They worshipped together in the same church.

Mr. Young never was known to flog one of his slaves or sell one. He fed and clothed them well, and never over-worked them. He allowed each family a small house to themselves with a little garden spot, whereon to raise their own vegetables; and a part of the day on Saturdays was allowed them to cultivate it.

In process of time he became deeply involved in debt by endorsing notes, and his property was all advertised to be sold by the sheriff at public auction. It consisted in slaves, many of whom were his brothers and sisters in the church.

On the day of sale there were slave traders and speculators on the ground to buy. The slaves were offered on the auction block one after another, until they were all sold before their old master's face. The first man offered on the block was an old gray-headed slave by the name of Richard. His wife followed him up to the block, and when they had bid him up to seventy or eighty dollars one of the bidders asked Mr. Young what he could do, as he looked very old and infirm? Mr. Young replied by saying, "he is not able to accomplish much manual labor, from his extreme age and hard labor in early life. Yet I would rather have him than many of those who are young and vigorous; who are able to perform twice as much labor—because I know him to be faithful and trustworthy, a Christian in good standing in my church. I can trust him anywhere with confidence. He has toiled many long years on my plantation and I have always found him faithful."

This giving him a good Christian character caused them to run him up to near two hundred dollars. His poor old companion stood by weeping and pleading that they might not be separated. But the marriage relation was soon dissolved by the sale, and they were separated never to meet again.

Another man was called up whose wife followed him with her infant in her arms, beseeching to be sold with her husband, which proved to be all in vain. After the men were all sold they then sold the women and children. They ordered the first woman to lay down her child and mount the auction block; she refused to give up her little one and clung to it as long as she could, while the cruel lash was applied to her back for disobedience. She pleaded for mercy in the name of God. But the child was torn from the arms of its mother amid the most heart-rending shrieks from the mother and child on the one hand, and bitter oaths and cruel lashes from the tyrants on the other. Finally the poor little child was torn from the mother while she was sacrificed to the highest bidder. In this way the sale was carried on from beginning to end.

There was each speculator with his hand-cuffs to bind his victims after the sale; and while they were doing their writings, the Christian portion of the slaves asked permission to kneel in prayer on the ground before they separated, which was granted. And while bathing each other with tears of sorrow on the verge of their final separation, their eloquent appeals in prayer to the Most High seemed to cause an unpleasant sensation upon the ears of their tyrants, who ordered them to rise and make ready their limbs for the coffles. And as they happened not to bound at the first sound, they were soon raised from their knees by the sound of the lash, and the rattle of the chains, in which they were soon taken off by their respective masters,—husbands from wives, and children from parents, never expecting to meet until the judgment of the great day. Then Christ shall say to the slaveholding professors of religion, "Inasmuch as ye did it unto one of the least of these little ones, my brethren, ye did it unto me."

Having thus tried to show the best side of slavery that I can conceive of, the reader can exercise his own judgment in deciding whether a man can be a Bible Christian, and yet hold his Christian brethren as property, so that they may be sold at any time in market, as sheep or oxen, to pay his debts.

During my life in slavery I have been sold by professors of religion several times. In 1836 "Bro." Albert G. Sibley, of Bedford, Kentucky, sold me for $850 to "Bro." John Sibley; and in the same year he sold me to "Bro." Wm. Gatewood of Bedford, for $850. In 1839 "Bro." Gatewood sold me to Madison Garrison, a slave trader, of Louisville, Kentucky, with my wife and child—at a depreciated price because I was a runaway. In the same year he sold me with my family to "Bro." Whitfield, in the city of New Orleans, for $1200. In 1841 "Bro." Whitfield sold me from my family to Thomas Wilson and Co., blacklegs. In the same year they sold me to a "Bro." in the Indian Territory. I think he was a member of the Presbyterian Church. F. E. Whitfield was a deacon in regular standing in the Baptist Church. A. Sibley was a Methodist exhorter of the M.E. Church in good standing. J. Sibley was a class-leader in the same church; and Wm. Gatewood was also an acceptable member of the same church.

Is this Christianity? Is it honest or right? Is it doing as we would be done by? Is it in accordance with the principles of humanity or justice?

I believe slaveholding to be a sin against God and man under all circumstances. I have no sympathy with the person or persons who tolerate and support the system willingly and knowingly, morally, religiously or politically.

Prayerfully and earnestly relying on the power of truth, and the aid of the divine providence, I trust that this little volume will bear some humble part in lighting up the path of freedom and revolutionizing public opinion upon this great subject. And I here pledge myself, God being my helper, ever to contend for the natural equality of the human family, without regard to color, which is but fading *matter,* while *mind* makes the man.

New York City, *May* 1, 1849.

Henry Bibb.

Narrative of
WILLIAM WELLS BROWN

A Fugitive Slave
written by himself

TO WELLS BROWN, OF OHIO

Thirteen years ago, I came to your door, a weary fugitive from chains and stripes. I was a stranger, and you took me in. I was hungry, and you fed me. Naked was I, and you clothed me. Even a name by which to be known among men, slavery had denied me. You bestowed upon me your own. Base indeed should I be, if I ever forget what I owe to you, or do anything to disgrace that honored name!

As a slight testimony of my gratitude to my earliest benefactor, I take the liberty to inscribe to you this little Narrative of the sufferings from which I was fleeing when you had compassion upon me. In the multitude that you have succored, it is very possible that you may not remember me; but until I forget God and myself, I can never forget you.

Your grateful friend,

WILLIAM WELLS BROWN

LETTER FROM EDMUND QUINCY, ESQ.

DEDHAM, JULY 1, 1847.

TO WILLIAM W. BROWN.

MY DEAR FRIEND:—I heartily thank you for the privilege of reading the manuscript of your Narrative. I have read it with deep interest and strong emotion. I am much mistaken if it be not greatly successful and eminently useful. It presents a different phase of the infernal slave-system from that portrayed in the admirable story of Mr. Douglass, and gives us a glimpse of its hideous cruelties in other portions of its domain.

Your opportunities of observing the workings of this accursed system have been singularly great. Your experiences in the Field, in the House, and especially on the River in the service of the slave-trader, Walker, have been such as few individuals have had;—no one, certainly, who has been competent to describe them. What I have admired, and marvelled at, in your Narrative, is the simplicity and calmness with which you describe scenes and actions which might well "move the very stones to rise and mutiny" against the National Institution which makes them possible.

You will perceive that I have made very sparing use of your flattering permission to alter what you had written. To correct a few errors, which appeared to be merely clerical ones, committed in the hurry of composition, under unfavorable circumstances, and to suggest a few curtailments, is all that I have ventured to do. I should be a bold man, as well as a vain one, if I should attempt to improve your descriptions of what you have seen and suffered. Some of the scenes are not unworthy of De Foe himself.

I trust and believe that your Narrative will have a wide circulation. I am sure it deserves it. At least, a man must be differently constituted from me, who can rise from the perusal of your Narrative without feeling that he understands slavery better, and hates it worse, than he ever did before.

I am, very faithfully and respectfully,

Your friend,
EDMUND QUINCY

PREFACE

The friends of freedom may well congratulate each other on the appearance of the following Narrative. It adds another volume to the rapidly increasing anti-slavery literature of the age. It has been remarked by a close observer of human nature, "Let me make the songs of a nation, and I care not who makes its laws;" and it may with equal truth be said, that, among a reading people like our own, their books will at least give character to their laws. It is an influence which goes forth noiselessly upon its mission, but fails not to find its way to many a warm heart, to kindle on the altar thereof the fires of freedom, which will one day break forth in a living flame to consume oppression.

This little book is a voice from the prison-house, unfolding the deeds of darkness which are there perpetrated. Our cause has received efficient aid from this source. The names of those who have come from thence, and battled manfully for the right, need not to be recorded here. The works of some of them are an enduring monument of praise, and their perpetual record shall be found in the grateful hearts of the redeemed bondman.

Few persons have had greater facilities for becoming acquainted with slavery, in all its horrible aspects, than William W. Brown. He has been behind the curtain. He has visited its secret chambers. Its iron has entered his own soul. The dearest ties of nature have been riven in his own person. A mother has been cruelly scourged before his own eyes. A father,—alas! slaves have no father. A brother has been made the subject of its tender mercies. A sister has been given up to the irresponsible control of the pale-faced oppressor. This nation looks on approvingly. The American Union sanctions the deed. The Constitution shields the criminals. American religion sanctifies the crime. But the tide is turning. Already, a mighty undercurrent is sweeping onward. The voice of warning, of remonstrance, of rebuke, of entreaty, has gone forth. Hand is linked in hand, and heart mingles with heart, in this great work of the slave's deliverance.

The convulsive throes of the monster, even now, give evidence of deep wounds.

The writer of this Narrative was hired by his master to a *"soul-driver,"* and has witnessed all the horrors of the traffic, from the buying up of human cattle in the slave-breeding States, which produced a constant scene of separating the victims from all those whom they loved, to their final sale in the southern market, to be worked up in seven years, or given over to minister to the lust of southern *Christians.*

Many harrowing scenes are graphically portrayed; and yet with that simplicity and ingenuousness which carries with it a conviction of the truthfulness of the picture.

This book will do much to unmask those who have "clothed themselves in the livery of the court of heaven" to cover up the enormity of their deeds.

During the past three years, the author has devoted his entire energies to the anti-slavery cause. Laboring under all the disabilities and disadvantages growing out of his education in slavery—subjected, as he had been from his birth, to all the wrongs and deprivations incident to his condition—he yet went forth, impelled to the work by a love of liberty—stimulated by the remembrance of his own sufferings—urged on by the consideration that a mother, brothers, and sister, were still grinding in the prison-house of bondage, in common with three millions of our Father's children—sustained by an unfaltering faith in the omnipotence of truth and the final triumph of justice—to plead the cause of the slave, and by the eloquence of earnestness carried conviction to many minds, and enlisted the sympathy and secured the co-operation of many to the cause.

His labors have been chiefly confined to Western New York, where he has secured many warm friends, by his untiring zeal, persevering energy, continued fidelity, and universal kindness.

Reader, are you an Abolitionist? What have you done for the slave? What are you doing in his behalf? What do you purpose to do? There is a great work before us. Who will be an idler now? This is the great humanitary movement of the age, swallowing up, for the time being, all other questions, comparatively speaking. The course of human events, in obedience to the unchangeable laws of our being, is fast hastening the final crisis, and

Have ye chosen, O my people, on whose party ye shall stand,
Ere the Doom from its worn sandal shakes the dust against our land?

Are you a Christian? This is the carrying out of practical Christianity; and there is no other. Christianity is *practical* in its very nature and essence. It is a life, springing out of a soul imbued with its spirit. Are you a friend of the missionary cause? This is the greatest missionary enterprise of the day. Three millions of *Christian,* law-manufactured heathen are longing for the glad tidings of the Gospel of freedom. Are you a friend of the Bible? Come, then, and help us to restore to these millions, whose eyes have been bored out by slavery, their sight, that they may see to read the Bible. Do you love God whom you have not seen? Then manifest that love, by restoring to your brother whom you have seen, his rightful inheritance, of which he has been so long and so cruelly deprived.

It is not for a single generation alone, numbering three millions —sublime as would be that effort—that we are working. It is for HUMANITY, the wide world over, not only now, but for all coming time, and all future generations:—

> For he who settles Freedom's principles,
> Writes the death-warrant of all tyranny.

It is a vast work—a glorious enterprise—worthy of the unswerving devotion of the entire lifetime of the great and the good.

Slaveholding and slaveholders must be rendered disreputable and odious. They must be stripped of their respectability and Christian reputation. They must be treated as "MEN-STEALERS—guilty of the highest kind of theft, and sinners of the first rank." Their more guilty accomplices in the persons of *northern apologists,* both in Church and State, must be placed in the same category. Honest men must be made to look upon their crimes with the same abhorrence and loathing with which they regard the less guilty robber and assassin, until

> The common damned shun their society,
> And look upon themselves as fiends less foul.

When a just estimate is placed upon the crime of slaveholding, the work will have been accomplished, and the glorious day ushered in

> When man nor woman in all our wide domain,
> Shall buy, or sell, or hold, or be a slave.

J. C. HATHAWAY.

Farmington, N. Y., 1847

I

I was born in Lexington, Ky. The man who stole me as soon as I was born, recorded the births of all the infants which he claimed to be born his property, in a book which he kept for that purpose. My mother's name was Elizabeth. She had seven children, viz: Solomon, Leander, Benjamin, Joseph, Millford, Elizabeth, and myself. No two of us were children of the same father. My father's name, as I learned from my mother, was George Higgins. He was a

Editor's note: Brown's *Narrative* was first published by the Anti-Slavery Office, Boston, in 1847.

white man, a relative of my master, and connected with some of the first families in Kentucky.

My master owned about forty slaves, twenty-five of whom were field hands. He removed from Kentucky to Missouri, when I was quite young, and settled thirty or forty miles above St. Charles, on the Missouri, where, in addition to his practice as a physician, he carried on milling, merchandizing and farming. He had a large farm, the principal productions of which were tobacco and hemp. The slave cabins were situated on the back part of the farm, with the house of the overseer, whose name was Grove Cook, in their midst. He had the entire charge of the farm, and having no family, was allowed a woman to keep house for him, whose business it was to deal out the provisions for the hands.

A woman was also kept at the quarters to do the cooking for the field hands, who were summoned to their unrequited toil every morning at four o'clock, by the ringing of a bell, hung on a post near the house of the overseer. They were allowed half an hour to eat their breakfast, and get to the field. At half past four, a horn was blown by the overseer, which was the signal to commence work; and every one that was not on the spot at the time, had to receive ten lashes from the negro-whip, with which the overseer always went armed. The handle was about three feet long, with the butt-end filled with lead, and the lash six or seven feet in length, made of cowhide, with platted wire on the end of it. This whip was put in requisition very frequently and freely, and a small offence on the part of a slave furnished an occasion for its use. During the time that Mr. Cook was overseer, I was a house servant—a situation preferable to that of a field hand, as I was better fed, better clothed, and not obliged to rise at the ringing of the bell, but about half an hour after. I have often laid and heard the crack of the whip, and the screams of the slave. My mother was a field hand, and one morning was ten or fifteen minutes behind the others in getting into the field. As soon as she reached the spot where they were at work, the overseer commenced whipping her. She cried, "Oh! pray—Oh! pray—Oh! pray"—these are generally the words of slaves when imploring mercy at the hands of their oppressors. I heard her voice, and knew it, and jumped out of my bunk, and went to the door. Though the field was some distance from the house, I could hear every crack of the whip, and every groan and cry of my poor mother. I remained at the door, not daring to venture any farther.

The cold chills ran over me, and I wept aloud. After giving her ten lashes, the sound of the whip ceased, and I returned to my bed, and found no consolation but in my tears. It was not yet daylight.

II

My master being a political demagogue, soon found those who were ready to put him into office, for the favors he could render them; and a few years after his arrival in Missouri, he was elected to a seat in the Legislature. In his absence from home, everything was left in charge of Mr. Cook, the overseer, and he soon became more tyrannical and cruel. Among the slaves on the plantation, was one by the name of Randall. He was a man about six feet high, and well-proportioned, and known as a man of great strength and power. He was considered the most valuable and able-bodied slave on the plantation; but no matter how good or useful a slave may be, he seldom escapes the lash. But it was not so with Randall. He had been on the plantation since my earliest recollection, and I had never known of his being flogged. No thanks were due to the master or overseer for this. I have often heard him declare, that no white man should ever whip him—that he would die first.

Cook, from the time that he came upon the plantation, had frequently declared, that he could and would flog any nigger that was put into the field to work under him. My master had repeatedly told him not to attempt to whip Randall, but he was determined to try it. As soon as he was left sole dictator, he thought the time had come to put his threats into execution. He soon began to find fault with Randall, and threatened to whip him, if he did not do better. One day he gave him a very hard task,—more than he could possibly do; and at night, the task not being performed, he told Randall that he should remember him the next morning. On the following morning, after the hands had taken breakfast, Cook called out to Randall, and told him that he intended to whip him, and ordered him to cross his hands and be tied. Randall asked why he wished to whip him. He answered, because he had not finished his task the day before. Randall said that the task was too great, or he should have done it. Cook said it made no difference,—he should whip him. Randall stood silent for a moment, and then said, "Mr. Cook, I have always tried to please you since you have been on the plantation, and I find you are determined not to be satisfied with my work, let me do as well as I may. No man has laid hands on me, to whip me, for the last ten years, and I have long since come to the conclusion not to be whipped by any man living." Cook, finding by Randall's determined look and gestures, that he would resist, called three of the hands from their work, and commanded them to seize Randall, and tie him. The hands stood still;—they knew Randall—and they also knew him to be a powerful man, and were afraid to grapple with him. As soon as Cook had ordered the men to seize him, Randall turned to them, and said—"Boys, you all know me; you know that I can handle any three of you, and the man that lays hands on me shall die. This white man can't whip me himself, and therefore he has called you to help him." The overseer was unable to prevail upon them to seize and secure Randall, and finally ordered them all to go to their work together.

Nothing was said to Randall by the overseer, for more than a week. One morning, however, while the hands were at work in the field, he came into it, accompanied by three friends of his, Thompson, Woodbridge and Jones. They came up to where Randall was at work, and Cook ordered him to leave his work, and go with them to the barn. He refused to go; whereupon he was attacked by the overseer and his companions, when he turned upon them, and laid them, one after another, prostrate on the ground. Woodbridge drew out his pistol, and fired at him, and brought him to the ground by a pistol ball. The others rushed upon him with their clubs, and beat him over the head and face, until they succeeded in tying him. He was then taken to the barn, and tied to a beam. Cook gave him over one hundred lashes with a heavy cowhide, had him washed with salt and water, and left him tied during the day. The next day he was untied, and taken to a blacksmith's shop, and had a ball and chain attached to his leg. He was compelled to labor in the field, and perform the same amount of work that the other hands did. When his master returned home, he was much pleased to find that Randall had been subdued in his absence.

III

Soon afterwards, my master removed to the city of St. Louis, and purchased a farm four miles from there, which he placed under the charge of an overseer by the name of Friend Haskell. He was a regular Yankee from New England. The Yankees are noted for making the most cruel overseers.

My mother was hired out in the city, and I was also hired out there to Major Freeland, who kept a public house. He was formerly from Virginia, and was a horse-racer, cock-fighter, gambler, and withal an inveterate drunkard. There were ten or twelve servants in the house, and when he was present, it was cut and slash—knock down and drag out. In his fits of anger, he would take up a chair, and throw it at at a servant; and in his more rational moments, when he wished to chastise one, he would tie them up in the smoke-house, and whip them; after which, he would cause a fire to be made of tobacco stems, and smoke them. This he called *"Virginia play."*

I complained to my master of the treatment which I received from Major Freeland; but it made no difference. He cared nothing about it, so long as he received the money for my labor. After living with Major Freeland five or six months, I ran away, and went into the woods back of the city; and when night came on, I made my way to my master's farm, but was afraid to be seen, knowing that if Mr. Haskell, the overseer, should discover me, I should be again carried back to Major Freeland; so I kept in the woods. One day, while in the woods, I heard the barking and howling of dogs, and in a short time they came so near, that I knew them to be the bloodhounds of Major Benjamin O'Fallon. He kept five or six, to hunt runaway slaves with.

As soon as I was convinced that it was them, I knew there was no chance of escape. I took refuge in the top of a tree, and the hounds were soon at its base, and there remained until the hunters came up in a half or three quarters of an hour afterwards. There were two men with the dogs, who, as soon as they came up, ordered me to descend. I came down, was tied, and taken to St. Louis jail. Major

Freeland soon made his appearance, and took me out, and ordered me to follow him, which I did. After we returned home, I was tied up in the smokehouse, and was very severely whipped. After the Major had flogged me to his satisfaction, he sent out his son Robert, a young man eighteen or twenty years of age, to see that I was well smoked. He made a fire of tobacco stems, which soon set me to coughing and sneezing. This, Robert told me, was the way his father used to do to his slaves in Virginia. After giving me what they conceived to be a decent smoking, I was untied and again set to work.

Robert Freeland was a "chip off the old block." Though quite young, it was not unfrequently that he came home in a state of intoxication. He is now, I believe, a popular commander of a steamboat on the Mississippi River. Major Freeland soon after failed in business, and I was put on board the steamboat Missouri, which plied between St. Louis and Galena. The commander of the boat was William B. Culver. I remained on her during the sailing season, which was the most pleasant time for me that I had ever experienced. At the close of navigation, I was hired to Mr. John Colburn, keeper of the Missouri Hotel. He was from one of the Free States; but a more inveterate hater of the negro, I do not believe ever walked on God's green earth. This hotel was at that time one of the largest in the city, and there were employed in it twenty or thirty servants, mostly slaves.

Mr. Colburn was very abusive, not only to the servants, but to his wife also, who was an excellent woman, and one from whom I never knew a servant to receive a harsh word; but never did I know a kind one to a servant from her husband. Among the slaves employed in the hotel, was one by the name of Aaron, who belonged to Mr. John F. Darby, a lawyer. Aaron was the knife-cleaner. One day, one of the knives was put on the table, not as clean as it might have been. Mr. Colburn, for this offence, tied Aaron up in the wood-house, and gave him over fifty lashes on the bare back with a cowhide, after which, he made me wash him down with rum. This seemed to put him into more agony than the whipping. After being untied, he went home to his master, and complained of the treatment which he had received. Mr. Darby would give no heed to anything he had to say, but sent him directly back. Colburn, learning that he had been to his master with complaints, tied him up again, and gave him a more severe whipping than before. The poor fellow's back was literally cut to pieces; so much so, that he was not able to work for ten or twelve days.

There was also, among the servants, a girl whose master resided in the country. Her name was Patsey. Mr. Colburn tied her up one evening, and whipped her until several of the boarders came out and begged him to desist. The reason for whipping her was this. She was engaged to be married to a man belonging to Major William Christy, who resided four or five miles north of the city. Mr. Colburn had forbid her to see John Christy. The reason of this was said to be the regard which he himself had for Patsey. She went to meeting that evening, and John returned home with her. Mr. Colburn had intended to flog John, if he came within the inclosure; but John knew too well the temper of his rival, and kept at a safe distance;—so he took vengeance on the poor girl. If all the slave-drivers had been called together, I do not think a more cruel man than John Colburn,—and he too a northern man,—could have been found among them.

While living at the Missouri Hotel, a circumstance occurred which caused me great unhappiness. My master sold my mother, and all her children, except myself. They were sold to different persons in the city of St. Louis.

IV

I was soon after taken from Mr. Colburn's, and hired to Elijah P. Lovejoy,* who was at that time publisher and editor of the "St. Louis Times." My work, while with him, was mainly in the printing office, waiting on the hands, working the press, &c. Mr. Lovejoy was a very good man, and decidedly the best master that I had ever had. I am chiefly indebted to him, and to my employment in the printing office, for what little learning I obtained while in slavery.

Though slavery is thought, by some, to be mild in Missouri, when compared with the cotton, sugar and rice growing States, yet no part of our slaveholding country, is more noted for the barbarity of

* [This is the famous Elijah Parish Lovejoy who was killed by a proslavery mob on November 7, 1837, while defending his fourth press from destruction.]

its inhabitants, than St. Louis. It was here that Col. Harney, a United States officer, whipped a slave woman to death. It was here that Francis McIntosh, a free colored man from Pittsburgh, was taken from the steamboat Flora, and burned at the stake. During a residence of eight years in this city, numerous cases of extreme cruelty came under my own observation;—to record them all, would occupy more space than could possibly be allowed in this little volume. I shall, therefore, give but a few more, in addition to what I have already related.

Capt. J. B. Brunt, who resided near my master, had a slave named John. He was his body servant, carriage driver, &c. On one occasion, while driving his master through the city,—the streets being very muddy, and the horses going at a rapid rate,—some mud spattered upon a gentleman by the name of Robert More. More was determined to be revenged. Some three or four months after this occurrence, he purchased John, for the express purpose, as he said, "to tame the d——d nigger." After the purchase, he took him to a blacksmith's shop, and had a ball and chain fastened to his leg, and then put him to driving a yoke of oxen, and kept him at hard labor, until the iron around his leg was so worn into the flesh, that it was thought mortification would ensue. In addition to this, John told me that his master whipped him regularly three times a week for the first two months:—and all this to *"tame him."* A more noble looking man than he, was not to be found in all St. Louis, before he fell into the hands of More; and a more degraded and spirit-crushed looking being was never seen on a southern plantation, after he had been subjected to this *"taming"* process for three months. The last time that I saw him, he had nearly lost the entire use of his limbs.

While living with Mr. Lovejoy, I was often sent on errands to the office of the "Missouri Republican," published by Mr. Edward Charles. Once, while returning to the office with type, I was attacked by several large boys, sons of slave-holders, who pelted me with snow-balls. Having the heavy form of type in my hands, I could not make my escape by running; so I laid down the type and gave them batttle. They gathered around me, pelting me with stones and sticks, until they overpowered me, and would have captured me, if I had not resorted to my heels. Upon my retreat, they took possession of the type; and what to do to regain it I could not devise. Knowing Mr. Lovejoy to be a very humane man, I went to the office, and laid the case before him. He told me to remain in the office. He took one of the apprentices with him, and went after the type, and soon returned with it; but on his return informed me that Samuel McKinney had told him that he would whip me, because I had hurt his boy. Soon after, McKinney was seen making his way to the office by one of the printers, who informed me to the fact, and I made my escape through the back door.

McKinney not being able to find me on his arrival, left the office in a great rage, swearing that he would whip me to death. A few days after, as I was walking along Main Street, he seized me by the collar, and struck me over the head five or six times with a large cane, which caused the blood to gush from my nose and ears in such a manner that my clothes were completely saturated with blood. After beating me to his satisfaction, he let me go, and I returned to the office so weak from the loss of blood, that Mr. Lovejoy sent me home to my master. It was five weeks before I was able to walk again. During this time, it was necessary to have some one to supply my place at the office, and I lost the situation.

After my recovery, I was hired to Capt. Otis Reynolds, as a waiter on board the steamboat Enterprize, owned by Messrs. John and Edward Walsh, commission merchants at St. Louis. This boat was then running on the upper Mississippi. My employment on board was to wait on gentlemen, and the captain being a good man, the situation was a pleasant one to me;—but in passing from place to place, and seeing new faces every day, and knowing that they could go where they pleased, I soon became unhappy, and several times thought of leaving the boat at some landing place, and trying to make my escape to Canada, which I had heard much about as a place where the slave might live, be free, and be protected.

But whenever such thoughts would come into my mind, my resolution would soon be shaken by the remembrance that my dear mother was a slave in St. Louis, and I could not bear the idea of leaving her in that condition. She had often taken me upon her knee, and told me how she had carried me upon her back to the field when I was an infant—how often she had been whipped for leaving her work to nurse me—and how happy I would appear when she would take me into her arms. When these thoughts came over me, I would resolve never to leave the land of slavery without my mother. I thought that to leave her in slavery, after she had undergone and suffered so much for me, would be proving recreant to the duty which I owed to her. Besides this, I had three brothers and a sister there,—two of my brothers having died.

My mother, my brothers Joseph and Millford, and my sister Elizabeth, belonged to Mr. Isaac Mansfield, formerly from one of the Free States, (Massachusetts, I believe.) He was a tinner by trade, and carried on a large manufacturing establishment. Of all my relatives, mother was first, and sister next. One evening, while visiting them, I made some allusion to a proposed journey to Canada, and my sister took her seat by my side, and taking my hand in hers, said, with tears in her eyes,—

"Brother, you are not going to leave mother and your dear sister here without a friend, are you?"

I looked into her face, as the tears coursed swiftly down her cheeks, and bursting into tears myself, said—

"No, I will never desert you and mother." She clasped my hand in hers, and said—

"Brother, you have often declared that you would not end your days in slavery. I see no possible way in which you can escape with us; and now, brother, you are on a steamboat where there is some chance for you to escape to a land of liberty. I beseech you not to let us hinder you. If we cannot get our liberty, we do not wish to be the means of keeping you from a land of freedom."

I could restrain my feelings no longer, and an outburst of my own feelings, caused her to cease speaking upon that subject. In opposition to their wishes, I pledged myself not to leave them in the hand of the oppressor. I took leave of them, and returned to the boat, and laid down in my bunk; but "sleep departed from my eyes, and slumber from my eyelids."

A few weeks after, on our downward passage, the boat took on board, at Hannibal, a drove of slaves, bound for the New Orleans market. They numbered from fifty to sixty, consisting of men and women from eighteen to forty years of age. A drove of slaves on a southern steamboat, bound for the cotton or sugar regions, is an occurrence so common, that no one, not even the passengers, appear to notice it, though they clank their chains at every step. There was, however, one in this gang that attracted the attention of the passengers and crew. It was a beautiful girl, apparently about twenty years of age, perfectly white, with straight light hair and blue eyes. But it was not the whiteness of her skin that created such a sensation among those who gazed upon her—it was her almost unparalleled beauty. She had been on the boat but a short time, before the attention of all the passengers, including the ladies, had been called to her, and the common topic of conversation was about the beautiful slave-girl. She was not in chains. The man who claimed this article of human merchandise was a Mr. Walker,—a well known slave-trader, residing in St. Louis. There was a general anxiety among the passengers and crew to learn the history of the girl. Her master kept close by her side, and it would have been considered impudent for any of the passengers to have spoken to her, and the crew were not allowed to have any conversation with them. When we reached St. Louis, the slaves were removed to a boat bound for New Orleans, and the history of the beautiful slave-girl remained a mystery.

I remained on the boat during the season, and it was not an unfrequent occurrence to have on board gangs of slaves on their way to the cotton, sugar and rice plantations of the South.

Toward the latter part of the summer, Captain Reynolds left the boat, and I was sent home. I was then placed on the farm under Mr. Haskell, the overseer. As I had been some time out of the field, and not accustomed to work in the burning sun, it was very hard; but I was compelled to keep up with the best of the hands.

I found a great difference between the work in a steamboat cabin and that in a corn-field.

My master, who was then living in the city, soon after removed to the farm, when I was taken out of the field to work in the house as a waiter. Though his wife was very peevish, and hard to please, I much preferred to be under her control than the overseer's. They brought with them Mr. Sloane, a Presbyterian minister; Miss Martha Tulley, a niece of theirs from Kentucky; and their nephew William. The latter had been in the family a number of years, but the others were all new-comers.

Mr. Sloane was a young minister, who had been at the South but a short time, and it seemed as if his whole aim was to please the slaveholders, especially my master and mistress. He was intending to make a visit during the winter, and he not only tried to please them, but I think he succeeded admirably. When they wanted singing, he sung; when they wanted praying, he prayed; when they wanted a story told, he told a story. Instead of his teaching my master theology, my master taught theology to him. While I was with Captain

Reynolds, my master "got religion," and new laws were made on the plantation. Formerly, we had the privilege of hunting, fishing, making splint brooms, baskets, &c. on Sunday; but this was all stopped. Every Sunday, we were all compelled to attend meeting. Master was so religious, that he induced some others to join him in hiring a preacher to preach to the slaves.

V

My master had family worship, night and morning. At night, the slaves were called in to attend; but in the mornings, they had to be at their work, and master did all the praying. My master and mistress were great lovers of mint julep, and every morning, a pitcher-full was made, of which they all partook freely, not excepting little master William. After drinking freely all round, they would have family worship, and then breakfast. I cannot say but I loved the julep as well as any of them, and during prayer was always careful to seat myself close to the table where it stood, so as to help myself when they were all busily engaged in their devotions. By the time prayer was over, I was about as happy as any of them. A sad accident happened one morning. In helping myself, and at the same time keeping an eye on my old mistress, I accidentally let the pitcher fall upon the floor, breaking it in pieces, and spilling the contents. This was a bad affair for me; for as soon as prayer was over, I was taken and severely chastised.

My master's family consisted of himself, his wife, and their nephew, William Moore. He was taken into the family, when only a few weeks of age. His name being that of my own, mine was changed, for the purpose of giving precedence to his, though I was his senior by ten or twelve years. The plantation being four miles from the city, I had to drive the family to church. I always dreaded the approach of the Sabbath; for, during service, I was obliged to stand by the horses in the hot broiling sun, or in the rain, just as it happened.

One Sabbath, as we were driving past the house of D. D. Page, a gentleman who owned a large baking establishment, as I was sitting upon the box of the carriage, which was very much elevated, I saw Mr. Page pursuing a slave around the yard, with a long whip, cutting him at every jump. The man soon escaped from the yard, and was followed by Mr. Page. They came running past us, and the slave perceiving that he would be overtaken, stopped suddenly, and Page stumbled over him, and falling on the stone pavement, fractured one of his legs, which crippled him for life. The same gentleman, but a short time previous, tied up a woman of his, by the name of Delphia, and whipped her nearly to death; yet he was a deacon in the Baptist church, in good and regular standing. Poor Delphia! I was well acquainted with her, and called to see her while upon her sick bed; and I shall never forget her appearance. She was a member of the same church with her master.

Soon after this, I was hired out to Mr. Walker; the same man whom I have mentioned as having carried a gang of slaves down the river, on the steamboat Enterprize. Seeing me in the capacity of steward on the boat, and thinking that I would make a good hand to take care of slaves, he determined to have me for that purpose; and finding that my master would not sell me, he hired me for the term of one year.

When I learned the fact of my having been hired to a negro speculator, or a "soul-driver" as they are generally called among slaves, no one can tell my emotions. Mr. Walker had offered a high price for me, as I afterwards learned, but I suppose my master was restrained from selling me by the fact that I was a near relative of his. On entering the service of Mr. Walker, I found that my opportunity of getting to a land of liberty was gone, at least for the time being. He had a gang of slaves in readiness to start for New Orleans, and in a few days we were on our journey. I am at a loss for language to express my feelings on that occasion. Although my master had told me that he had not sold me, and Mr. Walker had told me that he had not purchased me, I did not believe them; and not until I had been to New Orleans, and was on my return, did I believe that I was not sold.

There was on the boat a large room on the lower deck, in which the slaves were kept, men and women, promiscuously—all chained two and two, and a strict watch kept that they did not get loose; for cases have occurred in which slaves have got off their chains, and made their escape at landing-places, while the boats were taking in wood;—and with all our care, we lost one woman who had been taken from her husband and children, and having no desire to live without them, in the agony of her soul jumped overboard, and drowned herself. She was not chained.

It was almost impossible to keep that part of the boat clean.

On landing at Natchez, the slaves were all carried to the slave-pen, and there kept one week, during which time, several of them were sold. Mr. Walker fed his slaves well. We took on board, at St. Louis, several hundred pounds of bacon (smoked meat) and corn-meal, and his slaves were better fed than slaves generally were in Natchez, so far as my observation extended.

At the end of a week, we left for New Orleans, the place of our final destination, which we reached in two days. Here the slaves were placed in a negro-pen, where those who wished to purchase could call and examine them. The negro-pen is a small yard, surrounded by buildings, from fifteen to twenty feet wide, with the exception of a large gate with iron bars. The slaves are kept in the buildings during the night, and turned out into the yard during the day. After the best of the stock was sold at private sale at the pen, the balance were taken to the Exchange Coffee House Auction Rooms, kept by Isaac L. McCoy, and sold at public auction. After the sale of this lot of slaves, we left New Orleans for St. Louis.

VI

On our arrival at St. Louis, I went to Dr. Young, and told him that I did not wish to live with Mr. Walker any longer. I was heart-sick at seeing my fellow-creatures bought and sold. But the Dr. had hired me for the year, and stay I must. Mr. Walker again commenced purchasing another gang of slaves. He bought a man of Colonel John O'Fallon, who resided in the suburbs of the city. This man had a wife and three children. As soon as the purchase was made, he was put in jail for safe keeping, until we should be ready to start for New Orleans. His wife visited him while there, several times, and several times when she went for that purpose was refused admittance.

In the course of eight or nine weeks Mr. Walker had his cargo of human flesh made up. There was in this lot a number of old men and women, some of them with gray locks. We left St. Louis in the steamboat Carlton, Captain Swan, bound for New Orleans. On our way down, and before we reached Rodney,* the place where we made our first stop, I had to prepare the old slaves for market. I was ordered to have the old men's whiskers shaved off, and the gray hairs plucked out where they were not too numerous, in which case he had a preparation of blacking to color it, and with a blacking-brush we would put it on. This was new business to me, and was performed in a room where the passengers could not see us. These slaves were also taught how old they were by Mr. Walker, and after going through the blacking process, they looked ten or fifteen years younger; and I am sure that some of those who purchased slaves of Mr. Walker, were dreadfully cheated, especially in the ages of the slaves which they bought.

We landed at Rodney, and the slaves were driven to the pen in the back part of the village. Several were sold at this place, during our stay of four or five days, when we proceeded to Natchez. There we landed at night, and the gang were put in the warehouse until morning, when they were driven to the pen. As soon as the slaves are put in these pens, swarms of planters may be seen in and about them. They knew when Walker was expected, as he always had the time advertised beforehand when he would be in Rodney, Natchez, and New Orleans. These were the principal places where he offered his slaves for sale.

When at Natchez the second time, I saw a slave very cruelly whipped. He belonged to a Mr. Broadwell, a merchant who kept a store on the wharf. The slave's name was Lewis. I had known him several years, as he was formerly from St. Louis. We were expecting a steamboat down the river, in which we were to take passage for New Orleans. Mr. Walker sent me to the landing to watch for the boat, ordering me to inform him on its arrival. While there, I went into the store to see Lewis. I saw a slave in the store, and asked him where Lewis was. Said he, "They have got Lewis hanging between the heavens and the earth." I asked him what he meant by that. He told me to go into the warehouse and see. I went in, and found Lewis there. He was tied up to a beam, with his toes just touching the floor. As there was no one in the warehouse but

* [Mississippi.]

himself, I inquired the reason of his being in that situation. He said Mr. Broadwell had sold his wife to a planter six miles from the city, and that he had been to visit her,—that he went in the night, expecting to return before daylight, and went without his master's permission. The patrol had taken him up before he reached his wife. He was put in jail, and his master had to pay for his catching and keeping, and that was what he was tied up for.

Just as he finished his story, Mr. Broadwell came in, and inquired what I was doing there. I knew not what to say, and while I was thinking what reply to make, he struck me over the head with the cowhide, the end of which struck me over my right eye, sinking deep into the flesh, leaving a scar which I carry to this day. Before I visited Lewis, he had received fifty lashes. Mr. Broadwell gave him fifty more after I came out, as I was afterwards informed by Lewis himself.

The next day we proceeded to New Orleans, and put the gang in the same negro-pen which we occupied before. In a short time, the planters came flocking to the pen to purchase slaves. Before the slaves were exhibited for sale, they were dressed and driven out into the yard. Some were set to dancing, some to jumping, some to singing, and some to playing cards. This was done to make them appear cheerful and happy. My business was to see that they were placed in those situations before the arrival of the purchasers, and I have often set them to dancing when their cheeks were wet with tears. As slaves were in good demand at that time, they were all soon disposed of, and we again set out for St. Louis.

On our arrival, Mr. Walker purchased a farm five or six miles from the city. He had no family, but made a housekeeper of one of his female slaves. Poor Cynthia! I knew her well. She was a quadroon, and one of the most beautiful women I ever saw. She was a native of St. Louis, and bore an irreproachable character for virtue and propriety of conduct. Mr. Walker bought her for the New Orleans market, and took her down with him on one of the trips that I made with him. Never shall I forget the circumstances of that voyage! On the first night that we were on board the steamboat, he directed me to put her into a stateroom he had provided for her, apart from the other slaves. I had seen too much of the workings of slavery, not to know what this meant. I accordingly watched him into the state-room, and listened to hear what passed between them. I heard him make his base offers, and her reject them. He told her that if she would accept his vile proposals, he would take her back with him to St. Louis, and establish her as his housekeeper at his farm. But if she persisted in rejecting them, he would sell her as a field hand on the worst plantation on the river. Neither threats nor bribes prevailed, however, and he retired, disappointed of his prey.

The next morning, poor Cynthia told me what had past, and bewailed her sad fate with floods of tears. I comforted and encouraged her all I could; but I foresaw but too well what the result must be. Without entering into any farther particulars, suffice it to say that Walker performed his part of the contract, at that time. He took her back to St. Louis, established her as his mistress and housekeeper at his farm, and before I left, he had two children by her. But, mark the end! Since I have been at the North, I have been credibly informed that Walker has been married, and, as a previous measure, sold poor Cynthia and her four children (she having had two more since I came away) into hopeless bondage!

He soon commenced purchasing to make up the third gang. We took steamboat, and went to Jefferson City, a town on the Missouri river. Here we landed, and took stage for the interior of the State. He bought a number of slaves as he passed the different farms and villages. After getting twenty-two or twenty-three men and women, we arrived at St. Charles, a village on the banks of the Missouri. Here he purchased a woman who had a child in her arms, appearing to be four or five weeks old.

We had been travelling by land for some days, and were in hopes to have found a boat at this place for St. Louis, but were disappointed. As no boat was expected for some days, we started for St. Louis by land. Mr. Walker had purchased two horses. He rode one, and I the other. The slaves were chained together, and we took up our line of march, Mr. Walker taking the lead, and I bringing up the rear. Though the distance was not more than twenty miles, we did not reach it the first day. The road was worse than any that I have ever travelled.

Soon after we left St. Charles, the young child grew very cross, and kept up a noise during the greater part of the day. Mr. Walker complained of its crying several times, and told the mother to stop the child's d——d noise, or he would. The woman tried to keep the child from crying, but could not. We put up at night with an acquaintance of Mr. Walker, and in the morning, just as we were about to start, the child again commenced crying. Walker stepped up to her, and told her to give the child to him. The mother tremblingly obeyed. He took the child by one arm, as you would a cat by the leg, walked into the house, and said to the lady,

"Madam, I will make you a present of this little nigger; it keeps such a noise that I can't bear it."

"Thank you, sir," said the lady.

The mother, as soon as she saw that her child was to be left, ran up to Mr. Walker, and falling upon her knees begged him to let her have her child; she clung around his legs, and cried, "Oh, my child! my child! master, do let me have my child! oh, do, do, do. I will stop its crying, if you will only let me have it again." When I saw this woman crying for her child so piteously, a shudder,—a feeling akin to horror, shot through my frame. I have often since in imagination heard her crying for her child:—

O, master, let me stay to catch
My baby's sobbing breath,
His little glassy eye to watch,
And smooth his limbs in death,

And cover him with grass and leaf,
Beneath the large oak tree:
It is not sullenness, but grief,—
O, master, pity me!

The morn was chill—I spoke no word,
But feared my babe might die,
And heard all day, or thought I heard,
My little baby cry.

At noon, oh, how I ran and took
My baby to my breast!
I lingered—and the long lash broke
My sleeping infant's rest.

I worked till night—till darkest night,
In torture and disgrace;
Went home and watched till morning light,

To see my baby's face.
Then give me but one little hour—
O! do not lash me so!

One little hour—one little hour—
And gratefully I'll go.

Mr. Walker commanded her to return into the ranks with the other slaves. Women who had children were not chained, but those that had none were. As soon as her child was disposed of, she was chained in the gang.

The following song I have often heard the slaves sing, when about to be carried to the far south. It is said to have been composed by a slave.

See these poor souls from Africa
Transported to America;
We are stolen, and sold to Georgia,
Will you go along with me?
We are stolen, and sold to Georgia,
Come sound the jubilee!

See wives and husbands sold apart,
Their children's screams will break my heart;—
There's a better day a coming,
Will you go along with me?
There's a better day a coming,
Go sound the jubilee!

O, gracious Lord! when shall it be,
That we poor souls shall all be free;
Lord, break them slavery powers—
Will you go along with me?
Lord break them slavery powers,
Go sound the jubilee!

Dear Lord, dear Lord, when slavery'll cease,
Then we poor souls will have our peace;—
There's a better day a coming,
Will you go along with me?
There's a better day a coming,
Go sound the jubilee!"

We finally arrived at Mr. Walker's farm. He had a house built during our absence to put slaves in. It was a kind of domestic jail. The slaves were put in the jail at night, and worked on the farm during the day. They were kept here until the gang was completed, when we again started for New Orleans, on board the steamboat North America, Capt. Alexander Scott. We had a large number of slaves in this gang. One, by the name of Joe, Mr. Walker was training up to take my place, as my time was nearly out, and glad was I. We made our first stop at Vicksburg, where we remained one week and sold several slaves.

Mr. Walker, though not a good master, had not flogged a slave since I had been with him, though he had threatened me. The slaves were kept in the pen, and he always put up at the best hotel, and kept his wines in his room, for the accommodation of those who called to negotiate with him for the purchase of slaves. One day while we were at Vicksburg, several gentlemen came to see him for this purpose, and as usual the wine was called for. I took the tray and started around with it, and having accidentally filled some of the glasses too full, the gentlemen spilled the wine on their clothes as they went to drink. Mr. Walker apologized to them for my carelessness, but looked at me as though he would see me again on this subject.

After the gentlemen had left the room, he asked me what I meant by my carelessness, and said that he would attend to me. The next morning, he gave me a note to carry to the jailer, and a dollar in money to give to him. I suspected that all was not right, so I went down near the landing where I met with a sailor, and walking up to him, asked him if he would be so kind as to read the note for me. He read it over, and then looked at me. I asked him to tell me what was in it. Said he,

"They are going to give you hell."

"Why?" said I.

He said, "This is a note to have you whipped, and says that you have a dollar to pay for it."

He handed me back the note, and off I started. I knew not what to do, but was determined not to be whipped. I went up to the jail—took a look at it, and walked off again. As Mr. Walker was acquainted with the jailer, I feared that I should be found out if I did not go, and be treated in consequence of it still worse.

While I was meditating on the subject, I saw a colored man about my size walk up, and the thought struck me in a moment to send him with my note. I walked up to him, and asked him who he belonged to. He said he was a free man, and had been in the city but a short time. I told him I had a note to go into the jail, and get a trunk to carry to one of the steamboats; but was so busily engaged that I could not do it, although I had a dollar to pay for it.

He asked me if I would not give him the job. I handed him the note and the dollar, and off he started for the jail.

I watched to see that he went in, and as soon as I saw the door close behind him, I walked around the corner, and took my station, intending to see how my friend looked when he came out. I had been there but a short time, when a colored man came around the corner, and said to another colored man with whom he was acquainted—

"They are giving a nigger scissors in the jail."

"What for?" said the other. The man continued,

"A nigger came into the jail, and asked for the jailer. The jailer came out, and he handed him a note, and said he wanted to get a trunk. The jailer told him to go with him, and he would give him the trunk. So he took him into the room, and told the nigger to give up the dollar. He said a man had given him the dollar to pay for getting the trunk. But that lie would not answer. So they made him strip himself, and then they tied him down, and are now whipping him."

I stood by all the while listening to their talk, and soon found out that the person alluded to was my customer. I went into the street opposite the jail, and concealed myself in such a manner that I could not be seen by any one coming out. I had been there but a short time, when the young man made his appearance, and looked around for me. I, unobserved, came forth from my hiding-place, behind a pile of brick, and he pretty soon saw me and came up to me complaining bitterly, saying that I had played a trick upon him. I denied any knowledge of what the note contained, and asked him what they had done to him. He told me in substance what I heard the man tell who had come out of the jail.

"Yes," said he, "they whipped me and took my dollar, and gave me this note."

He showed me the note which the jailer had given him, telling him to give it to his master. I told him I would give him fifty cents for it,—that being all the money I had. He gave it to me, and took his money. He had received twenty lashes on his bare back, with the negro-whip.

I took the note and started for the hotel where I had left Mr. Walker. Upon reaching the hotel, I handed it to a stranger whom I had not seen before, and requested him to read it to me. As near as I can recollect, it was as follows:—

Dear Sir:—By your direction, I have given your boy twenty lashes. He is a very saucy boy, and tried to make me believe that he did not belong to you, and I put it on to him well for lying to me.

I remain,

Your obedient servant.

It is true that in most of the slave-holding cities, when a gentleman wishes his servants whipped, he can send him to the jail and have it done. Before I went in where Mr. Walker was, I wet my cheeks a little, as though I had been crying. He looked at me, and inquired what was the matter. I told him that I had never had such a whipping in my life, and handed him the note. He looked at it and laughed;—"and so you told him that you did not belong to me." "Yes, sir," said I. "I did not know that there was any harm in that." He told me I must behave myself, if I did not want to be whipped again.

This incident shows how it is that slavery makes its victims lying and mean; for which vices it afterwards reproaches them, and uses them as arguments to prove that they deserve no better fate. I have often, since my escape, deeply regretted the deception I practised upon this poor fellow; and I heartily desire that it may be, at some time or other, in my power to make him amends for his vicarious sufferings in my behalf.

VII

In a few days we reached New Orleans, and arriving there in the night, remained on board until morning. While at New Orleans this time, I saw a slave killed; an account of which had been published by Theodore D. Weld, in his book entitled, "Slavery as it is."* The circumstances were as follows. In the evening, between seven and eight o'clock, a slave came running down the levee, followed by several men and boys. The whites were crying out, "Stop that

* [Theodore Dwight Weld was one of the leading evangelical abolitionists of his generation. His book, *American Slavery As It Is,* was the most popular antislavery tract prior to the publication of Harriet Beecher Stowe's *Uncle Tom's Cabin.*]

nigger, stop that nigger;" while the poor panting slave, in almost breathless accents, was repeating, "I did not steal the meat—I did not steal the meat." The poor man at last took refuge in the river. The whites who were in pursuit of him, ran on board of one of the boats to see if they could discover him. They finally espied him under the bow of the steamboat Trenton. They got a pike-pole, and tried to drive him from his hiding place. When they would strike at him, he would dive under the water. The water was so cold, that it soon became evident that he must come out or be drowned.

While they were trying to drive him from under the bow of the boat or drown him, he would in broken and imploring accents say, "I did not steal the meat; I did not steal the meat. My master lives up the river. I want to see my master. I did not steal the meat. Do let me go home to master." After punching him, and striking him over the head for some time, he at last sunk in the water, to rise no more alive.

On the end of the pike-pole with which they were striking him was a hook which caught in his clothing, and they hauled him on the bow of the boat. Some said he was dead, others said he was *"playing possum,"* while others kicked him to make him get up, but it was of no use—he was dead.

As soon as they became satisfied of this, they commenced leaving, one after another. One of the hands on the boat informed the captain that they had killed the man, and that the dead body was lying on the deck. The captain came on deck, and said to those who were remaining, "You have killed this nigger; now take him off of my boat." The captain's name was Hart. The dead body was dragged on shore and left there. I went on board of the boat where our gang of slaves were, and during the whole night my mind was occupied with what I had seen. Early in the morning, I went on shore to see if the dead body remained there. I found it in the same position that it was left the night before. I watched to see what they would do with it. It was left there until between eight and nine o'clock, when a cart, which takes up the trash out of the streets, came along, and the body was thrown in, and in a few minutes more was covered over with dirt which they were removing from the streets. During the whole time, I did not see more than six or seven persons around it, who, from their manner, evidently regarded it as no uncommon occurrence.

During our stay in the city, I met with a young white man with whom I was well acquainted in St. Louis. He had been sold into slavery, under the following circumstances. His father was a drunkard, and very poor, with a family of five or six children. The father died, and left the mother to take care of and provide for the children as best she might. The eldest was a boy, named Burrill, about thirteen years of age, who did chores in a store kept by Mr. Riley, to assist his mother in procuring a living for the family. After working with him two years, Mr. Riley took him to New Orleans to wait on him while in that city on a visit, and when he returned to St. Louis, he told the mother of the boy that he had died with the yellow fever. Nothing more was heard from him, no one supposing him to be alive. I was much astonished when Burrill told me his story. Though I sympathized with him, I could not assist him. We were both slaves. He was poor, uneducated, and without friends; and if living, is, I presume, still held as a slave.

After selling out this cargo of human flesh, we returned to St. Louis, and my time was up with Mr. Walker. I had served him one year, and it was the longest year I ever lived.

VIII

I was sent home, and was glad enough to leave the service of one who was tearing the husband from the wife, the child from the mother, and the sister from the brother,—but a trial more severe and heart-rending than any which I had yet met with awaited me. My dear sister had been sold to a man who was going to Natchez, and was lying in jail awaiting the hour of his departure. She had expressed her determination to die, rather than go to the far south, and she was put in jail for safe keeping. I went to the jail the same day that I arrived, but as the jailor was not in, I could not see her.

I went home to my master, in the country, and the first day after my return, he came where I was at work, and spoke to me very politely. I knew from his appearance that something was the matter. After talking about my several journeys to New Orleans with Mr. Walker, he told me that he was hard pressed for money, and as he had sold my mother and all her children except me, he thought it would be better to sell me than any other one, and that as I had been used to living in the city, he thought it probable that I would prefer it to a country life. I raised up my head, and looked him full in the face. When my eyes caught his, he immediately looked to the ground. After a short pause, I said,

"Master, mother has often told me that you are a near relative of mine, and I have often heard you admit the fact; and after you have hired me out, and received, as I once heard you say, nine hundred dollars for my services,—after receiving this large sum, will you sell me to be carried to New Orleans or some other place?"

"No," said he, "I do not intend to sell you to a negro trader. If I had wished to have done that, I might have sold you to Mr. Walker for a large sum, but I would not sell you to a negro trader. You may go to the city, and find you a good master."

"But," said I, "I cannot find a good master in the whole city of St. Louis."

"Why?" said he.

"Because there are no good masters in the State."

"Do you not call me a good master?"

"If you were, you would not sell me."

"Now I will give you one week to find a master in, and surely you can do it in that time."

The price set by my evangelical master upon my soul and body was the trifling sum of five hundred dollars. I tried to enter into some arrangement by which I might purchase my freedom; but he would enter into no such arrangement.

I set out for the city with the understanding that I was to return in a week with some one to become my new master. Soon after reaching the city, I went to the jail, to learn if I could once more see my sister; but could not gain admission. I then went to mother, and learned from her that the owner of my sister intended to start for Natchez in a few days.

I went to the jail again the next day, and Mr. Simonds, the keeper, allowed me to see my sister for the last time. I cannot give a just description of the scene at that parting interview. Never, never can be erased from my heart the occurrences of that day! When I entered the room where she was, she was seated in one corner, alone. There were four other women in the same room, belonging to the same man. He had purchased them, he said, for his own use. She was seated with her face towards the door where I entered, yet she did not look up until I walked up to her. As soon as she observed me, she sprung up, threw her arms around my neck, leaned her head upon my breast, and, without uttering a word, burst into tears. As soon as she recovered herself sufficiently to speak, she advised me to take mother, and try to get out of slavery. She said there was no hope for herself,—that she must live and die a slave. After giving her some advice, and taking from my finger a ring and placing it upon hers, I bade her farewell forever, and returned to my mother, and then and there made up my mind to leave for Canada as soon as possible.

I had been in the city nearly two days, and as I was to be absent only a week, I thought best to get on my journey as soon as possible. In conversing with mother, I found her unwilling to make the attempt to reach a land of liberty, but she counselled me to get my liberty if I could. She said, as all her children were in slavery, she did not wish to leave them. I could not bear the idea of leaving her among those pirates, when there was a prospect of being able to get away from them. After much persuasion, I succeeded in inducing her to make the attempt to get away.

The time fixed for our departure was the next night. I had with me a little money that I had received, from time to time, from gentlemen for whom I had done errands. I took my scanty means and purchased some dried beef, crackers and cheese, which I carried to mother, who had provided herself with a bag to carry it in. I occasionally thought of my old master, and of my mission to the city to find a new one. I waited with the most intense anxiety for the appointed time to leave the land of slavery, in search of a land of liberty.

The time at length arrived, and we left the city just as the clock struck nine. We proceeded to the upper part of the city, where I had been two or three times during the day, and selected a skiff to carry us across the river. The boat was not mine, nor did I know to whom it did belong; neither did I care. The boat was fastened with a small pole, which, with the aid of a rail, I soon loosened from its moorings. After hunting round and finding a board to use as an oar, I turned to the city, and bidding it a long farewell, pushed off my boat. The current running very swift, we had not reached the middle of the stream before we were directly opposite the city.

We were soon upon the Illinois shore, and, leaping from the boat, turned it adrift, and the last I saw of it, it was going down the river at good speed. We took the main road to Alton, and passed through just at daylight, when we made for the woods, where we remained during the day. Our reason for going into the woods was, that we expected that Mr. Mansfield (the man who owned my mother) would start in pursuit of her as soon as he discovered that she was missing. He also knew that I had been in the city looking for a new master, and we thought probably he would go out to my master's to see if he could find my mother, and in so doing, Dr. Young might be led to suspect that I had gone to Canada to find a purchaser.

We remained in the woods during the day, and as soon as darkness overshadowed the earth, we started again on our gloomy way, having no guide but the North Star. We continued to travel by night, and secrete ourselves in woods by day; and every night, before emerging from our hiding-place, we would anxiously look for our friend and leader,—the North Star.

IX

As we travelled towards a land of liberty, my heart would at times leap for joy. At other times, being, as I was, almost constantly on my feet, I felt as though I could travel no further. But when I thought of slavery with its Democratic whips—its Republican chains—its evangelical blood-hounds, and its religious slave-holders—when I thought of all this paraphernalia of American Democracy and Religion behind me, and the prospect of liberty before me, I was encouraged to press forward, my heart was strengthened, and I forgot that I was tired or hungry.

On the eighth day of our journey, we had a very heavy rain, and in a few hours after it commenced, we had not a dry thread upon our bodies. This made our journey still more unpleasant. On the tenth day, we found ourselves entirely destitute of provisions, and how to obtain any we could not tell. We finally resolved to stop at some farmhouse, and try to get something to eat. We had no sooner determined to do this, than we went to a house, and asked them for some food. We were treated with great kindness, and they not only gave us something to eat, but gave us provisions to carry with us.

They advised us to travel by day, and lie by at night. Finding ourselves about one hundred and fifty miles from St. Louis, we concluded that it would be safe to travel by daylight, and did not leave the house until the next morning. We travelled on that day through a thickly settled country, and through one small village. Though we were fleeing from a land of oppression, our hearts were still there. My dear sister and two beloved brothers were behind us, and the idea of giving them up, and leaving them forever, made us feel sad. But with all this depression of heart, the thought that I should one day be free, and call my body my own, buoyed me up, and made my heart leap for joy. I had just been telling mother how I should try to get employment as soon as we reached Canada, and how I intended to purchase us a little farm, and how I would earn money enough to buy sister and brothers, and how happy we would be in our own FREE HOME,—when three men came up on horseback, and ordered us to stop.

I turned to the one who appeared to be the principal man, and asked him what he wanted. He said he had a warrant to take us up. The three immediately dismounted, and one took from his pocket a handbill, advertising us as runaways, and offering a reward of two hundred dollars for our apprehension, and delivery in the city of St. Louis. The advertisement had been put out by Isaac Mansfield and John Young.

While they were reading the advertisement, mother looked me in the face, and burst into tears. A cold chill ran over me, and such a sensation I never experienced before, and I hope never to again. They took out a rope and tied me, and we were taken back about six miles, to the house of the individual who appeared to be the leader. We reached there about seven o'clock in the evening, had supper, and were separated for the night. Two men remained in the room during the night. Before the family retired to rest, they were all called together to attend prayers. The man who but a few hours before had bound my hands together with a strong cord, read a chapter from the Bible, and then offered up prayer, just as though God sanctioned the act he had just committed upon a poor panting, fugitive slave.

The next morning, a blacksmith came in, and put a pair of handcuffs on me, and we started on our journey back to the land of whips, chains and Bibles. Mother was not tied, but was closely watched at night. We were carried back in a wagon, and after four days travel, we came in sight of St. Louis. I cannot describe my feelings upon approaching the city.

As we were crossing the ferry, Mr. Wiggins, the owner of the ferry, came up to me, and inquired what I had been doing that I was in chains. He had not heard that I had run away. In a few minutes, we were on the Missouri side, and were taken directly to the jail. On the way thither, I saw several of my friends, who gave me a nod of recognition as I passed them. After reaching the jail, we were locked up in different apartments.

X

I had been in jail but a short time when I heard that my master was sick, and nothing brought more joy to my heart than that intelligence. I prayed fervently for him—not for his recovery, but for his death. I knew he would be exasperated at having to pay for my apprehension, and knowing his cruelty, I feared him. While in jail, I learned that my sister Elizabeth, who was in prison when we left the city, had been carried off four days before our arrival.

I had been in jail but a few hours when three negro-traders, learning that I was secured thus for running away, came to my prison-house and looked at me, expecting that I would be offered for sale. Mr. Mansfield, the man who owned mother, came into the jail as soon as Mr. Jones, the man who arrested us, informed him that he had brought her back. He told her that he would not whip her, but would sell her to a negro-trader, or take her to New Orleans himself. After being in jail about one week, master sent a man to take me out of jail, and send me home. I was taken out and carried home, and the old man was well enough to sit up. He had me brought into the room where he was, and as I entered, he asked me where I had been? I told I had acted according to his orders. He had told me to look for a master, and I had been to look for one. He answered that he did not tell me to go to Canada to look for a master. I told him that as I had served him faithfully, and had been the means of putting a number of hundreds of dollars into his pocket, I thought I had a right to my liberty. He said he had promised my father that I should not be sold to supply the New Orleans market, or he would sell me to a negro-trader.

I was ordered to go into the field to work, and was closely watched by the overseer during the day, and locked up at night. The overseer gave me a severe whipping on the second day that I was in the field. I had been at home but a short time, when master was able to ride to the city; and on his return, he informed me that he had sold me to Samuel Willi, a merchant tailor. I knew Mr. Willi. I had lived with him three or four months some years before, when he hired me of my master.

Mr. Willi was not considered by his servants as a very bad man, nor was he the best of masters. I went to my new home, and found my new mistress very glad to see me. Mr. Willi owned two servants before he purchased me,—Robert and Charlotte. Robert was an excellent white-washer, and hired his time from his master, paying him one dollar per day, besides taking care of himself. He was known in the city by the name of Bob Music. Charlotte was an old woman, who attended to the cooking, washing, &c. Mr. Willi was not a wealthy man, and did not feel able to keep many servants around his house; so he soon decided to hire me out, and as I had been accustomed to service in steamboats, he gave me the privilege of finding such employment.

I soon secured a situation on board the steamer Otto, Capt. J. B. Hill, which sailed from St. Louis to Independence, Missouri. My former master, Dr. Young, did not let Mr. Willi know that I had run away, or he would not have permitted me to go on board a steamboat. The boat was not quite ready to commence running, and therefore I had to remain with Mr. Willi. But during this time, I had to undergo a trial, for which I was entirely unprepared. My mother, who had been in jail since her return until the present time, was now about being carried to New Orleans, to die on a cotton, sugar, or rice plantation!

I had been several times to the jail, but could obtain no interview with her. I ascertained, however, the time the boat in which she was to embark would sail, and as I had not seen mother since her being thrown into prison, I felt anxious for the hour of sailing to come. At last, the day arrived when I was to see her for the first time after our painful separation, and, for aught I knew, for the last time in this world!

At about ten o'clock in the morning I went on board of the boat, and found her there in company with fifty or sixty other slaves. She was chained to another woman. On seeing me, she immediately dropped her head upon her heaving bosom. She moved not, neither did she weep. Her emotions were too deep for tears. I approached, threw my arms around her neck, kissed her, and fell upon my knees, begging her forgiveness, for I thought myself to blame for her sad condition; for if I had not persuaded her to accompany me, she would not then have been in chains.

She finally raised her head, looked me in the face (and such a look none but an angel can give!) and said, *"My dear son, you are not to blame for my being here. You have done nothing more nor less than your duty. Do not, I pray you, weep for me. I cannot last long upon a cotton plantation. I feel that my heavenly master will soon call me home, and then I shall be out of the hands of the slaveholders!"*

I could bear no more—my heart struggled to free itself from the human form. In a moment she saw Mr. Mansfield coming toward that part of the boat, and she whispered into my ear, *"My child, we must soon part to meet no more this side of the grave. You have ever said that you would not die a slave; that you would be a freeman. Now try to get your liberty! You will soon have no one to look after but yourself!"* and just as she whispered the last sentence into my ear, Mansfield came up to me, and with an oath, said, "Leave here this instant; you have been the means of my losing one hundred dollars to get this wench back,"—at the same time kicking me with a heavy pair of boots. As I left her, she gave one shriek, saying, "God be with you!" It was the last time that I saw her, and the last word I heard her utter.

I walked on shore. The bell was tolling. The boat was about to start. I stood with a heavy heart, waiting to see her leave the wharf. As I thought of my mother, I could but feel that I had lost

——the glory of my life,
My blessing and my pride!
I half forgot the name of slave,
When she was by my side.

XI

The love of liberty that had been burning in my bosom, had well nigh gone out. I felt as though I was ready to die. The boat moved gently from the wharf, and while she glided down the river, I realized that my mother was indeed

Gone,—gone,—sold and gone,
To the rice swamp dank and lone!

After the boat was out of sight, I returned home; but my thoughts were so absorbed in what I had witnessed, that I knew not what I was about half of the time. Night came, but it brought no sleep to my eyes.

In a few days, the boat upon which I was to work being ready, I went on board to commence. This employment suited me better than living in the city, and I remained until the close of navigation; though it proved anything but pleasant. The captain was a drunken, profligate, hard-hearted creature, not knowing how to treat himself, or any other person.

The boat, on its second trip, brought down Mr. Walker, the man of whom I have spoken in a previous chapter, as hiring my time. He had between one and two hundred slaves, chained and manacled. Among them was a man that formerly belonged to my old master's brother, Aaron Young. His name was Solomon. He was a preacher, and belonged to the same church with his master. I was glad to see the old man. He wept like a child when he told me how he had been sold from his wife and children.

The boat carried down, while I remained on board, four or five gangs of slaves. Missouri, though a comparatively new State, is very much engaged in raising slaves to supply the southern market. In a former chapter, I have mentioned that I was once in the employ of a slave-trader, or driver, as he is called at the south. For fear that some may think that I have misrepresented a slave-driver, I will here give an extract from a paper published in a slaveholding state, Tennessee, called the "Millennial Trumpeter."

"Droves of negroes, chained together in dozens and scores, and hand-cuffed, have been driven through our country in numbers far surpassing any previous year, and these vile slave-drivers and dealers are swarming like buzzards around a carrion. Through this country, you cannot pass a few miles in the great roads without having every feeling of humanity insulted and lacerated by this spectacle, nor can you go into any county or any neighborhood, scarcely, without seeing or hearing of some of these despicable creatures, called negro-drivers.

"Who is a negro-driver? One whose eyes dwell with delight on lacerated bodies of helpless men, women and children; whose soul feels diabolical raptures at the chains, and hand-cuffs, and cart-whips, for inflicting tortures on weeping mothers torn from helpless babes, and on husbands and wives torn asunder forever!"

Dark and revolting as is the picture here drawn, it is from the pen of one living in the midst of slavery. But though these men may cant about negro-drivers, and tell what despicable creatures they are, who is it, I ask, that supplies them with the human beings that they are tearing asunder? I answer, as far as I have any knowledge of the State where I came from, that those who raise slaves for the market are to be found among all classes, from Thomas H. Benton down to the lowest political demagogue, who may be able to purchase a woman for the purpose of raising stock, and from the Doctor of Divinity down to the most humble lay member in the church.

It was not uncommon in St. Louis to pass by an auction-stand, and behold a woman upon the auction-block, and hear the seller crying out, *"How much is offered for this woman? She is a good cook, good washer, a good obedient servant. She has got religion!"* Why should this man tell the purchasers that she has religion? I answer, because in Missouri, and as far as I have any knowledge of slavery in the other States, the religious teaching consists in teaching the slave that he must never strike a white man; that God made him for a slave; and that, when whipped, he must not find fault,—for the Bible says, "He that knoweth his master's will, and doeth it not, shall be beaten with many stripes!" And slaveholders find such religion very profitable to them.

After leaving the steamer Ohio, I resided at home, in Mr. Willi's family, and again began to lay my plans for making my escape from slavery. The anxiety to be a freeman would not let me rest day or night. I would think of the northern cities that I had heard so much about;—of Canada, where so many of my acquaintances had found refuge. I would dream at night that I was in Canada, a freeman, and on waking in the morning, weep to find myself so sadly mistaken.

I would think of Victoria's domain,
And in a moment I seemed to be there!
But the fear of being taken again,
Soon hurried me back to despair.

Mr. Willi treated me better than Dr. Young ever had; but instead of making me contented and happy, it only rendered me the more miserable, for it enabled me to better appreciate liberty. Mr. Willi was a man who loved money as most men do, and without looking for an opportunity to sell me, he found one in the offer of Captain Enoch Price, a steamboat owner and commission merchant, living in the city of St. Louis. Captain Price tendered seven hundred dollars, which was two hundred more than Mr. Willi had paid. He therefore thought best to accept the offer. I was wanted for a carriage driver, and Mrs. Price was very much pleased with the captain's bargain. His family consisted besides of one child. He had three servants beside myself—one man and two women.

Mrs. Price was very proud of her servants, always keeping them well dressed, and as soon as I had been purchased, she resolved to have a new carriage. And soon one was procured, and all preparations were made for a turn-out in grand style, I being the driver.

One of the female servants was a girl some eighteen or twenty years of age, named Maria. Mrs. Price was very soon determined to have us united, if she could so arrange matters. She would often urge upon me the necessity of having a wife, saying that it would be so pleasant for me to take one in the same family! But getting married, while in slavery, was the last of my thoughts; and had I been ever so inclined, I should not have married Maria, as my love had already gone in another quarter. Mrs. Price soon found out that her efforts at this match-making between Maria and myself would not prove successful. She also discovered (or thought she had) that I was rather partial to a girl named Eliza, who was owned by Dr. Mills. This induced her at once to endeavor the purchase of Eliza, so great was her desire to get me a wife!

Before making the attempt, however, she deemed it best to talk to me a little upon the subject of love, courtship, and marriage.

Accordingly one afternoon she called me into her room—telling me to take a chair and sit down. I did so, thinking it rather strange, for servants are not very often asked thus to sit down in the same room with the master or mistress. She said that she had found out that I did not care enough about Maria to marry her. I told her that was true. She then asked me if there was not a girl in the city that I loved. Well, now, this was coming into too close quarters with me! People, generally, don't like to tell their love stories to everybody that think fit to ask about them, and it was so with me. But, after blushing awhile and recovering myself, I told her that I did not want a wife. She then asked me, if I did not think something of Eliza. I told her that I did. She then said that if I wished to marry Eliza, she would purchase her if she could.

I gave but little encouragement to this proposition, as I was determined to make another trial to get my liberty, and I knew that if I should have a wife, I should not be willing to leave her behind; and if I should attempt to bring her with me, the chances would be difficult for success. However, Eliza was purchased, and brought into the family.

XII

But the more I thought of the trap laid by Mrs. Price to make me satisfied with my new home, by getting me a wife, the more I determined never to marry any woman on earth until I should get my liberty. But this secret I was compelled to keep to myself, which placed me in a very critical position. I must keep upon good terms with Mrs. Price and Eliza. I therefore promised Mrs. Price that I would marry Eliza; but said that I was not then ready. And I had to keep upon good terms with Eliza, for fear that Mrs. Price would find out that I did not intend to get married.

I have here spoken of marriage, and it is very common among slaves themselves to talk of it. And it is common for slaves to be married; or at least have the marriage ceremony performed. But there is no such thing as slaves being lawfully married. There has never yet a case occurred where a slave has been tried for bigamy. The man may have as many women as he wishes, and the women as many men; and the law takes no cognizance of such acts among slaves. And in fact some masters, when they have sold the husband from the wife, compel her to take another.

There lived opposite Captain Price's, Doctor Farrar, well known in St. Louis. He sold a man named Ben, to one of the traders. He also owned Ben's wife, and in a few days he compelled Sally (that was her name) to marry Peter, another man belonging to him. I asked Sally "why she married Peter so soon after Ben was sold." She said, "because master made her do it."

Mr. John Calvert, who resided near our place, had a woman named Lavinia. She was quite young, and a man to whom she was about to be married was sold, and carried into the country near St. Charles, about twenty miles from St. Louis. Mr. Calvert wanted her to get a husband; but she had resolved not to marry any other man, and she refused. Mr. Calvert whipped her in such a manner that it was thought she would die. Some of the citizens had him arrested, but it was soon hushed up. And that was the last of it. The woman did not die, but it would have been the same if she had.

Captain Price purchased me in the month of October, and I remained with him until December, when the family made a voyage to New Orleans, in a boat owned by himself, and named the "Chester." I served on board, as one of the stewards. On arriving at New Orleans, about the middle of the month, the boat took in freight for Cincinnati; and it was decided that the family should go up the river in her, and what was of more interest to me, I was to accompany them.

The long looked for opportunity to make my escape from slavery was near at hand.

Captain Price had some fears as to the propriety of taking me near a free State, or a place where it was likely I could run away, with a prospect of liberty. He asked me if I had ever been in a free State. "Oh yes," said I, "I have been in Ohio; my master carried me into that State once, but I never like a free State."

It was soon decided that it would be safe to take me with them, and what made it more safe, Eliza was on the boat with us, and Mrs. Price, to try me, asked if I thought as much as ever of Eliza. I told her that Eliza was very dear to me indeed, and that nothing but death should part us. It was the same as if we were married. This had the desired effect. The boat left New Orleans, and proceeded up the river.

I had at different times obtained little sums of money, which I had reserved for a "rainy day." I procured some cotton cloth, and made me a bag to carry provisions in. The trials of the past were all lost in hopes for the future. The love of liberty, that had been burning in my bosom for years, and had been well nigh extinguished, was now resuscitated. At night, when all around was peaceful, I would walk the decks, meditating upon my happy prospects.

I should have stated, that before leaving St. Louis, I went to an old man named Frank, a slave, owned by a Mr. Sarpee. This old man was very distinguished (not only among the slave population, but also the whites) as a fortune-teller. He was about seventy years of age, something over six feet high, and very slender. Indeed, he was so small around his body that it looked as though it was not strong enough to hold up his head.

Uncle Frank was a very great favorite with the young ladies, who would go to him in great numbers to get their fortunes told. And it was generally believed that he could really penetrate into the mysteries of futurity. Whether true or not, he had the *name*, and that is about half of what one needs in this gullible age. I found Uncle Frank seated in the chimney corner, about ten o'clock at night. As soon as I entered, the old man left his seat. I watched his movement as well as I could by the dim light of the fire. He soon lit a lamp, and coming up, looked me full in the face, saying, "Well, my son, you have come to get uncle to tell your fortune, have you?" "Yes," said I. But how the old man should know what I had come for, I could not tell. However, I paid the fee of twenty-five cents, and he commenced by looking into a gourd, filled with water. Whether the old man was a prophet, or the son of a prophet, I cannot say; but there is one thing certain, many of his predictions were verified.

I am no believer in soothsaying; yet I am sometimes at a loss to know how Uncle Frank could tell so accurately what would occur in the future. Among the many things he told was one which was enough to pay me for all the trouble of hunting him up. It was that *I should be free!* He further said, that in trying to get my liberty, I would meet with many severe trials. I thought to myself, any fool could tell me that!

The first place in which we landed in a free State was Cairo, a small village at the mouth of the Ohio River. We remained here but a few hours, when we proceeded to Louisville. After unloading some of the cargo, the boat started on her upward trip. The next day was the first of January. I had looked forward to New Year's day as the commencement of a new era in the history of my life. I had decided upon leaving the peculiar institution that day.

During the last night that I served in slavery, I did not close my eyes a single moment. When not thinking of the future, my mind dwelt on the past. The love of a dear mother, a dear sister, and three dear brothers, yet living, caused me to shed many tears. If I could only have been assured of their being dead, I should have felt satisfied; but I imagined I saw my dear mother in the cotton-field, followed by a merciless task-master, and no one to speak a consoling word to her! I beheld my dear sister in the hands of a slave-driver, and compelled to submit to his cruelty! None but one placed in such a situation can for a moment imagine the intense agony to which these reflections subjected me.

XIII

At last the time for action arrived. The boat landed at a point which appeared to me the place of all others to start from. I found that it would be impossible to carry anything with me, but what was upon my person. I had some provisions, and a single suit of clothes, about half worn. When the boat was discharging her cargo, and the passengers engaged carrying their baggage on and off shore, I improved the opportunity to convey myself with my little effects on land. Taking up a trunk, I went up the wharf, and was soon out of the crowd. I made directly for the woods, where I remained until night, knowing well that I could not travel, even in the State of Ohio, during the day, without danger of being arrested.

I had long since made up my mind that I would not trust myself in the hands of any man, white or colored. The slave is brought up to look upon every white man as an enemy to him and his race; and twenty-one years in slavery had taught me that there were traitors, even among colored people. After dark, I emerged from the woods into a narrow path, which led me into the main travelled road. But I knew not which way to go. I did not know North from South,

East from West. I looked in vain for the North Star; a heavy cloud hid it from my view. I walked up and down the road until near midnight, when the clouds disappeared, and I welcomed the sight of my friend,—truly the slave's friend,—the North Star!

As soon as I saw it, I knew my course, and before daylight I travelled twenty or twenty-five miles. It being in the winter, I suffered intensely from the cold; being without an overcoat, and my other clothes rather thin for the season. I was provided with a tinder-box, so that I could make up a fire when necesssary. And but for this, I should certainly have frozen to death; for I was determined not to go to any house for shelter. I knew of a man belonging to Gen. Ashly, of St. Louis, who had run away near Cincinnati, on the way to Washington, but had been caught and carried back into slavery; and I felt that a similar fate awaited me, should I be seen by any one. I travelled at night, and lay by during the day.

On the fourth day, my provisions gave out, and then what to do I could not tell. Have something to eat, I must; but how to get it was the question! On the first night after my food was gone, I went to a barn on the road-side, and there found some ears of corn. I took ten or twelve of them, and kept on my journey. During the next day, while in the woods, I roasted my corn and feasted upon it, thanking God that I was so well provided for.

My escape to a land of freedom now appeared certain, and the prospects of the future occupied a great part of my thoughts. What should be my occupation, was a subject of much anxiety to me; and the next thing what should be my name? I have before stated that my old master, Dr. Young, had no children of his own, but had with him a nephew, the son of his brother, Benjamin Young. When this boy was brought to Doctor Young, his name being William, the same as mine, my mother was ordered to change mine to something else. This, at the time, I thought to be one of the most cruel acts that could be committed upon my rights; and I received several very severe whippings for telling people that my name was William, after orders were given to change it. Though young, I was old enough to place a high appreciation upon my name. It was decided, however, to call me "Sandford," and this name I was known by, not only upon my master's plantation, but up to the time that I made my escape. I was sold under the name of Sandford.

But as soon as the subject came to my mind, I resolved on adopting my old name of William, and let Sandford go by the board, for I always hated it. Not because there was anything peculiar in the name; but because it had been forced upon me. It is sometimes common at the south, for slaves to take the name of their masters. Some have a legitimate right to do so. But I always detested the idea of being called by the name of either of my masters. And as for my father, I would rather have adopted the name of "Friday," and been known as the servant of some Robinson Crusoe, than to have taken his name. So I was not only hunting for my liberty, but also hunting for a name; though I regarded the latter as of little consequence, if I could but gain the former. Travelling along the road, I would sometimes speak to myself, sounding my name over, by way of getting used to it, before I should arrive among civilized human beings. On the fifth or sixth day, it rained very fast, and it froze about as fast as it fell, so that my clothes were one glare of ice. I travelled on at night until I became so chilled and benumbed—the wind blowing into my face—that I found it impossible to go any further, and accordingly took shelter in a barn, where I was obliged to walk about to keep from freezing.

I have ever looked upon that night as the most eventful part of my escape from slavery. Nothing but the providence of God, and that old barn, saved me from freezing to death. I received a very severe cold, which settled upon my lungs, and from time to time my feet had been frost-bitten, so that it was with difficulty I could walk. In this situation I travelled two days, when I found that I must seek shelter somewhere, or die.

The thought of death was nothing frightful to me, compared with that of being caught, and again carried back into slavery. Nothing but the prospect of enjoying liberty could have induced me to undergo such trials, for

Behind I left the whips and chains,
Before me were sweet Freedom's plains!

This, and this alone, cheered me onward. But I at last resolved to seek protection from the inclemency of the weather, and therefore I secured myself behind some logs and brush, intending to wait there until some one should pass by; for I thought it probable that I might see some colored person, or, if not, some one who was not a slaveholder; for I had an idea that I should know a slaveholder as far as I could see him.

XIV

The first person that passed was a man in a buggy-wagon. He looked too genteel for me to hail him. Very soon, another passed by on horseback. I attempted speaking to him, but fear made my voice fail me. As he passed, I left my hiding-place, and was approaching the road, when I observed an old man walking towards me, leading a white horse. He had on a broad-brimmed hat and a very long coat, and was evidently walking for exercise. As soon as I saw him, and observed his dress, I thought to myself, "You are the man that I have been looking for!" Nor was I mistaken. He was the very man!

On approaching me, he asked me, "if I was not a slave." I looked at him some time, and then asked him "if he knew of any one who would help me, as I was sick." He answered that he would; but again asked, if I was not a slave. I told him I was. He then said that I was in a very pro-slavery neighborhood, and if I would wait until he went home, he would get a covered wagon for me. I promised to remain. He mounted his horse, and was soon out of sight.

After he was gone, I meditated whether to wait or not; being apprehensive that he had gone for some one to arrest me. But I finally concluded to remain until he should return; removing some few rods to watch his movements. After a suspense of an hour and a half or more, he returned with a two horse covered-wagon, such as are usually seen under the shed of a Quaker meeting-house on Sundays and Thursdays; for the old man proved to be a Quaker of the George Fox stamp.

He took me to his house, but it was some time before I could be induced to enter it; not until the old lady came out, did I venture into the house. I thought I saw something in the old lady's cap that told me I was not only safe, but welcome, in her house. I was not, however, prepared to receive their hospitalities. The only fault I found with them was their being too kind. I had never had a white man to treat me as an equal, and the idea of a white lady waiting on me at the table was still worse! Though the table was loaded with the good things of this life, I could not eat. I thought if I could only be allowed the privilege of eating in the kitchen, I should be more than satisfied!

Finding that I could not eat, the old lady, who was a "Thomsonian," made me a cup of "composition," or "number six;" but it was so strong and hot, that I called it *"number seven!"** However, I soon found myself at home in this family. On different occasions, when telling these facts, I have been asked how I felt upon finding myself regarded as a man by a white family; especially just having run away from one. I cannot say that I have ever answered the question yet.

The fact that I was in all probability a freeman, sounded in my ears like a charm. I am satisfied that none but a slave could place such an appreciation upon liberty as I did at that time. I wanted to see mother and sister, that I might tell them "I was free!" I wanted to see my fellow slaves in St. Louis, and let them know that the chains were no longer upon my limbs. I wanted to see Captain Price, and let him learn from my own lips that I was no more a chattel, but a man! I was anxious, too, thus to inform Mrs. Price that she must get another coachman. And I wanted to see Eliza more than I did either Mr. or Mrs. Price!

The fact that I was a freeman—could walk, talk, eat and sleep as a man, and no one to stand over me with the blood-clotted cowhide—all this made me feel that I was not myself.

The kind friend that had taken me in was named Wells Brown. He was a devoted friend of the slave; but was very old, and not in the enjoyment of good health. After being by the fire awhile, I found that my feet had been very much frozen. I was seized with a fever which threatened to confine me to my bed. But my Thomsonian friends soon raised me, treating me as kindly as if I had been one of their own children. I remained with them twelve or fifteen days, during which time they made me some clothing, and the old gentleman purchased me a pair of boots.

I found that I was about fifty or sixty miles from Dayton, in the State of Ohio, and between one and two hundred miles from Cleveland, on Lake Erie, a place I was desirous of reaching on my way

* [Thomsonians were followers of Dr. Samuel Thomson (1769–1843) of Massachusetts. Dr. Thomson was a believer in vegetable preparations and steam baths. His name was synonymous with practitioners of herb medicine for a century.]

to Canada. This I know will sound strangely to the ears of people in foreign lands, but it is nevertheless true. An American citizen was fleeing from a Democratic, Republican, Christian government, to receive protection under the monarchy of Great Britain. While the people of the United States boast of their freedom, they at the same time keep three millions of their own citizens in chains; and while I am seated here in sight of Bunker Hill Monument, writing this narrative, I am a slave, and no law, not even in Massachusetts, can protect me from the hands of the slaveholder!

Before leaving this good Quaker friend, he inquired what my name was besides William. I told him that I had no other name. "Well," said he, "thee must have another name. Since thee has got out of slavery, thee has become a man, and men always have two names."

I told him that he was the first man to extend the hand of friendship to me, and I would give him the privilege of naming me.

"If I name thee," said he, "I shall call thee Wells Brown, after myself."

"But," said I, "I am not willing to lose my name of William. As it was taken from me once against my will, I am not willing to part with it again upon any terms."

"Then," said he, "I will call thee William Wells Brown."

"So be it," said I; and I have been known by that name ever since I left the house of my first white friend, Wells Brown.

After giving me some little change, I again started for Canada. In four days I reached a public house, and went in to warm myself. I there learned that some fugitive slaves had just passed through the place. The men in the bar-room were talking about it, and I thought that it must have been myself they referred to, and I was therefore afraid to start, fearing they would seize me; but I finally mustered courage enough, and took my leave. As soon as I was out of sight, I went into the woods, and remained there until night, when I again regained the road, and travelled on until the next day.

Not having had any food for nearly two days, I was faint with hunger, and was in a dilemma what to do, as the little cash supplied me by my adopted father, and which had contributed to my comfort, was now all gone. I however concluded to go to a farmhouse, and ask for something to eat. On approaching the door of the first one presenting itself, I knocked, and was soon met by a man who asked me what I wanted. I told him that I would like something to eat. He asked where I was from, and where I was going. I replied that I had come some way, and was going to Cleveland.

After hesitating a moment or two, he told me that he could give me nothing to eat, adding, "that if I would work, I could get something to eat."

I felt bad, being thus refused something to sustain nature, but did not dare tell him that I was a slave.

Just as I was leaving the door, with a heavy heart, a woman, who proved to be the wife of this gentleman, came to the door, and asked her husband what I wanted? He did not seem inclined to inform her. She therefore asked me herself. I told her that I had asked for something to eat. After a few other questions, she told me to come in, and that she would give me something to eat.

I walked up to the door, but the husband remained in the passage, as if unwilling to let me enter.

She asked him two or three times to get out of the way, and let me in. But as he did not move, she pushed him on one side, bidding me walk in! I was never before so glad to see a woman push a man aside! Ever since that act, I have been in favor of "woman's rights"!

After giving me as much food as I could eat, she presented me with ten cents, all the money then at her disposal, accompanied with a note to a friend, a few miles further on the road. Thanking this angel of mercy from an overflowing heart, I pushed on my way, and in three days arrived at Cleveland, Ohio.

Being an entire stranger in this place, it was difficult for me to find where to stop. I had no money, and the lake being frozen, I saw that I must remain until the opening of navigation, or go to Canada by way of Buffalo. But believing myself to be somewhat out of danger, I secured an engagement at the Mansion House, as a table waiter, in payment for my board. The proprietor, however, whose name was E. M. Segur, in a short time, hired me for twelve dollars per month; on which terms I remained until spring, when I found good employment on board a lake steamboat.

I purchased some books, and at leisure moments perused them with considerable advantage to myself. While at Cleveland, I saw, for the first time, an anti-slavery newspaper. It was the *Genius of*

Universal Emancipation, published by Benjamin Lundy,* and though I had no home, I subscribed for the paper. It was my great desire, being out of slavery myself, to do what I could for the emancipation of my brethren yet in chains, and while on Lake Erie, I found many opportunities of "helping their cause along."

It is well known, that a great number of fugitives make their escape to Canada, by way of Cleveland; and while on the lake, I always made arrangement to carry them on the boat to Buffalo or Detroit, and thus effect their escape to the "promised land." The friends of the slave, knowing that I would transport them without charge, never failed to have a delegation when the boat arrived at Cleveland. I have sometimes had four or five on board, at one time.

In the year 1842, I conveyed, from the first of May to the first of December, sixty-nine fugitives over Lake Erie to Canada. In 1843, I visited Malden, in Upper Canada, and counted seventeen, in that small village, who owed their escape to my humble efforts.

Soon after coming North, I subscribed for the *Liberator,* edited by that champion of freedom, William Lloyd Garrison. I labored a season to promote the temperance cause among the colored people, but for the last three years, have been pleading for the victims of American slavery.

WILLIAM WELLS BROWN

Boston, Mass., June, 1847.

* [The *Genius,* founded in 1821, was one of the earliest American antislavery newspapers. It ceased publication on Lundy's death on August 22, 1839.]

Twelve Years A Slave
Narrative of
SOLOMON NORTHUP

A Citizen of New York, kidnapped in Washington City in 1841 and rescued in 1853 from a cotton plantation near the Red River in Louisiana

I

Introductory.—Ancestry.—The Northup family.—Birth and parentage.—Mintus Northup—Marriage with Anne Hampton.—Good resolutions.—Champlain Canal.—Rafting excursion to Canada.—Farming.—The violin.—Cooking.—Removal to Saratoga.—Parker and Perry.—Slaves and slavery.—The children.—The beginning of sorrow.

Having been born a freeman, and for more than thirty years enjoyed the blessings of liberty in a free State—and having at the end of that time been kidnapped and sold into slavery, where I remained, until happily rescued in the month of January, 1853, after a bondage of twelve years—it has been suggested that an account of my life and fortunes would not be uninteresting to the public.

Since my return to liberty, I have not failed to perceive the increasing interest throughout the Northern States, in regard to the subject of Slavery. Works of fiction, professing to portray its features in their more pleasing as well as more repugnant aspects, have been circulated to an extent unprecedented, and, as I understand, have created a fruitful topic of comment and discussion.

I can speak of Slavery only so far as it came under my own observation—only so far as I have known and experienced it in my own person. My object is, to give a candid and truthful statement of facts: to repeat the story of my life, without exaggeration, leaving it for others to determine, whether even the pages of fiction present a picture of more cruel wrong or a severer bondage.

As far back as I have been able to ascertain, my ancestors on the paternal side were slaves in Rhode Island. They belonged to a family by the name of Northup, one of whom, removing to the State of New-York, settled at Hoasic, in Rensselaer county. He brought with him Mintus Northup, my father. On the death of this gentleman, which must have occurred some fifty years ago, my father became free, having been emancipated by a direction in his will.

Editor's note: *Twelve Years a Slave* was first published by Derby and Miller in Auburn, New York, in 1853.

Henry B. Northup, Esq., of Sandy Hill, a distinguished counselor at law, and the man to whom, under Providence, I am indebted for my present liberty, and my return to the society of my wife and children, is a relative of the family in which my forefathers were thus held to service, and from which they took the name I bear. To this fact may be attributed the persevering interest he has taken in my behalf.

Sometime after my father's liberation, he removed to the town of Minerva, Essex County, N.Y., where I was born, in the month of July, 1808. How long he remained in the latter place I have not the means of definitely ascertaining. From thence he removed to Granville, Washington County, near a place known as Slyborough, where, for some years, he labored on the farm of Clark Northup, also a relative of his old master; from thence he removed to the Alden farm, at Moss Street, a short distance north of the village of Sandy Hill; and from thence to the farm now owned by Russel Pratt, situated on the road leading from Fort Edward to Argyle, where he continued to reside until his death, which took place on the 22d day of November, 1829. He left a widow and two children —myself, and Joseph, an elder brother. The latter is still living in the county of Oswego, near the city of that name; my mother died during the period of my captivity.

Though born a slave, and laboring under the disadvantages to which my unfortunate race is subjected, my father was a man respected for his industry and integrity, as many now living, who well remember him, are ready to testify. His whole life was passed in the peaceful pursuits of agriculture, never seeking employment in those more menial positions, which seem to be especially allotted to the children of Africa. Besides giving us an education surpassing that ordinarily bestowed upon children in our condition, he acquired, by his diligence and economy, a sufficient property qualification to entitle him to the right of suffrage. He was accustomed to speak to us of his early life; and although at all times cherishing the warmest emotions of kindness, and even of affection towards the family, in whose house he had been a bondsman, he nevertheless comprehended the system of Slavery, and dwelt with sorrow on the degradation of his race. He endeavored to imbue our minds with sentiments of morality, and to teach us to place our trust and confidence in Him who regards the humblest as well as the highest of his creatures. How often since that time has the recollection of his paternal counsels occurred to me, while lying in a slave hut in the distant and sickly regions of Louisiana, smarting with the undeserved wounds which an inhuman master had inflicted, and longing only for the grave which had covered him, to shield me also from the lash of the oppressor. In the church-yard at Sandy Hill, an humble stone marks the spot where he reposes, after having worthily performed the duties appertaining to the lowly sphere wherein God had appointed him to walk.

Up to this period I had been principally engaged with my father in the labors of the farm. The leisure hours allowed me were generally either employed over my books, or playing on the violin—an amusement which was the ruling passion of my youth. It has also been the source of consolation since, affording pleasure to the simple beings with whom my lot was cast, and beguiling my own thoughts, for many hours, from the painful contemplation of my fate.

On Christmas day, 1829, I was married to Anne Hampton, a colored girl then living in the vicinity of our residence. The ceremony was performed at Fort Edward, by Timothy Eddy, Esq., a magistrate of that town, and still a prominent citizen of the place. She had resided a long time at Sandy Hill, with Mr. Baird, proprietor of the Eagle Tavern, and also in the family of Rev. Alexander Proudfit, of Salem. This gentleman for many years had presided over the Presbyterian society at the latter place, and was widely distinguished for his learning and piety. Anne still holds in grateful remembrance the exceeding kindness and the excellent counsels of that good man. She is not able to determine the exact line of her descent, but the blood of three races mingles in her veins. It is difficult to tell whether the red, white, or black predominates. The union of them all, however, in her origin, has given her a singular but pleasing expression, such as is rarely to be seen. Though somewhat resembling, yet she cannot properly be styled a quadroon, a class to which, I have omitted to mention, my mother belonged.

I had just now passed the period of my minority, having reached the age of twenty-one years in the month of July previous. Deprived of the advice and assistance of my father, with a wife dependent upon me for support, I resolved to enter upon a life of industry; and notwithstanding the obstacle of color, and the consciousness of my lowly state, indulged in pleasant dreams of a good time coming, when the possession of some humble habitation, with a few surrounding acres, should reward my labors, and bring me the means of happiness and comfort.

From the time of my marriage to this day the love I have borne my wife has been sincere and unabated; and only those who have felt the glowing tenderness a father cherishes for his offspring, can appreciate my affection for the beloved children which have since been born to us. This much I deem appropriate and necessary to say, in order that those who read these pages, may comprehend the poignancy of those sufferings I have been doomed to bear.

Immediately upon our marriage we commenced house-keeping, in the old yellow building then standing at the southern extremity of Fort Edward village, and which has since been transformed into a modern mansion, and lately occupied by Captain Lathrop. It is known as the Fort House. In this building the courts were sometime held after the organization of the county. It was also occupied by Burgoyne in 1777, being situated near the old Fort on the left bank of the Hudson.

During the winter I was employed with others repairing the Champlain Canal, on that section over which William Van Nortwick was superintendent. David McEachron had the immediate charge of the men in whose company I labored. By the time the canal opened in the spring, I was enabled, from the savings of my wages, to purchase a pair of horses, and other things necessarily required in the business of navigation.

Having hired several efficient hands to assist me, I entered into contracts for the transportation of large rafts of timber from Lake Champlain to Troy. Dyer Beckwith and a Mr. Bartemy, of Whitehall, accompanied me on several trips. During the season I became perfectly familiar with the art and mysteries of rafting—a knowledge which afterwards enabled me to render profitable service to a worthy master, and to astonish the simple-witted lumbermen on the banks of the Bayou Bœuf.

In one of my voyages down Lake Champlain, I was induced to make a visit to Canada. Repairing to Montreal, I visited the cathedral and other places of interest in that city, from whence I continued my excursion to Kingston and other towns, obtaining a knowledge of localities, which was also of service to me afterwards, as will appear towards the close of this narrative.

Having completed my contracts on the canal satisfactorily to myself and to my employer, and not wishing to remain idle, now that the navigation of the canal was again suspended, I entered into another contract with Medad Gunn, to cut a large quantity of wood. In this business I was engaged during the winter of 1831-32.

With the return of spring, Anne and myself conceived the project of taking a farm in the neighborhood. I had been accustomed from earliest youth to agricultural labors, and it was an occupation congenial to my tastes. I accordingly entered into arrangements for a part of the old Alden farm, on which my father formerly resided. With one cow, one swine, a yoke of fine oxen I had lately purchased of Lewis Brown, in Hartford, and other personal property and effects, we proceeded to our new home in Kingsbury. That year I planted twenty-five acres of corn, sowed large fields of oats, and commenced forming upon as large a scale as my utmost means would permit. Anne was diligent about the house affairs, while I toiled laboriously in the field.

On this place we continued to reside until 1834. In the winter season I had numerous calls to play on the violin. Wherever the young people assembled to dance, I was almost invariably there. Throughout the surrounding villages my fiddle was notorious. Anne, also, during her long residence at the Eagle Tavern, had become somewhat famous as a cook. During court weeks, and on public occasions, she was employed at high wages in the kitchen at Sherrill's Coffee House.

We always returned home from the performance of these services with money in our pockets; so that, with fiddling, cooking, and farming, we soon found ourselves in the possession of abundance, and, in fact, leading a happy and prosperous life. Well, indeed, would it have been for us had we remained on the farm at Kingsbury; but the time came when the next step was to be taken towards the cruel destiny that awaited me.

In March, 1834, we removed to Saratoga Springs. We occupied a house belonging to Daniel O'Brien, on the north side of Washington street. At that time Isaac Taylor kept a large boarding house, known as Washington Hall, at the north end of Broadway. He employed me to drive a hack, in which capacity I worked for him two years. After this time I was generally employed through the visiting season, as also was Anne, in the United States Hotel, and other public houses of the place. In winter season I relied upon my violin, though during the construction of the Troy and Saratoga railroad, I performed many hard days' labor upon it.

I was in the habit, at Saratoga, of purchasing articles necessary for my family at the stores of Mr. Cephas Parker and Mr. William Perry, gentlemen towards whom, for many acts of kindness, I entertained feelings of strong regard. It was for this reason that, twelve years afterwards, I caused to be directed to them the letter, which is hereinafter inserted, and which was the means, in the hands of Mr. Northup, of my fortunate deliverance.

While living at the United States Hotel, I frequently met with slaves, who had accompanied their masters from the South. They were always well dressed and well provided for, leading apparently an easy life, with but few of its ordinary troubles to perplex them. Many times they entered into conversation with me on the subject of Slavery. Almost uniformly I found they cherished a secret desire for liberty. Some of them expressed the most ardent anxiety to escape, and consulted me on the best method of effecting it. The fear of punishment, however, which they knew was certain to attend their re-capture and return, in all cases proved sufficient to deter them from the experiment. Having all my life breathed the free air of the North, and conscious that I possessed the same feelings and affections that find a place in the white man's breast; conscious, moreover, of an intelligence equal to that of some men, at least, with a fairer skin, I was too ignorant, perhaps too independent, to conceive how any one could be content to live in the abject condition of a slave. I could not comprehend the justice of that law, or that religion, which upholds or recognizes the principle of Slavery; and never once, I am proud to say, did I fail to counsel any one who came to me, to watch his opportunity, and strike for freedom.

I continued to reside at Saratoga until the spring of 1841. The flattering anticipations which, seven years before, had seduced us from the quiet farm-house, on the east side of the Hudson, had not been realized. Though always in comfortable circumstances, we had not prospered. The society and associations at that world-renowned watering place, were not calculated to preserve the simple habits of industry and economy to which I had been accustomed, but, on the contrary, to substitute others in their stead, tending to shiftlessness and extravagance.

At this time we were the parents of three children—Elizabeth,

Margaret, and Alonzo. Elizabeth, the eldest, was in her tenth year; Margaret was two years younger, and little Alonzo had just passed his fifth birth-day. They filled our house with gladness. Their young voices were music in our ears. Many an airy castle did their mother and myself build for the little innocents. When not at labor I was always walking with them, clad in their best attire, through the streets and groves of Saratoga. Their presence was my delight; and I clasped them to my bosom with as warm and tender love as if their clouded skins had been as white as snow.

Thus far the history of my life presents nothing whatever unusual —nothing but the common hopes, and loves, and labors of an obscure colored man, making his humble progress in the world. But now I had reached a turning point in my existence—reached the threshold of unutterable wrong, and sorrow, and despair. Now had I approached within the shadow of the cloud, into the thick darkness whereof I was soon to disappear, thenceforward to be hidden from the eyes of all my kindred, and shut out from the sweet light of liberty, for many a weary year.

II

The two strangers.—The circus company.—Departure from Saratoga.—Ventriloquism and legerdemain.—Journey to New York.—Free papers.—Brown and Hamilton.—The haste to reach the circus.—Arrival in Washington.—Funeral of Harrison.—The sudden sickness.—The torment of thirst. —The receding light.—Insensibility.—Chains and darkness.

One morning, towards the latter part of the month of March, 1841, having at that time no particular business to engage my attention, I was walking about the village of Saratoga Springs, thinking to myself where I might obtain some present employment, until the busy season should arrive. Anne, as was her usual custom, had gone over to Sandy Hill, a distance of some twenty miles, to take charge of the culinary department at Sherrill's Coffee House, during the session of the court. Elizabeth, I think, had accompanied her. Margaret and Alonzo were with their aunt at Saratoga.

On the corner of Congress street and Broadway, near the tavern, then, and for aught I know to the contrary, still kept by Mr. Moon, I was met by two gentlemen of respectable appearance, both of whom were entirely unknown to me. I have the impression that they were introduced to me by some one of my acquaintances, but who, I have in vain endeavored to recall, with the remark that I was an expert player on the violin.

At any rate, they immediately entered into conversation on that subject, making numerous inquiries touching my proficiency in that respect. My responses being to all appearances satisfactory, they proposed to engage my services for a short period, stating, at the same time, I was just such a person as their business required. Their names, as they afterwards gave them to me, were Merrill Brown and Abram Hamilton, though whether these were their true appellations, I have strong reasons to doubt. The former was a man apparently forty years of age, somewhat short and thick-set, with a countenance indicating shrewdness and intelligence. He wore a black frock coat and black hat, and said he resided either at Rochester or at Syracuse. The latter was a young man of fair complexion and light eyes, and, I should judge, had not passed the age of twenty-five. He was tall and slender, dressed in a snuff-colored coat, with glossy hat, and vest of elegant pattern. His whole apparel was in the extreme of fashion. His appearance was somewhat effeminate, but prepossessing, and there was about him an easy air, that showed he had mingled with the world. They were connected, as they informed me, with a circus company, then in the city of Washington; that they were on their way thither to rejoin it, having left it for a short time to make an excursion northward, for the purpose of seeing the country, and were paying their expenses by an occasional exhibition. They also remarked that they had found much difficulty in procuring music for their entertainments, and that if I would accompany them as far as New-York, they would give me one dollar for each day's services, and three dollars in addition for every night I played at their performances, besides sufficient to pay the expenses of my return from New-York to Saratoga.

I at once accepted the tempting offer, both for the reward it promised, and from a desire to visit the metropolis. They were anxious to leave immediately. Thinking my absence would be brief, I did not deem it necessary to write to Anne whither I had gone; in fact supposing that my return, perhaps, would be as soon as hers. So taking a change of linen and my violin, I was ready to depart. The carriage was brought round—a covered one, drawn by a pair of noble bays, altogether forming an elegant establishment. Their baggage, consisting of three large trunks, was fastened on the rack, and mounting to the driver's seat, while they took their places in the rear, I drove away from Saratoga on the road to Albany, elated with my new position, and happy as I had ever been, on any day in all my life.

We passed through Ballston, and striking the ridge road, as it is called, if my memory correctly serves me, followed it direct to Albany. We reached that city before dark, and stopped at a hotel southward from the Museum.

This night I had an opportunity of witnessing one of their performances—the only one, during the whole period I was with them. Hamilton was stationed at the door; I formed the orchestra, while Brown provided the entertainment. It consisted in throwing balls, dancing on the rope, frying pancakes in a hat, causing invisible pigs to squeal, and other like feats of ventriloquism and legerdemain. The audience was extraordinarily sparse, and not of the selectest character at that, and Hamilton's report of the proceeds presented but a "beggarly account of empty boxes."

Early next morning we renewed our journey. The burden of their conversation now was the expression of an anxiety to reach the circus without delay. They hurried forward, without again stopping to exhibit, and in due course of time, we reached New-York, taking lodgings at a house on the west side of the city, in a street running from Broadway to the river. I supposed my journey was at an end, and expected in a day or two at least, to return to my friends and family at Saratoga. Brown and Hamilton, however, began to importune me to continue with them to Washington. They alleged that immediately on their arrival, now that the summer season was approaching, the circus would set out for the north. They promised me a situation and high wages if I would accompany them. Largely did they expatiate on the advantages that would result to me, and such were the flattering representations they made, that I finally concluded to accept the offer.

The next morning they suggested that, inasmuch as we were about entering a slave State, it would be well, before leaving New-York, to procure free papers. The idea struck me as a prudent one, though I think it would scarcely have occurred to me, had they not proposed it. We proceeded at once to what I understood to be the Custom House. They made oath to certain facts showing I was a free man. A paper was drawn up and handed us, with the direction to take it to the clerk's office. We did so, and the clerk having added something to it, for which he was paid six shillings, we returned again to the Custom House. Some further formalities were gone through with before it was completed, when, paying the officer two dollars, I placed the papers in my pocket, and started with my two friends to our hotel. I thought at the time, I must confess, that the papers were scarcely worth the cost of obtaining them—the apprehension of danger to my personal safety never having suggested itself to me in the remotest manner. The clerk, to whom we were directed, I remember, made a memorandum in a large book, which, I presume, is in the office yet. A reference to the entries during the latter part of March, or first of April, 1841, I have no doubt will satisfy the incredulous, at least so far as this particular transaction is concerned.

With the evidence of freedom in my possession, the next day after our arrival in New-York, we crossed the ferry to Jersey City, and took the road to Philadelphia. Here we remained one night, continuing our journey towards Baltimore early in the morning. In due time, we arrived in the latter city, and stopped at a hotel near the railroad depot, either kept by a Mr. Rathbone, or known as the Rathbone House. All the way from New-York, their anxiety to reach the circus seemed to grow more and more intense. We left the carriage at Baltimore, and entering the cars, proceeded to Washington, at which place we arrived just at nightfall, the evening previous to the funeral of General Harrison, and stopped at Gadsby's Hotel, on Pennsylvania Avenue.

After supper they called me to their apartments, and paid me forty-three dollars, a sum greater than my wages amounted to, which act of generosity was in consequence, they said, of their not having exhibited as often as they had given me to anticipate, during our trip from Saratoga. They moreover informed me that it had been the intention of the circus company to leave Washington the next morning, but that on account of the funeral, they had concluded to remain another day. They were then, as they had been from the time of our first meeting, extremely kind. No opportunity was omitted of addressing me in the language of approbation;

while, on the other hand, I was certainly much prepossessed in their favor. I gave them my confidence without reserve, and would freely have trusted them to almost any extent. Their constant conversation and manner towards me—their foresight in suggesting the idea of free papers, and a hundred other little acts, unnecessary to be repeated—all indicated that they were friends indeed, sincerely solicitous for my welfare. I know not but they were. I know not but they were innocent of the great wickedness of which I now believe them guilty. Whether they were accessory to my misfortunes—subtle and inhuman monsters in the shape of men—designedly luring me away from home and family, and liberty, for the sake of gold—those who read these pages will have the same means of determining as myself. If they were innocent, my sudden disappearance must have been unaccountable indeed; but revolving in my mind all the attending circumstances, I never yet could indulge, towards them, so charitable a supposition.

After receiving the money from them, of which they appeared to have an abundance, they advised me not to go into the streets that night, inasmuch as I was unacquainted with the customs of the city. Promising to remember their advice, I left them together, and soon after was shown by a colored servant to a sleeping room in the back part of the hotel, on the ground floor. I laid down to rest, thinking of home and wife, and children, and the long distance that stretched between us, until I fell asleep. But no good angel of pity came to my bedside, bidding me to fly—no voice of mercy forewarned me in my dreams of the trials that were just at hand.

The next day there was a great pageant in Washington. The roar of cannon and the tolling of bells filled the air, while many houses were shrouded with crape, and the streets were black with people. As the day advanced, the procession made its appearance, coming slowly through the Avenue, carriage after carriage, in long succession, while thousands upon thousands followed on foot—all moving to the sound of melancholy music. They were bearing the dead body of Harrison to the grave.

From early in the morning, I was constantly in the company of Hamilton and Brown. They were the only persons I knew in Washington. We stood together as the funeral pomp passed by. I remember distinctly how the window glass would break and rattle to the ground, after each report of the cannon they were firing in the burial ground. We went to the Capitol, and walked a long time about the grounds. In the afternoon, they strolled towards the President's House, all the time keeping me near to them, and pointing out various places of interest. As yet, I had seen nothing of the circus. In fact, I had thought of it but little, if at all, amidst the excitement of the day.

My friends, several times during the afternoon, entered drinking saloons, and called for liquor. They were by no means in the habit, however, so far as I knew them, of indulging to excess. On these occasions, after serving themselves, they would pour out a glass and hand it to me. I did not become intoxicated, as may be inferred from what subsequently occurred. Towards evening, and soon after partaking of one of these potations, I began to experience most unpleasant sensations. I felt extremely ill. My head commenced aching—a dull, heavy pain, inexpressibly disagreeable. At the supper table, I was without appetite; the sight and flavor of food was nauseous. About dark the same servant conducted me to the room I had occupied the previous night. Brown and Hamilton advised me to retire, commiserating me kindly, and expressing hopes that I would be better in the morning. Divesting myself of coat and boots merely, I threw myself upon the bed. It was impossible to sleep. The pain in my head continued to increase, until it became almost unbearable. In a short time I became thirsty. My lips were parched. I could think of nothing but water—of lakes and flowing rivers, of brooks where I had stopped to drink, and of the dripping bucket, rising with its cool and overflowing nectar, from the bottom of the well. Towards midnight, as near as I could judge, I arose, unable longer to bear such intensity of thirst. I was a stranger in the house, and knew nothing of its apartments. There was no one up, as I could observe. Groping about at random, I knew not where, I found the way at last to a kitchen in the basement. Two or three colored servants were moving through it, one of whom, a woman, gave me two glasses of water. It afforded momentary relief, but by the time I had reached my room again, the same burning desire of drink, the same tormenting thirst, had again returned. It was even more torturing than before, as was also the wild pain in my head, if such a thing could be. I was in sore distress—in most excruciating agony! I seemed to stand on the brink of madness! The memory of that night of horrible suffering will follow me to the grave.

In the course of an hour or more after my return from the kitchen, I was conscious of some one entering my room. There seemed to be several—a mingling of various voices,—but how many, or who they were, I cannot tell. Whether Brown and Hamilton were among them, is a mere matter of conjecture. I only remember, with any degree of distinctness, that I was told it was necessary to go to a physician and procure medicine, and that pulling on my boots, without coat or hat, I followed them through a long passage-way, or alley, into the open street. It ran out at right angles from Pennsylvania Avenue. On the opposite side there was a light burning in a window. My impression is there were then three persons with me, but it is altogether indefinite and vague, and like the memory of a painful dream. Going towards the light, which I imagined proceeded from a physician's office, and which seemed to recede as I advanced, is the last glimmering recollection I can now recall. From that moment I was insensible. How long I remained in that condition—whether only that night, or many days and nights—I do not know; but when consciousness returned, I found myself alone, in utter darkness, and in chains.

The pain in my head had subsided in a measure, but I was very faint and weak. I was sitting upon a low bench, made of rough boards, and without coat or hat. I was hand-cuffed. Around my ankles also were a pair of heavy fetters. One end of a chain was fastened to a large ring in the floor, the other to the fetters on my ankles. I tried in vain to stand upon my feet. Waking from such a painful trance, it was some time before I could collect my thoughts. Where was I? What was the meaning of these chains? Where were Brown and Hamilton? What had I done to deserve imprisonment in such a dungeon? I could not comprehend. There was a blank of some indefinite period, preceding my awakening in that lonely place, the events of which the utmost stretch of memory was unable to recall. I listened intently for some sign or sound of life, but nothing broke the oppressive silence, save the clinking of my chains, whenever I chanced to move. I spoke aloud, but the sound of my voice startled me. I felt of my pockets, so far as the fetters would allow—far enough, indeed, to ascertain that I had not only been robbed of liberty, but that my money and free papers were also gone! Then did the idea begin to break upon my mind, at first dim and confused, that I had been kidnapped. But that I thought was incredible. There must have been some misapprehension—some unfortunate mistake. It could not be that a free citizen of New-York, who had wronged no man, nor violated any law, should be dealt with thus inhumanly. The more I contemplated my situation, however, the more I became confirmed in my suspicions. It was a desolate thought, indeed. I felt there was no trust or mercy in unfeeling man; and commending myself to the God of the oppressed, bowed my head upon my fettered hands, and wept most bitterly.

III

Painful meditations.—James H. Burch.—Williams' slave pen in Washington.—The lackey, Radburn.—Assert my freedom. —The anger of the trader.—The paddle and cat-o'-ninetails. —The whipping.—New Acquaintances.—Ray, Williams, and Randall.—Arrival of little Emily and her mother in the pen. —Maternal sorrows.—The story of Eliza.

Some three hours elapsed, during which time I remained seated on the low bench, absorbed in painful meditations. At length I heard the crowing of a cock, and soon a distant rumbling sound, as of carriages hurrying through the streets, came to my ears, and I knew that it was day. No ray of light, however, penetrated my prison. Finally, I heard footsteps immediately overhead, as of some one walking to and fro. It occurred to me then that I must be in an underground apartment, and the damp, mouldy odors of the place confirmed the supposition. The noise above continued for at least an hour, when, at last, I heard footsteps approaching from without. A key rattled in the lock—a strong door swung back upon its hinges, admitting a flood of light, and two men entered and stood before me. One of them was a large, powerful man, forty years of age, perhaps, with dark, chestnut-colored hair, slightly interspersed with gray. His face was full, his complexion flush, his features grossly coarse, expressive of nothing but cruelty and cunning. He was about five feet ten inches high, of full habit, and without prejudice, I must be allowed to say, was a man whose whole appearance was sinister and repugnant. His name was James H. Burch, as I learned afterwards—a well-known slave-dealer in Washington; and then, or lately, connected in business, as a partner, with Theophilus Freeman, of New-Orleans. The person who accompanied him was a simple lackey, named Ebenezer Radburn, who acted merely in the capacity of turnkey. Both of these men still live in Washington, or did, at the time of my return through that city from slavery in January last.

The light admitted through the open door enabled me to observe the room in which I was confined. It was about twelve feet square —the walls of solid masonry. The floor was of heavy plank. There was one small window, crossed with great iron bars, with an outside shutter, securely fastened.

An iron-bound door led into an adjoining cell, or vault, wholly destitute of windows, or any means of admitting light. The furniture of the room in which I was, consisted of the wooden bench on which I sat, an old-fashioned, dirty box stove, and besides these, in either cell, there was neither bed, nor blanket, nor any other thing whatever. The door, through which Burch and Radburn entered, led through a small passage, up a flight of steps into a yard, surrounded by a brick wall ten or twelve feet high, immediately in rear of a building of the same width as itself. The yard extended rearward from the house about thirty feet. In one part of the wall there was a strongly ironed door, opening into a narrow, covered passage, leading along one side of the house into the street. The doom of the colored man, upon whom the door leading out of that narrow passage closed, was sealed. The top of the wall supported one end of a roof, which ascended inwards, forming a kind of open shed. Underneath the roof there was a crazy loft all round, where slaves, if so disposed, might sleep at night, or in inclement weather seek shelter from the storm. It was like a farmer's barnyard in most respects, save it was so constructed that the outside world could never see the human cattle that were herded there.

The building to which the yard was attached, was two stories high, fronting on one of the public streets of Washington. Its outside presented only the appearance of a quiet private residence. A stranger looking at it, would never have dreamed of its execrable uses. Strange as it may seem, within plain sight of this same house, looking down from its commanding height upon it, was the Capitol. The voices of patriotic representatives boasting of freedom and equality, and the rattling of the poor slave's chains, almost commingled. A slave pen within the very shadow of the Capitol!

Such is a correct description as it was in 1841, of Williams' slave pen in Washington, in one of the cellars of which I found myself so unaccountably confined.

"Well, my boy, how do you feel now?" said Burch, as he entered through the open door. I replied that I was sick, and inquired the cause of my imprisonment. He answered that I was his slave—that he had bought me, and that he was about to send me to New-Orleans. I asserted, aloud and boldly, that I was a free man—a resident of Saratoga, where I had a wife and children, who were also free, and that my name was Northup. I complained bitterly of the strange treatment I had received, and threatened, upon my liberation, to have satisfaction for the wrong. He denied that I was free, and with an emphatic oath, declared that I came from Georgia. Again and again I asserted I was no man's slave, and insisted upon his taking off my chains at once. He endeavored to hush me, as if he feared my voice would be overheard. But I would not be silent, and denounced the authors of my imprisonment, whoever they might be, as unmitigated villains. Finding he could not quiet me, he flew into a towering passion. With blasphemous oaths, he called me a black liar, a runaway from Georgia, and every other profane and vulgar epithet that the most indecent fancy could conceive.

During this time Radburn was standing silently by. His business was, to oversee this human, or rather inhuman stable, receiving slaves, feeding and whipping them, at the rate of two shillings a head per day. Turning to him, Burch ordered the paddle and cat-o'-ninetails to be brought in. He disappeared, and in a few moments returned with these instruments of torture. The paddle, as it is termed in slave-beating parlance, or at least the one with which I first became acquainted, and of which I now speak, was a piece of hard-wood board, eighteen or twenty inches long, moulded to the shape of an old-fashioned pudding stick, or ordinary oar. The flattened portion, which was about the size in circumference of two open hands, was bored with a small auger in numerous places. The cat was a large rope of many strands—the strands unraveled, and a knot tied at the extremity of each.

As soon as these formidable whips appeared, I was seized by both of them, and roughly divested of my clothing. My feet, as has been stated, were fastened to the floor. Drawing me over the bench, face downwards, Radburn placed his heavy foot upon the fetters, between my wrists, holding them painfully to the floor.

With the paddle, Burch commenced beating me. Blow after blow was inflicted upon my naked body. When his unrelenting arm grew tired, he stopped and asked if I still insisted I was a free man. I did insist upon it, and then the blows were renewed, faster and more energetically, if possible, than before. When again tired, he would repeat the same question, and receiving the same answer, continue his cruel labor. All this time, the incarnate devil was uttering most fiendish oaths. At length the paddle broke, leaving the useless handle in his hand. Still I would not yield. All his brutal blows could not force from my lips the foul lie that I was a slave. Casting madly on the floor the handle of the broken paddle, he seized the rope. This was far more painful than the other. I struggled with all my power, but it was in vain. I prayed for mercy, but my prayer was only answered with imprecations and with stripes. I thought I must die beneath the lashes of the accursed brute. Even now the flesh crawls upon my bones, as I recall the scene. I was all on fire. My sufferings I can compare to nothing else than the burning agonies of hell!

At last I became silent to his repeated questions. I would make no reply. In fact, I was becoming almost unable to speak. Still he plied the lash without stint upon my poor body, until it seemed that the lacerated flesh was stripped from my bones at every stroke. A man with a particle of mercy in his soul would not have beaten even a dog so cruelly. At length Radburn said that it was useless to whip me any more—that I would be sore enough. There upon, Burch desisted, saying, with an admonitory shake of his fist in my face, and hissing the words through his firm-set teeth, that if ever I dared to utter again that I was entitled to my freedom, that I had been kidnapped, or any thing whatever of the kind, the castigation I had just received was nothing in comparison with what would follow. He swore that he would either conquer or kill me. With these consolatory words, the fetters were taken from my wrists, my feet still remaining fastened to the ring; the shutter of the little barred window, which had been opened, was again closed, and going out, locking the great door behind them, I was left in darkness as before.

In an hour, perhaps two, my heart leaped to my throat, as the key rattled in the door again. I, who had been so lonely, and who had longed so ardently to see some one, I cared not who, now shuddered at the thought of man's approach. A human face was fearful to me, especially a white one. Radburn entered, bringing with him, on a tin plate, a piece of shriveled fried pork, a slice of bread and a cup of water. He asked me how I felt, and remarked that I had received a pretty severe flogging. He remonstrated with me against the propriety of asserting my freedom. In rather a patronizing and confidential manner, he gave it to me as his advice, that the less I said on that subject the better it would be for me. The man evidently endeavored to appear kind—whether touched at the sight of my sad condition, or with the view of silencing, on my part, any further expression of my rights, it is not necessary now to conjecture. He unlocked the fetters from my ankles, opened the shutters of the little window, and departed, leaving me again alone.

By this time I had become stiff and sore; my body was covered with blisters, and it was with great pain and difficulty that I could move. From the window I could observe nothing but the roof resting on the adjacent wall. At night I laid down upon the damp, hard floor, without any pillow or covering whatever. Punctually, twice a day, Radburn came in, with his pork, and bread, and water. I had but little appetite, though I was tormented with continual thirst. My wounds would not permit me to remain but a few minutes in any one position; so, sitting, or standing, or moving slowly round, I passed the days and nights. I was heart sick and discouraged. Thoughts of my family, of my wife and children, continually occupied my mind. When sleep overpowered me I dreamed of them—dreamed I was again in Saratoga—that I could see their faces, and hear their voices calling me. Awakening from the pleasant phantasms of sleep to the bitter realities around me, I could but groan and weep. Still my spirit was not broken. I indulged the anticipation of escape, and that speedily. It was impossible, I reasoned, that men could be so unjust as to detain me as a slave, when the truth of my case was known. Burch, ascertaining I was no runaway from Georgia, would certainly let me go. Though suspicions of Brown and Hamilton were not unfrequent, I could not reconcile myself to the idea that they were instrumental to my imprisonment. Surely they would seek me out—they would deliver me from thraldom. Alas! I had not then learned the measure of "man's inhumanity to man," nor to what limitless extent of wickedness he will go for the love of gain.

In the course of several days the outer door was thrown open, allowing me the liberty of the yard. There I found three slaves—

one of them a lad of ten years, the others young men of about twenty and twenty-five. I was not long in forming an acquaintance, and learning their names and the particulars of their history.

The eldest was a colored man named Clemens Ray. He had lived in Washington; had driven a hack, and worked in a livery stable there for a long time. He was very intelligent, and fully comprehended his situation. The thought of going south overwhelmed him with grief. Burch had purchased him a few days before, and had placed him there until such time as he was ready to send him to the New-Orleans market. From him I learned for the first time that I was in William's Slave Pen, a place I had never heard of previously. He described to me the uses for which it was designed. I repeated to him the particulars of my unhappy story, but he could only give me the consolation of his sympathy. He also advised me to be silent henceforth on the subject of my freedom; for, knowing the character of Burch, he assured me that it would only be attended with renewed whipping. The next eldest was named John Williams. He was raised in Virginia, not far from Washington. Burch had taken him in payment of a debt, and he constantly entertained the hope that his master would redeem him—a hope that was subsequently realized. The lad was a sprightly child, that answered to the name of Randall. Most of the time he was playing about the yard, but occasionally would cry, calling for his mother, and wondering when she would come. His mother's absence seemed to be the great and only grief in his little heart. He was too young to realize his condition, and when the memory of his mother was not in his mind, he amused us with his pleasant pranks.

At night, Ray, Williams, and the boy, slept in the loft of the shed, while I was locked in the cell. Finally we were each provided with blankets, such as are used upon horses—the only bedding I was allowed to have for twelve years afterwards. Ray and Williams asked me many questions about New-York—how colored people were treated there; how they could have homes and families of their own, with none to disturb and oppress them; and Ray, especially, sighed continually for freedom. Such conversations, however, were not in the hearing of Burch, or the keeper Radburn. Aspirations such as these would have brought down the lash upon our backs.

It is necessary in this narrative, in order to present a full and truthful statement of all the principal events in the history of my life, and to portray the institution of Slavery as I have seen and known it, to speak of well-known places, and of many persons who are yet living. I am, and always was, an entire stranger in Washington and its vicinity—aside from Burch and Radburn, knowing no man there, except as I have heard of them through my enslaved companions. What I am about to say, if false, can be easily contradicted.

I remained in Williams' slave pen about two weeks. The night previous to my departure a woman was brought in, weeping bitterly, and leading by the hand a little child. They were Randall's mother and half-sister. On meeting them he was overjoyed, clinging to her dress, kissing the child, and exhibiting every demonstration of delight. The mother also clasped him in her arms, embraced him tenderly, and gazed at him fondly through her tears, calling him by many an endearing name.

Emily, the child, was seven or eight years old, of light complexion, and with a face of admirable beauty. Her hair fell in curls around her neck, while the style and richness of her dress, and the neatness of her whole appearance indicated she had been brought up in the midst of wealth. She was a sweet child indeed. The woman also was arrayed in silk, with rings upon her fingers, and golden ornaments suspended from her ears. Her air and manners, the correctness and propriety of her language—all showed, evidently, that she had sometime stood above the common level of a slave. She seemed to be amazed at finding herself in such a place as that. It was plainly a sudden and unexpected turn of fortune that had brought her there. Filling the air with her complainings, she was hustled, with the children and myself, into the cell. Language can convey but an inadequate impression of the lamentations to which she gave incessant utterance. Throwing herself upon the floor, and encircling the children in her arms, she poured forth such touching words as only maternal love and kindness can suggest. They nestled closely to her, as if *there* only was there any safety or protection. At last they slept, their heads resting upon her lap. While they slumbered, she smoothed the hair back from their little foreheads, and talked to them all night long. She called them her darlings—her sweet babes—poor innocent things, that knew not the misery they were destined to endure. Soon they would have no mother to comfort them—they would be taken from her. What would become of them? Oh! she could not live away from her little

Emmy and her dear boy. They had always been good children, and had such loving ways. It would break her heart, God knew, she said, if they were taken from her; and yet she knew they meant to sell them, and, may be, they would be separated, and could never see each other any more. It was enough to melt a heart of stone to listen to the pitiful expressions of that desolate and distracted mother. Her name was Eliza; and this was the story of her life, as she afterwards related it:

She was the slave of Elisha Berry, a rich man, living in the neighborhood of Washington. She was born, I think she said, on his plantation. Years before, he had fallen into dissipated habits, and quarreled with his wife. In fact, soon after the birth of Randall, they separated. Leaving his wife and daughter in the house they had always occupied, he erected a new one near by, on the estate. Into this house he brought Eliza; and, on condition of her living with him, she and her children were to be emancipated. She resided with him there nine years, with servants to attend upon her, and provided with every comfort and luxury of life. Emily was his child! Finally, her young mistress, who had always remained with her mother at the homestead, married a Mr. Jacob Brooks. At length, for some cause (as I gathered from her relation) beyond Berry's control, a division of his property was made. She and her children fell to the share of Mr. Brooks. During the nine years she had lived with Berry, in consequence of the position she was compelled to occupy, she and Emily had become the object of Mrs. Berry and her daughter's hatred and dislike. Berry himself she represented as a man of naturally a kind heart, who always promised her that she should have her freedom, and who, she had no doubt, would grant it to her then, if it were only in his power. As soon as they thus came into possession and control of the daughter, it became very manifest they would not live long together. The sight of Eliza seemed to be odious to Mrs. Brooks; neither could she bear to look upon the child, half-sister, and beautiful as she was!

The day she was led into the pen, Brooks had brought her from the estate into the city, under pretence that the time had come when her free papers were to be executed, in fulfillment of her master's promise. Elated at the prospect of immediate liberty, she decked herself and little Emmy in their best apparel, and accompanied him with a joyful heart. On their arrival in the city, instead of being baptized into the family of freemen, she was delivered to the trader Burch. The paper that was executed was a bill of sale. The hope of years was blasted in a moment. From the height of most exulting happiness to the utmost depths of wretchedness, she had that day descended. No wonder that she wept, and filled the pen with wailings and expressions of heart-rending woe.

Eliza is now dead. Far up the Red River, where it pours its waters sluggishly through the unhealthy low lands of Louisiana, she rests in the grave at last—the only resting place of the poor slave! How all her fears were realized—how she mourned day and night, and never would be comforted—how, as she predicted, her heart did indeed break, with the burden of maternal sorrow, will be seen as the narrative proceeds.

IV

Eliza's sorrows.—Preparation to embark.—Driven through the streets of Washington.—Hail, Columbia.—The tomb of Washington.—Clem Ray.—The breakfast on the steamer.—The happy birds.—Aquia Creek.—Fredericksburgh.—Arrival in Richmond.—Goodin and his slave pen.—Robert, of Cincinnati.—David and his wife.—Mary and Lethe.—Clem's return.— His subsequent escape to Canada.— The brig Orleans.—James H. Burch.

At intervals during the first night of Eliza's incarceration in the pen, she complained bitterly of Jacob Brooks, her young mistress' husband. She declared that had she been aware of the deception he intended to practice upon her, he never would have brought her there alive. They had chosen the opportunity of getting her away when Master Berry was absent from the plantation. He had always been kind to her. She wished that she could see him; but she knew that even he was unable now to rescue her. Then would she commence weeping again—kissing the sleeping children—talking first to one, then to the other, as they lay in their unconscious slumbers, with their heads upon her lap. So wore the long night away; and when the morning dawned, and night had come again, still she kept mourning on, and would not be consoled.

About midnight following, the cell door opened, and Burch and Radburn entered, with lanterns in their hands. Burch, with an oath, ordered us to roll up our blankets without delay, and get ready to go on board the boat. He swore we would be left unless we hurried fast. He aroused the children from their slumbers with a rough shake, and said they were d——d sleepy, it appeared. Going out into the yard, he called Clem Ray, ordering him to leave the loft and come into the cell, and bring his blanket with him. When Clem appeared, he placed us side by side, and fastened us together with hand-cuffs—my left hand to his right. John Williams had been taken out a day or two before, his master having redeemed him, greatly to his delight. Clem and I were ordered to march, Eliza and the children following. We were conducted into the yard, from thence into the covered passage, and up a flight of steps through a side door into the upper room, where I had heard the walking to and fro. Its furniture was a stove, a few old chairs, and a long table, covered with papers. It was a white-washed room, without any carpet on the floor, and seemed a sort of office. By one of the windows, I remember, hung a rusty sword, which attracted my attention. Burch's trunk was there. In obedience to his orders, I took hold of one of its handles with my unfettered hand, while he taking hold of the other, we proceeded out of the front door into the street in the same order as we had left the cell.

It was a dark night. All was quiet. I could see lights, or the reflection of them, over towards Pennsylvania Avenue, but there was no one, not even a straggler, to be seen. I was almost resolved to attempt to break away. Had I not been hand-cuffed the attempt would certainly have been made, whatever consequence might have followed. Radburn was in the rear, carrying a large stick, and hurrying up the children as fast as the little ones could walk. So we passed, hand-cuffed and in silence, through the streets of Washington—through the Capital of a nation, whose theory of government, we are told, rests on the foundation of man's inalienable right to life, LIBERTY, and the pursuit of happiness! Hail! Columbia, happy land, indeed!

Reaching the steamboat, we were quickly hustled into the hold, among barrels and boxes of freight. A colored servant brought a light, the bell rung, and soon the vessel started down the Potomac, carrying us we knew not where. The bell tolled as we passed the tomb of Washington! Burch, no doubt, with uncovered head, bowed reverently before the sacred ashes of the man who devoted his illustrious life to the liberty of his country.

None of us slept that night but Randall and little Emmy. For the first time Clem Ray was wholly overcome. To him the idea of going south was terrible in the extreme. He was leaving the friends and associations of his youth—every thing that was dear and precious to his heart—in all probability never to return. He and Eliza mingled their tears together, bemoaning their cruel fate. For my own part, difficult as it was, I endeavored to keep up my spirits. I resolved in my mind a hundred plans of escape, and fully determined to make the attempt the first desperate chance that offered. I had by this time become satisfied, however, that my true policy was to say nothing further on the subject of my having been born a freeman. It would but expose me to mal-treatment, and diminish the chances of liberation.

After sunrise in the morning we were called up on deck to breakfast. Burch took our hand-cuffs off, and we sat down to table. He asked Eliza if she would take a dram. She declined, thanking him politely. During the meal we were all silent—not a word passed between us. A mulatto woman who served at table seemed to take an interest in our behalf—told us to cheer up, and not to be so cast down. Breakfast over, the hand-cuffs were restored, and Burch ordered us out on the stern deck. We sat down together on some boxes, still saying nothing in Burch's presence. Occasionally a passenger would walk out to where we were, look at us for a while, then silently return.

It was a very pleasant morning. The fields along the river were covered with verdure, far in advance of what I had been accustomed to see at that season of the year. The sun shone out warmly; the birds were singing in the trees. The happy birds—I envied them. I wished for wings like them, that I might cleave the air to where my birdlings waited vainly for their father's coming, in the cooler region of the North.

In the forenoon the streamer reached Aquia Creek. There the passengers took stages—Burch and his five slaves occupying one exclusively. He laughed with the children, and at one stopping place went so far as to purchase them a piece of gingerbread. He told me to hold up my head and look smart. That I might, perhaps, get a good master if I behaved myself. I made him no reply. His face was hateful to me, and I could not bear to look upon it. I sat in the corner, cherishing in my heart the hope, not yet extinct, of some day meeting the tyrant on the soil of my native State.

At Fredericksburgh we were transferred from the stage coach to a car, and before dark arrived in Richmond, the chief city of Virginia. At this city we were taken from the cars, and driven through the street to a slave pen, between the railroad depot and the river, kept by a Mr. Goodin. This pen is similar to Williams' in Washington, except it is somewhat larger; and besides, there were two small houses standing at opposite corners within the yard. These houses are usually found within slave yards, being used as rooms for the examination of human chattels by purchasers before concluding a bargain. Unsoundness in a slave, as well as in a horse, detracts materially from his value. If no warranty is given, a close examination is a matter of particular importance to the negro jockey.

We were met at the door of Goodin's yard by that gentleman himself—a short, fat man, with a round, plump face, black hair and whiskers, and a complexion almost as dark as some of his own negroes. He had a hard, stern look, and was perhaps about fifty years of age. Burch and he met with great cordiality. They were evidently old friends. Shaking each other warmly by the hand, Burch remarked he had brought some company, inquired at what time the brig would leave, and was answered that it would probably leave the next day at such an hour. Goodin then turned to look at me, took hold of my arm, turned me partly round, looked at me sharply with the air of one who considered himself a good judge of property, and as if estimating in his own mind about how much I was worth.

"Well, boy, where did you come from?"

Forgetting myself, for a moment, I answered, "From New-York."

"New-York! H——l! what have you been doing up there?" was his astonished interrogatory.

Observing Burch at this moment looking at me with an angry expression that conveyed a meaning it was not difficult to understand, I immediately said, "O, I have only been up that way a piece," in a manner intended to imply that although I might have been as far as New-York, yet I wished it distinctly understood that I did not belong to that free State, nor to any other.

Goodin then turned to Clem, and then to Eliza and the children, examining them severally, and asking various questions. He was pleased with Emily, as was every one who saw the child's sweet countenance. She was not as tidy as when I first beheld her; her hair was now somewhat disheveled; but through its unkempt and soft profusion there still beamed a little face of most surpassing loveliness. "Altogether we were a fair lot—a devilish good lot," he said, enforcing that opinion with more than one emphatic adjective not found in the Christian vocabulary. Thereupon we passed into the yard. Quite a number of slaves, as many as thirty I should say, were moving about, or sitting on benches under the shed. They were all cleanly dressed—the men with hats, the women with handkerchiefs tied about their heads.

Burch and Goodin, after separating from us, walked up the steps at the back part of the main building, and sat down upon the door sill. They entered into conversation, but the subject of it I could not hear. Presently Burch came down into the yard, unfettered me, and led me into one of the small houses.

"You told that man you came from New-York," said he.

I replied, "I told him I had been up as far as New-York, to be sure, but did not tell him I belonged there, nor that I was a freeman. I meant no harm at all, Master Burch. I would not have said it had I thought."

He looked at me a moment as if he was ready to devour me, then turning round went out. In a few minutes he returned. "If ever I hear you say a word about New-York, or about your freedom, I will be the death of you—I will kill you; you may rely on that," he ejaculated fiercely.

I doubt not he understood then better than I did, the danger and the penalty of selling a free man into slavery. He felt the necessity of closing my mouth against the crime he knew he was committing. Of course, my life would not have weighed a feather, in any emergency requring such a sacrifice. Undoubtedly, he meant precisely what he said.

Under the shed on one side of the yard, there was constructed a rough table, while overhead were sleeping lofts—the same as in the pen at Washington. After partaking at this table of our supper of pork and bread, I was hand-cuffed to a large yellow man, quite stout and fleshy, with a countenance expressive of the utmost melancholy. He was a man of intelligence and information. Chained together, it was not long before we became acquainted with each other's history. His name was Robert. Like myself, he had been born free, and had a wife and two children in Cincinnati. He said he had come south with two men, who had hired him in the city of his residence. Without free papers, he had been seized at Fredericksburgh, placed in confinement, and beaten until he had learned, as I had, the necessity and the policy of silence. He had been in Goodin's pen about three weeks. To this man I became much attached. We could sympathize with, and understand each other. It was with tears and a heavy heart, not many days subsequently, that I saw him die, and looked for the last time upon his lifeless form!

Robert and myself, with Clem, Eliza and her children, slept that night upon our blankets, in one of the small houses in the yard. There were four others, all from the same plantation, who had been sold, and were now on their way south, who also occupied it with us. David and his wife, Caroline, both mulattoes, were exceedingly affected. They dreaded the thought of being put into the cane and cotton fields; but their greatest source of anxiety was the apprehension of being separated. Mary, a tall, lithe girl, of a most jetty black, was listless and apparently indifferent. Like many of the class, she scarcely knew there was such a word as freedom. Brought up in the ignorance of a brute, she possessed but little more than a brute's intelligence. She was one of those, and there are very many, who fear nothing but their master's lash, and know no further duty than to obey his voice. The other was Lethe. She was of an entirely different character. She had long, straight hair, and bore more the appearance of an Indian than a negro woman. She had sharp and spiteful eyes, and continually gave utterance to the language of hatred and revenge. Her husband had been sold. She knew not where she was. An exchange of masters, she was sure, could not be for the worse. She cared not whither they might carry her. Pointing to the scars upon her face, the desperate creature wished that she might see the day when she could wipe them off in some man's blood!

While we were thus learning the history of each other's wretchedness, Eliza was seated in a corner by herself, singing hymns and praying for her children. Wearied from the loss of so much sleep, I could no longer bear up against the advances of that "sweet restorer," and laying down by the side of Robert, on the floor, soon forgot my troubles, and slept until the dawn of day.

In the morning, having swept the yard, and washed ourselves under Goodin's superintendence, we were ordered to roll up our blankets, and make ready for the continuance of our journey. Clem Ray was informed that he would go no further, Burch, for some cause, having concluded to carry him back to Washington. He was much rejoiced. Shaking hands, we parted in the slave pen at Richmond, and I have not seen him since. But, much to my surprise, since my return, I learned that he had escaped from bondage, and on his way to the free soil of Canada, lodged one night at the house of my brother-in-law in Saratoga, informing my family of the place and the condition in which he left me.

In the afternoon we were drawn up, two abreast, Robert and myself in advance, and in this order, driven by Burch and Goodin from the yard, through the streets of Richmond to the brig Orleans. She was a vessel of respectable size, full rigged, and freighted principally with tobacco. We were all on board by five o'clock. Burch brought us each a tin cup and a spoon. There were forty of us in the brig, being all, except Clem, that were in the pen.

With a small pocket knife that had not been taken from me, I began cutting the initials of my name upon the tin cup. The others immediately flocked round me, requesting me to mark theirs in a similar manner. In time, I gratified them all, of which they did not appear to be forgetful.

We were all stowed away in the hold at night, and the hatch barred down. We laid on boxes, or wherever there was room enough to stretch our blankets on the floor.

Burch accompanied us no farther than Richmond, returning from that point to the capital with Clem. Not until the lapse of almost twelve years, to wit, in January last, in the Washington police office, did I set my eyes upon his face again.

James H. Burch was a slave-trader—buying men, women and children at low prices, and selling them at an advance. He was a speculator in human flesh—a disreputable calling—and so considered at the South. For the present he disappears from the scenes recorded in this narrative, but he will appear again before its close, not in the character of a man-whipping tyrant, but as an arrested, cringing criminal in a court of law, that failed to do him justice.

V

Arrival at Norfolk.—Frederick and Maria.—Arthur, the freeman.—Appointed steward.—Jim, Cuffee, and Jenny.—The storm.—Bahama banks.—The calm.—The conspiracy.—The long boat.—The small-pox.—Death of Robert.—Manning, the sailor.—The meeting in the forecastle.—The letter.—Arrival at New-Orleans.—Arthur's rescue.—Theophilus Freeman, the consignee.—Platt.—First night in the New-Orleans slave pen.

After we were all on board, the brig Orleans proceeded down James River. Passing into Chesapeake Bay, we arrived next day opposite the city of Norfolk. While lying at anchor, a lighter approached us from the town, bringing four more slaves. Frederick, a boy of eighteen, had been born a slave, as also had Henry, who was some years older. They had both been house servants in the city. Maria was a rather genteel looking colored girl, with a faultless form, but ignorant and extremely vain. The idea of going to New-Orleans was pleasing to her. She entertained an extravagantly high opinion of her own attractions. Assuming a haughty mien, she declared to her companions, that immediately on our arrival in New-Orleans, she had no doubt, some wealthy single gentleman of good taste would purchase her at once!

But the most prominent of the four, was a man named Arthur. As the lighter approached, he struggled stoutly with his keepers. It was with main force that he was dragged aboard the brig. He protested, in a loud voice, against the treatment he was receiving, and demanded to be released. His face was swollen, and covered with wounds and bruises, and, indeed, one side of it was a complete raw sore. He was forced, with all haste, down the hatchway into the hold. I caught an outline of his story as he was borne struggling along, of which he afterwards gave me a more full relation, and it was as follows: He had long resided in the city of Norfolk, and was a free man. He had a family living there, and was a mason by trade. Having been unusually detained, he was returning late one night to his house in the suburbs of the city, when he was attacked by a gang of persons in an unfrequented street. He fought until his strength failed him. Overpowered at last, he was gagged and bound with ropes, and beaten, until he became insensible. For several days they secreted him in the slave pen at Norfolk —a very common establishment, it appears, in the cities of the South. The night before, he had been taken out and put on board the lighter, which, pushing out from shore, had awaited our arrival. For some time he continued his protestations, and was altogether irreconcilable. At length, however, he became silent. He sank into a gloomy and thoughtful mood, and appeared to be counseling with himself. There was in the man's determined face, something that suggested the thought of desperation.

After leaving Norfolk the hand-cuffs were taken off, and during the day we were allowed to remain on deck. The captain selected Robert as his waiter, and I was appointed to superintend the cooking department, and the distribution of food and water. I had three assistants, Jim, Cuffee and Jenny. Jenny's business was to prepare the coffee, which consisted of corn meal scorched in a kettle, boiled and sweetened with molasses. Jim and Cuffee baked the hoe-cake and boiled the bacon.

Standing by a table, formed of a wide board resting on the heads of the barrels, I cut and handed to each a slice of meat and a "dodger" of the bread, and from Jenny's kettle also dipped out for each a cup of the coffee. The use of plates was dispensed with, and their sable fingers took the place of knives and forks. Jim and Cuffee were very demure and attentive to business, somewhat inflated with their situation as second cooks, and without doubt feeling that there was a great responsibility resting on them. I was called steward—a name given me by the captain.

The slaves were fed twice a day, at ten and five o'clock—always receiving the same kind and quantity of fare, and in the same manner as above described. At night we were driven into the hold, and securely fastened down.

Scarcely were we out of sight of land before we were overtaken by a violent storm. The brig rolled and plunged until we feared she would go down. Some were sea-sick, others on their knees praying, while some were fast holding to each other, paralyzed with fear. The sea-sickness rendered the place of our confinement loathsome and disgusting. It would have been a happy thing for most of us—it would have saved the agony of many hundred lashes, and miserable deaths at last—had the compassionate sea snatched us that day from the clutches of remorseless men. The thought of Randall and little Emmy sinking down among the monsters of the deep, is a more pleasant contemplation than to think of them as they are now, perhaps, dragging out lives of unrequited toil.

When in sight of the Bahama Banks, at a place called Old Point Compass, or the Hole in the Wall, we were becalmed three days. There was scarcely a breath of air. The waters of the gulf presented a singularly white appearance, like lime water.

In the order of events, I come now to the relation of an occurrence, which I never call to mind but with sensations of regret. I thank God, who has since permitted me to escape from the thralldom of slavery, that through his merciful interposition I was prevented from imbruing my hands in the blood of his creatures. Let not those who have never been placed in like circumstances, judge me harshly. Until they have been chained and beaten—until they find themselves in the situation I was, borne away from home and family towards a land of bondage—let them refrain from saying what they would not do for liberty. How far I should have been justified in the sight of God and man, it is unnecessary now to speculate upon. It is enough to say that I am able to congratulate myself upon the harmless termination of an affair which threatened, for a time, to be attended with serious results.

Towards evening, on the first day of the calm, Arthur and myself were in the bow of the vessel, seated on the windlass. We were conversing together of the probable destiny that awaited us, and mourning together over our misfortunes. Arthur said, and I agreed with him, that death was far less terrible than the living prospect that was before us. For a long time we talked of our children, our past lives, and of the probabilities of escape. Obtaining possession of the brig was suggested by one of us. We discussed the possibility of our being able, in such an event, to make our way to the harbor of New-York. I knew little of the compass; but the idea of risking the experiment was eagerly entertained. The chances, for and against us, in an encounter with the crew, was canvassed. Who could be relied upon, and who could not, the proper time and manner of the attack, were all talked over and over again. From the moment the plot suggested itself I began to hope. I revolved it constantly in my mind. As difficulty after difficulty arose, some ready conceit was at hand, demonstrating how it could be overcome. While others slept, Arthur and I were maturing our plans. At length, with much caution, Robert was gradually made acquainted with our intentions. He approved of them at once, and entered into the conspiracy with a zealous spirit. There was not another slave we dared to trust. Brought up in fear and ignorance as they are, it can scarcely be conceived how servilely they will cringe before a white man's look. It was not safe to deposit so bold a secret with any of them, and finally we three resolved to take upon ourselves alone the fearful responsibility of the attempt.

At night, as has been said, we were driven into the hold, and the hatch barred down. How to reach the deck was the first difficulty that presented itself. On the bow of the brig, however, I had observed the small boat lying bottom upwards. It occurred to me that by secreting ourselves underneath it, we would not be missed from the crowd, as they were hurried down into the hold at night. I was selected to make the experiment, in order to satisfy ourselves of its feasibility. The next evening, accordingly, after supper, watching my opportunity, I hastily concealed myself beneath it. Lying close upon the deck, I could see what was going on around me, while wholly unperceived myself. In the morning, as they came up, I slipped from my hiding place without being observed. The result was entirely satisfactory.

The captain and mate slept in the cabin of the former. From Robert, who had frequent occasion, in his capacity of waiter, to make observations in that quarter, we ascertained the exact position of their respective berths. He further informed us that there were always two pistols and a cutlass lying on the table. The crew's cook slept in the cook galley on deck, a sort of vehicle on wheels, that could be moved about as convenience required, while the sailors, numbering only six, either slept in the forecastle, or in hammocks swung among the rigging.

Finally our arrangements were all completed. Arthur and I were to steal silently to the captain's cabin, seize the pistols and cutlass, and as quickly as possible despatch him and the mate. Robert, with a club, was to stand by the door leading from the deck down into the cabin, and, in case of necessity, beat back the sailors, until we could hurry to his assistance. We were to proceed then as circumstances might require. Should the attack be so sudden and successful as to prevent resistance, the hatch was to remain barred down;

otherwise the slaves were to be called up, and in the crowd, and hurry, and confusion of the time, we resolved to regain our liberty or lose our lives. I was then to assume the unaccustomed place of pilot, and, steering northward, we trusted that some lucky wind might bear us to the soil of freedom.

The mate's name was Biddee, the captain's I cannot now recall, though I rarely ever forget a name once heard. The captain was a small, genteel man, erect and prompt, with a proud bearing, and looked the personification of courage. If he is still living, and these pages should chance to meet his eye, he will learn a fact connected with the voyage of the brig, from Richmond to New-Orleans, in 1841, not entered on his log-book.

We were all prepared, and impatiently waiting an opportunity of putting our designs into execution, when they were frustrated by a sad and unforeseen event. Robert was taken ill. It was soon announced that he had the small-pox. He continued to grow worse, and four days previous to our arrival in New-Orleans he died. One of the sailors sewed him in his blanket, with a large stone from the ballast at his feet, and then laying him on a hatchway, and elevating it with tackles above the railing, the inanimate body of poor Robert was consigned to the white waters of the gulf.

We were all panic-stricken by the appearance of the small-pox. The captain ordered lime to be scattered through the hold, and other prudent precautions to be taken. The death of Robert, however, and the presence of the malady, oppressed me sadly, and I gazed out over the great waste of waters with a spirit that was indeed disconsolate.

An evening or two after Robert's burial, I was leaning on the hatchway near the forecastle, full of desponding thoughts, when a sailor in a kind voice asked me why I was so down-hearted. The tone and manner of the man assured me, and I answered, because I was a freeman, and had been kidnapped. He remarked that it was enough to make any one down-hearted, and continued to interrogate me until he learned the particulars of my whole history. He was evidently much interested in my behalf, and, in the blunt speech of a sailor, swore he would aid me all he could, if it "split his timbers." I requested him to furnish me pen, ink and paper, in order that I might write to some of my friends. He promised to obtain them—but how I could use them undiscovered was a difficulty. If I could only get into the forecastle while his watch was off, and the other sailors asleep, the thing could be accomplished. The small boat instantly occurred to me. He thought we were not far from the Balize, at the mouth of the Mississippi, and it was necessary that the letter be written soon, or the opportunity would be lost. Accordingly, by arrangement, I managed the next night to secret myself again under the long-boat. His watch was off at twelve. I saw him pass into the forecastle, and in about an hour followed him. He was nodding over a table, half asleep, on which a sickly light was flickering, and on which also was a pen and sheet of paper. As I entered he aroused, beckoned me to a seat beside him, and pointed to the paper. I directed the letter to Henry B. Northup, of Sandy Hill—stating that I had been kidnapped, was then on board the brig Orleans, bound for New-Orleans; that it was then impossible for me to conjecture my ultimate destination, and requesting he would take measures to rescue me. The letter was sealed and directed, and Manning, having read it, promised to deposit it in the New-Orleans post-office. I hastened back to my place under the long-boat, and in the morning, as the slaves came up and were walking around, crept out unnoticed and mingled with them.

My good friend, whose name was John Manning, was an Englishman by birth, and a noble-hearted, generous sailor as ever walked a deck. He had lived in Boston—was a tall, well-built man, about twenty-four years old, with a face somewhat pock-marked, but full of benevolent expression.

Nothing to vary the monotony of our daily life occurred, until we reached New-Orleans. On coming to the levee, and before the vessel was made fast, I saw Manning leap on shore and hurry away into the city. As he started off he looked back over his shoulder significantly, giving me to understand the object of his errand. Presently he returned, and passing close by me, hunched me with his elbow, with a peculiar wink, as much as to say, "it is all right."

The letter, as I have since learned, reached Sandy Hill. Mr. Northup visited Albany and laid it before Governor Seward, but inasmuch as it gave no definite information as to my probable locality, it was not, at that time, deemed advisable to institute measures for my liberation. It was concluded to delay, trusting that a knowledge of where I was might eventually be obtained.

A happy and touching scene was witnessed immediately upon our reaching the levee. Just as Manning left the brig, on his way to the post office, two men came up and called aloud for Arthur. The latter, as he recognized them, was almost crazy with delight. He could hardly be restrained from leaping over the brig's side; and when they met soon after, he grasped them by the hand, and clung to them a long, long time. They were men from Norfolk, who had come on to New-Orleans to rescue him. His kidnappers, they informed him, had been arrested, and were then confined in the Norfolk prison. They conversed a few moments with the captain, and then departed with the rejoicing Arthur.

But in all the crowd that thronged the wharf, there was no one who knew or cared for me. Not one. No familiar voice greeted my ears, nor was there a single face that I had ever seen. Soon Arthur would rejoin his family, and have the satisfaction of seeing his wrongs avenged: my family, alas, should I ever see them more? There was a feeling of utter desolation in my heart, filling it with a despairing and regretful sense, that I had not gone down with Robert to the bottom of the sea.

Very soon traders and consignees came on board. One, a tall, thin-faced man, with light complexion and a little bent, made his appearance, with a paper in his hand. Burch's gang, consisting of myself, Eliza and her children, Harry, Lethe, and some others, who had joined us at Richmond, were consigned to him. This gentleman was Mr. Theophilus Freeman. Reading from his paper, he called, "Platt." No one answered. The name was called again and again, but still there was no reply. Then Lethe was called, then Eliza, then Harry, until the list was finished, each one stepping forward as his or her name was called.

"Captain, where's Platt?" demanded Theophilus Freeman.

The captain was unable to inform him, no one being on board answering to that name.

"Who shipped *that* nigger?" he again inquired of the captain, pointing to me.

"Burch," replied the captain.

"Your name is Platt—you answer my description. Why don't you come forward?" he demanded of me, in an angry tone.

I informed him that was not my name; that I had never been called by it, but that I had no objection to it as I knew of.

"Well, I will learn you your name," said he; "and so you won't forget it either, by——," he added.

Mr. Theophilus Freeman, by the way, was not a whit behind his partner, Burch, in the matter of blasphemy. On the vessel I had gone by the name of "Steward," and this was the first time I had ever been designated as Platt—the name forwarded by Burch to his consignee. From the vessel I observed the chain-gang at work on the levee. We passed near them as we were driven to Freeman's slave pen. This pen is very similar to Goodin's in Richmond, except the yard was enclosed by plank, standing upright, with ends sharpened, instead of brick walls.

Including us, there were now at least fifty in this pen. Depositing our blankets in one of the small buildings in the yard, and having been called up and fed, we were allowed to saunter about the enclosure until night, when we wrapped our blankets round us and laid down under the shed, or in the loft, or in the open yard, just as each one preferred.

It was but a short time I closed my eyes that night. Thought was busy in my brain. Could it be possible that I was thousands of miles from home—that I had been driven through the streets like a dumb beast—that I had been chained and beaten without mercy—that I was even then herded with a drove of slaves, a slave myself? Were the events of the last few weeks realities indeed?—or was I passing only through the dismal phases of a long, protracted dream? It was no illusion. My cup of sorrow was full to overflowing. Then I lifted up my hands to God, and in the still watches of the night, surrounded by the sleeping forms of my companions, begged for mercy on the poor, forsaken captive. To the Almighty Father of us all—the freeman and the slave—I poured forth the supplications of a broken spirit, imploring strength from on high to bear up against the burden of my troubles, until the morning light aroused the slumberers, ushering in another day of bondage.

VI

Freeman's industry.—Cleanliness and clothes.—Exercising in the show room.—The dance.—Bob, the fiddler.—Arrival of customers.—Slaves examined.—The old gentleman of New-Orleans.—Sale of David, Caroline and Lethe.—Parting of Randall and Eliza.—Small pox.—The hospital.—Recovery and return to freeman's slave pen.—The purchaser of Eliza, Harry and Platt.—Eliza's agony on parting from little Emily.

The very amiable, pious-hearted Mr. Theophilus Freeman, partner or consignee of James H. Burch, and keeper of the slave pen in New-Orleans, was out among his animals early in the morning. With an occasional kick of the older men and women, and many a sharp crack of the whip about the ears of the younger slaves, it was not long before they were all astir, and wide awake. Mr. Theophilus Freeman bustled about in a very industrious manner, getting his property ready for the sales-room, intending, no doubt, to do that day a rousing business.

In the first place we were required to wash thoroughly, and those with beards, to shave. We were then furnished with a new suit each, cheap, but clean. The men had hat, coat, shirt, pants and shoes; the women frocks of calico, and handkerchiefs to bind about their heads. We were now conducted into a large room in the front part of the building to which the yard was attached, in order to be properly trained, before the admission of customers. The men were arranged on one side of the room, the women on the other. The tallest was placed at the head of the row, then the next tallest, and so on in the order of their respective heights. Emily was at the foot of the line of women. Freeman charged us to remember our places; exhorted us to appear smart and lively,—sometimes threatening, and again, holding out various inducements. During the day he exercised us in the art of "looking smart," and of moving to our places with exact precision.

After being fed, in the afternoon, we were again paraded and made to dance. Bob, a colored boy, who had some time belonged to Freeman, played on the violin. Standing near him, I made bold to inquire if he could play the "Virginia Reel." He answered he could not, and asked me if I could play. Replying in the affirmative, he handed me the violin. I struck up a tune, and finished it. Freeman ordered me to continue playing, and seemed well pleased, telling Bob that I far excelled him—a remark that seemed to grieve my musical companion very much.

Next day many customers called to examine Freeman's "new lot." The latter gentleman was very loquacious, dwelling at much length upon our several good points and qualities. He would make us hold up our heads, walk briskly back and forth, while customers would feel of our hands and arms and bodies, turn us about, ask us what we could do, make us open our mouths and show our teeth, precisely as a jockey examines a horse which he is about to barter for or purchase. Sometimes a man or woman was taken back to the small house in the yard, stripped, and inspected more minutely. Scars upon a slave's back were considered evidence of a rebellious or unruly spirit, and hurt his sale.

One old gentleman, who said he wanted a coachman, appeared to take a fancy to me. From his conversation with Freeman, I learned he was a resident in the city. I very much desired that he would buy me, because I conceived it would not be difficult to make my escape from New-Orleans on some northern vessel. Freeman asked him fifteen hundred dollars for me. The old gentleman insisted it was too much, as times were very hard. Freeman, however, declared that I was sound and healthy, of a good constitution, and intelligent. He made it a point to enlarge upon my musical attainments. The old gentleman argued quite adroitly that there was nothing extraordinary about the nigger, and finally, to my regret, went out, saying he would call again. During the day, however, a number of sales were made. David and Caroline were purchased together by a Natchez planter. They left us, grinning broadly, and in the most happy state of mind, caused by the fact of their not being separated. Lethe was sold to a planter of Baton Rouge, her eyes flashing with anger as she was led away.

The same man also purchased Randall. The little fellow was made to jump, and run across the floor, and perform many other feats, exhibiting his activity and condition. All the time the trade was going on, Eliza was crying aloud, and wringing her hands. She besought the man not to buy him, unless he also bought herself and Emily. She promised, in that case, to be the most faithful slave that ever lived. The man answered that he could not afford it, and then Eliza burst into a paroxysm of grief, weeping plaintively. Freeman turned round to her, savagely, with his whip in his uplifted hand, ordering her to stop her noise, or he would flog her. He would not have such work—such snivelling; and unless she ceased that minute, he would take her to the yard and give her a hundred lashes. Yes, he would take the nonsense out of her pretty quick—if he didn't, might he be d——d. Eliza shrunk before him, and tried to wipe away her tears, but it was all in vain. She wanted to be with her children, she said, the little time she had to live. All the frowns and threats of Freeman, could not wholly silence the afflicted mother. She kept on begging and beseeching them, most piteously, not to separate the three. Over and over again she told them how she loved her boy. A great many times she repeated her former promises—how very faithful and obedient she would be; how hard she would labor day and night, to the last moment of her life, if he would only buy them all together. But it was of no avail; the man could not afford it. The bargain was agreed upon, and Randall must go alone. Then Eliza ran to him; embraced him passionately; kissed him again and again; told him to remember her—all the while her tears falling in the boy's face like rain.

Freeman damned her, calling her a blubbering, bawling wench, and ordered her to go to her place, and behave herself, and be somebody. He swore he wouldn't stand such stuff but a little longer. He would soon give her something to cry about, if she was not mighty careful, and that she might depend upon.

The planter from Baton Rouge, with his new purchases, was ready to depart.

"Don't cry, mama. I will be a good boy. Don't cry," said Randall, looking back, as they passed out of the door.

What has become of the lad, God knows. It was a mournful scene indeed. I would have cried myself if I had dared.

That night, nearly all who came in on the brig Orleans, were taken ill. They complained of violent pain in the head and back. Little Emily—a thing unusual with her—cried constantly. In the morning a physician was called in, but was unable to determine the nature of our complaint. While examining me, and asking questions touching my symptoms, I gave it as my opinion that it was an attack of small-pox—mentioning the fact of Robert's death as the reason of my belief. It might be so indeed, he thought, and he would send for the head physician of the hospital. Shortly, the head physician came—a small, light-haired man, whom they called Dr. Carr. He pronounced it small-pox, whereupon there was much alarm throughout the yard. Soon after Dr. Carr left, Eliza, Emmy, Harry and myself were put into a hack and driven to the hospital—a large white marble building, standing on the outskirts of the city. Harry and I were placed in a room in one of the upper stories. I became very sick. For three days I was entirely blind. While lying in this state one day, Bob came in, saying to Dr. Carr that Freeman had sent him over to inquire how we were getting on. Tell him, said the doctor, that Platt is very bad, but that if he survives until nine o'clock, he may recover.

I expected to die. Though there was little in the prospect before me worth living for, the near approach of death appalled me. I thought I could have been resigned to yield up my life in the bosom of my family, but to expire in the midst of strangers, under such circumstances, was a bitter reflection.

There were a great number in the hospital, of both sexes, and of all ages. In the rear of the building coffins were manufactured. When one died, the bell tolled—a signal to the undertaker to come and bear away the body to the potter's field. Many times, each day and night, the tolling bell sent forth its melancholy voice, announcing another death. But my time had not yet come. The crisis having passed, I began to revive, and at the end of two weeks and two days, returned with Harry to the pen, bearing upon my face the effects of the malady, which to this day continues to disfigure it. Eliza and Emily were also brought back next day in a hack, and again were we paraded in the sales-room, for the inspection and examination of purchasers. I still indulged the hope that the old gentleman in search of a coachman would call again, as he had promised, and purchase me. In that event I felt an abiding confidence that I would soon regain my liberty. Customer after customer entered, but the old gentleman never made his appearance.

At length, one day, while we were in the yard, Freeman came out and ordered us to our places, in the great room. A gentleman was waiting for us as we entered, and inasmuch as he will be often mentioned in the progress of this narrative, a description of his personal appearance, and my estimation of his character, at first sight, may not be out of place.

He was a man above the ordinary height somewhat bent and stooping forward. He was a good looking man, and appeared to have reached about the middle age of life. There was nothing repulsive in his presence; but on the other hand, there was something cheerful and attractive in his face, and in his tone of voice. The finer elements were all kindly mingled in his breast, as any one could see. He moved about among us, asking many questions, as to what we could do, and what labor we had been accustomed to; if we thought we would like to live with him, and would be good boys if he would buy us, and other interrogatories of like character.

After some further inspection, and conversation touching prices, he finally offered Freeman one thousand dollars for me, nine hundred for Harry, and seven hundred for Eliza. Whether the small-pox had depreciated our value, or from what cause Freeman had concluded to fall five hundred dollars from the price I was before held at, I cannot say. At any rate, after a little shrewd reflection, he announced his acceptance of the offer.

As soon as Eliza heard it, she was in an agony again. By this time she had become haggard and hollow-eyed with sickness and with sorrow. It would be a relief if I could consistently pass over in silence the scene that now ensued. It recalls memories more mournful and affecting than any language can portray. I have seen mothers kissing for the last time the faces of their dead offspring; I have seen them looking down into the grave, as the earth fell with a dull sound upon their coffins, hiding them from their eyes forever; but never have I seen such an exhibition of intense, unmeasured, and unbounded grief, as when Eliza was parted from her child. She broke from her place in the line of women, and rushing down where Emily was standing, caught her in her arms. The child, sensible of some impending danger, instinctively fastened her hands around her mother's neck, and nestled her little head upon her bosom. Freeman sternly ordered her to be quiet, but she did not heed him. He caught her by the arm and pulled her rudely, but she only clung the closer to the child. Then, with a volley of great oaths, he struck her such a heartless blow, that she staggered backward, and was like to fall. Oh! how piteously then did she beseech and beg and pray that they might not be separated. Why could they not be purchased together? Why not let her have one of her dear children? "Mercy, mercy, master!" she cried, falling on her knees. "Please, master, buy Emily. I can never work any if she is taken from me: I will die."

Freeman interfered again, but, disregarding him, she still plead most earnestly, telling how Randall had been taken from her—how she never would see him again, and now it was too bad—oh, God! it was too bad, too cruel, to take her away from Emily—her pride—her only darling, that could not live, it was so young, without its mother!

Finally, after much more of supplication, the purchaser of Eliza stepped forward, evidently affected, and said to Freeman he would buy Emily, and asked him what her price was.

"What is her *price? Buy* her?" was the responsive interrogatory of Theophilus Freeman. And instantly answering his own inquiry, he added, "I won't sell her. She's not for sale."

The man remarked he was not in need of one so young—that it would be of no profit to him, but since the mother was so fond of her, rather than see them separated, he would pay a reasonable price. But to this humane proposal Freeman was entirely deaf. He would not sell her then on any account whatever. There were heaps and piles of money to be made of her, he said, when she was a few years older. There were men enough in New-Orleans who would give five thousand dollars for such an extra, handsome, fancy piece as Emily would be, rather than not get her. No, no, he would not sell her then. She was a beauty—a picture—a doll—one of the regular bloods—none of your thick-lipped, bullet-headed, cotton-picking niggers—if she was might he be d——d.

When Eliza heard Freeman's determination not to part with Emily, she became absolutely frantic.

"I will *not* go without her. They shall *not* take her from me," she fairly shrieked, her shrieks commingling with the loud and angry voice of Freeman, commanding her to be silent.

Meantime Harry and myself had been to the yard and returned with our blankets, and were at the front door ready to leave. Our purchaser stood near us, gazing at Eliza with an expression indicative of regret at having bought her at the expense of so much sorrow. We waited some time, when, finally, Freeman, out of patience, tore Emily from her mother by main force, the two clinging to each other with all their might.

"Don't leave me, mama—don't leave me," screamed the child, as its mother was pushed harshly forward; "Don't leave me—come back, mama," she still cried, stretching forth her little arms imploringly. But she cried in vain. Out of the door and into the street we were quickly hurried. Still we could hear her calling to her mother, "Come back—don't leave me—come back, mama," until her infant voice grew faint and still more faint, and gradually died away, as distance intervened, and finally was wholly lost.

Eliza never after saw or heard of Emily or Randall. Day nor night, however, were they ever absent from her memory. In the cotton field, in the cabin, always and everywhere, she was talking of them—often *to* them, as if they were actually present. Only when absorbed in that illusion, or asleep, did she ever have a moment's comfort afterwards.

She was no common slave, as has been said. To a large share of natural intelligence which she possessed, was added a general knowledge and information on most subjects. She had enjoyed opportunities such as are afforded to a very few of her oppressed class. She had been lifted up into the regions of a higher life. Freedom—freedom for herself and for her offspring, for many years had been her cloud by day, her pillar of fire by night. In her pilgrimage through the wilderness of bondage, with eyes fixed upon that hope-inspiring beacon, she had at length ascended to "the top of Pisgah," and beheld "the land of promise." In an unexpected moment she was utterly overwhelmed with disappointment and despair. The glorious vision of liberty faded from her sight as they led her away into captivity. Now "she weepeth sore in the night, and tears are on her cheeks, all her friends have dealt treacherously with her: they have become her enemies."

VII

The steamboat Rodolph.—Departure from New-Orleans.—William Ford.—Arrival at Alexandria, on Red River.—Resolutions.—The great pine woods.—Wild cattle.—Martin's summer residence.—The Texas road.—Arrival at Master Ford's.—Rose.—Mistress Ford.—Sally, and her children.—John, the cook.—Walter, Sam, and Antony.—The mills on Indian Creek.—Sabbath days.—Sam's conversion.—The profit of kindness.—Rafting.—Adam Taydem, the little white man.—Cascalla and his tribe.—The Indian ball.—John M. Tibeats.—The storm approaching.

On leaving the New-Orleans slave pen, Harry and I followed our new master through the streets, while Eliza, crying and turning back, was forced along by Freeman and his minions, until we found ourselves on board the steamboat Rodolph, then lying at the levee. In the course of half an hour we were moving briskly up the Mississippi, bound for some point on Red River. There were quite a number of slaves on board beside ourselves, just purchased in the New-Orleans market. I remember a Mr. Kelsow, who was said to be a well known and extensive planter, had in charge a gang of women.

Our master's name was William Ford. He resided then in the "Great Pine Woods," in the parish of Avoyelles, situated on the right bank of Red River, in the heart of Louisiana. He is now a Baptist preacher. Throughout the whole parish of Avoyelles, and especially along both shores of Bayou Bœuf, where he is more intimately known, he is accounted by his fellow-citizens as a worthy minister of God. In many northern minds, perhaps, the idea of a man holding his brother man in servitude, and the traffic in human flesh, may seem altogether incompatible with their conceptions of a moral or religious life. From descriptions of such men as Burch and Freeman, and others hereinafter mentioned, they are led to despise and execrate the whole class of slaveholders, indiscriminately. But I was sometime his slave, and had an opportunity of learning well his character and disposition, and it is but simple justice to him when I say, in my opinion, there never was a more kind, noble, candid, Christian man than William Ford. The influences and associations that had always surrounded him, blinded him to the inherent wrong at the bottom of the system of Slavery. He never doubted the moral right of one man holding another in subjection. Looking through the same medium with his fathers before him, he saw things in the same light. Brought up under other circumstances and other influences, his notions would undoubtedly have been different. Nevertheless, he was a model master, walking uprightly, according to the light of his understanding, and fortunate was the slave who came to his possession. Were all men such as he, Slavery would be deprived of more than half its bitterness.

Wc were two days and three nights on board the steamboat Rodolph, during which time nothing of particular interest occurred. I was now known as Platt, the name given me by Burch, and by which I was designated through the whole period of my servitude. Eliza was sold by the name of "Dradey." She was so distinguished in the conveyance to Ford, now on record in the recorder's office in New-Orleans.

On our passage I was constantly reflecting on my situation, and consulting with myself on the best course to pursue in order to effect my ultimate escape. Sometimes, not only then, but afterwards, I was almost on the point of disclosing fully to Ford the facts of my history. I am inclined now to the opinion it would have resulted in my benefit. This course was often considered, but through fear of its miscarriage, never put into execution, until eventually by transfer and his pecuniary embarrassments rendered it evidently unsafe. Afterwards, under other masters, unlike William Ford, I knew well enough the slightest knowledge of my real character would consign me at once to the remoter depths of Slavery. I was too costly a chattel to be lost, and was well aware that I would be taken farther on, into some by-place, over the Texan border, perhaps, and sold; that I would be disposed of as the thief disposes of his stolen horse, if my right to freedom was even whispered. So I resolved to lock the secret closely in my heart—never to utter one word or syllable as to who or what I was—trusting in Providence and my own shrewdness for deliverance.

At length we left the steamboat Rodolph at a place called Alexandria, several hundred miles from New-Orleans. It is a small town on the southern shore of Red River. Having remained there over night, we entered the morning train of cars, and were soon at Bayou Lamourie, a still smaller place, distant eighteen miles from Alexandria. At that time it was the termination of the railroad. Ford's plantation was situated on the Texas road, twelve miles from Lamourie, in the Great Pine Woods. This distance, it was announced to us, must be traveled on foot, there being public conveyances no farther. Accordingly we all set out in the company of Ford. It was an excessively hot day. Harry, Eliza, and myself were yet weak, and the bottoms of our feet were very tender from the effects of the small-pox. We proceeded slowly, Ford telling us to take our time and sit down and rest whenever we desired—a privilege that was taken advantage of quite frequently. After leaving Lamourie and crossing two plantations, one belonging to Mr. Carnell, the other to a Mr. Flint, we reached the Pine Woods, a wilderness that stretches to the Sabine River.

The whole country about Red River is low and marshy. The Pine Woods, as they are called, is comparatively upland, with frequent small intervals, however, running through them. This upland is covered with numerous trees—the white oak, the chincopin, resembling chestnut, but principally the yellow pine. They are of great size, running up sixty feet, and perfectly straight. The woods were full of cattle, very shy and wild, dashing away in herds, with a loud snuff, at our approach. Some of them were marked or branded, the rest appeared to be in their wild and untamed state. They are much smaller than northern breeds, and the peculiarity about them that most attracted my attention was their horns. They stand out from the sides of the head precisely straight, like two iron spikes.

At noon we reached a cleared piece of ground containing three or four acres. Upon it was a small, unpainted, wooden house, a corn crib, or, as we would say, a barn, and a log kitchen, standing about a rod from the house. It was the summer residence of Mr. Martin. Rich planters, having large establishments on Bayou Bœuf, are accustomed to spend the warmer season in these woods. Here they find clear water and delightful shades. In fact, these retreats are to the planters of that section of the country what Newport and Saratoga are to the wealthier inhabitants of northern cities.

We were sent around into the kitchen, and supplied with sweet potatoes, corn-bread, and bacon, while Master Ford dined with Martin in the house. There were several slaves about the premises. Martin came out and took a look at us, asking Ford the price of each, if we were green hands, and so forth, and making inquiries in relation to the slave market generally.

After a long rest we set forth again, following the Texas road, which had the appearance of being very rarely traveled. For five miles we passed through continuous woods without observing a single habitation. At length, just as the sun was sinking in the west, we entered another opening, containing some twelve or fifteen acres.

In this opening stood a house much larger than Mr. Martin's. It was two stories high, with a piazza in front. In the rear of it was also a log kitchen, poultry house, corncribs, and several negro cabins. Near the house was a peach orchard, and gardens of orange and pomegranate trees. The space was entirely surrounded by woods, and covered with a carpet of rich, rank verdure. It was a quiet, lonely, pleasant place—literally a green spot in the wilderness. It was the residence of my master, William Ford.

As we approached, a yellow girl—her name was Rose—was standing on the piazza. Going to the door, she called her mistress, who presently came running out to meet her lord. She kissed him, and laughingly demanded if he had bought "those niggers." Ford said he had, and told us to go round to Sally's cabin and rest ourselves. Turning the corner of the house, we discovered Sally washing—her two baby children near her, rolling on the grass. They jumped up and toddled towards us, looked at us a moment like a brace of rabbits, then ran back to their mother as if afraid of us.

Sally conducted us into the cabin, told us to lay down our bundles and be seated, for she was sure that we were tired. Just then John, the cook, a boy some sixteen years of age, and blacker than any crow, came running in, looked steadily in our faces, then turning round, without saying as much as "how d'ye do," ran back to the kitchen, laughing loudly, as if our coming was a great joke indeed.

Much wearied with our walk, as soon as it was dark, Harry and I wrapped our blankets round us, and laid down upon the cabin floor. My thoughts, as usual, wandered back to my wife and children. The consciousness of my real situation; the hopelessness of any effort to escape through the wide forests of Avoyelles, pressed heavily upon me, yet my heart was at home in Saratoga.

I was awakened early in the morning by the voice of Master Ford, calling Rose. She hastened into the house to dress the children, Sally to the field to milk the cows, while John was busy in the kitchen preparing breakfast. In the meantime Harry and I were strolling about the yard, looking at our new quarters. Just after breakfast a colored man, driving three yoke of oxen, attached to a wagon load of lumber, drove into the opening. He was a slave of Ford's, named Walton, the husband of Rose. By the way, Rose was a native of Washington, and had been brought from thence five years before. She had never seen Eliza, but she had heard of Berry, and they knew the same streets, and the same people, either personally, or by reputation. They became fast friends immediately, and talked a great deal together of old times, and of friends they had left behind.

Ford was at that time a wealthy man. Besides his seat in the Pine Woods, he owned a large lumbering establishment on Indian Creek, four miles distant, and also, in his wife's right, an extensive plantation and many slaves on Bayou Bœuf.

Walton had come with his load of lumber from the mills on Indian Creek. Ford directed us to return with him, saying he would follow us as soon as possible. Before leaving, Mistress Ford called me into the storeroom, and handed me, as it is there termed, a tin bucket of molasses for Harry and myself.

Eliza was still ringing her hands and deploring the loss of her children. Ford tried as much as possible to console her—told her she need not work very hard; that she might remain with Rose, and assist the madam in the house affairs.

Riding with Walton in the wagon, Harry and I became quite well acquainted with him long before reaching Indian Creek. He was a "born thrall" of Ford's, and spoke kindly and affectionately of him, as a child would speak of his own father. In answer to his inquiries from whence I came, I told him from Washington. Of that city, he had heard much from his wife, Rose, and all the way plied me with many extravagant and absurd questions.

On reaching the mills at Indian Creek, we found two more of Ford's slaves, Sam and Antony. Sam, also, was a Washingtonian, having been brought out in the same gang with Rose. He had worked on a farm near Georgetown. Antony was a blacksmith, from Kentucky, who had been in his present master's service about ten years. Sam knew Burch, and when informed that he was the trader who had sent me on from Washington, it was remarkable how well we agreed upon the subject of his superlative rascality. He had forwarded Sam, also.

On Ford's arrival at the mill, we were employed in piling lumber, and chopping logs, which occupation we continued for the remainder of the summer.

We usually spent our Sabbaths at the opening, on which days our master would gather all his slaves about him, and read and expound the Scriptures. He sought to inculcate in our minds feelings of kindness towards each other, of dependence upon God—setting forth the rewards promised unto those who lead an upright and prayerful life. Seated in the doorway of his house, surrounded by his man-servants and his maid-servants, who looked earnestly into the good man's face, he spoke of the loving kindness of the Creator, and of the life that is to come. Often did the voice of prayer ascend from his lips to heaven, the only sound that broke the solitude of the place.

In the course of the summer Sam became deeply convicted, his mind dwelling intensely on the subject of religion. His mistress gave him a Bible, which he carried with him to his work. Whatever leisure time was allowed him, he spent in perusing it, though it was only with great difficulty that he could master any part of it. I often read to him, a favor which he well repaid me by many expressions of gratitude. Sam's piety was frequently observed by white men who came to the mill, and the remark it most generally provoked was, that a man like Ford, who allowed his slaves to have Bibles, was "not fit to own a nigger."

He, however, lost nothing by his kindness. It is a fact I have more than once observed, that those who treated their slaves most leniently, were rewarded by the greatest amount of labor. I know it from my own experience. It was a source of pleasure to surprise Master Ford with a greater day's work than was required, while, under subsequent masters, there was no prompter to extra effort but the overseer's lash.

It was the desire of Ford's approving voice that suggested to me an idea that resulted to his profit. The lumber we were manufacturing was contracted to be delivered at Lamourie. It had hitherto been transported by land, and was an important item of expense. Indian Creek, upon which the mills were situated, was a narrow but deep stream emptying into Bayou Bœuf. In some places it was not more than twelve feet wide, and much obstructed with trunks of trees. Bayou Bœuf was connected with Bayou Lamourie. I ascertained the distance from the mills to the point on the latter bayou, where our lumber was to be delivered, was but a few miles less by land than by water. Provided the creek could be made navigable for rafts, it occurred to me that the expense of transportation would be materially diminished.

Adam Taydem, a little white man, who had been a soldier in Florida, and had strolled into that distant region, was foreman and superintendent of the mills. He scouted the idea; but Ford, when I laid it before him, received it favorably, and permitted me to try the experiment.

Having removed the obstructions, I made up a narrow raft, consisting of twelve cribs. At this business I think I was quite skillful, not having forgotten my experience years before on the Champlain canal. I labored hard, being extremely anxious to succeed, both from a desire to please my master, and to show Adam Taydem that my scheme was not such a visionary one as he incessantly pronounced it. One hand could manage three cribs. I took charge of the forward three, and commenced poling down the creek. In due time we entered the first bayou, and finally reached our destination in a shorter period of time than I had anticipated.

The arrival of the raft at Lamourie created a sensation, while Mr. Ford loaded me with commendations. On all sides I heard Ford's Platt pronounced the "smartest nigger in the Pine Woods"—in fact I was the Fulton of Indian Creek. I was not insensible to the praise bestowed upon me, and enjoyed, especially, my triumph over Taydem, whose half-malicious ridicule had stung my pride. From this time the entire control of bringing the lumber to Lamourie was placed in my hands until the contract was fulfilled.

Indian Creek, in its whole length, flows through a magnificent forest. There dwells on its shore a tribe of Indians, a remnant of the Chickasaws or Chickopees, if I remember rightly. They live in simple huts, ten or twelve feet square, constructed of pine poles and covered with bark. They subsist principally on the flesh of the deer, the coon, and opossum, all of which are plenty in these woods. Sometimes they exchange venison for a little corn and whisky with the planters on the bayous. Their usual dress is buckskin breeches and calico hunting shirts of fantastic colors, buttoned from belt to chin. They wear brass rings on their wrists, and in their ears and noses. The dress of the squaws is very similar. They are fond of dogs and horses—owning many of the latter, of a small, tough breed—and are skillful riders. Their bridles, girths and saddles were made of raw skins of animals; their stirrups of a certain kind of wood. Mounted astride their ponies, men and women, I have seen them dash out into the woods at the utmost of their speed, following narrow winding paths, and dodging trees, in a manner that eclipsed the most miraculous feats of civilized equestrianism. Circling away in various directions, the forest echoing and re-echoing with their whoops, they would presently return at the same dashing, headlong speed with which they started. Their village was on Indian Creek, known as Indian Castle, but their range extended to the Sabine River. Occasionally a tribe from Texas would come over on a visit, and then there was indeed a carnival in the "Great Pine Woods." Chief of the tribe was Cascalla; second in rank, John Baltese, his son-in-law; with both of whom, as with many others of the tribe, I became acquainted during my frequent voyages down the creek with rafts. Sam and myself would often visit them when the day's task was done. They were obedient to the chief; the word of Cascalla was their law. They were a rude but harmless people, and enjoyed their wild mode of life. They had little fancy for the open country, the cleared lands on the shores of the bayous, but preferred to hide themselves within the shadows of the forest. They worshiped the Great Spirit, loved whisky, and were happy.

On one occasion I was present at a dance, when a roving herd from Texas had encamped in their village. The entire carcass of a deer was roasting before a large fire, which threw its light a long distance among the trees under which they were assembled. When they had formed in a ring, men and squaws alternately, a sort of Indian fiddle set up an indescribable tune. It was a continuous, melancholy kind of wavy sound, with the slightest possible variation. At the first note, if indeed there was more than one note in the whole tune, they circled around, trotting after each other, and giving utterance to a guttural, sing-song noise, equally as nondescript as the music of the fiddle. At the end of the third circuit, they would stop suddenly, whoop as if their lungs would crack, then break from the ring, forming in couples, man and squaw, each jumping backwards as far as possible from the other, then forwards —which graceful feat having been twice or thrice accomplished, they would form in a ring, and go trotting round again. The best dancer appeared to be considered the one who could whoop the loudest, jump the farthest, and utter the most excruciating noise. At intervals, one or more would leave the dancing circle, and going to the fire, cut from the roasting carcass a slice of venison.

In a hole, shaped like a mortar, cut in the trunk of a fallen tree, they pounded corn with a wooden pestle, and of the meal made cake. Alternately they danced and ate. Thus were the visitors from Texas entertained by the dusky sons and daughters of the Chicopees, and such is a description, as I saw it, of an Indian ball in the Pine Woods of Avoyelles.

In the autumn, I left the mills, and was employed at the opening. One day the mistress was urging Ford to procure a loom, in order that Sally might commence weaving cloth for the winter garments of the slaves. He could not imagine where one was to be found, when I suggested that the easiest way to get one would be to make it, informing him at the same time, that I was a sort of "Jack of all trades," and would attempt it, with his permission. It was granted very readily, and I was allowed to go to a neighboring planter's to inspect one before commencing the undertaking. At length it was finished and pronounced by Sally to be perfect. She could easily weave her task of fourteen yards, milk the cows, and have leisure time besides each day. It worked so well, I was continued in the employment of making looms, which were taken down to the plantation on the bayou.

At this time one John M. Tibeats, a carpenter, came to the opening to do some work on master's house. I was directed to quit the looms and assist him. For two weeks I was in his company, planing and matching boards for ceiling, a plastered room being a rare thing in the parish of Avoyelles.

John M. Tibeats was the opposite of Ford in all respects. He was a small, crabbed, quick-tempered, spiteful man. He had no fixed residence that I ever heard of, but passed from one plantation to another, wherever he could find employment. He was without standing in the community, not esteemed by white men, nor even respected by slaves. He was ignorant, withal, and of a revengeful disposition. He left the parish long before I did, and I know not whether he is at present alive or dead. Certain it is, it was a most unlucky day for me that brought us together. During my residence with Master Ford I had seen only the bright side of slavery. His was no heavy hand crushing us to the earth. He pointed upwards, and with benign and cheering words addressed us as his fellow-mortals, accountable, like himself, to the Maker of us all. I think of him with affection, and had my family been with me, could have borne his gentle servitude, without murmuring, all my days. But clouds were gathering in the horizon—forerunners of a pitiless storm that was soon to break over me. I was doomed to endure such bitter trials as the poor slave only knows, and to lead no more the comparatively happy life which I had led in the "Great Pine Woods."

VIII

Ford's embarrassments.—The sale to Tibeats.—The chattel mortgage.—Mistress Ford's plantation on Bayou Bœuf.—Description of the latter.—Ford's brother-in-law, Peter Tanner.

—Meeting with Eliza.—She still mourns for her children.—Ford's overseer, Chapin.—Tibeat's abuse.—The keg of nails.—The first fight with Tibeats.—His discomfiture and castigation.—The attempt to hang me.—Chapin's interference and speech.—Unhappy reflections.—Abrupt departure of Cook, and Ramsay.—Lawson and the brown mule.—Message to the pine woods.

William Ford unfortunately became embarrassed in his pecuniary affairs. A heavy judgment was rendered against him in consequence of his having become security for his brother, Franklin Ford, residing on Red River, above Alexandria, and who had failed to meet his liabilities. He was also indebted to John M. Tibeats to a considerable amount in consideration of his services in building the mills on Indian Creek, and also a weaving-house, corn-mill and other erections on the plantation at Bayou Bœuf, not yet completed. It was therefore necessary, in order to meet these demands, to dispose of eighteen slaves, myself among the number. Seventeen of them, including Sam and Harry, were purchased by Peter Compton, a planter also residing on Red River.

I was sold to Tibeats, in consequence, undoubtedly, of my slight skill as a carpenter. This was in the winter of 1842. The deed of myself from Freeman to Ford, as I ascertained from the public records in New-Orleans on my return, was dated June 23d, 1841. At the time of my sale to Tibeats, the price agreed to be given for me being more than the debt, Ford took a chattel mortgage of four hundred dollars. I am indebted for my life, as will hereafter be seen, to that mortgage.

I bade farewell to my good friends at the opening, and departed with my new master Tibeats. We went down to the plantation on Bayou Bœuf, distant twenty-seven miles from the Pine Woods, to complete the unfinished contract. Bayou Bœuf is a sluggish, winding stream—one of those stagnant bodies of water common in that region, setting back from Red River. It stretches from a point not far from Alexandria, in a south-easterly direction, and following its tortuous course, is more than fifty miles in length. Large cotton and sugar plantations line each shore, extending back to the borders of interminable swamps. It is alive with alligators, rendering it unsafe for swine, or unthinking slave children to stroll along its banks.

Upon a bend in this bayou, a short distance from Cheneyville, was situated the plantation of Madam Ford—her brother, Peter Tanner, a great landholder, living on the opposite side.

On my arrival at Bayou Bœuf, I had the pleasure of meeting Eliza, whom I had not seen for several months. She had not pleased Mrs. Ford, being more occupied in brooding over her sorrows than in attending to her business, and had, in consequence, been sent down to work in the field on the plantation. She had grown feeble and emaciated, and was still mourning for her children. She asked me if I had forgotten them, and a great many times inquired if I still remembered how handsome little Emily was—how much Randall loved her—and wondered if they were living still, and where the darlings could then be. She had sunk beneath the weight of an excessive grief. Her drooping form and hollow cheeks too plainly indicated that she had well nigh reached the end of her weary road.

Ford's overseer on this plantation, and who had the exclusive charge of it, was a Mr. Chapin, a kindly-disposed man, and a native of Pennsylvania. In common with others, he held Tibeats in light estimation, which fact, in connection with the four hundred dollar mortgage, was fortunate for me.

I was now compelled to labor very hard. From earliest dawn until late at night, I was not allowed to be a moment idle. Notwithstanding which, Tibeats was never satisfied. He was continually cursing and complaining. He never spoke to me a kind word. I was his faithful slave, and earned him large wages every day, and yet I went to my cabin nightly, loaded with abuse and stinging epithets.

We had completed the corn mill, the kitchen, and so forth, and were at work upon the weaving-house, when I was guilty of an act, in that State punishable with death. It was my first fight with Tibeats. The weaving-house we were erecting stood in the orchard a few rods from the residence of Chapin, or the "great house," as it was called. One night, having worked until it was too dark to see, I was ordered by Tibeats to rise very early in the morning, procure a keg of nails from Chapin, and commence putting on the clapboards. I retired to the cabin extremely tired, and having cooked a supper of bacon and corn cake, and conversed a while with Eliza, who occupied the same cabin, as also did Lawson and his wife Mary, and a slave named Bristol, laid down upon the ground floor, little dreaming of the sufferings that awaited me on the morrow.

Before daylight I was on the piazza of the "great house," awaiting the appearance of overseer Chapin. To have aroused him from his slumbers and stated my errand, would have been an unpardonable boldness. At length he came out. Taking off my hat, I informed him Master Tibeats had directed me to call upon him for a keg of nails. Going into the store-room, he rolled it out, at the same time saying, if Tibeats preferred a different size, he would endeavor to furnish them, but that I might use those until further directed. Then mounting his horse, which stood saddled and bridled at the door, he rode away into the field, whither the slaves had preceded him, while I took the keg on my shoulder, and proceeding to the weaving-house, broke in the head, and commenced nailing on the clapboards.

As the day began to open, Tibeats came out of the house to where I was, hard at work. He seemed to be that morning even more morose and disagreeable than usual. He was my master, entitled by law to my flesh and blood, and to exercise over me such tyrannical control as his mean nature prompted; but there was no law that could prevent my looking upon him with intense contempt. I despised both his disposition and his intellect. I had just come round to the keg for a further supply of nails, as he reached the weaving-house.

"I thought I told you to commence putting on weather-boards this morning," he remarked.

"Yes, master, and I am about it," I replied.

"Where?" he demanded.

"On the other side," was my answer.

He walked round to the other side, examined my work for a while, muttering to himself in a fault-finding tone.

"Didn't I tell you last night to get a keg of nails of Chapin?" he broke forth again.

"Yes, master, and so I did; and overseer said he would get another size for you, if you wanted them, when he came back from the field."

Tibeats walked to the keg, looked a moment at the contents, then kicked it violently. Coming towards me in a great passion, he exclaimed,

"G—d d—n you! I thought you *knowed* something."

I made answer: "I tried to do as you told me, master. I didn't mean anything wrong. Overseer said—" But he interrupted me with such a flood of curses that I was unable to finish the sentence.

At length he ran towards the house, and going to the piazza, took down one of the overseer's whips. The whip had a short wooden stock, braided over with leather, and was loaded at the butt. The lash was three feet long, or thereabouts, and made of raw-hide strands.

At first I was somewhat frightened, and my impulse was to run. There was no one about except Rachel, the cook, and Chapin's wife, and neither of them were to be seen. The rest were in the field. I knew he intended to whip me, and it was the first time any one had attempted it since my arrival at Avoyelles. I felt, moreover, that I had been faithful—that I was guilty of no wrong whatever, and deserved commendation rather than punishment. My fear changed to anger, and before he reached me I had made up my mind fully not to be whipped, let the result be life or death.

Winding the lash around his hand, and taking hold of the small end of the stock, he walked up to me, and with a malignant look, ordered me to strip.

"Master Tibeats," said I, looking him boldly in the face, "I will *not.*" I was about to say something further in justification, but with concentrated vengeance, he sprang upon me, seizing me by the throat with one hand, raising the whip with the other, in the act of striking. Before the blow descended, however, I had caught him by the collar of the coat, and drawn him closely to me. Reaching down, I seized him by the ankle, and pushing him back with the other hand, he fell over on the ground. Putting one arm around his leg, and holding it to my breast, so that his head and shoulders only touched the ground, I placed my foot upon his neck. He was completely in my power. My blood was up. It seemed to course through my veins like fire. In the frenzy of my madness I snatched the whip from his hand. He struggled with all his power; swore that I should not live to see another day; and that he would tear out my heart. But his struggles and his threats were alike in vain. I cannot tell how many times I struck him. Blow after blow fell fast and heavy upon his wriggling form. At length he screamed—cried murder—and at last the blasphemous tyrant called on God for mercy. But he who had never shown mercy did not receive it. The stiff stock of the whip warped round his cringing body until my right arm ached.

Until this time I had been too busy to look about me. Desisting for a moment, I saw Mrs. Chapin looking from the window, and

Rachel standing in the kitchen door. Their attitudes expressed the utmost excitement and alarm. His screams had been heard in the field. Chapin was coming as fast as he could ride. I struck him a blow or two more, then pushed him from me with such a well-directed kick that he went rolling over on the ground.

Rising to his feet, and brushing the dirt from his hair, he stood looking at me, pale with rage. We gazed at each other in silence. Not a word was uttered until Chapin galloped up to us.

"What is the matter?" he cried out.

"Master Tibeats wants to whip me for using the nails you gave me," I replied.

"What is the matter with the nails?" he inquired, turning to Tibeats.

Tibeats answered to the effect that they were too large, paying little heed, however, to Chapin's question, but still keeping his snakish eyes fastened maliciously on me.

"I am overseer here," Chapin began. "I told Platt to take them and use them, and if they were not of the proper size I would get others on returning from the field. It is not his fault. Besides, I shall furnish such nails as I please. I hope you will understand *that,* Mr. Tibeats."

Tibeats made no reply, but, grinding his teeth and shaking his fist, swore he would have satisfaction, and that it was not half over yet. Thereupon he walked away, followed by the overseer, and entered the house, the latter talking to him all the while in a suppressed tone, and with earnest gestures.

I remained where I was, doubting whether it was better to fly or abide the result, whatever it might be. Presently Tibeats came out of the house, and, saddling his horse, the only property he possessed besides myself, departed on the road to Cheneyville.

When he was gone, Chapin came out, visibly excited, telling me not to stir, not to attempt to leave the plantation on any account whatever. He then went to the kitchen, and calling Rachel out, conversed with her some time. Coming back, he again charged me with great earnestness not to run, saying my master was a rascal; that he had left on no good errand, and that there might be trouble before night. But at all events, he insisted upon it, I must not stir.

As I stood there, feelings of unutterable agony overwhelmed me. I was conscious that I had subjected myself to unimaginable punishment. The reaction that followed my extreme ebullition of anger produced the most painful sensations of regret. An unfriended, helpless slave—what could I *do,* what could I *say,* to justify, in the remotest manner, the heinous act I had committed, of resenting a *white* man's contumely and abuse. I tried to pray—I tried to beseech my Heavenly Father to sustain me in my sore extremity, but emotion choked my utterance, and I could only bow my head upon my hands and weep. For at least an hour I remained in this situation, finding relief only in tears, when, looking up, I beheld Tibeats, accompanied by two horsemen, coming down the bayou. They rode into the yard, jumped from their horses, and approached me with large whips, one of them also carrying a coil of rope.

"Cross your hands," commanded Tibeats, with the addition of such a shuddering expression of blasphemy as is not decorous to repeat.

"You need not bind me, Master Tibeats, I am ready to go with you anywhere," said I.

One of his companions then stepped forward, swearing if I made the least resistance he would break my head—he would tear me limb from limb—he would cut my black throat—and giving wide scope to other similar expressions. Perceiving any importunity altogether vain, I crossed my hands, submitting humbly to whatever disposition they might please to make of me. Thereupon Tibeats tied my wrists, drawing the rope around them with his utmost strength. Then he bound my ankles in the same manner. In the meantime the other two had slipped a cord within my elbows, running it across my back, and tying it firmly. It was utterly impossible to move hand or foot. With a remaining piece of rope Tibeats made an awkward noose, and placed it about my neck.

"Now, then," inquired one of Tibeats' companions, "where shall we hang the nigger?"

One proposed such a limb, extending from the body of a peach tree, near the spot where we were standing. His comrade objected to it, alleging it would break, and proposed another. Finally they fixed upon the latter.

During this conversation, and all the time they were binding me, I uttered not a word. Overseer Chapin, during the progress of the scene, was walking hastily back and forth on the piazza. Rachel was crying by the kitchen door, and Mrs. Chapin was still looking from the window. Hope died within my heart. Surely my time had come. I should never behold the light of another day—never behold the faces of my children—the sweet anticipation I had cherished with such fondness. I should that hour struggle through the fearful agonies of death! None would mourn for me—none revenge me. Soon my form would be mouldering in that distant soil, or, perhaps, be cast to the slimy reptiles that filled the stagnant waters of the bayou! Tears flowed down my cheeks, but they only afforded a subject of insulting comment for my executioners.

At length, as they were dragging me towards the tree, Chapin, who had momentarily disappeared from the piazza, came out of the house and walked towards us. He had a pistol in each hand, and as near as I can now recall to mind, spoke in a firm, determined manner as follows:

"Gentlemen, I have a few words to say. You had better listen to them. Whoever moves that slave another foot from where he stands is a dead man. In the first place, he does not deserve this treatment. It is a shame to murder him in this manner. I never knew a more faithful boy than Platt. You, Tibeats, are in the fault yourself. You are pretty much of a scoundrel, and I know it, and you richly deserve the flogging you have received. In the next place, I have been overseer on this plantation seven years, and, in the absence of William Ford, am master here. My duty is to protect his interests, and that duty I shall perform. You are not responsible—you are a worthless fellow. Ford holds a mortgage on Platt of four hundred dollars. If you hang him he loses his debt. Until that is canceled you have no right to take his life. You have no right to take it any way. There is a law for the slave as well as for the white man. You are no better than a murderer.

"As for you," addressing Cook and Ramsay, a couple of overseers from neighboring plantations, "as for you—begone! If you have any regard for your own safety, I say, begone."

Cook and Ramsay, without a further word, mounted their horses and rode away. Tibeats, in a few minutes, evidently in fear, and overawed by the decided tone of Chapin, sneaked off like a coward, as he was, and mounting his horse, followed his companions.

I remained standing where I was, still bound, with the rope around my neck. As soon as they were gone, Chapin called Rachel, ordering her to run to the field, and tell Lawson to hurry to the house without delay, and bring the brown mule with him, an animal much prized for its unusual fleetness. Presently the boy appeared.

"Lawson," said Chapin, "you must go to the Pine Woods. Tell your Master Ford to come here at once—that he must not delay a single moment. Tell him they are trying to murder Platt. Now hurry, boy. Be at the Pine Woods by noon if you kill the mule."

Chapin stepped into the house and wrote a pass. When he returned, Lawson was at the door, mounted on his mule. Receiving the pass, he plied the whip right smartly to the beast, dashed out of the yard, and turning up the bayou on a hard gallop, in less time than it has taken me to describe the scene, was out of sight.

IX

The hot sun.—Yet bound.—The cords sink into my flesh.—Chapin's uneasiness.—Speculation.—Rachel, and her cup of water.—Suffering increases.—The happiness of slavery.—Arrival of Ford.—He cuts the cords which bind me, and takes the rope from my neck.—Misery.—The gathering of the slaves in Eliza's cabin.—Their kindness.—Rachel repeats the occurrences of the day.—Lawson entertains his companions with an account of his ride.—Chapin's apprehensions of Tibeats.—Hired to Peter Tanner.—Peter expounds the scriptures.—Description of the stocks.

As the sun approached the meridian that day it became insufferably warm. Its hot rays scorched the ground. The earth almost blistered the foot that stood upon it. I was without coat or hat, standing bareheaded, exposed to its burning blaze. Great drops of perspiration rolled down my face, drenching the scanty apparel wherewith I was clothed. Over the fence, a very little way off, the peach trees cast their cool, delicious shadows on the grass. I would gladly have given a long year of service to have been enabled to exchange the heated oven, as it were, wherein I stood, for a seat beneath their branches. But I was yet bound, the rope still dangling from my neck, and standing in the same tracks where Tibeats and his comrades left me. I could not move an inch, so firmly had I been bound. To have been enabled to lean against the weaving house would have been a luxury indeed. But it was far beyond my reach, though distant less than twenty feet. I wanted to lie down, but knew I could not rise again. The ground was so parched and boiling hot I was aware it would but add to the discomfort of my situation. If I could have only moved my position, however slightly, it would have been relief unspeakable. But the hot rays of a southern sun, beating all the long summer day on my bare head, produced not half the suffering I experienced from my aching limbs. My wrists and ankles, and the cords of my legs and arms began to swell, burying the rope that bound them into the swollen flesh.

All day Chapin walked back and forth upon the stoop, but not once approached me. He appeared to be in a state of great uneasiness, looking first towards me, and then up the road, as if expecting some arrival every moment. He did not go to the field, as was his custom. It was evident from his manner that he supposed Tibeats would return with more and better armed assistance, perhaps, to renew the quarrel, and it was equally evident he had prepared his mind to defend my life at whatever hazard. Why he did not relieve me—why he suffered me to remain in agony the whole weary day, I never knew. It was not for want of sympathy, I am certain. Perhaps he wished Ford to see the rope about my neck, and the brutal manner in which I had been bound; perhaps his interference with another's property in which he had no legal interest might have been a trespass, which would have subjected him to the penalty of the law. Why Tibeats was all day absent was another mystery I never could divine. He knew well enough that Chapin would not harm him unless he persisted in his design against me. Lawson told me afterwards, that, as he passed the plantation of John David Cheney, he saw the three, and that they turned and looked after him as he flew by. I think his supposition was, that Lawson had been sent out by Overseer Chapin to arouse the neighboring planters, and to call on them to come to his assistance. He, therefore, undoubtedly, acted on the principle, that "discretion is the better part of valor," and kept away.

But whatever motive may have governed the cowardly and malignant tyrant, it is of no importance. There I still stood in the noon-tide sun, groaning with pain. From long before daylight I had not eaten a morsel. I was growing faint from pain, and thirst, and hunger. Once only, in the very hottest portion of the day, Rachel, half fearful she was acting contrary to the overseer's wishes, ventured to me, and held a cup of water to my lips. The humble creature never knew, nor could she comprehend if she had heard them, the blessings I invoked upon her, for that balmy draught. She could only say, "Oh, Platt, how I do pity you," and then hastened back to her labors in the kitchen.

Never did the sun move so slowly through the heavens—never did it shower down such fervent and fiery rays, as it did that day. At least, so it appeared to me. What my meditations were—the innumerable thoughts that thronged through my distracted brain —I will not attempt to give expression to. Suffice it to say, during the whole long day I came not to the conclusion, even once, that the southern slave, fed, clothed, whipped and protected by his master, is happier than the free colored citizen of the North. To that conclusion I have never since arrived. There are many, however, even in the Northern States, benevolent and well-disposed men, who will pronounce my opinion erroneous, and gravely proceed to substantiate the assertion with an argument. Alas! they have never drunk, as I have, from the bitter cup of slavery. Just at sunset my heart leaped with unbounded joy, as Ford came riding into the yard, his horse covered with foam. Chapin met him at the door, and after conversing a short time, he walked directly to me.

"Poor Platt, you are in a bad state," was the only expression that escaped his lips.

"Thank God!" said I, "thank God, Master Ford, that you have come at last."

Drawing a knife from his pocket, he indignantly cut the cord from my wrists, arms, and ankles, and slipped the noose from my neck. I attempted to walk, but staggered like a drunken man, and fell partially to the ground.

Ford returned immediately to the house, leaving me alone again. As he reached the piazza, Tibeats and his two friends rode up. A long dialogue followed. I could hear the sound of their voices, the mild tones of Ford mingling with the angry accents of Tibeats, but was unable to distinguish what was said. Finally the three departed again, apparently not well pleased.

I endeavored to raise the hammer, thinking to show Ford how willing I was to work, by proceeding with my labors on the weaving-house, but it fell from my nerveless hand. At dark I crawled into the cabin, and laid down. I was in great misery—all sore and swollen—the slightest movement producing excruciating suffering. Soon the hands came in from the field. Rachel, when she went after

Lawson, had told them what had happened. Eliza and Mary broiled me a piece of bacon, but my appetite was gone. Then they scorched some corn meal and made coffee. It was all that I could take. Eliza consoled me and was very kind. It was not long before the cabin was full of slaves. They gathered round me, asking many questions about the difficulty with Tibeats in the morning—and the particulars of all the occurrences of the day. Then Rachel came in, and in her simple language, repeated it over again—dwelling emphatically on the kick that sent Tibeats rolling over on the ground—whereupon there was a general titter throughout the crowd. Then she described how Chapin walked out with his pistols and rescued me, and how Master Ford cut the ropes with his knife, just as if he was mad.

By this time Lawson had returned. He had to regale them with an account of his trip to the Pine Woods—how the brown mule bore him faster than a "streak o' lightnin' "—how he astonished everybody as he flew along—how Master Ford started right away—how he said Platt was a good nigger, and they shouldn't kill him, concluding with pretty strong intimations that there was not another human being in the wide world, who could have created such a universal sensation on the road, or performed such a marvelous John Gilpin feat, as he had done that day on the brown mule.

The kind creatures loaded me with the expression of their sympathy—saying, Tibeats was a hard, cruel man, and hoping "Massa Ford" would get me back again. In this manner they passed the time, discussing, chatting, talking over and over again the exciting affair, until suddenly Chapin presented himself at the cabin door and called me.

"Platt," said he, "you will sleep on the floor in the great house tonight; bring your blanket with you."

I arose as quickly as I was able, took my blanket in my hand, and followed him. On the way he informed me that he should not wonder if Tibeats was back again before morning—that he intended to kill me—and that he did not mean he should do it without witnesses. Had he stabbed me to the heart in the presence of a hundred slaves, not one of them, by the laws of Louisiana, could have given evidence against him. I laid down on the floor in the "great house"—the first and the last time such a sumptuous resting place was granted me during my twelve years of bondage—and tried to sleep. Near midnight the dog began to bark. Chapin arose, looked from the window, but could discover nothing. At length the dog was quiet. As he returned to his room, he said,

"I believe, Platt, that scoundrel is skulking about the premises somewhere. If the dog barks again, and I am sleeping, wake me."

I promised to do so. After the lapse of an hour or more, the dog re-commenced his clamor, running towards the gate, then back again, all the while barking furiously.

Chapin was out of bed without waiting to be called. On this occasion, he stepped forth upon the piazza, and remained standing there a considerable length of time. Nothing, however, was to be seen, and the dog returned to his kennel. We were not disturbed again during the night. The excessive pain that I suffered, and the dread of some impending danger, prevented any rest whatever. Whether or not Tibeats did actually return to the plantation that night, seeking an opportunity to wreak his vengeance upon me, is a secret known only to himself, perhaps. I thought then, however, and have the strong impression still, that he was there. At all events, he had the disposition of an assassin—cowering before a brave man's words, but ready to strike his helpless or unsuspecting victim in the back, as I had reason afterwards to know.

At daylight in the morning, I arose, sore and weary, having rested little. Nevertheless, after partaking breakfast, which Mary and Eliza had prepared for me in the cabin, I proceeded to the weaving-house and commenced the labors of another day. It was Chapin's practice, as it is the practice of overseers generally, immediately on arising, to bestride his horse, always saddled and bridled and ready for him—the particular business of some slave—and ride into the field. This morning, on the contrary, he came to the weaving-house, asking if I had seen anything of Tibeats yet. Replying in the negative, he remarked there was something not right about the fellow—there was bad blood in him—that I must keep a sharp watch of him, or he would do me wrong some day when I least expected it.

While he was yet speaking, Tibeats rode in, hitched his horse, and entered the house. I had little fear of him while Ford and Chapin were at hand, but they could not be near me always.

Oh! how heavily the weight of slavery pressed upon me then. I must toil day after day, endure abuse and taunts and scoffs, sleep on the hard ground, live on the coarsest fare, and not only this, but live the slave of a blood-seeking wretch, of whom I must stand henceforth in continued fear and dread. Why had I not died in my young years—before God had given me children to love and live for? What unhappiness and suffering and sorrow it would have prevented. I sighed for liberty; but the bondman's chain was round me, and could not be shaken off. I could only gaze wistfully towards the North, and think of the thousands of miles that stretched between me and the soil of freedom, over which a *black* freeman may not pass.

Tibeats, in the course of half an hour, walked over to the weaving-house, looked at me sharply, then returned without saying anything. Most of the forenoon he sat on the piazza, reading a newspaper and conversing with Ford. After dinner, the latter left for the Pine Woods, and it was indeed with regret that I beheld him depart from the plantation.

Once more during the day Tibeats came to me, gave me some order, and returned.

During the week the weaving-house was completed—Tibeats in the meantime making no allusion whatever to the difficulty—when I was informed he had hired me to Peter Tanner, to work under another carpenter by the name of Myers. This announcement was received with gratification, as any place was desirable that would relieve me of his hateful presence.

Peter Tanner, as the reader has already been informed, lived on the opposite shore, and was the brother of Mistress Ford. He is one of the most extensive planters on Bayou Bœuf, and owns a large number of slaves.

Over I went to Tanner's joyfully enough. He had heard of my late difficulties—in fact, I ascertained the flogging of Tibeats was soon blazoned far and wide. This affair, together with my rafting experiment, had rendered me somewhat notorious. More than once I heard it said that Platt Ford, now Platt Tibeats—a slave's name changes with his change of master—was "a devil of a nigger." But I was destined to make a still further noise, as will presently be seen, throughout the little world of Bayou Bœuf.

Peter Tanner endeavored to impress upon me the idea that he was quite severe, though I could perceive there was a vein of good humor in the old fellow, after all.

"You're the nigger," he said to me on my arrival—"You're the nigger that flogged your master, eh? You're the nigger that kicks, and holds carpenter Tibeats by the leg, and wallops him, are ye?

I'd like to see you hold me by the leg—I should. You're a 'portant character—you're a great nigger—very remarkable nigger, ain't ye? *I'd* lash you—*I'd* take the tantrums out of ye. Jest take hold of my leg, if you please. None of your pranks here, my boy, remember *that.* Now go to work, you *kickin'* rascal," concluded Peter Tanner, unable to suppress a half-comical grin at his own wit and sarcasm.

After listening to this salutation, I was taken charge of by Myers, and labored under his direction for a month, to his and my own satisfaction.

Like William Ford, his brother-in-law, Tanner was in the habit of reading the Bible to his slaves on the Sabbath, but in a somewhat different spirit. He was an impressive commentator on the New Testament. The first Sunday after my coming to the plantation, he called them together, and began to read the twelfth chapter of Luke. When he came to the 47th verse, he looked deliberately around him, and continued—"And that servant which knew his lord's *will,"*—here he paused, looking around more deliberately than before, and again proceeded—"which knew his lord's *will,* and *prepared* not himself"—here was another pause—*"prepared* not himself, neither did *according* to his will, shall be beaten with many *stripes."*

"D'ye hear that?" demanded Peter, emphatically. *"Stripes,"* he repeated, slowly and distinctly, taking off his spectacles, preparatory to making a few remarks.

"That nigger that don't take care—that don't obey his lord—that's his master—d'ye see?—that *'ere* nigger shall be beaten with many stripes. Now, 'many' signifies a *great* many—forty, a hundred, a hundred and fifty lashes. *That's* Scripter!" and so Peter continued to elucidate the subject for a great length of time, much to the edification of his sable audience.

At the conclusion of the exercises, calling up three of his slaves, Warner, Will and Major, he cried out to me—

"Here, Platt, you held Tibeats by the legs; now I'll see if you can hold these rascals in the same way, till I get back from meetin'."

Thereupon he ordered them to the stocks—a common thing on plantations in the Red River country. The stocks are formed of two planks, the lower one made fast at the ends to two short posts, driven firmly into the ground. At regular distances half circles are cut in the upper edge. The other plank is fastened to one of the posts by a hinge, so that it can be opened or shut down, in the same manner as the blade of a pocket-knife is shut or opened. In the lower edge of the upper plank corresponding half circles are also cut, so that when they close, a row of holes is formed large enough to admit a negro's leg above the ankle, but not large enough to enable him to draw out his foot. The other end of the upper plank, opposite the hinge, is fastened to its post by lock and key. The slave is made to sit upon the ground, when the uppermost plank is elevated, his legs, just above the ankles, placed in the sub-half circles, and shutting it down again, and locking it, he is held secure and fast. Very often the neck instead of the ankle is enclosed. In this manner they are held during the operation of whipping.

Warner, Will and Major, according to Tanner's account of them, were melon-stealing, Sabbath-breaking niggers, and not approving of such wickedness, he felt it his duty to put them in the stocks. Handing me the key, himself, Myers, Mistress Tanner and the children entered the carriage and drove away to church at Cheneyville. When they were gone, the boys begged me to let them out. I felt sorry to see them sitting on the hot ground, and remembered my own sufferings in the sun. Upon their promise to return to the stocks at any moment they were required to do so, I consented to release them. Grateful for the lenity shown them, and in order in some measure to repay it, they could do no less, of course, than pilot me to the melon-patch. Shortly before Tanner's return, they were in the stocks again. Finally he drove up, and looking at the boys, said, with a chuckle,—

"Aha! ye haven't been strolling about much to-day, any way. *I'll* teach you what's what. *I'll* tire ye of eating water-melons on the Lord's day, ye Sabbath-breaking niggers."

Peter Tanner prided himself upon his strict religious observances: he was a deacon in the church.

But I have now reached a point in the progress of my narrative, when it becomes necessary to turn away from these light descriptions, to the more grave and weighty matter of the second battle with Master Tibeats, and the flight through the great Pacoudrie Swamp.

X

Return to Tibeats.—Impossibility of pleasing him.—He attacks me with a hatchet.—The struggle over the broad axe.—The temptation to murder him.—Escape across the plantation.—Observations from the fence.—Tibeats approaches, followed by the hounds.—They take my track.—Their loud yells.—They almost overtake me.—I reach the water.—The hounds confused.—Moccasin snakes.—Alligators.—Night in the "Great Pacoudrie Swamp".—The sounds of life.—Northwest course.—Emerge into the Pine Woods.—The slave and his young master.—Arrival at Ford's.—Food and rest.

At the end of a month, my services being no longer required at Tanner's I was sent over the bayou again to my master, whom I found engaged in building the cotton press. This was situated at some distance from the great house, in a rather retired place. I commenced working once more in company with Tibeats, being entirely alone with him most part of the time. I remembered the words of Chapin, his precautions, his advice to beware, lest in some unsuspecting moment he might injure me. They were always in my mind, so that I lived in a most uneasy state of apprehension and fear. One eye was on my work, the other on my master. I determined to give him no cause of offence, to work still more diligently, if possible, than I had done, to bear whatever abuse he might heap upon me, save bodily injury, humbly and patiently, hoping thereby to soften in some degree his manner towards me, until the blessed time might come when I should be delivered from his clutches.

The third morning after my return, Chapin left the plantation for Cheneyville, to be absent until night. Tibeats, on that morning, was attacked with one of those periodical fits of spleen and ill-humor to which he was frequently subject, rendering him still more disagreeable and venomous than usual.

It was about nine o'clock in the forenoon, when I was busily employed with the jack-plane on one of the sweeps. Tibeats was standing by the work-bench, fitting a handle into the chisel, with which he had been engaged previously in cutting the thread of the screw.

"You are not planing that down enough," said he.

"It is just even with the line," I replied.

"You're a d——d liar," he exclaimed passionately.

"Oh, well, master," I said, mildly, "I will plane it down more if you say so," at the same time proceeding to do as I supposed he desired. Before one shaving had been removed, however, he cried out, saying I had now planed it too deep—it was too small—I had spoiled the sweep entirely. Then followed curses and imprecations. I had endeavored to do exactly as he directed, but nothing would satisfy the unreasonable man. In silence and in dread I stood by the sweep, holding the jack-plane in my hand, not knowing what to do, and not daring to be idle. His anger grew more and more violent, until, finally, with an oath, such a bitter, frightful oath as only Tibeats could utter, he seized a hatchet from the work-bench and darted towards me, swearing he would cut my head open.

It was a moment of life or death. The sharp, bright blade of the hatchet glittered in the sun. In another instant it would be buried in my brain, and yet in that instant—so quick will a man's thoughts come to him in such a fearful strait—I reasoned with myself. If I stood still, my doom was certain; if I fled, ten chances to one the hatchet, flying from his hand with a too-deadly and unerring aim, would strike me in the back. There was but one course to take. Springing towards him with all my power, and meeting him full half-way, before he could bring down the blow, with one hand I caught his uplifted arm, with the other seized him by the throat. We stood looking each other in the eyes. In his I could see murder. I felt as if I had a serpent by the neck, watching the slightest relaxation of my grip, to coil itself round my body, crushing and stinging it to death. I thought to scream aloud, trusting that some ear might catch the sound—but Chapin was away; the hands were in the field; there was no living soul in sight or hearing.

The good genius, which thus far through life has saved me from the hands of violence, at that moment suggested a lucky thought. With a vigorous and sudden kick, that brought him on one knee, with a groan, I released my hold upon his throat, snatched the hatchet, and cast it beyond reach.

Frantic with rage, maddened beyond control, he seized a white oak stick, five feet long, perhaps, and as large in circumference as his hand could grasp, which was lying on the ground. Again he rushed towards me, and again I met him, seized him about the waist, and being the stronger of the two, bore him to the earth. While in that position I obtained possession of the stick, and rising, cast it from me, also.

He likewise arose and ran for the broad-axe, on the work-bench. Fortunately, there was a heavy plank lying upon its broad blade, in such a manner that he could not extricate it, before I had sprung upon his back. Pressing him down closely and heavily on the plank, so that the axe was held more firmly to its place, I endeavored, but in vain, to break his grasp upon the handle. In that position we remained some minutes.

There have been hours in my unhappy life, many of them, when the contemplation of death as the end of earthly sorrow—of the grave as a resting place for the tired and worn out body—has been pleasant to dwell upon. But such contemplations vanish in the hour of peril. No man, in his full strength, can stand undismayed, in the presence of the "king of terrors." Life is dear to every living thing; the worm that crawls upon the ground will struggle for it. At that moment it was dear to me, enslaved and treated as I was.

Not able to unloose his hand, once more I seized him by the throat, and this time, with a vise-like grip that soon relaxed his hold. He became pliant and unstrung. His face, that had been white with passion, was now black from suffocation. Those small serpent eyes that spat such venom, were now full of horror—two great white orbs starting from their sockets!

There was "a lurking devil" in my heart that prompted me to kill the human blood-hound on the spot—to retain the grip on his accursed throat till the breath of life was gone! I dared not murder him, and I dared not let him live. If I killed him, my life must pay the forfeit—if he lived, my life only would satisfy his vengeance. A voice within whispered me to fly. To be a wanderer among the swamps, a fugitive and a vagabond on the face of the earth, was preferable to the life that I was leading.

My resolution was soon formed, and swinging him from the work-bench to the ground, I leaped a fence near by, and hurried across the plantation, passing the slaves at work in the cotton field. At the end of a quarter of a mile I reached the wood-pasture, and it was a short time indeed that I had been running it. Climbing on to a high fence, I could see the cotton press, the great house, and the space between. It was a conspicuous position, from whence the whole plantation was in view. I saw Tibeats cross the field towards the house, and enter it—then he came out, carrying his saddle, and presently mounted his horse and galloped away.

I was desolate, but thankful. Thankful that my life was spared, —desolate and discouraged with the prospect before me. What would become of me? Who would befriend me? Whither should I fly? Oh, God! Thou who gavest me life, and implanted in my bosom the love of life—who filled it with emotions such as other men, thy creatures, have, do not forsake me. Have pity on the poor slave—let me not perish. If thou dost not protect me, I am lost—lost! Such supplications, silently and unuttered, ascended from my inmost heart to Heaven. But there was no answering voice—no sweet, low tone, coming down from on high, whispering to my soul, "It is I, be not afraid." I was the forsaken of God, it seemed—the despised and hated of men!

In about three-fourths of an hour several of the slaves shouted and made signs for me to run. Presently, looking up the bayou, I saw Tibeats and two others on horse-back, coming at a fast gait, followed by a troop of dogs. There were as many as eight or ten. Distant as I was, I knew them. They belonged on the adjoining plantation. The dogs used on Bayou Bœuf for hunting slaves are a kind of blood-hound, but a far more savage breed than is found in the Northern States. They will attack a negro, at their master's bidding, and cling to him as the common bull-dog will cling to a four footed animal. Frequently their loud bay is heard in the swamps, and then there is speculation as to what point the runaway will be overhauled—the same as a New-York hunter spots to listen to the hounds coursing along the hillsides, and suggests to his companion that the fox will be taken at such a place. I never knew a slave escaping with his life from Bayou Bœuf. One reason is, they are not allowed to learn the art of swimming, and are incapable of crossing the most inconsiderable stream. In their flight they can go in no direction but a little way without coming to a bayou, when the inevitable alternative is presented, of being drowned or overtaken by the dogs. In youth I had practised in the clear streams that flow through my native district, until I had become an expert swimmer, and felt at home in the watery element.

I stood upon the fence until the dogs had reached the cotton press. In an instant more, their long, savage yells announced they were on my track. Leaping down from my position, I ran towards the swamp. Fear gave me strength, and I exerted it to the utmost. Every few moments I could hear the yelpings of the dogs. They were gaining upon me. Every howl was nearer and nearer. Each moment I expected they would spring upon my back—expected to feel their long teeth sinking into my flesh. There were so many of them, I knew they would tear me to pieces, that they would worry me, at once, to death. I gasped for breath—gasped forth a half-uttered, choking prayer to the Almighty to save me—to give me strength to reach some wide, deep bayou where I could throw them off the track, or sink into its waters. Presently I reached a thick palmetto bottom. As I fled through them they made a loud rustling noise, not loud enough, however, to drown the voices of the dogs.

Continuing my course due south, as nearly as I can judge, I came at length to water just over shoe. The hounds at that moment could not have been five rods behind me. I could hear them crashing and plunging through the palmettoes, their loud, eager yells making the whole swamp clamorous with the sound. Hope revived a little as I reached the water. If it were only deeper, they might lose the scent, and thus disconcerted, afford me the opportunity of evading them. Luckily, it grew deeper the farther I proceeded—now over my ankles—now half-way to my knees—now sinking a moment to my waist, and then emerging presently into more shallow places. The dogs had not gained upon me since I struck the water. Evidently they were confused. Now their savage intonations grew more and more distant, assuring me that I was leaving them. Finally I stopped to listen, but the long howl came booming on the air again, telling me I was not yet safe. From bog to bog, where I had stepped, they could still keep upon the track, though impeded by the water. At length, to my great joy, I came to a wide bayou, and plunging in, had soon stemmed its sluggish current to the other side. There, certainly, the dogs would be confounded—the current carrying down the stream all traces of that slight, mysterious scent, which enables the quick-smelling hound to follow in the track of the fugitive.

After crossing this bayou the water became so deep I could not run. I was now in what I afterwards learned was the "Great Pacoudrie Swamp." It was filled with immense trees—the sycamore, the gum, the cotton wood and cypress, and extends, I am informed, to the shore of the Calcasieu River. For thirty or forty miles it is without inhabitants, save wild beasts—the bear, the wild-cat, the tiger, and great slimy reptiles, that are crawling through it everywhere. Long before I reached the bayou, in fact, from the time I struck the water until I emerged from the swamp on my return, these reptiles surrounded me. I saw hundreds of moccasin snakes. Every log and bog—every trunk of a fallen tree, over which I was compelled to step or climb, was alive with them. They crawled away at my approach, but sometimes in my haste, I almost placed my hand or foot upon them. They are poisonous serpents—their bite more fatal than the rattlesnake's. Besides, I had lost one shoe, the sole having come entirely off, leaving the upper only dangling to my ankle.

I saw also many alligators, great and small, lying in the water, or on pieces of floodwood. The noise I made usually startled them, when they moved off and plunged into the deepest places. Sometimes, however, I would come directly upon a monster before observing it. In such cases, I would start back, run a short way round, and in that manner shun them. Straight forward, they will run a short distance rapidly, but do not possess the power of turning. In a crooked race, there is no difficulty in evading them.

About two o'clock in the afternoon, I heard the last of the hounds. Probably they did not cross the bayou. Wet and weary, but relieved from the sense of instant peril, I continued on, more cautious and afraid, however, of the snakes and alligators than I had been in the earlier portion of my flight. Now, before stepping into a muddy pool, I would strike the water with stick. If the waters moved, I would go around it, if not, I would venture through.

At length the sun went down, and gradually night's trailing mantle shrouded the great swamp in darkness. Still I staggered on, fearing every instant I should feel the dreadful sting of the moccasin, or be crushed within the jaws of some disturbed alligator. The dread of them now almost equaled the fear of the pursuing hounds. The moon arose after a time, its mild light creeping through the overspreading branches, loaded with long, pendent moss. I kept traveling forwards until after midnight, hoping all the while that I would soon emerge into some less desolate and dangerous region. But the water grew deeper and the walking more difficult than ever. I perceived it would be impossible to proceed much farther, and knew not, moreover, what hands I might fall into, should I succeed in reaching a human habitation. Not provided with a pass, any white man would be at liberty to arrest me, and place me in prison until such time as my master should "prove property, pay charges, and take me away." I was an estray, and if so unfortunate as to meet a law-abiding citizen of Louisiana, he would deem it his duty to his neighbor, perhaps, to put me forthwith in the pound. Really, it was difficult to determine which I had most reason to fear—dogs, alligators or men!

After midnight, however, I came to a halt. Imagination cannot picture the dreariness of the scene. The swamp was resonant with the quacking of innumerable ducks! Since the foundation of the earth, in all probability, a human footstep had never before so far penetrated the recesses of the swamp. It was not silent now—silent to a degree that rendered it oppressive,—as it was when the sun was shining in the heavens. My midnight intrusion had awakened the feathered tribes, which seemed to throng the morass in hundreds of thousands, and their garrulous throats poured forth such multitudinous sounds—there was such a fluttering of wings—such sullen plunges in the water all around me—that I was affrighted and appalled. All the fowls of the air, and all the creeping things of the earth appeared to have assembled together in that particular place, for the purpose of filling it with clamor and confusion. Not by human dwellings—not in crowded cities alone, are the sights and sounds of life. The wildest places of the earth are full of them. Even in the heart of that dismal swamp, God had provided a refuge and a dwelling place for millions of living things.

The moon had now risen above the trees, when I resolved upon a new project. Thus far I had endeavored to travel as nearly south as possible. Turning about I proceeded in a north-west direction, my object being to strike the Pine Woods in the vicinity of Master Ford's. Once within the shadow of his protection, I felt I would be comparatively safe.

My clothes were in tatters, my hands, face, and body covered with scratches, received from the sharp knots of fallen trees, and in climbing over piles of brush and floodwood. My bare foot was full of thorns. I was besmeared with muck and mud, and the green slime that had collected on the surface of the dead water, in which I had been immersed to the neck many times during the day and night. Hour after hour, and tiresome indeed had they become, I continued to plod along on my north-west course. The water began to grow less deep, and the ground more firm under my feet. At last I reached the Pacoudrie, the same wide bayou I had swam while "outward bound." I swam it again, and shortly after thought I heard a cock crow, but the sound was faint, and it might have been a mockery of the ear. The water receded from my advancing footsteps—now I had left the bogs behind me—now I was on dry land that gradually ascended to the plain, and I knew I was somewhere in the "Great Pine Woods."

Just at day-break I came to an opening—a sort of small plantation—but one I had never seen before. In the edge of the woods I came upon two men, a slave and his young master, engaged in catching wild hogs. The white man I knew would demand my pass, and not able to give him one, would take me into possession. I was too wearied to run again, and too desperate to be taken, and therefore adopted a ruse that proved entirely successful. Assuming a fierce expression, I walked directly towards him, looking him steadily in the face. As I approached, he moved backwards with an air of alarm. It was plain he was much affrighted—that he looked upon me as some infernal goblin, just arisen from the bowels of the swamp!

"Where does William Ford live?" I demanded, in no gentle tone.

"He lives seven miles from here," was the reply.

"Which is the way to his place?" I again demanded, trying to look more fiercely than ever.

"Do you see those pine trees yonder?" he asked, pointing to two, a mile distant, that rose far above their fellows, like a couple of tall sentinels, overlooking the broad expanse of forest.

"I see them," was the answer.

"At the feet of those pine trees," he continued, "runs the Texas road. Turn to the left, and it will lead you to William Ford's."

Without further parley, I hastened forward, happy as he was, no doubt, to place the widest possible distance between us. Striking the Texas road, I turned to the left hand, as directed, and soon passed a great fire, where a pile of logs were burning. I went to it, thinking I would dry my clothes; but the gray light of the morning was fast breaking away,—some passing white man might observe me; besides, the heat overpowered me with the desire of sleep: so, lingering no longer, I continued my travels, and finally, about eight o'clock, reached the house of Master Ford.

The slaves were all absent from the quarters, at their work. Stepping on to the piazza, I knocked at the door, which was soon opened by Mistress Ford. My appearance was so changed—I was in such a woebegone and forlorn condition, she did not know me. Inquiring if Master Ford was at home, that good man made his appearance, before the question could be answered. I told him of my flight, and all the particulars connected with it. He listened attentively, and when I had concluded, spoke to me kindly and sympathetically, and taking me to the kitchen, called John, and ordered him to prepare me food. I had tasted nothing since daylight the previous morning.

When John had set the meal before me, the madam came out with a bowl of milk, and many little delicious dainties, such as rarely please the palate of a slave. I was hungry, and I was weary, but neither food nor rest afforded half the pleasure as did the blessed voices speaking kindness and consolation. It was the oil and the wine which the Good Samaritan in the "Great Pine Woods" was ready to pour into the wounded spirit of the slave, who came to him, stripped of his raiment and half-dead.

They left me in the cabin, that I might rest. Blessed be sleep! It visiteth all alike, descending as the dews of heaven on the bond and free. Soon it nestled to my bosom, driving away the troubles that oppressed it, and bearing me to that shadowy region, where I saw again the faces, and listened to the voices of my children, who, alas, for aught I knew in my waking hours, had fallen into the arms of that *other* sleep, from which they *never* would arouse.

XI

The mistress' garden.—The crimson and golden fruit.—Orange and pomegranate trees.—Return to Bayou Bœuf.—Master Ford's remarks on the way.—The meeting with Tibeats.—His account of the chase.—Ford censures his brutality.—Arrival at the plantation.—Astonishment of the slaves on seeing me.—The anticipated flogging.—Kentucky John.—Mr. Eldret, the planter.—Eldret's Sam.—Trip to the "Big Cane Brake".—The tradition of "Sutton's Field".—For-

est trees.—Gnats and mosquitoes.—The arrival of black women in the big cane.—Lumber women.—Sudden appearance of Tibeats.—His provoking treatment.—Visit to Bayou Bœuf.—The slave pass.—Southern hospitality.—The last of Eliza.—Sale to Edwin Epps.

After a long sleep, sometime in the afternoon I awoke, refreshed, but very sore and stiff. Sally came in and talked with me, while John cooked me some dinner. Sally was in great trouble, as well as myself, one of her children being ill, and she feared it could not survive. Dinner over, after walking about the quarters for a while, visiting Sally's cabin and looking at the sick child, I strolled into the madam's garden. Though it was a season of the year when the voices of the birds are silent, and the trees are stripped of their summer glories in more frigid climes, yet the whole variety of roses were then blooming there, and the long, luxuriant vines creeping over the frames. The crimson and golden fruit hung half hidden amidst the younger and older blossoms of the peach, the orange, the plum, and the pomegranate; for, in that region of almost perpetual warmth, the leaves are falling and the buds bursting into bloom the whole year long.

I indulged the most grateful feelings towards Master and Mistress Ford, and wishing in some manner to repay their kindness, commenced trimming the vines, and afterwards weeding out the grass from among the orange and pomegranate trees. The latter grows eight or ten feet high, and its fruit, though larger, is similar in appearance to the jelly-flower. It has the luscious flavor of the strawberry. Oranges, peaches, plums, and most other fruits are indigenous to the rich, warm soil of Avoyelles; but the apple, most common of them all in colder latitudes, is rarely to be seen.

Mistress Ford came out presently, saying it was praise-worthy in me, but I was not in a condition to labor, and might rest myself at the quarters until master should go down to Bayou Bœuf, which would not be that day, and it might not be the next. I said to her—to be sure, I felt bad, and was stiff, and that my foot pained me, the stubs and thorns having so torn it; but thought such exercise would not hurt me, and that it was a great pleasure to work for so good a mistress. Thereupon she returned to the great house, and for three days I was diligent in the garden, cleaning the walks, weeding the flower beds, and pulling up the rank grass beneath the jessamine vines, which the gentle and generous hand of my protectress had taught to clamber along the walls.

The fourth morning, having become recruited and refreshed, Master Ford ordered me to make ready to accompany him to the bayou. There was but one saddle horse at the opening, all the others with the mules having been sent down to the plantation. I said I could walk, and bidding Sally and John goodbye, left the opening, trotting along by the horse's side.

That little paradise in the Great Pine Woods was the oasis in the desert, towards which my heart turned lovingly, during many years of bondage. I went forth from it now with regret and sorrow, not so overwhelming, however, as if it had then been given me to know that I should never return to it again.

Master Ford urged me to take his place occasionally on the horse, to rest me; but I said no, I was not tired, and it was better for me to walk than him. He said many kind and cheering things to me on the way, riding slowly, in order that I might keep pace with him. The goodness of God was manifest, he declared, in my miraculous escape from the swamp. As Daniel came forth unharmed from the den of lions, and as Jonah had been preserved in the whale's belly, even so had I been delivered from evil by the Almighty. He interrogated me in regard to the various fears and emotions I had experienced during the day and night, and if I had felt, at any time, a desire to pray. I felt forsaken of the whole world, I answered him, and was praying mentally all the while. At such times, said he, the heart of man turns instinctively towards his Maker. In prosperity, and when there is nothing to injure or make him afraid, he remembers Him not, and is ready to defy Him; but place him in the midst of dangers, cut him off from human aid, let the grave open before him—then it is, in the time of his tribulation, that the scoffer and unbelieving man turns to God for help, feeling there is no other hope, or refuge, or safety, save in his protecting arm.

So did that benignant man speak to me of this life and of the life hereafter; of the goodness and power of God, and of the vanity of earthly things, as we journeyed along the solitary road towards Bayou Bœuf.

When within some five miles of the plantation, we discovered a horseman at a distance, galloping towards us. As he came near I saw that it was Tibeats! He looked at me a moment, but did not address me, and turning about, rode along side by side with Ford. I trotted silently at their horses' heels, listening to their conversation. Ford informed him of my arrival in the Pine Woods three days before, of the sad plight I was in, and of the difficulties and dangers I had encountered.

"Well," exclaimed Tibeats, omitting his usual oaths in the presence of Ford, "I never saw such running before. I'll bet him against a hundred dollars, he'll beat any nigger in Louisiana. I offered John David Cheney twenty-five dollars to catch him, dead or alive, but he outran his dogs in a fair race. Them Cheney dogs ain't much, after all. Dunwoodie's hounds would have had him down before he touched the palmettoes. Somehow the dogs got off the track, and we had to give up the hunt. We rode the horses as far as we could, and then kept on foot till the water was three feet deep. The boys said he was drowned, sure. I allow I wanted a shot at him mightily. Ever since, I have been riding up and down the bayou, but hadn't much hope of catching him—thought he was dead, *sartin.* Oh, he's a cuss to run—that nigger is!"

In this way Tibeats ran on, describing his search in the swamp, the wonderful speed with which I had fled before the hounds, and when he had finished, Master Ford responded by saying, I had always been a willing and faithful boy with him; that he was sorry we had such trouble; that, according to Platt's story, he had been inhumanly treated, and that he, Tibeats, was himself in fault. Using hatchets and broad-axes upon slaves was shameful, and should not be allowed, he remarked. "This is no way of dealing with them, when first brought into the country. It will have a pernicious influence, and set them all running away. The swamps will be full of them. A little kindness would be far more effectual in restraining them, and rendering them obedient, than the use of such deadly weapons. Every planter on the bayou should frown upon such inhumanity. It is for the interest of all to do so. It is evident enough, Mr. Tibeats, that you and Platt cannot live together. You dislike him, and would not hesitate to kill him, and knowing it, he will run from you again through fear of his life. Now, Tibeats, you must sell him, or hire him out, at least. Unless you do so, I shall take measures to get him out of your possession."

In this spirit Ford addressed him the remainder of the distance. I opened not my mouth. On reaching the plantation they entered the great house, while I repaired to Eliza's cabin. The slaves were astonished to find me there, on returning from the field, supposing I was drowned. That night, again, they gathered about the cabin to listen to the story of my adventure. They took it for granted I would be whipped, and that it would be severe, the well-known penalty of running away being five hundred lashes.

"Poor fellow," said Eliza, taking me by the hand, "it would have been better for you if you had drowned. You have a cruel master, and he will kill you yet, I am afraid."

Lawson suggested that it might be, overseer Chapin would be appointed to inflict the punishment, in which case it would not be severe, whereupon Mary, Rachel, Bristol, and others hoped it would be Master Ford, and then it would be no whipping at all. They all pitied me and tried to console me, and were sad in view of the castigation that awaited me, except Kentucky John. There were no bounds to his laughter; he filled the cabin with cachinnations, holding his sides to prevent an explosion, and the cause of his noisy mirth was the idea of my outstripping the hounds. Somehow, he looked at the subject in a comical light. "I *know'd* dey wouldn't cotch him, when he run cross de plantation. O, de lor', didn't Platt pick his feet right up, tho', hey? When dem dogs got whar he was, he wasn't *dar*—haw, haw, haw! O, de lor' a' mity!"—and then Kentucky John relapsed into another of his boisterous fits.

Early the next morning, Tibeats left the plantation. In the course of the forenoon, while sauntering about the gin-house, a tall, good-looking man came to me, and inquired if I was Tibeats' boy, that youthful appellation being applied indiscriminately to slaves even though they may have passed the number of three score years and ten. I took off my hat, and answered that I was.

"How would you like to work for me?" he inquired.

"Oh, I would like to, very much," said I, inspired with a sudden hope of getting away from Tibeats.

"You worked under Myers at Peter Tanner's, didn't you?"

I replied I had, adding some complimentary remarks that Myers had made concerning me.

"Well, boy," said he, "I have hired you of your master to work for me in the 'Big Cane Brake,' thirty-eight miles from here, down on Red River."

This man was Mr. Eldret, who lived below Ford's, on the same side of the bayou. I accompanied him to his plantation, and in the morning started with his slave Sam, and a wagon-load of provisions, drawn by four mules, for the Big Cane, Eldret and Myers having preceded us on horseback. This Sam was a native of Charleston, where he had a mother, brother and sisters. He "allowed"—a common word among both black and white—that Tibeats was a mean man, and hoped, as I most earnestly did also, that his master would buy me.

We proceeded down the south shore of the bayou, crossing it at Carey's plantation; from thence to Huff Power, passing which, we came upon the Bayou Rouge road, which runs towards Red River. After passing through Bayou Rouge Swamp, and just at sunset, turning from the highway, we struck off into the "Big Cane Brake." We followed an unbeaten track, scarcely wide enough to admit the wagon. The cane, such as are used for fishing-rods, were as thick as they could stand. A person could not be seen through them the distance of a rod. The paths of wild beasts run through them in various directions—the bear and the American tiger abounding in these brakes, and wherever there is a basin of stagnant water, it is full of alligators.

We kept on our lonely course through the "Big Cane" several miles, when we entered a clearing, known as "Sutton's Field." Many years before, a man by the name of Sutton had penetrated the wilderness of cane to this solitary place. Tradition has it, that he fled thither, a fugitive, not from service, but from justice. Here he lived alone—recluse and hermit of the swamp—with his own hands planting the seed and gathering in the harvest. One day a band of Indians stole upon his solitude, and after a bloody battle, overpowered and massacred him. For miles the country round, in the slaves' quarters, and on the piazzas of "great houses," where white children listen to superstitious tales, the story goes, that that spot, in the heart of the "Big Cane," is a haunted place. For more than a quarter of a century, human voices had rarely, if ever, disturbed the silence of the clearing. Rank and noxious weeds had overspread the once cultivated field—serpents sunned themselves on the doorway of the crumbling cabin. It was indeed a dreary picture of desolation.

Passing "Sutton's Field," we followed a new-cut road two miles farther, which brought us to its termination. We had now reached the wild lands of Mr. Eldret, where he contemplated clearing up an extensive plantation. We went to work next morning with our cane-knives, and cleared a sufficient space to allow the erection of two cabins—one for Myers and Eldret, the other for Sam, myself, and the slaves that were to join us. We were now in the midst of trees of enormous growth, whose wide-spreading branches almost shut out the light of the sun, while the space between the trunks was an impervious mass of cane, with here and there an occasional palmetto.

The bay and the sycamore, the oak and the cypress, reach a growth unparalleled, in those fertile lowlands bordering the Red River. From every tree, moreover, hang long, large masses of moss, presenting to the eye unaccustomed to them, a striking and singular appearance. This moss, in large quantities, is sent north, and there used for manufacturing purposes.

We cut down oaks, split them into rails, and with these erected temporary cabins. We covered the roofs with the broad palmetto leaf, an excellent substitute for shingles, as long as they last.

The greatest annoyance I met with here were small flies, gnats and mosquitoes. They swarmed the air. They penetrated the porches of the ear, the nose, the eyes, the mouth. They sucked themselves beneath the skin. It was impossible to brush or beat them off. It seemed, indeed, as if they would devour us—carry us away piecemeal, in their small tormenting mouths.

A lonelier spot, or one more disagreeable, than the centre of the "Big Cane Brake," it would be difficult to conceive; yet to me it was a paradise, in comparison with any other place in the company of Master Tibeats. I labored hard, and oft-times was weary and fatigued, yet I could lie down at night in peace, and arise in the morning without fear.

In the course of a fortnight, four black girls came down from Eldret's plantation—Charlotte, Fanny, Cresia and Nelly. They were all large and stout. Axes were put into their hands, and they were sent out with Sam and myself to cut trees. They were excellent choppers, the largest oak or sycamore standing but a brief season before their heavy and well-directed blows. At piling logs, they were equal to any man. There are lumberwomen as well as lumbermen in the forests of the South. In fact, in the region of the Bayou Bœuf they perform their share of all the labor required on the plantation. They plough, drag, drive team, clear wild lands, work on the highway, and so forth. Some planters, owning large cotton and sugar plantations, have none other than the labor of slave women. Such an one is Jim Burns, who lives on the north shore of the bayou, opposite the plantation of John Fogaman.

On our arrival in the brake, Eldret promised me, if I worked well, I might go up to visit my friends at Ford's in four weeks. On Saturday night of the fifth week, I reminded him of his promise, when he told me I had done so well, that I might go. I had set my heart upon it, and Eldret's announcement thrilled me with pleasure. I was to return in time to commence the labors of the day on Tuesday morning.

While indulging the pleasant anticipation of so soon meeting my old friends again, suddenly the hateful form of Tibeats appeared among us. He inquired how Myers and Platt got along together, and was told, very well, and that Platt was going up to Ford's plantation in the morning on a visit.

"Poh, poh!" sneered Tibeats; "it isn't worth while—the nigger will get unsteady. He can't go."

But Eldret insisted I had worked faithfully—that he had given me his promise, and that, under the circumstances, I ought not to be disappointed. They then, it being about dark, entered one cabin and I the other. I could not give up the idea of going; it was a sore disappointment. Before morning I resolved, if Eldret made no objection, to leave at all hazards. At daylight I was at his door, with my blanket rolled up into a bundle, and hanging on a stick over my shoulder, waiting for a pass. Tibeats came out presently in one of his disagreeable moods, washed his face, and going to a stump near by, sat down upon it, apparently busily thinking with himself. After standing there a long time, impelled by a sudden impulse of impatience, I started off.

"Are you going without a pass?" he cried out to me.

"Yes, master, I thought I would," I answered.

"How do you think you'll get there?" demand he.

"Don't know," was all the reply I made him.

"You'd be taken and sent to jail, where you ought to be, before you got half-way there," he added, passing into the cabin as he said it. He came out soon with the pass in his hand, and calling me a "d——d nigger that deserved a hundred lashes," threw it on the ground. I picked it up, and hurried away right speedily.

A slave caught off his master's plantation without a pass, may be seized and whipped by any white man whom he meets. The one I now received was dated, and read as follows:

Platt has permission to go to Ford's plantation, on Bayou Bœuf, and return by Tuesday Morning.

JOHN M. TIBEATS.

This is the usual form. On the way, a great many demanded it, read it, and passed on. Those having the air and appearance of gentlemen, whose dress indicated the possession of wealth, frequently took no notice of me whatever; but a shabby fellow, an unmistakable loafer, never failed to hail me, and to scrutinize and examine me in the most thorough manner. Catching runaways is sometimes a money-making business. If, after advertising, no owner appears, they may be sold to the highest bidder; and certain fees are allowed the finder for his services, at all events, even if reclaimed. "A mean white," therefore,—a name applied to the species loafer—considers it a god-send to meet an unknown negro without a pass.

There are no inns along the highways in that portion of the State where I sojourned. I was wholly destitute of money, neither did I carry any provisions, on my journey from the Big Cane to Bayou Bœuf; nevertheless, with his pass in his hand, a slave need never suffer from hunger or from thirst. It is only necessary to present it to the master or overseer of a plantation, and state his wants, when he will be sent round to the kitchen and provided with food or shelter, as the case may require. The traveler stops at any house and calls for a meal with as much freedom as if it was a public tavern. It is the general custom of the country. Whatever their faults may be, it is certain the inhabitants along Red River, and around the bayous in the interior of Louisiana are not wanting in hospitality.

I arrived at Ford's plantation towards the close of the afternoon, passing the evening in Eliza's cabin, with Lawson, Rachel, and others of my acquaintance. When we left Washington Eliza's form was round and plump. She stood erect, and in her silks and jewels, presented a picture of graceful strength and elegance. Now she was but a thin shadow of her former self. Her face had become ghastly haggard, and the once straight and active form was bowed down, as if bearing the weight of a hundred years. Crouching on her cabin floor, and clad in the coarse garments of a slave, old Elisha Berry would not have recognized the mother of his child. I never saw her afterwards. Having become useless in the cotton-field, she was bartered for a trifle, to some man residing in the vicinity of Peter Compton's. Grief had gnawed remorselessly at her heart, until her strength was gone; and for that, her last master, it is said, lashed and abused her most unmercifully. But he could not whip back the departed vigor of her youth, nor straighten up that bended body to its full height, such as it was when her children were around her, and the light of freedom was shining on her path.

I learned the particulars relative to her departure from this world, from some of Compton's slaves, who had come over Red River to the bayou, to assist young Madam Tanner during the "busy season." She became at length, they said, utterly helpless, for several weeks lying on the ground floor in a dilapidated cabin, dependent upon the mercy of her fellow-thralls for an occasional drop of water, and a morsel of food. Her master did not "knock her on the head," as is sometimes done to put a suffering animal out of misery, but left her unprovided for, and unprotected, to linger through a life of pain and wretchedness to its natural close. When the hands returned from the field one night they found her dead! During the day, the Angel of the Lord, who moveth invisibly over all the earth, gathering in his harvest of departing souls, had silently entered the cabin of the dying woman, and taken her from thence. She was *free* at last!

Next day, rolling up my blanket, I started on my return to the Big Cane. After traveling five miles, at a place called Huff Power, the ever-present Tibeats met me in the road. He inquired why I was going back so soon, and when informed I was anxious to return by the time I was directed, he said I need go no farther than the next plantation, as he had that day sold me to Edwin Epps. We walked down into the yard, where we met the latter gentleman, who examined me, and asked me the usual questions propounded by purchasers. Having been duly delivered over, I was ordered to the quarters, and at the same time directed to make a hoe and axe handle for myself.

I was now no longer the property of Tibeats—his dog, his brute, dreading his wrath and cruelty day and night; and whoever or whatever my new master might prove to be, I could not, certainly, regret the change. So it was good news when the sale was announced, and with a sigh of relief I sat down for the first time in my new abode.

Tibeats soon after disappeared from that section of the country. Once afterwards, and only once, I caught a glimpse of him. It was many miles from Bayou Bœuf. He was seated in the doorway of a low groggery. I was passing, in a drove of slaves, through St. Mary's parish.

XII

Personal appearance of Epps.—Epps, drunk and sober.—A glimpse of his history.—Cotton growing.—The mode of ploughing and preparing ground.—Of planting.—Of hoeing, of picking, of treating raw hands.—The difference in cotton pickers.—Patsey a remarkable one.—Tasked according to ability.—Beauty of a cotton field.—The slave's labors.—Fear on approaching the gin-house.—Weighing.—"Chores".—Cabin life.—The corn mill.—The uses of the gourd.—Fear of oversleeping.—Fear continually.—Mode of cultivating corn.—Sweet potatoes.—Fertility of the soil.—Fattening hogs.—Preserving bacon.—Raising cattle.—Shooting-matches.—Garden products.—Flowers and verdure.

Edwin Epps, of whom much will be said during the remainder of this history, is a large, portly, heavy-bodied man with light hair, high cheek bones, and a Roman nose of extraordinary dimensions. He has blue eyes, a fair complexion, and is, as I should say, full six feet high. He has the sharp, inquisitive expression of a jockey. His manners are repulsive and coarse, and his language gives speedy and unequivocal evidence that he has never enjoyed the advantages of an education. He has the faculty of saying most provoking things, in that respect even excelling old Peter Tanner. At the time I came into his possession, Edwin Epps was fond of the bottle, his "sprees" sometimes extending over the space of two whole weeks. Latterly, however, he had reformed his habits, and when I left him, was as strict a specimen of temperance as could be found on Bayou Bœuf. When "in his cups," Master Epps was a roystering, blustering, noisy fellow, whose chief delight was in dancing with his "niggers," or lashing them about the yard with his long whip, just for the pleasure of hearing them screech and scream, as the great welts were planted on their backs. When sober, he was silent, reserved and cunning, not beating us indiscriminately, as in his drunken moments, but sending the end of his rawhide to some tender spot of a lagging slave, with a sly dexterity peculiar to himself.

He had been a driver and overseer in his younger years, but at this time was in possession of a plantation on Bayou Huff Power, two and a half miles from Holmesville, eighteen from Marksville, and twelve from Cheneyville. It belonged to Joseph B. Roberts, his wife's uncle, and was leased by Epps. His principal business was raising cotton, and inasmuch as some may read this book who have never seen a cotton field, a description of the manner of its culture may not be out of place.

The ground is prepared by throwing up beds or ridges, with the plough—back-furrowing, it is called. Oxen and mules, the latter almost exclusively, are used in ploughing. The women as frequently as the men perform this labor, feeding, currying, and taking care of their teams, and in all respects doing the field and stable work, precisely as do the ploughboys of the North.

The beds, or ridges, are six feet wide, that is, from water furrow to water furrow. A plough drawn by one mule is then run along the top of the ridge or center of the bed, making the drill, into which a girl usually drops the seed, which she carries in a bag hung round her neck. Behind her comes a mule and harrow, covering up the seed, so that two mules, three slaves, a plough and harrow, are employed in planting a row of cotton. This is done in the months of March and April. Corn is planted in February. When there are no cold rains, the cotton usually makes its appearance in a week. In the course of eight or ten days afterwards the first hoeing is commenced. This is performed in part, also, by the aid of the plough and mule. The plough passes as near as possible to the cotton on both sides, throwing the furrow from it. Slaves follow with their hoes, cutting up the grass and cotton, leaving hills two feet and a half apart. This is called scraping cotton. In two weeks more commences the second hoeing. This time the furrow is thrown towards the cotton. Only one stalk, the largest, is now left standing in each hill. In another fortnight it is hoed the third time, throwing the furrow towards the cotton in the same manner as before, and killing all the grass between the rows. About the first of July, when it is a foot high or thereabouts, it is hoed the fourth and last time.

Now the whole space between the rows is ploughed, leaving a deep water furrow in the center. During all these hoeings the overseer or driver follows the slaves on horseback with a whip, such as has been described. The fastest hoer takes the lead row. He is usually about a rod in advance of his companions. If one of them passes him, he is whipped. If one falls behind or is a moment idle, he is whipped. In fact, the lash is flying from morning until night, the whole day long. The hoeing season thus continues from April until July, a field having no sooner been finished once, than it is commenced again.

In the latter part of August begins the cotton picking season. At this time each slave is presented with a sack. A strap is fastened to it, which goes over the neck, holding the mouth of the sack breast high, while the bottom reaches nearly to the ground. Each one is also presented with a large basket that will hold about two barrels. This is to put the cotton in when the sack is filled. The baskets are carried to the field and placed at the beginning of the rows.

When a new hand, one unaccustomed to the business, is sent for the first time into the field, he is whipped up smartly, and made for that day to pick as fast as he can possibly. At night it is weighed, so that his capability in cotton picking is known. He must bring in the same weight each night following. If it falls short, it is considered evidence that he has been laggard, and a greater or less number of lashes is the penalty.

An ordinary day's work is two hundred pounds. A slave who is accustomed to picking, is punished, if he or she brings in a less quantity than that. There is a great difference among them as regards this kind of labor. Some of them seem to have a natural knack, or quickness, which enables them to pick with great celerity, and with both hands, while others, with whatever practice or industry, are utterly unable to come up to the ordinary standard. Such hands are taken from the cotton field and employed in other business. Patsey, of whom I shall have more to say, was known as the most remarkable cotton picker on Bayou Bœuf. She picked with both hands and with such surprising rapidity, that five hundred pounds a day was not unusual for her.

Each one is tasked, therefore, according to his picking abilities, none, however, to come short of two hundred weight. I, being unskillful always in that business, would have satisfied my master by bringing in the latter quantity, while on the other hand, Patsey would surely have been beaten if she failed to produce twice as much.

The cotton grows from five to seven feet high, each stalk having a great many branches, shooting out in all directions, and lapping each other above the water furrow.

There are few sights more pleasant to the eye, than a wide cotton field when it is in the bloom. It presents an appearance of purity, like an immaculate expanse of light, new-fallen snow.

Sometimes the slave picks down one side of a row, and back upon the other, but more usually, there is one on either side, gathering all that has blossomed, leaving the unopened bolls for a succeeding picking. When the sack is filled, it is emptied into the basket and trodden down. It is necessary to be extremely careful the first time going through the field, in order not to break the branches off the stalks. The cotton will not bloom upon a broken branch. Epps never failed to inflict the severest chastisement on the unlucky servant who, either carelessly or unavoidably, was guilty in the least degree in this respect.

The hands are required to be in the cotton field as soon as it is light in the morning, and, with the exception of ten or fifteen minutes, which is given them at noon to swallow their allowance of cold bacon, they are not permitted to be a moment idle until it is too dark to see, and when the moon is full, they often times labor till the middle of the night. They do not dare to stop even at dinner time, nor return to the quarters, however late it be, until the order to halt is given by the driver.

The day's work over in the field, the baskets are "toted," or in other words, carried to the gin-house, where the cotton is weighed. No matter how fatigued and weary he may be—no matter how much he longs for sleep and rest—a slave never approaches the gin-house with his basket of cotton but with fear. If it falls short in weight—if he has not performed the full task appointed him, he knows that he must suffer. And if he has exceeded it by ten or twenty pounds, in all probability his master will measure the next day's task accordingly. So, whether he has too little or too much, his approach to the gin-house is always with fear and trembling. Most frequently they have too little, and therefore it is they are not anxious to leave the field. After weighing, follow the whippings; and then the baskets are carried to the cotton house, and their contents stored away like hay, all hands being sent in to tramp it down. If the cotton is not dry, instead of taking it to the gin-house at once, it is laid upon platforms, two feet high, and some three times as wide, covered with boards or plank, with narrow walks running between them.

This done, the labor of the day is not yet ended, by any means. Each one must then attend to his respective chores. One feeds the mules, another the swine—another cuts the wood, and so forth; besides, the packing is all done by candle light. Finally, at a late hour, they reach the quarters, sleepy and overcome with the long day's toil. Then a fire must be kindled in the cabin, the corn ground in the small hand-mill, and supper, and dinner for the next day in the field, prepared. All that is allowed them is corn and bacon, which is given out at the corncrib and smoke-house every Sunday morning. Each one receives, as his weekly allowance, three and a half pounds of bacon, and corn enough to make a peck of meal. That is all—no tea, coffee, sugar, and with the exception of a very scanty sprinkling now and then, no salt. I can say, from a ten years' residence with Master Epps, that no slave of his is ever likely to suffer from the gout, superinduced by excessive high living. Master Epps' hogs were fed on *shelled* corn—it was thrown out to his "niggers" in the ear. The former, he thought, would fatten faster by shelling, and soaking it in the water—the latter, perhaps, if treated in the same manner, might grow too fat to labor. Master Epps was a shrewd calculator and knew how to manage his own animals, drunk or sober.

The corn mill stands in the yard beneath a shelter. It is like a common coffee mill, the hopper holding about six quarts. There was one privilege which Master Epps granted freely to every slave he had. They might grind their corn nightly, in such small quantities as their daily wants required, or they might grind the whole week's allowance at one time, on Sundays, just as they preferred. A very generous man was Master Epps!

I kept my corn in a small wooden box, the meal in a gourd; and, by the way, the gourd is one of the most convenient and necessary utensils on a plantation. Besides supplying the place of all kinds of crockery in a slave cabin, it is used for carrying water to the fields. Another, also, contains the dinner. It dispenses with the necessity of pails, dippers, basins, and such tin and wooden superfluities altogether.

When the corn is ground, and fire is made, the bacon is taken down from the nail on which it hangs, a slice cut off and thrown upon the coals to broil. The majority of slaves have no knife, much less a fork. They cut their bacon with the axe at the woodpile. The corn meal is mixed with a little water, placed in the fire, and baked. When it is "done brown," the ashes are scraped off, and being placed upon a chip, which answers for a table, the tenant of the slave hut is ready to sit down upon the ground to supper. By this time it is usually midnight. The same fear of punishment with which they approach the gin-house, possesses them again on lying down to get a snatch of rest. It is the fear of oversleeping in the morning. Such an offence would certainly be attended with not less than twenty lashes. With a prayer that he may be on his feet and wide awake at the first sound of the horn, he sinks to his slumbers nightly.

The softest couches in the world are not to be found in the log mansion of the slave. The one whereon I reclined year after year, was a plank twelve inches wide and ten feet long. My pillow was a stick of wood. The bedding was a coarse blanket, and not a rag or shred beside. Moss might be used, were it not that it directly breeds a swarm of fleas.

The cabin is constructed of logs, without floor or window. The latter is altogether unnecessary, the crevices between the logs admitting sufficient light. In stormy weather the rain drives through them, rendering it comfortless and extremely disagreeable. The rude door hangs on great wooden hinges. In one end is constructed an awkward fire-place.

An hour before day light the horn is blown. Then the slaves arouse, prepare their breakfast, fill a gourd with water, in another deposit their dinner of cold bacon and corn cake, and hurry to the field again. It is an offence invariably followed by a flogging, to be found at the quarters after daybreak. Then the fears and labors of another day begin; and until its close there is no such thing as rest. He fears he will be caught lagging through the day; he fears to approach the gin-house with his basket-load of cotton at night; he fears, when he lies down, that he will oversleep himself in the morning. Such is a true, faithful, unexaggerated picture and description of the slave's daily life, during the time of cotton-picking, on the shores of Bayou Bœuf.

In the month of January, generally, the fourth and last picking is completed. Then commences the harvesting of corn. This is considered a secondary crop, and receives far less attention than the cotton. It is planted, as already mentioned, in February. Corn is grown in that region for the purpose of fattening hogs and feeding slaves; very little, if any, being sent to market. It is the white variety, the ear of great size, and the stalk growing to the height of eight, and often times ten feet. In August the leaves are stripped off, dried in the sun, bound in small bundles, and stored away as provender for the mules and oxen. After this the slaves go through the field, turning down the ear, for the purpose of keeping the rains from penetrating to the grain. It is left in this condition until after cotton-picking is over, whether earlier or later. Then the ears are separated from the stalks, and deposited in the corncrib with the husks on; otherwise, stripped of the husks, the weevil would destroy it. The stalks are left standing in the field.

The Carolina, or sweet potato, is also grown in that region to some extent. They are not fed, however, to hogs or cattle, and are considered but of small importance. They are preserved by placing them upon the surface of the ground, with a slight covering of earth or cornstalks. There is not a cellar on Bayou Bœuf. The ground is so low it would fill with water. Potatoes are worth from two to three "bits," or shillings a barrel; corn, except when there is an unusual scarity, can be purchased at the same rate.

As soon as the cotton and corn crops are secured, the stalks are pulled up, thrown into piles and burned. The ploughs are started at the same time, throwing up the beds again, preparatory to another planting. The soil, in the parishes of Rapides and Avoyelles, and throughout the whole country, so far as my observation extended, is of exceeding richness and fertility. It is a kind of marl, of a brown or reddish color. It does not require those invigorating composts necessary to more barren lands, and on the same field the same crop is grown for many successive years.

Ploughing, planting, picking cotton, gathering the corn, and pulling and burning stalks, occupies the whole of the four seasons of the year. Drawing and cutting wood, pressing cotton, fattening and killing hogs, are but incidental labors.

In the month of September or October, the hogs are run out of the swamps by dogs, and confined in pens. On a cold morning, generally about New Year's day, they are slaughtered. Each carcass is cut into six parts, and piled one above the other in salt, upon large tables in the smoke-house. In this condition it remains a fortnight, when it is hung up, and a fire built, and continued more than half the time during the remainder of the year. This thorough smoking is necessary to prevent the bacon from becoming infested with worms. In so warm a climate it is difficult to preserve it, and very many times myself and my companions have received our weekly allowance of three pounds and a half, when it was full of these disgusting vermin.

Although the swamps are overrun with cattle, they are never made the source of profit, to any considerable extent. The planter cuts his mark upon the ear, or brands his initials upon the side, and turns them into the swamps, to roam unrestricted within their almost limitless confines. They are the Spanish breed, small and spike-horned. I have known of droves being taken from Bayou Bœuf, but it is of very rare occurrence. The value of the best cows is about five dollars each. Two quarts at one milking, would be considered an unusual large quantity. They furnish little tallow, and that of a soft, inferior quality. Notwithstanding the great number of cows that throng the swamps, the planters are indebted to the North for their cheese and butter, which is purchased in the New-Orleans market. Salted beef is not an article of food either in the great house, or in the cabin.

Master Epps was accustomed to attend shooting matches for the purpose of obtaining what fresh beef he required. These sports occurred weekly at the neighboring village of Holmesville. Fat beeves are driven thither and shot at, a stipulated price being demanded for the privilege. The lucky marksman divides the flesh among his fellows, and in this manner the attending planters are supplied.

The great number of tame and untamed cattle which swarm the woods and swamps of Bayou Bœuf, most probably suggested that appellation to the French, inasmuch as the term, translated, signifies the creek or river of the wild ox.

Garden products, such as cabbages, turnips and the like, are cultivated for the use of the master and his family. They have greens and vegetables at all times and seasons of the year. "The grass withereth and the flower fadeth" before the desolating winds of autumn in the chill northern latitudes, but perpetual verdure overspreads the hot lowlands, and flowers bloom in the heart of winter, in the region of Bayou Bœuf.

There are no meadows appropriated to the cultivation of the

grasses. The leaves of the corn supply a sufficiency of food for the laboring cattle, while the rest provide for themselves all the year in the ever-growing pasture.

There are many other peculiarities of climate, habit, custom, and of the manner of living and laboring at the South, but the foregoing, it is supposed, will give the reader an insight and general idea of life on a cotton plantation in Louisiana. The mode of cultivating cane, and the process of sugar manufacturing, will be mentioned in another place.

XIII

The curious axe-helve.—Symptoms of approaching illness.—Continue to decline.—The whip ineffectual.—Confined to the cabin.—Visit by Dr. Wines.—Partial recovery.—Failure at cotton picking.—What may be heard on Epps' plantation.—Lashes graduated.—Epps in a whipping mood.—Epps in a dancing mood.—Description of the dance.—Loss of rest no excuse.—Epps' characteristics.—Jim Burns' removal from Huff Power to Bayou Bœuf.—Description of Uncle Abram; of Wiley; of Aunt Phebe; of Bob, Henry, and Edward; of Patsey; with a genealogical account of each.—Something of their past history, and peculiar characteristics.—Jealousy and lust.—Patsey, the victim.

On my arrival at Master Epps', in obedience to his order, the first business upon which I entered was the making of an axe-helve. The handles in use there are simply a round, straight stick. I made a crooked one, shaped like those to which I had been accustomed at the North. When finished, and presented to Epps, he looked at it with astonishment, unable to determine exactly what it was. He had never before seen such a handle, and when I explained its conveniences, he was forcibly struck with the novelty of the idea. He kept it in the house a long time, and when his friends called, was wont to exhibit it as a curiosity.

It was now the season of hoeing. I was first sent into the cornfield, and afterwards set to scraping cotton. In this employment I remained until hoeing time was nearly passed, when I began to experience the symptoms of approaching illness. I was attacked with chills, which were succeeded by a burning fever. I became weak and emaciated, and frequently so dizzy that it caused me to reel and stagger like a drunken man. Nevertheless, I was compelled to keep up my row. When in health I found little difficulty in keeping pace with my fellow-laborers, but now it seemed to be an utter impossibility. Often I fell behind, when the driver's lash was sure to greet my back, infusing into my sick and drooping body a little temporary energy. I continued to decline until at length the whip became entirely ineffectual. The sharpest sting of the rawhide could not arouse me. Finally, in September, when the busy season of cotton picking was at hand, I was unable to leave my cabin. Up to this time I had received no medicine, nor any attention from my master or mistress. The old cook visited me occasionally, preparing me corn-coffee, and sometimes boiling a bit of bacon, when I had grown too feeble to accomplish it myself.

When it was said that I would die, Master Epps, unwilling to bear the loss, which the death of an animal worth a thousand dollars would bring upon him, concluded to incur the expense of sending to Holmesville for Dr. Wines. He announced to Epps that it was the effect of the climate, and there was a probability of his losing me. He directed me to eat no meat, and to partake of no more food than was absolutely necessary to sustain life. Several weeks elapsed, during which time, under the scanty diet to which I was subjected, I had partially recovered. One morning, long before I was in a proper condition to labor, Epps appeared at the cabin door, and, presenting me a sack, ordered me to the cotton field. At this time I had had no experience whatever in cotton picking. It was an awkward business indeed. While others used both hands, snatching the cotton and depositing it in the mouth of the sack, with a precision and dexterity that was incomprehensible to me, I had to seize the boll with one hand, and deliberately draw out the white, gushing blossom with the other.

Depositing the cotton in the sack, moreover, was a difficulty that demanded the exercise of both hands and eyes. I was compelled to pick it from the ground where it would fall, nearly as often as from the stalk where it had grown. I made havoc also with the branches, loaded with the yet unbroken bolls, the long, cumbersome sack swinging from side to side in a manner not allowable in the cotton field. After a most laborious day I arrived at the gin-house with my load. When the scale determined its weight to be only ninety-five pounds, not half the quantity required of the poorest picker, Epps threatened the severest flogging, but in consideration of my being a "raw hand," concluded to pardon me on that occasion. The following day, and many days succeeding, I returned at night with no better success—I was evidently not designed for that kind of labor. I had not the gift—the dexterous fingers and quick motion of Patsey, who could fly along one side of a row of cotton, stripping it of its undefiled and fleecy whiteness miraculously fast. Practice and whipping were alike unavailing, and Epps, satisfied of it at last, swore I was a disgrace—that I was not fit to associate with a cotton-picking "nigger"—that I could not pick enough in a day to pay the trouble of weighing it, and that I should go into the cotton field no more. I was now employed in cutting and hauling wood, drawing cotton from the field to the gin-house, and performed whatever other service was required. Suffice to say, I was never permitted to be idle.

It was rarely that a day passed by without one or more whippings. This occurred at the time the cotton was weighed. The delinquent, whose weight had fallen short, was taken out, stripped, made to lie upon the ground, face downwards, when he received a punishment proportioned to his offence. It is the literal, unvarnished truth, that the crack of the lash, and the shrieking of the slaves, can be heard from dark till bed time, on Epps' plantation, any day almost during the entire period of the cotton-picking season.

The number of lashes is graduated according to the nature of the case. Twenty-five are deemed a mere brush, inflicted, for instance, when a dry leaf or piece of boll is found in the cotton, or when a branch is broken in the field; fifty is the ordinary penalty following all delinquencies of the next higher grade; one hundred is called severe: it is the punishment inflicted for the serious offence of standing idle in the field; from one hundred and fifty to two hundred is bestowed upon him who quarrels with his cabin-mates, and five hundred, well laid on, besides the mangling of the dogs, perhaps, is certain to consign the poor, unpitied runaway to weeks of pain and agony.

During the two years Epps remained on the plantation at Bayou Huff Power, he was in the habit, as often as once in a fortnight at least, of coming home intoxicated from Holmesville. The shooting-matches almost invariably concluded with a debauch. At such times he was boisterous and half-crazy. Often he would break the dishes, chairs, and whatever furniture he could lay his hands on. When satisfied with his amusement in the house, he would seize the whip and walk forth into the yard. Then it behooved the slaves to be watchful and exceeding wary. The first one who came within reach felt the smart of his lash. Sometimes for hours he would keep them running in all directions, dodging around the corners of the cabins. Occasionally he would come upon one unawares, and if he succeeded in inflicting a fair, round blow, it was a feat that much delighted him. The younger children, and the aged, who had become inactive, suffered then. In the midst of the confusion he would slily take his stand behind a cabin, waiting with raised whip, to dash it into the first black face that peeped cautiously around the corner.

At other times he would come home in a less brutal humor. Then there must be a merry-making. Then all must move to the measure of a tune. Then Master Epps must needs regale his melodious ears with the music of a fiddle. Then did he become buoyant, elastic, gaily "tripping the light fantastic toe" around the piazza and all through the house.

Tibeats, at the time of my sale, had informed him I could play on the violin. He had received his information from Ford. Through the importunities of Mistress Epps, her husband had been induced to purchase me one during a visit to New-Orleans. Frequently I was called into the house to play before the family, mistress being passionately fond of music.

All of us would be assembled in the large room of the great house, whenever Epps came home in one of his dancing moods. No matter how worn out and tired we were, there must be a general dance. When properly stationed on the floor, I would strike up a tune.

"Dance, you d——d niggers, dance," Epps would shout.

Then there must be no halting or delay, no slow or languid movements; all must be brisk, and lively, and alert. "Up and down, heel and toe, and away we go," was the order of the hour. Epps' portly form mingled with those of his dusky slaves, moving rapidly through all the mazes of the dance.

Usually his whip was in his hand, ready to fall about the ears of the presumptuous thrall, who dared to rest a moment, or even stop to catch his breath. When he was himself exhausted, there would be a brief cessation, but it would be very brief. With a slash, and crack, and flourish of the whip, he would shout again, "Dance, niggers, dance," and away they would go once more, pell-mell, while I, spurred by an occasional sharp touch of the lash, sat in a corner, extracting from my violin a marvelous quick-stepping tune. The mistress often upbraided him, declaring she would return to her father's house at Cheneyville; nevertheless, there were times she could not restrain a burst of laughter, on witnessing his uproarious pranks. Frequently, we were thus detained until almost morning. Bent with excessive toil—actually suffering for a little refreshing rest, and feeling rather as if we could cast ourselves upon the earth and weep, many a night in the house of Edwin Epps have his unhappy slaves been made to dance and laugh.

Notwithstanding these deprivations in order to gratify the whim of an unreasonable master, we had to be in the field as soon as it was light, and during the day perform the ordinary and accustomed task. Such deprivations could not be urged at the scales in extenuation of any lack of weight, or in the cornfield for not hoeing with the usual rapidity. The whippings were just as severe as if we had gone forth in the morning, strengthened and invigorated by a night's repose. Indeed, after such frantic revels, he was always more sour and savage than before, punishing for slighter causes, and using the whip with increased and more vindictive energy.

Ten years I toiled for that man without reward. Ten years of my incessant labor has contributed to increase the bulk of his possessions. Ten years I was compelled to address him with down-cast eyes and uncovered head—in the attitude and language of a slave. I am indebted to him for nothing, save undeserved abuse and stripes.

Beyond the reach of his inhuman thong, and standing on the soil of the free State where I was born, thanks be to Heaven, I can raise my head once more among men. I can speak of the wrongs I have suffered, and of those who inflicted them, with upraised eyes. But I have no desire to speak of him or any other one otherwise than truthfully. Yet to speak truthfully of Edwin Epps would be to say—he is a man in whose heart the quality of kindness or of justice is not found. A rough, rude energy, united with an uncultivated mind and an avaricious spirit, are his prominent characteristics. He is known as a "nigger breaker," distinguished for his faculty of subduing the spirit of the slave, and priding himself upon his reputation in this respect, as a jockey boasts of his skill in managing a refractory horse. He looked upon a colored man, not as a human being, responsible to his Creator for the small talent entrusted to him, but as a "chattel personal," as mere live property, no better, except in value, than his mule or dog. When the evidence, clear and indisputable, was laid before him that I was a free man, and as much entitled to my liberty as he—when, on the day I left, he was informed that I had a wife and children, as dear to me as his own babes to him, he only raved and swore, denouncing the law that tore me from him, and declaring he would find out the man who had forwarded the letter that disclosed the place of my captivity, if there was any virtue or power in money, and would take his life. He thought of nothing but his loss, and cursed me for having been born free. He could have stood unmoved and seen the tongues of his poor slaves torn out by the roots—he could have seen them burned to ashes over a slow fire, or gnawed to death by dogs, if it only brought him profit. Such a hard, cruel, unjust man is Edwin Epps.

There was but one greater savage on Bayou Bœuf than he. Jim Burns' plantation was cultivated, as already mentioned, exclusively by women. That barbarian kept their backs so sore and raw, that they could not perform the customary labor demanded daily of the slave. He boasted of his cruelty, and through all the country round was accounted a more thorough-going, energetic man than even Epps. A brute himself, Jim Burns had not a particle of mercy for his subject brutes, and like a fool, whipped and scourged away the very strength upon which depended his amount of gain.

Epps remained on Huff Power two years, when, having accumulated a considerable sum of money, he expended it in the purchase of the plantation on the east bank of Bayou Bœuf, where he still continues to reside. He took possession of it in 1845, after the holidays were passed. He carried thither with him nine slaves, all of whom, except myself, and Susan, who has since died, remain there yet. He made no addition to this force, and for eight years the following were my companions in his quarters, viz: Abram, Wiley, Phebe, Bob, Henry, Edward, and Patsey. All these, except Edward, born since, were purchased out of a drove by Epps during the time he was overseer for Archy B. Williams, whose plantation is situated on the shore of Red River, not far from Alexandria.

Abram was tall, standing a full head above any common man. He is sixty years of age, and was born in Tennessee. Twenty years ago, he was purchased by a trader, carried into South Carolina, and sold to James Buford, of Williamsburgh county, in that State. In his youth he was renowned for his great strength, but age and unremitting toil have somewhat shattered his powerful frame and enfeebled his mental faculties.

Wiley is forty-eight. He was born on the estate of William Tassle, and for many years took charge of that gentleman's ferry over the Big Black River, in South Carolina.

Phebe was a slave of Buford, Tassle's neighbor, and having married Wiley, he bought the latter, at her instigation. Buford was a kind master, sheriff of the county, and in those days a man of wealth.

Bob and Henry are Phebe's children, by a former husband, their father having been abandoned to give place to Wiley. That seductive youth had insinuated himself into Phebe's affections, and therefore the faithless spouse had gently kicked her first husband out of her cabin door. Edward had been born to them on Bayou Huff Power.

Patsey is twenty-three—also from Buford's plantation. She is in no wise connected with the others, but glories in the fact that she is the offspring of a "Guinea nigger," brought over to Cuba in a slave ship, and in the course of trade transferred to Buford, who was her mother's owner.

This, as I learned from them, is a genealogical account of my master's slaves. For years they had been together. Often they recalled the memories of other days, and sighed to retrace their steps to the old home in Carolina. Troubles came upon their master Buford, which brought far greater troubles upon them. He became involved in debt, and unable to bear up against his failing fortunes, was compelled to sell these, and others of his slaves. In a chain gang they had been driven from beyond the Mississippi to the plantation of Archy B. Williams. Edwin Epps, who, for a long while had been his driver and overseer, was about establishing himself in business on his own account, at the time of their arrival, and accepted them in payment of his wages.

Old Abram was a kind-hearted being—a sort of patriarch among us, fond of entertaining his younger brethren with grave and serious discourse. He was deeply versed in such philosophy as is taught in the cabin of the slave; but the great absorbing hobby of Uncle Abram was General Jackson, whom his young master in Tennessee had followed to the wars. He loved to wander back, in imagination, to the place where he was born, and to recount the scenes of his youth during those stirring times when the nation was in arms. He had been athletic, and more keen and powerful than the generality of his race, but now his eye had become dim, and his natural force abated. Very often, indeed, while discussing the best method of baking the hoe-cake, or expatiating at large upon the glory of Jackson, he would forget where he left his hat, or his hoe, or his basket; and then would the old man be laughed at, if Epps was absent, and whipped if he was present. So was he perplexed continually, and sighed to think that he was growing aged and going to decay. Philosophy and Jackson and forgetfulness had played the mischief with him, and it was evident that all of them combined were fast bringing down the gray hairs of Uncle Abram to the grave.

Aunt Phebe had been an excellent field hand, but latterly was put into the kitchen, where she remained, except occasionally, in a time of uncommon hurry. She was a sly old creature, and when not in the presence of her mistress or her master, was garrulous in the extreme.

Wiley, on the contrary, was silent. He performed his task without murmur or complaint, seldom indulging in the luxury of speech, except to utter a wish that he was away from Epps, and back once more in South Carolina.

Bob and Henry had reached the ages of twenty and twenty-three, and were distinguished for nothing extraordinary or unusual, while Edward, a lad of thirteen, not yet able to maintain his row in the corn or the cotton field, was kept in the great house, to wait on the little Eppses.

Patsey was slim and straight. She stood erect as the human form is capable of standing. There was an air of loftiness in her movement, that neither labor, nor weariness, nor punishment could destroy. Truly, Patsey was a splendid animal, and were it not that bondage had enshrouded her intellect in utter and everlasting darkness, would have been chief among ten thousand of her people. She could leap the highest fences, and a fleet hound it was indeed, that could outstrip her in a race. No horse could fling her from his back. She was a skillful teamster. She turned as true a furrow as the best, and at splitting rails there were none who could excel her. When the order to halt was heard at night, she would have her mules at the crib, unharnessed, fed and curried, before uncle Abram had found his hat. Not, however, for all or any of these, was she chiefly famous. Such lightning-like motion was in her fingers as no other fingers ever possessed, and therefore it was, that in cotton picking time, Patsey was queen of the field.

She had a genial and pleasant temper, and was faithful and obedient. Naturally, she was a joyous creature, a laughing, light-hearted girl, rejoicing in the mere sense of existence. Yet Patsey wept oftener, and suffered more, than any of her companions. She had been literally excoriated. Her back bore the scars of a thousand stripes; not because she was backward in her work, nor because she was of an unmindful and rebellious spirit, but because it had fallen to her lot to be the slave of a licentious master and a jealous mistress. She shrank before the lustful eye of the one, and was in danger even of her life at the hands of the other, and between the two, she was indeed accursed. In the great house, for days together, there were high and angry words, poutings and estrangement, whereof she was the innocent cause. Nothing delighted the mistress so much as to see her suffer, and more than once, when Epps had refused to sell her, has she tempted me with bribes to put her secretly to death, and bury her body in some lonely place in the margin of the swamp. Gladly would Patsey have appeased this unforgiving spirit, if it had been in her power, but not like Joseph, dared she escape from Master Epps, leaving her garment in his hand. Patsey walked under a cloud. If she uttered a word in opposition to her master's will, the lash was resorted to at once, to bring her to subjection; if she was not watchful when about her cabin, or when walking in the yard, a billet of wood, or a broken bottle perhaps, hurled from her mistress' hand, would smite her unexpectedly in the face. The enslaved victim of lust and hate, Patsey had no comfort of her life.

These were my companions and fellow-slaves, with whom I was accustomed to be driven to the field, and with whom it has been my lot to dwell for ten years in the log cabins of Edwin Epps. They, if living, are yet toiling on the banks of Bayou Bœuf, never destined to breathe, as I now do, the blessed air of liberty, nor to shake off the heavy shackles that enthrall them, until they shall lie down forever in the dust.

XIV

Destruction of the cotton crop in 1845.—Demand for laborers in St. Mary's Parish.—Sent thither in a drove.—The order of the march.—The grand coteau.—Hired to judge Turner on Bayou Salle.—Appointed driver in his sugar house.—Sunday services.—Slave furniture, how obtained.—The party at Yarney's in Centreville.—Good fortune.—The captain of the steamer.—His refusal to secrete me.—Return to Bayou Bœuf.—Sight of Tibeats.—Patsey's sorrows.—Tumult and contention.—Hunting the coon and opossum.—The cunning of the latter.—The lean condition of the slave.—Description of the fish trap.—The murder of the man from Natchez.—Epps challenged by Marshall.—The influence of slavery.—The love of freedom.

The first year of Epps' residence on the bayou, 1845, the caterpillars almost totally destroyed the cotton crop throughout that region. There was little to be done, so that the slaves were necessarily idle half the time. However, there came a rumor to Bayou Bœuf that wages were high, and laborers in great demand on the sugar plantations in St. Mary's parish. This parish is situated on the coast of the Gulf of Mexico, about one hundred and forty miles from Avoyelles. The Rio Teche, a considerable stream, flows through St. Mary's to the gulf.

It was determined by the planters, on the receipt of this intelligence, to make up a drove of slaves to be sent down to Tuckapaw in St. Mary's, for the purpose of hiring them out in the cane fields. Accordingly, in the month of September, there were one hundred and forty-seven collected at Holmesville, Abram, Bob and myself among the number. Of these about one-half were women. Epps, Alonson Pierce, Henry Toler, and Addison Roberts, were the white men, selected to accompany, and take charge of the drove. They had a two-horse carriage and two saddle horses for their use. A large wagon, drawn by four horses, and driven by John, a boy belonging to Mr. Roberts, carried the blankets and provisions.

About 2 o'clock in the afternoon, having been fed, preparations were made to depart. The duty assigned me was, to take charge of the blankets and provisions, and see that none were lost by the way. The carriage proceeded in advance, the wagon following; behind this slaves were arranged, while the two horsemen brought up the rear, and in this order the procession moved out of Holmesville.

That night we reached a Mr. McCrow's plantation, a distance of ten or fifteen miles, when we were ordered to halt. Large fires were built, and each one spreading his blanket on the ground, laid down upon it. The white men lodged in the great house. An hour before day we were aroused by the drivers coming among us, cracking their whips and ordering us to arise. Then the blankets were rolled up, and being severally delivered to me and deposited in the wagon, the procession set forth again.

The following night it rained violently. We were all drenched, our clothes saturated with mud and water. Reaching an open shed, formerly a gin-house, we found beneath it such shelter as it afforded. There was not room for all of us to lay down. There we remained, huddled together, through the night, continuing our march, as usual, in the morning. During the journey we were fed twice a day, boiling our bacon and baking our corn-cake at the fires in the same manner as in our huts. We passed through Lafayetteville, Mountsville, New-Town, to Centreville, where Bob and Uncle Abram were hired. Our number decreased as we advanced—nearly every sugar plantation requiring the services of one or more.

On our route we passed the Grand Coteau or prairie, a vast space of level, monotonous country, without a tree, except an occasional one which had been transplanted near some dilapidated dwelling. It was once thickly populated, and under cultivation, but for some cause had been abandoned. The business of the scattered inhabitants that now dwell upon it is principally raising cattle. Immense herds were feeding upon it as we passed. In the centre of the Grand Coteau one feels as if he were on the ocean, out of sight of land. As far as the eye can see, in all directions, it is but a ruined and deserted waste.

I was hired to Judge Turner, a distinguished man and extensive planter, whose large estate is situated on Bayou Salle, within a few miles of the gulf. Bayou Salle is a small stream flowing into the bay of Atchafalaya. For some days I was employed at Turner's in repairing his sugar house, when a cane knife was put into my hand, and with thirty or forty others, I was sent into the field. I found no such difficulty in learning the art of cutting cane that I had in picking cotton. It came to me naturally and intuitively, and in a short time I was able to keep up with the fastest knife. Before the cutting was over, however, Judge Turner transferred me from the field to the sugar house, to act there in the capacity of driver. From the time of the commencement of sugar making to the close, the grinding and boiling does not cease day or night. The whip was given me with directions to use it upon any one who was caught standing idle. If I failed to obey them to the letter, there was another one for my own back. In addition to this my duty was to call on and off the different gangs at the proper time. I had no regular periods of rest, and could never snatch but a few moments of sleep at a time.

It is the custom in Louisiana, as I presume it is in other slave States, to allow the slave to retain whatever compensation he may obtain for services performed on Sundays. In this way, only, are they able to provide themselves with any luxury or convenience whatever. When a slave, purchased, or kidnapped in the North, is transported to a cabin on Bayou Bœuf, he is furnished with neither knife, nor fork, nor dish, nor kettle, nor any other thing in the shape of crockery, or furniture of any nature or description. He is furnished with a blanket before he reaches there, and wrapping that around him, he can either stand up, or lie down upon the ground, or on a board, if his master has no use for it. He is at liberty to find a gourd in which to keep his meal, or he can eat his corn from the cob, just as he pleases. To ask the master for a knife, or skillet, or any small convenience of the kind, would be answered with a kick, or laughed at as a joke. Whatever necessary article of this nature is found in a cabin has been purchased with Sunday money. However injurious to the morals, it is certainly a blessing to the physical condition of the slave, to be permitted to break the Sabbath. Otherwise there would be no way to provide himself with any utensils, which seem to be indispensable to him who is compelled to be his own cook.

On cane plantations in sugar time, there is no distinction as to the days of the week. It is well understood that all hands must labor on the Sabbath, and it is equally well understood that those especially who are hired, as I was to Judge Turner, and others in succeeding years, shall receive remuneration for it. It is usual, also, in the most hurrying time of cotton-picking, to require the same extra service. From this source, slaves generally are afforded an opportunity of earning sufficient to purchase a knife, a kettle, tobacco and so forth. The females, discarding the latter luxury, are apt to expend their little revenue in the purchase of gaudy ribbons, wherewithal to deck their hair in the merry season of the holidays.

I remained in St. Mary's until the first of January, during which time my Sunday money amounted to ten dollars. I met with other good fortune, for which I was indebted to my violin, my constant companion, the source of profit, and soother of my sorrows during years of servitude. There was a grand party of whites assembled at Mr. Yarney's, in Centreville, a hamlet in the vicinity of Turner's plantation. I was employed to play for them, and so well pleased were the merry-makers with my performance, that a contribution was taken for my benefit, which amounted to seventeen dollars.

With this sum in possession, I was looked upon by my fellows as a millionaire. It afforded me great pleasure to look at it—to count it over and over again, day after day. Visions of cabin furniture, of water pails, of pocket knives, new shoes and coat and hats, floated through my fancy, and up through all rose the triumphant contemplation, that I was the wealthiest "nigger" on Bayou Bœuf.

Vessels run up the Rio Teche to Centreville. While there, I was bold enough one day to present myself before the captain of a steamer, and beg permission to hide myself among the freight. I was emboldened to risk the hazard of such a step, from overhearing a conversation, in the course of which I ascertained he was a native of the North. I did not relate to him the particulars of my history, but only expressed an ardent desire to escape from slavery to a free State. He pitied me, but said it would be impossible to avoid the vigilant custom house officers in New-Orleans, and that detection would subject him to punishment, and his vessel to confiscation. My earnest entreaties evidently excited his sympathies, and doubtless he would have yielded to them, could he have done so with any kind of safety. I was compelled to smother the sudden flame that lighted up my bosom with sweet hopes of liberation, and turn my steps once more towards the increasing darkness of despair.

Immediately after this event the drove assembled at Centreville, and several of the owners having arrived and collected the monies due for our services, we were driven back to Bayou Bœuf. It was on our return, while passing through a small village, that I caught sight of Tibeats, seated in the door of a dirty grocery, looking somewhat seedy and out of repair. Passion and poor whisky, I doubt not, have ere this laid him on the shelf.

During our absence, I learned from Aunt Phebe and Patsey, that the latter had been getting deeper and deeper into trouble. The poor girl was truly an object of pity. "Old Hogjaw," the name by which Epps was called, when the slaves were by themselves, had beaten her more severely and frequently than ever. As surely as he came from Holmesville, elated with liquor—and it was often in those days—he would whip her, merely to gratify the mistress; would punish her to an extent almost beyond endurance, for an offence of which he himself was the sole and irresistible cause. In his sober moments he could not always be prevailed upon to indulge his wife's insatiable thirst for vengeance.

To be rid of Patsey—to place her beyond sight or reach, by sale, or death, or in any other manner, of late years, seemed to be the ruling thought and passion of my mistress. Patsey had been a favorite when a child, even in the great house. She had been petted and admired for her uncommon sprightliness and pleasant disposition. She had been fed many a time, so Uncle Abram said, even on biscuit and milk, when the madam, in her younger days, was wont to call her to the piazza, and fondle her as she would a playful kitten. But a sad change had come over the spirit of the woman. Now, only black and angry fiends ministered in the temple of her heart, until she could look on Patsey but with concentrated venom.

Mistress Epps was not naturally such an evil woman, after all. She was possessed of the devil, jealousy, it is true, but aside from that, there was much in her character to admire. Her father, Mr. Roberts, resided in Cheneyville, an influential and honorable man, and as much respected throughout the parish as any other citizen. She had been well educated at some institution this side the Mississippi; was beautiful, accomplished, and usually good-humored. She was kind to all of us but Patsey—frequently, in the absence of her husband, sending out to us some little dainty from her own table. In other situations—in a different society from that which exists on the shores of Bayou Bœuf, she would have been pronounced an elegant and fascinating woman. An ill wind it was that blew her into the arms of Epps.

He respected and loved his wife as much as a coarse nature like his is capable of loving, but supreme selfishness always overmastered conjugal affection.

He loved as well as baser natures can,
But a mean heart and soul were in that man.

He was ready to gratify any whim—to grant any request she made, provided it did not cost too much. Patsey was equal to any two of his slaves in the cotton field. He could not replace her with the same money she would bring. The idea of disposing of her, therefore, could not be entertained. The mistress did not regard her at all in that light. The pride of the haughty woman was aroused; the blood of the fiery southern boiled at the sight of Patsey, and nothing less than trampling out the life of the helpless bondwoman would satisfy her.

Sometimes the current of her wrath turned upon him whom she had just cause to hate. But the storm of angry words would pass over at length, and there would be a season of calm again. At such times Patsey trembled with fear, and cried as if her heart would break, for she knew from painful experience, that if mistress should work herself to the red-hot pitch of rage, Epps would quiet her at last with a promise that Patsey should be flogged—a promise he was sure to keep. Thus did pride, and jealousy, and vengeance war with avarice and brute-passion in the mansion of my master, filling it with daily tumult and contention. Thus, upon the head of Patsey—the simpleminded slave, in whose heart God had implanted the seeds of virtue—the force of all these domestic tempests spent itself at last.

During the summer succeeding my return from St. Mary's parish, I conceived a plan of providing myself with food, which, though simple, succeeded beyond expectation. It has been followed by many others in my condition, up and down the bayou, and of such benefit has it become that I am almost persuaded to look upon myself as a benefactor. That summer the worms got into the bacon. Nothing but ravenous hunger could induce us to swallow it. The weekly allowance of meal scarcely sufficed to satisfy us. It was customary with us, as it is with all in that region, where the allowance is exhausted before Saturday night, or is in such a state as to render it nauseous and disgusting, to hunt in the swamps for coon and opossum. This, however, must be done at night, after the day's work is accomplished. There are planters whose slaves, for months at a time, have no other meat than such as is obtained in this manner. No objections are made to hunting, inasmuch as it dispenses with drafts upon the smoke-house, and because every marauding coon that is killed is so much saved from the standing corn. They are hunted with dogs and clubs, slaves not being allowed the use of fire-arms.

The flesh of the coon is palatable, but verily there is nothing in all butcherdom so delicious as a roasted 'possum. They are a round, rather long-bodied, little animal, of a whitish color, with nose like a pig, and caudal extremity like a rat. They burrow among the roots and in the hollows of the gum tree, and are clumsy and slow of motion. They are deceitful and cunning creatures. On receiving the slightest tap of a stick, they will roll over on the ground and feign death. If the hunter leaves him, in pursuit of another, without first taking particular pains to break his neck, the chances are, on his return, he is not to be found. The little animal has outwitted the enemy—has "played 'possum"—and is off. But after a long and hard day's work, the weary slave feels little like going to the swamp for his supper, and half the time prefers throwing himself on the cabin floor without it. It is for the interest of the master that the servant should not suffer in health from starvation, and it is also for his interest that he should not become gross from over-feeding. In the estimation of the owner, a slave is the most serviceable when in rather a lean and lank condition, such a condition as the race-horse is in, when fitted for the course, and in that condition they are generally to be found on the sugar and cotton plantations along Red River.

My cabin was within a few rods of the bayou bank, and necessity being indeed the mother of invention, I resolved upon a mode of obtaining the requisite amount of food, without the trouble of resorting nightly to the woods. This was to construct a fish trap. Having, in my mind, conceived the manner in which it could be done, the next Sunday I set about putting it into practical execution. It may be impossible for me to convey to the reader a full and correct idea of its construction, but the following will serve as a general description:

A frame between two and three feet square is made, and of a

greater or less height, according to the depth of water. Boards or slats are nailed on three sides of this frame, not so closely, however, as to prevent the water circulating freely through it. A door is fitted into the fourth side, in such manner that it will slide easily up and down in the grooves cut in the two posts. A movable bottom is then so fitted that it can be raised to the top of the frame without difficulty. In the centre of the movable bottom an auger hole is bored, and into this one end of a handle or round stick is fastened on the under side so loosely that it will turn. The handle ascends from the centre of the movable bottom to the top of the frame, or as much higher as is desirable. Up and down this handle, in a great many places, are gimlet holes, through which small sticks are inserted, extending to opposite sides of the frame. So many of these small sticks are running out from the handle in all directions, that a fish of any considerable dimensions cannot pass through without hitting one of them. The frame is then placed in the water and made stationary.

The trap is "set" by sliding or drawing up the door, and kept in that position by another stick, one end of which rests in a notch on the inner side, the other end in a notch made in the handle, running up from the centre of the movable bottom. The trap is baited by rolling a handful of wet meal and cotton together until it becomes hard, and depositing it in the back part of the frame. A fish swimming through the upraised door towards the bait, necessarily strikes one of the small sticks turning the handle, which displacing the stick supporting the door, the latter falls, securing the fish within the frame. Taking hold of the top of the handle, the movable bottom is then drawn up to the surface of the water, and the fish taken out. There may have been other such traps in use before mine was constructed, but if there were I had never happened to see one. Bayou Bœuf abounds in fish of large size and excellent quality, and after this time I was very rarely in want of one for myself, or for my comrades. Thus a mine was opened—a new resource was developed, hitherto unthought of by the enslaved children of Africa, who toil and hunger along the shores of that sluggish, but prolific stream.

About the time of which I am now writing, an event occurred in our immediate neighborhood, which made a deep impression upon me, and which shows the state of society existing there, and the manner in which affronts are oftentimes avenged. Directly opposite our quarters, on the other side of the bayou, was situated the plantation of Mr. Marshall. He belonged to a family among the most wealthy and aristocratic in the country. A gentleman from the vicinity of Natchez had been negotiating with him for the purchase of the estate. One day a messenger came in great haste to our plantation, saying that a bloody and fearful battle was going on at Marshall's—that blood had been spilled—and unless the combatants were forthwith separated, the result would be disastrous.

On repairing to Marshall's house, a scene presented itself that beggars description. On the floor of one of the rooms lay the ghastly corpse of the man from Natchez, while Marshall, enraged and covered with wounds and blood, was stalking back and forth, "breathing out threatenings and slaughter." A difficulty had arisen in the course of their negotiation, high words ensued, when drawing their weapons, the deadly strife began that ended so unfortunately. Marshall was never placed in confinement. A sort of trial or investigation was had at Marksville, when he was acquitted, and returned to his plantation, rather more respected, as I thought, than ever, from the fact that the blood of a fellow being was on his soul.

Epps interested himself in his behalf, accompanying him to Marksville, and on all occasions loudly justifying him, but his services in this respect did not afterwards deter a kinsman of this same Marshall from seeking his life also. A brawl occurred between them over a gambling-table, which terminated in a deadly feud. Riding up on horseback in front of the house one day, armed with pistols and bowie knife, Marshall challenged him to come forth and make a final settlement of the quarrel, or he would brand him as a coward, and shoot him like a dog the first opportunity. Not through cowardice, nor from any conscientious scruples, in my opinion, but through the influence of his wife, he was restrained from accepting the challenge of his enemy. A reconciliation, however, was effected afterward, since which time they have been on terms of the closest intimacy.

Such occurrences, which would bring upon the parties concerned in them merited and condign punishment in the Northern States, are frequent on the bayou, and pass without notice, and almost without comment. Every man carries his bowie knife, and when two fall out, they set to work hacking and thrusting at each other, more like savages than civilized and enlightened beings.

The existence of Slavery in its most cruel form among them, has a tendency to brutalize the humane and finer feelings of their nature. Daily witnesses of human suffering—listening to the agonizing screeches of the slave—beholding him writhing beneath the merciless lash—bitten and torn by dogs—dying without attention, and buried without shroud or coffin—it cannot otherwise be expected, than that they should become brutified and reckless of human life. It is true there are many kind-hearted and good men in the parish of Avoyelles—such men as William Ford—who can look with pity upon the sufferings of a slave, just as there are, over all the world, sensitive and sympathetic spirits, who cannot look with indifference upon the sufferings of any creature which the Almighty has endowed with life. It is not the fault of the slaveholder that he is cruel, so much as it is the fault of the system under which he lives. He cannot withstand the influence of habit and associations that surround him. Taught from earliest childhood, by all that he sees and hears, that the rod is for the slave's back, he will not be apt to change his opinions in maturer years.

There may be humane masters, as there certainly are inhuman ones—there may be slaves well-clothed, well-fed, and happy, as there surely are those half-clad, half-starved and miserable; nevertheless, the institution that tolerates such wrong and inhumanity as I have witnessed, is a cruel, unjust, and barbarous one. Men may write fictions portraying lowly life as it is, or as it is not—may expatiate with owlish gravity upon the bliss of ignorance—discourse flippantly from arm chairs of the pleasures of slave life; but let them toil with him in the field—sleep with him in the cabin—feed with him on husks; let them behold him scourged, hunted, trampled on, and they will come back with another story in their mouths. Let them know the *heart* of the poor slave—learn his secret thoughts—thoughts he dare not utter in the hearing of the white man; let them sit by him in the silent watches of the night—converse with him in trustful confidence, of "life, liberty, and the pursuit of happiness," and they will find that ninety-nine out of every hundred are intelligent enough to understand their situation, and to cherish in their bosoms the love of freedom, as passionately as themselves.

XV

Labors on sugar plantations.—The mode of planting cane.—Of hoeing cane.—Cane ricks.—Cutting cane.—Description of the cane knife.—Winrowing.—Preparing for succeeding crops.—Description of Hawkins' sugar mill on Bayou Bœuf.—The Christmas holidays.—The carnival season of the children of bondage.—The Christmas supper.—Red, the favorite color.—The violin, and the consolation it afforded.—The Christmas dance.—Lively, the coquette.—Sam Roberts, and his rivals.—Slave songs.—Southern life as it is.—Three days in the year.—The system of marriage.—Uncle Abram's contempt of matrimony.

In consequence of my inability in cotton-picking, Epps was in the habit of hiring me out on sugar plantations during the season of cane-cutting and sugar-making. He received for my services a dollar a day, with the money supplying my place on his cotton plantation. Cutting cane was an employment that suited me, and for three successive years I held the lead row at Hawkins', leading a gang of from fifty to an hundred hands.

In a previous chapter the mode of cultivating cotton is described. This may be the proper place to speak of the manner of cultivating cane.

The ground is prepared in beds, the same as it is prepared for the reception of the cotton seed, except it is ploughed deeper. Drills are made in the same manner. Planting commences in January, and continues until April. It is necessary to plant a sugar field only once in three years. Three crops are taken before the seed or plant is exhausted.

Three gangs are employed in the operation. One draws the cane from the rick, or stack, cutting the top and flags from the stalk, leaving only that part which is sound and healthy. Each joint of the cane has an eye, like the eye of a potato, which sends forth a sprout when buried in the soil. Another gang lays the cane in the drill, placing two stalks side by side in such manner that joints will occur once in four or six inches. The third gang follows with hoes, drawing earth upon the stalks, and covering them to the depth of three inches.

In four weeks, at the farthest, the sprouts appear above the ground, and from this time forward grow with great rapidity. A sugar field is hoed three times, the same as cotton, save that a greater quantity of earth is drawn to the roots. By the first of August hoeing is usually over. About the middle of September, whatever is required for seed is cut and stacked in ricks, as they are termed. In October it is ready for the mill or sugar-house, and then the general cutting begins. The blade of a cane-knife is fifteen inches long, three inches wide in the middle, and tapering towards the point and handle. The blade is thin, and in order to be at all serviceable must be kept very sharp. Every third hand takes the lead of two others, one of whom is on each side of him. The lead hand, in the first place, with a blow of his knife shears the flags from the stalk. He next cuts off the top down as far as it is green. He must be careful to sever all the green from the ripe part, inasmuch as the juice of the former sours the molasses, and renders it unsalable. Then he severs the stalk at the root, and lays it directly behind him. His right and left hand companions lay their stalks, when cut in the same manner, upon his. To every three hands there is a cart, which follows, and the stalks are thrown into it by the younger slaves, when it is drawn to the sugar-house and ground.

If the planter apprehends a frost, the cane is winrowed. Winrowing is the cutting of the stalks at an early period and throwing them lengthwise in the water furrow in such a manner that the tops will cover the butts of the stalks. They will remain in this condition three weeks or a month without souring, and secure from frost. When the proper time arrives, they are taken up, trimmed and carted to the sugar-house.

In the month of January the slaves enter the field again to prepare for another crop. The ground is now strewn with the tops, and flags cut from the past year's cane. On a dry day fire is set to this combustible refuse, which sweeps over the field, leaving it bare and clean, and ready for the hoes. The earth is loosened about the roots of the old stubble, and in process of time another crop springs up from the last year's seed. It is the same the year following; but the third year the seed has exhausted its strength, and the field must be ploughed and planted again. The second year the cane is sweeter and yields more than the first, and the third year more than the second.

During the three seasons I labored on Hawkins' plantation, I was employed a considerable portion of the time in the sugar-house. He is celebrated as the producer of the finest variety of white sugar. The following is a general description of his sugar-house and the process of manufacture:

The mill is an immense brick building, standing on the shore of the bayou. Running out from the building is an open shed, at least an hundred feet in length and forty or fifty feet in width. The boiler in which the steam is generated is situated outside the main building; the machinery and engine rest on a brick pier, fifteen feet above the floor, within the body of the building. The machinery turns two great iron rollers, between two and three feet in diameter and six or eight feet in length. They are elevated above the brick pier, and roll in towards each other. An endless carrier, made of chain and wood, like leathern belts used in small mills, extends from the iron rollers out of the main building and through the entire length of the open shed. The carts in which the cane is brought from the field as fast as it is cut, are unloaded at the sides of the shed. All along the endless carrier are ranged slave children, whose business it is to place the cane upon it, when it is conveyed through the shed into the main building, where it falls between the rollers, is crushed, and drops upon another carrier that conveys it out of the main building in an opposite direction, depositing it in the top of a chimney upon a fire beneath, which consumes it. It is necessary to burn it in this manner, because otherwise it would soon fill the building, and more especially because it would soon sour and engender disease. The juice of the cane falls into a conductor underneath the iron rollers, and is carried into a reservoir. Pipes convey it from thence into five filterers, holding several hogsheads each. These filterers are filled with bone-black, a substance resembling pulverized charcoal. It is made of bones calcinated in close vessels, and is used for the purpose of decolorizing, by filtration, the cane juice before boiling. Through these five filterers it passes in succession, and then runs into a large reservoir underneath the ground floor, from whence it is carried up, by means of a steam pump, into a clarifier made of sheet iron, where it is heated by steam until it boils. From the first clarifier it is carried in pipes to a second and a third, and thence into close iron pans, through which tubes pass, filled with steam. While in a boiling state it flows through three pans in succession, and is then carried in other pipes down to the coolers on the ground floor. Coolers are wooden boxes with sieve bottoms made of the finest wire. As soon as the syrup passes into the coolers, and is met by the air, it grains, and the molasses at once escapes through the sieves into a cistern below. It is then white or loaf sugar of the finest kind—clear, clean, and as white as snow. When cool, it is taken out, packed in hogsheads, and is ready for market. The molasses is then carried from the cistern into the upper story again, and by another process converted into brown sugar.

There are larger mills, and those constructed differently from the one thus imperfectly described, but none, perhaps, more celebrated than this anywhere on Bayou Bœuf. Lambert, of New-Orleans, is a partner of Hawkins. He is a man of vast wealth, holding, as I have been told, an interest in over forty different sugar plantations in Louisiana.

The only respite from constant labor the slave has through the whole year, is during the Christmas holidays. Epps allowed us three—others allow four, five and six days, according to the measure of their generosity. It is the only time to which they look forward with any interest or pleasure. They are glad when night comes, not only because it brings them a few hours repose, but because it brings them one day nearer Christmas. It is hailed with equal delight by the old and the young; even Uncle Abram ceases to glorify Andrew Jackson, and Patsey forgets her many sorrows, amid the general hilarity of the holidays. It is the time of feasting, and frolicking, and fiddling—the carnival season with the children of bondage. They are the only days when they are allowed a little restricted liberty, and heartily indeed do they enjoy it.

It is the custom for one planter to give a "Christmas supper," inviting the slaves from neighboring plantations to join his own on the occasion; for instance, one year it is given by Epps, the next by Marshall, the next by Hawkins, and so on. Usually from three to five hundred are assembled, coming together on foot, in carts, on horseback, on mules, riding double and triple, sometimes a boy and girl, at others a girl and two boys, and at others again a boy, a girl and an old woman. Uncle Abram astride a mule, with Aunt Phebe and Patsey behind him, trotting towards a Christmas supper, would be no uncommon sight on Bayou Bœuf.

Then, too, "of all days i' the year," they array themselves in their best attire. The cotton coat has been washed clean, the stump of a tallow candle has been applied to the shoes, and if so fortunate as to possess a rimless or a crownless hat, it is placed jauntily on the head. They are welcomed with equal cordiality, however, if they come bare-headed and barefooted to the feast. As a general thing, the women wear handkerchiefs tied about their heads, but if chance has thrown in their way a fiery red ribbon, or a cast-off bonnet of their mistress' grandmother, it is sure to be worn on such occasions. Red—the deep blood red—is decidedly the favorite color among the enslaved damsels of my acquaintance. If a red ribbon does not encircle the neck, you will be certain to find all the hair of their wooly heads tied up with red strings of one sort or another.

The table is spread in the open air, and loaded with varieties of meat and piles of vegetables. Bacon and corn meal at such times are dispensed with. Sometimes the cooking is performed in the kitchen on the plantation, at others in the shade of wide branching trees. In the latter case, a ditch is dug in the ground, and wood laid in and burned until it is filled with glowing coals, over which chickens, ducks, turkeys, pigs, and not unfrequently the entire body of a wild ox, are roasted. They are furnished also with flour, of which biscuits are made, and often with peach and other preserves, with tarts, and every manner and description of pies, except the mince, that being an article of pastry as yet unknown among them. Only the slave who has lived all the years on his scanty allowance of meal and bacon, can appreciate such suppers. White people in great numbers assemble to witness the gastronomical enjoyments.

They seat themselves at the rustic table—the males on one side, the females on the other. The two between whom there may have been an exchange of tenderness, invariably manage to sit opposite; for the omnipresent Cupid disdains not to hurl his arrows into the simple hearts of slaves. Unalloyed and exulting happiness lights up the dark faces of them all. The ivory teeth, contrasting with their black complexions, exhibit two long, white streaks the whole extent of the table. All round the bountiful board a multitude of eyes roll in ecstacy. Giggling and laughter and the clattering of cutlery and crockery succeed. Cuffee's elbow hunches his neighbor's side, impelled by an involuntary impulse of delight; Nelly shakes her finger at Sambo and laughs, she knows not why, and so the fun and merriment flows on.

When the viands have disappeared, and the hungry maws of the children of toil are satisfied, then, next in the order of amusement, is the Christmas dance. My business on these gala days always was to play on the violin. The African race is a music-loving one, proverbially; and many there were among my fellowbondsmen whose organs of tune were strikingly developed, and who could thumb the banjo with dexterity; but at the expense of appearing egotistical, I must, nevertheless, declare, that I was considered the Ole Bull of Bayou Bœuf. My master often received letters, sometimes from a distance of ten miles, requesting him to send me to play at a ball or festival of the whites. He received his compensation, and usually I also returned with many picayunes jingling in my pockets—the extra contributions of those to whose delight I had administered. In this manner I became more acquainted than I otherwise would, up and down the bayou. The young men and maidens of Holmesville always knew there was to be a jollification somewhere, whenever Platt Epps was seen passing through the town with his fiddle in his hand. "Where are you going now, Platt?" and "What is coming off tonight, Platt?" would be interrogatories issuing from every door and window, and many a time when there was no special hurry, yielding to pressing importunities, Platt would draw his bow, and sitting astride his mule, perhaps, discourse musically to a crowd of delighted children, gathered around him in the street.

Alas! had it not been for my beloved violin, I scarcely can conceive how I could have endured the long years of bondage. It introduced me to great houses—relieved me of many days' labor in the field—supplied me with conveniences for my cabin—with pipes and tobacco, and extra pairs of shoes, and oftentimes led me away from the presence of a hard master, to witness scenes of jollity and mirth. It was my companion—the friend of my bosom—triumphing loudly when I was joyful, and uttering its soft, melodious consolations when I was sad. Often, at midnight, when sleep had fled affrighted from the cabin, and my soul was disturbed and troubled with the contemplation of my fate, it would sing me a song of peace. On holy Sabbath days, when an hour or two of leisure was allowed, it would accompany me to some quiet place on the bayou bank, and, lifting up its voice, discourse kindly and pleasantly indeed. It heralded my name round the country—made me friends, who, otherwise would not have noticed me—gave me an honored seat at the yearly feasts, and secured the loudest and heartiest welcome of them all at the Christmas dance. The Christmas dance! Oh, ye pleasure-seeking sons and daughters of idleness, who move with measured step, listless and snail-like, through the slow-winding cotillon, if ye wish to look upon the celerity, if not the "poetry of motion"—upon genuine happiness, rampant and unrestrained—go down to Louisiana, and see the slaves dancing in the starlight of a Christmas night.

On that particular Christmas I have now in my mind, a description whereof will serve as a description of the day generally, Miss Lively and Mr. Sam, the first belonging to Stewart, the latter to Roberts, started the ball. It was well known that Sam cherished an ardent passion for Lively, as also did one of Marshall's and another of Carey's boys; for Lively was *lively* indeed, and a heart-breaking coquette withal. It was a victory for Sam Roberts, when, rising from the repast, she gave him her hand for the first "figure" in preference to either of his rivals. They were somewhat crest-fallen, and, shaking their heads angrily, rather intimated they would like to pitch into Mr. Sam and hurt him badly. But not an emotion of wrath ruffled the placid bosom of Samuel, as his legs flew like drum-sticks down the outside and up the middle, by the side of his bewitching partner. The whole company cheered them vociferously, and, excited with the applause, they continued "tearing down" after all the others had become exhausted and halted a moment to recover breath. But Sam's superhuman exertions overcame him finally, leaving Lively alone, yet whirling like a top. Thereupon one of Sam's rivals, Pete Marshall, dashed in, and, with might and main, leaped and shuffled and threw himself into every conceivable shape, as if determined to show Miss Lively and all the world that Sam Roberts was of no account.

Pete's affection, however, was greater than his discretion. Such violent exercise took the breath out of him directly, and he dropped like an empty bag. Then was the time for Harry Carey to try his hand; but Lively also soon out-winded him, amidst hurrahs and shouts, fully sustaining her well-earned reputation of being the "fastest gal" on the bayou.

One "set" off, another takes its place, he or she remaining longest on the floor receiving the most uproarious commendation, and so the dancing continues until broad daylight. It does not cease with the sound of the fiddle, but in that case they set up a music peculiar to themselves. This is called "patting," accompanied with one of those unmeaning songs, composed rather for its adaptation to a certain tune or measure, than for the purpose of expressing any distinct idea. The patting is performed by striking the hands on the knees, then striking the hands together, then striking the right shoulder with one hand, the left with the other—all the while keeping time with the feet, and singing, perhaps, this song:

Harper's creek and roarin' ribber,
Thar, my dear, we'll live forebber;
Den we'll go to de Ingin nation,
All I want is dis creation,
Is pretty little wife and big plantation.
Chorus. Up dat oak and down dat ribber,
Two overseers and one little nigger.

Or, if these words are not adapted to the tune called for, it may be that "Old Hog Eye" *is*—a rather solemn and startling specimen of versification, not, however, to be appreciated unless heard at the South. It runneth as follows:

Who's been here since I've been gone?
Pretty little gal wid a josey on.
Hog Eye!
Old Hog Eye,
And Hosey too!

Never see de like since I was born,
Here come a little gal wid a josey on.
Hog eye!
Old Hog Eye!
And Hosey too!

Or, may be the following, perhaps, equally nonsensical, but full of melody, nevertheless, as it flows from the negro's mouth:

Ebo Dick and Jurdan's Jo,
Them two niggers stole my yo'.
Chorus. Hop Jim along,
Walk Jim along,
Talk Jim along, &c.

Old black Dan, as black as tar,
He dam glad he was not dar.
Hop Jim along, &c.

During the remaining holidays succeeding Christmas, they are provided with passes, and permitted to go where they please within a limited distance, or they may remain and labor on the plantation, in which case they are paid for it. It is very rarely, however, that the latter alternative is accepted. They may be seen at these times hurrying in all directions, as happy looking mortals as can be found on the face of the earth. They are different beings from what they are in the field; the temporary relaxation, the brief deliverance from fear, and from the lash, producing an entire metamorphosis in their appearance and demeanor. In visiting, riding, renewing old friendships, or, perchance, reviving some old attachment, or pursuing whatever pleasure may suggest itself, the time is occupied. Such is "southern life as it is," *three days in the year,* as I found it—the other three hundred and sixty-two being days of weariness, and fear, and suffering, and unremitting labor.

Marriage is frequently contracted during the holidays, if such an institution may be said to exist among them. The only ceremony required before entering into that "holy estate," is to obtain the consent of the respective owners. It is usually encouraged by the masters of female slaves. Either party can have as many husbands or wives as the owner will permit, and either is at liberty to discard the other at pleasure. The law in relation to divorce, or to bigamy, and so forth, is not applicable to property, of course. If the wife does not belong on the same plantation with the husband, the latter is permitted to visit her on Saturday nights, if the distance is not too far. Uncle Abram's wife lived seven miles from Epps', on Bayou Huff Power. He had permission to visit her once a fortnight, but he was growing old, as has been said, and truth to say, had latterly well nigh forgotten her. Uncle Abram had no time to spare from his meditations on General Jackson—connubial dalliance being well enough for the young and thoughtless, but unbecoming a grave and solemn philosopher like himself.

XVI

Overseers.—How they are armed and accompanied.—The homicide.—His execution at Marksville.—Slave-drivers.—Appointed driver on removing to Bayou Bœuf.—Practice makes perfect.—Epps' attempt to cut Platt's throat.—The escape from him.—Protected by the mistress.—Forbids reading and writing.—Obtain a sheet of paper after nine years' effort.—The letter.—Armsby, the mean white.—Partially confide in him.—His treachery.—Epps' suspicions.—How they were quieted.—Burning the letter.—Armsby leaves the Bayou.—Disappointment and despair.

With the exception of my trip to St. Mary's parish, and my absence during the cane-cutting seasons, I was constantly employed on the plantation of Master Epps. He was considered but a small planter, not having a sufficient number of hands to require the services of an overseer, acting in the latter capacity himself. Not able to increase his force, it was his custom to hire during the hurry of cotton-picking.

On larger estates, employing fifty or a hundred, or perhaps two hundred hands, an overseer is deemed indispensable. These gentlemen ride into the field on horseback, without an exception, to my knowledge, armed with pistols, bowie knife, whip, and accompanied by several dogs. They follow, equipped in this fashion, in rear of the slaves, keeping a sharp lookout upon them all. The requisite qualifications in an overseer are utter heartlessness, brutality and cruelty. It is his business to produce large crops, and if that is accomplished, no matter what amount of suffering it may have cost. The presence of the dogs are necessary to overhaul a fugitive who may take to his heels, as is sometimes the case, when faint or sick, he is unable to maintain his row, and unable, also, to endure the whip. The pistols are reserved for any dangerous emergency, there having been instances when such weapons were necessary. Goaded into uncontrollable madness, even the slave will sometimes turn upon his oppressor. The gallows were standing at Marksville last January, upon which one was executed a year ago for killing his overseer. It occurred not many miles from Epps' plantation on Red River. The slave was given his task at splitting rails. In the course of the day the overseer sent him on an errand, which occupied so much time that it was not possible for him to perform the task. The next day he was called to an account, but the loss of time occasioned by the errand was no excuse, and he was ordered to kneel and bare his back for the reception of the lash. They were in the woods alone—beyond the reach of sight or hearing. The boy submitted until maddened at such injustice, and insane with pain, he sprang to his feet, and seizing an axe, literally chopped the overseer in pieces. He made no attempt whatever at concealment, but hastening to his master, related the whole affair, and declared himself ready to expiate the wrong by the sacrifice of his life. He was led to the scaffold, and while the rope was around his neck, maintained an undismayed and fearless bearing, and with his last words justified the act.

Besides the overseer, there are drivers under him, the number being in proportion to the number of hands in the field. The drivers are black, who, in addition to the performance of their equal share of work, are compelled to do the whipping of their several gangs. Whips hang around their necks, and if they fail to use them thoroughly, are whipped themselves. They have a few privileges, however; for example, in cane-cutting the hands are not allowed to sit down long enough to eat their dinners. Carts filled with corn cake, cooked at the kitchen, are driven into the field at noon. The cake is distributed by the drivers, and must be eaten with the least possible delay.

When the slave ceases to perspire, as he often does when taxed beyond his strength, he falls to the ground and becomes entirely helpless. It is then the duty of the driver to drag him into the shade of the standing cotton or cane, or of a neighboring tree, where he dashes buckets of water upon him, and uses other means of bringing out perspiration again, when he is ordered to his place, and compelled to continue his labor.

At Huff Power, when I first came to Epps', Tom, one of Roberts' negroes, was driver. He was a burly fellow, and severe in the extreme. After Epps' removal to Bayou Bœuf, that distinguished honor was conferred upon myself. Up to the time of my departure I had to wear a whip about my neck in the field. If Epps was present, I dared not show any lenity, not having the Christian fortitude of a certain well-known Uncle Tom sufficiently to brave his wrath, by refusing to perform the office. In that way, only, I escaped the immediate martyrdom he suffered, and, withal, saved my companions much suffering, as it proved in the end. Epps, I soon found, whether actually in the field or not, had his eyes pretty generally upon us. From the piazza, from behind some adjacent tree, or other concealed point of observation, he was perpetually on the watch. If one of us had been backward or idle through the day, we were apt to be told all about it on returning to the quarters, and as it was a matter of principle with him to reprove every offence of that kind that came within his knowledge, the offender not only was certain of receiving a castigation for his tardiness, but I likewise was punished for permitting it.

If, on the other hand, he had seen me use the lash freely, the man was satisfied. "Practice makes perfect," truly; and during my eight years' experience as a driver, I learned to handle the whip with marvelous dexterity and precision, throwing the lash within a hair's breadth of the back, the ear, the nose, without, however, touching either of them. If Epps was observed at a distance, or we had reason to apprehend he was sneaking somewhere in the vicinity, I would commence plying the lash vigorously, when, according to arrangement, they would squirm and screech as if in agony, although not one of them had in fact been even grazed. Patsey would take occasion, if he made his appearance presently, to mumble in his hearing some complaints that Platt was lashing them the whole time, and Uncle Abram, with an appearance of honesty peculiar to himself, would declare roundly I had just whipped them worse than General Jackson whipped the enemy at New-Orleans. If Epps was not drunk, and in one of his beastly humors, this was, in general, satisfactory. If he was, some one or more of us must suffer, as a matter of course. Sometimes his violence assumed a dangerous form, placing the lives of his human stock in jeopardy. On one occasion the drunken madman thought to amuse himself by cutting my throat.

He had been absent at Holmesville, in attendance at a shooting-match, and none of us were aware of his return. While hoeing by the side of Patsey, she exclaimed, in a low voice, suddenly, "Platt, d'ye see old Hog-Jaw beckoning me to come to him?"

Glancing sideways, I discovered him in the edge of the field, motioning and grimacing, as was his habit when half-intoxicated. Aware of his lewd intentions, Patsey began to cry. I whispered her not to look up, and to continue at her work, as if she had not observed him. Suspecting the truth of the matter, however, he soon staggered up to me in a great rage.

"What did you say to Pats?" he demanded, with an oath. I made him some evasive answer, which only had the effect of increasing his violence.

"How long have you owned this plantation, *say*, you d——d

nigger?" he inquired, with a malicious sneer, at the same time taking hold of my shirt collar with one hand, and thrusting the other into his pocket. "Now I'll cut your black throat; that's what I'll do," drawing his knife from his pocket as he said it. But with one hand he was unable to open it, until finally seizing the blade in his teeth, I saw he was about to succeed, and felt the necessity of escaping from him, for in his present reckless state, it was evident he was not joking, by any means. My shirt was open in front, and as I turned round quickly and sprang from him, while he still retained his grip, it was stripped entirely from my back. There was no difficulty now in eluding him. He would chase me until out of breath, then stop until it was recovered, swear, and renew the chase again. Now he would command me to come to him, now endeavor to coax me, but I was careful to keep at a respectful distance. In this manner we made the circuit of the field several times, he making desperate plunges, and I always dodging them, more amused than frightened, well knowing that when his sober senses returned, he would laugh at his own drunken folly. At length I observed the mistress standing by the yard fence, watching our half-serious, half-comical manœuvres. Shooting past him, I ran directly to her. Epps, on discovering her, did not follow. He remained about the field an hour or more, during which time I stood by the mistress, having related the particulars of what had taken place. Now, *she* was aroused again, denouncing her husband and Patsey about equally. Finally, Epps came towards the house, by this time nearly sober, walking demurely, with his hands behind his back, and attempting to look as innocent as a child.

As he approached, nevertheless, Mistress Epps began to berate him roundly, heaping upon him many rather disrespectful epithets, and demanding for what reason he had attempted to cut my throat. Epps made wondrous strange of it all, and to my surprise, swore by all the saints in the calendar he had not spoken to me that day.

"Platt, you lying nigger, *have* I?" was his brazen appeal to me.

It is not safe to contradict a master, even by the assertion of a truth. So I was silent, and when he entered the house I returned to the field, and the affair was never after alluded to.

Shortly after this time a circumstance occurred that came nigh divulging the secret of my real name and history, which I had so long and carefully concealed, and upon which I was convinced depended my final escape. Soon after he purchased me, Epps asked me if I could write and read, and on being informed that I had received some instruction in those branches of education, he assured me, with emphasis, if he ever caught me with a book, or with pen and ink, he would give me a hundred lashes. He said he wanted me to understand that he bought "niggers" to work and not to educate. He never inquired a word of my past life, or from whence I came. The mistress, however, cross-examined me frequently about Washington, which she supposed was my native city, and more than once remarked that I did not talk nor act like the other "niggers," and she was sure I had seen more of the world than I admitted.

My great object always was to invent means of getting a letter secretly into the post-office, directed to some of my friends or family at the North. The difficulty of such an achievement cannot be comprehended by one unacquainted with the severe restrictions imposed upon me. In the first place, I was deprived of pen, ink, and paper. In the second place, a slave cannot leave his plantation without a pass, nor will a post-master mail a letter for one without written instructions from his owner. I was in slavery nine years, and always watchful and on the alert, before I met with the good fortune of obtaining a sheet of paper. While Epps was in New-Orleans, one winter, disposing of his cotton, the mistress sent me to Holmesville, with an order for several articles, and among the rest a quantity of foolscap. I appropriated a sheet concealing it in the cabin, under the board on which I slept.

After various experiments I succeeded in making ink, by boiling white maple bark, and with a feather plucked from the wing of a duck, manufactured a pen. When all were asleep in the cabin, by the light of the coals, lying upon my plank couch, I managed to complete a somewhat lengthy epistle. It was directed to an old acquaintance at Sandy Hill, stating my condition, and urging him to take measures to restore me to liberty. This letter I kept a long time, contriving measures by which it could be safely deposited in the post-office. At length, a low fellow, by the name of Armsby, hitherto a stranger, came into the neighborhood, seeking a situation as overseer. He applied to Epps, and was about the plantation for several days. He next went over to Shaw's, near by, and remained with him several weeks. Shaw was generally surrounded by such worthless characters, being himself noted as a gambler and unprincipled man. He had made a wife of his slave Charlotte, and a brood of young mulattoes were growing up in his house. Armsby became so much reduced at last, that he was compelled to labor with the slaves. A white man working in the field is a rare and unusual spectacle on Bayou Bœuf. I improved every opportunity of cultivating his acquaintance privately, desiring to obtain his confidence so far as to be willing to intrust the letter to his keeping. He visited Marksville repeatedly, he informed me, a town some twenty miles distant, and there, I proposed to myself, the letter should be mailed.

Carefully deliberating on the most proper manner of approaching him on the subject, I concluded finally to ask him simply if he would deposit a letter for me in the Marksville post-office the next time he visited that place, without disclosing to him that the letter was written, or any of the particulars it contained; for I had fears that he might betray me, and knew that some inducement must be held out to him of a pecuniary nature, before it would be safe to confide in him. As late as one o'clock one night I stole noiselessly from my cabin, and, crossing the field to Shaw's, found him sleeping on the piazza. I had but a few picayunes—the proceeds of my fiddling performances, but all I had in the world I promised him if he would do me the favor required. I begged him not to expose me if he could not grant the request. He assured me, upon his honor, he would deposit it in the Marksville post-office, and that he would keep it an inviolable secret forever. Though the letter was in my pocket at the time, I dared not then deliver it to him, but stating I would have it written in a day or two, bade him good night, and returned to my cabin. It was impossible for me to expel the suspicions I entertained, and all night I lay awake, revolving in my mind the safest course to pursue. I was willing to risk a great deal to accomplish my purpose, but should the letter by any means fall into the hands of Epps, it would be a death-blow to my aspirations. I was "perplexed in the extreme."

My suspicions were well-founded, as the sequel demonstrated. The next day but one, while scraping cotton in the field, Epps seated himself on the line fence between Shaw's plantation and his own, in such a position as to overlook the scene of our labors. Presently Armsby made his appearance, and, mounting the fence, took a seat beside him. They remained two or three hours, all of which time I was in an agony of apprehension.

That night, while broiling my bacon, Epps entered the cabin with his rawhide in his hand.

"Well, boy," said he, "I understand I've got a larned nigger, that writes letters, and tries to get white fellows to mail 'em. Wonder if you know who he is?"

My worst fears were realized, and although it may not be considered entirely creditable, even under the circumstances, yet a resort to duplicity and downright falsehood was the only refuge that presented itself.

"Don't know nothing about it, Master Epps," I answered him, assuming an air of ignorance and surprise; "Don't know nothing at all about it, sir."

"Wan't you over to Shaw's night before last?" he inquired.

"No, master," was the reply.

"Haven't you asked that fellow, Armsby, to mail a letter for you at Marksville?"

"Why, Lord, master, I never spoke three words to him in all my life. I don't know what you mean."

"Well," he continued, "Armsby told me to-day the devil was among my niggers; that I had one that needed close watching or he would run away; and when I axed him why, he said you come over to Shaw's, and waked him up in the night, and wanted him to carry a letter to Marksville. What have you got to say to that, ha?"

"All I've got to say, master," I replied, "is, there is no truth in it. How could I write a letter without any ink or paper? There is nobody I want to write to, 'cause I haint got no friends living as I know of. That Armsby is a lying, drunken fellow, they say, and nobody believes him anyway. You know I always tell the truth, and that I never go off the plantation without a pass. Now, master, I can see what that Armsby is after, plain enough. Didn't he want you to hire him for an overseer?"

"Yes, he wanted me to hire him," answered Epps.

"That's it," said I, "he wants to make you believe we're all going to run away, and then he thinks you'll hire an overseer to watch us. He just made that story out of whole cloth, 'cause he wants to get a situation. It's all a lie, master, you may depend on't."

Epps mused awhile, evidently impressed with the plausibility of my theory, and exclaimed,

"I'm d——d, Platt, if I don't believe you tell the truth. He must take me for a soft, to think he can come it over me with them kind of yarns, mustn't he? Maybe he thinks he can fool me; maybe he thinks I don't know nothing—can't take care of my own niggers, eh! Soft soap old Epps, eh! Ha, ha, ha! D—n Armsby! Set the dogs on him, Platt," and with many other comments descriptive of Armsby's general character, and his capability of taking care of his own business, and attending to his own "niggers," Master Epps left the cabin. As soon as he was gone I threw the letter in the fire, and, with a desponding and despairing heart, beheld the epistle which had cost me so much anxiety and thought, and which I fondly hoped would have been my forerunner to the land of freedom, writhe and shrivel on its bed of coals, and dissolve into smoke and ashes. Armsby, the treacherous wretch, was driven from Shaw's plantation not long subsequently, much to my relief, for I feared he might renew his conversation, and perhaps induce Epps to credit him.

I knew not now whither to look for deliverance. Hopes sprang up in my heart only to be crushed and blighted. The summer of my life was passing away; I felt I was growing prematurely old; that a few years more, and toil, and grief, and the poisonous miasmas of the swamps would accomplish their work upon me—would consign me to the grave's embrace, to moulder and be forgotten. Repelled, betrayed, cut off from the hope of succor, I could only prostrate myself upon the earth and groan in unutterable anguish. The hope of rescue was the only light that cast a ray of comfort on my heart. That was now flickering, faint and low; another breath of disappointment would extinguish it altogether, leaving me to grope in midnight darkness to the end of life.

XVII

Wiley disregards the counsels of Aunt Phebe and Uncle Abram, and is caught by the patrollers.—The organization and duties of the latter.—Wiley runs away.—Speculations in regard to him.—His unexpected return.—His capture on Red River, and confinement in Alexandria jail.—Discovered by Joseph B. Roberts.—Subduing dogs in anticipation of escape.—The fugitives in the Great Pine Woods.—Captured by

Adam Taydem and the Indians.—Augustus killed by dogs.—Nelly, Eldret's slave woman.—The story of Celeste.—The concerted movement.—Lew Cheney, the traitor.—The idea of insurrection.

The year 1850, down to which time I have now arrived, omitting many occurrences uninteresting to the reader, was an unlucky year for my companion Wiley, the husband of Phebe, whose taciturn and retiring nature has thus far kept him in the background. Notwithstanding Wiley seldom opened his mouth, and revolved in his obscure and unpretending orbit without a grumble, nevertheless the warm elements of sociality were strong in the bosom of that silent "nigger." In the exuberance of his self-reliance, disregarding the philosophy of Uncle Abram, and setting the counsels of Aunt Phebe utterly at naught, he had the fool-hardiness to essay a nocturnal visit to a neighboring cabin without a pass.

So attractive was the society in which he found himself, that Wiley took little note of the passing hours, and the light began to break in the east before he was aware. Speeding homeward as fast as he could run, he hoped to reach the quarters before the horn would sound; but, unhappily, he was spied on the way by a company of patrollers.

How it is in other dark places of slavery, I do not know, but on Bayou Bœuf there is an organization of patrollers, as they are styled, whose business it is to seize and whip any slave they may find wandering from the plantation. They ride on horseback, headed by a captain, armed, and accompanied by dogs. They have the right, either by law, or by general consent, to inflict discretionary chastisement upon a black man caught beyond the boundaries of his master's estate without a pass, and even to shoot him, if he attempts to escape. Each company has a certain distance to ride up and down the bayou. They are compensated by the planters, who contribute in proportion to the number of slaves they own. The clatter of their horses' hoofs dashing by can be heard at all hours of the night, and frequently they may be seen driving a slave before them, or leading him by a rope fastened around his neck, to his owner's plantation.

Wiley fled before one of these companies, thinking he could reach his cabin before they could overtake him; but one of their dogs, a great ravenous hound, gripped him by the leg, and held him fast. The patrollers whipped him severely, and brought him, a prisoner, to Epps. From him he received another flagellation still more severe, so that the cuts of the lash and the bites of the dog rendered him sore, stiff and miserable, insomuch he was scarcely able to move. It was impossible in such a state to keep up his row, and consequently there was not an hour in the day but Wiley felt the sting of his master's rawhide on his raw and bleeding back. His sufferings became intolerable, and finally he resolved to run away. Without disclosing his intentions to run away even to his wife Phebe, he proceeded to make arrangements for carrying his plan into execution. Having cooked his whole week's allowance, he cautiously left the cabin on a Sunday night, after the inmates of the quarters were asleep. When the horn sounded in the morning, Wiley did not make his appearance. Search was made for him in the cabins, in the corn-crib, in the cotton-house, and in every nook and corner of the premises. Each of us was examined, touching any knowledge we might have that could throw light upon his sudden disappearance or present whereabouts. Epps raved and stormed, and mounting his horse, galloped to neighboring plantations, making inquiries in all directions. The search was fruitless. Nothing whatever was elicited, going to show what had become of the missing man. The dogs were led to the swamp, but were unable to strike his trail. They would circle away through the forest, their noses to the ground, but invariably returned in a short time to the spot from whence they started.

Wiley had escaped, and so secretly and cautiously as to elude and baffle all pursuit. Days and even weeks passed away, and nothing could be heard of him. Epps did nothing but curse and swear. It was the only topic of conversation among us when alone. We indulged in a great deal of speculation in regard to him, one suggesting he might have been drowned in some bayou, inasmuch as he was a poor swimmer; another, that perhaps he might have been devoured by alligators, or stung by the venomous moccasin, whose bite is certain and sudden death. The warm and hearty sympathies of us all, however, were with poor Wiley, wherever he might be. Many an earnest prayer ascended from the lips of Uncle Abram, beseeching safety for the wanderer.

In about three weeks, when all hope of ever seeing him again was dismissed, to our surprise, he one day appeared among us. On leaving the plantation, he informed us, it was his intention to make his way back to South Carolina—to the old quarters of Master Buford. During the day he remained secreted, sometimes in the branches of a tree, and at night pressed forward through the swamps. Finally, one morning, just at dawn, he reached the shore of Red River. While standing on the bank, considering how he could cross it, a white man accosted him, and demanded a pass. Without one, and evidently a runaway, he was taken to Alexandria, the shire town of the parish of Rapides, and confined in prison. It happened several days after that Joseph B. Roberts, uncle of Mistress Epps, was in Alexandria, and going into the jail, recognized him. Wiley had worked on his plantation, when Epps resided at Huff Power. Paying the jail fee, and writing him a pass, underneath which was a note to Epps, requesting him not to whip him on his return, Wiley was sent back to Bayou Bœuf. It was the hope that hung upon this request, and which Roberts assured him would be respected by his master, that sustained him as he approached the house. The request, however, as may be readily supposed, was entirely disregarded. After being kept in suspense three days, Wiley was stripped, and compelled to endure one of those inhuman floggings to which the poor slave is so often subjected. It was the first and last attempt of Wiley to run away. The long scars upon his back, which he will carry with him to the grave, perpetually remind him of the dangers of such a step.

There was not a day throughout the ten years I belonged to Epps that I did not consult with myself upon the prospect of escape. I laid many plans, which at the time I considered excellent ones, but one after the other they were all abandoned. No man who has never been placed in such a situation, can comprehend the thousand obstacles thrown in the way of the flying slave. Every white man's hand is raised against him—the patrollers are watching for him—the hounds are ready to follow on his track, and the nature of the country is such as renders it impossible to pass through it with any safety. I thought, however, that the time might come, perhaps, when I should be running through the swamps again. I concluded, in that case, to be prepared for Epps' dogs, should they pursue me. He possessed several, one of which was a notorious slave-hunter, and the most fierce and savage of his breed. While out hunting the coon or the opossum, I never allowed an opportunity to escape, when alone, of whipping them severely. In this manner I succeeded at length in subduing them completely. They feared me, obeying my voice at once when others had no control over them whatever. Had they followed and overtaken me, I doubt not they would have shrank from attacking me.

Notwithstanding the certainty of being captured, the woods and swamps are, nevertheless, continually filled with runaways. Many of them, when sick, or so worn out as to be unable to perform their tasks, escape into the swamps, willing to suffer the punishment inflicted for such offences, in order to obtain a day or two of rest.

While I belonged to Ford, I was unwittingly the means of disclosing the hiding-place of six or eight, who had taken up their residence in the "Great Pine Woods." Adam Taydem frequently sent me from the mills over to the opening after provisions. The whole distance was then a thick pine forest. About ten o'clock of a beautiful moonlight night, while walking along the Texas road, returning to the mills, carrying a dressed pig in a bag swung over my shoulder, I heard footsteps behind me, and turning round, beheld two black men in the dress of slaves approaching at rapid pace. When within a short distance, one of them raised a club, as if intending to strike me; the other snatched at the bag. I managed to dodge them both, and seizing a pine knot, hurled it with such force against the head of one of them that he was prostrated apparently senseless to the ground. Just then two more made their appearance from one side of the road. Before they could grapple me, however, I succeeded in passing them, and taking to my heels, fled, much affrighted, towards the mills. When Adam was informed of the adventure, he hastened straightway to the Indian village, and arousing Cascalla and several of his tribe, started in pursuit of the highwaymen. I accompanied them to the scene of attack, when we discovered a puddle of blood in the road, where the man whom I had smitten with the pine knot had fallen. After searching carefully through the woods a long time, one of Cascalla's men discovered a smoke curling up through the branches of several prostrate pines, whose tops had fallen together. The rendezvous was cautiously surrounded, and all of them taken prisoners. They had escaped from a plantation in the vicinity of Lamourie, and had been secreted there three weeks. They had no evil design upon me, except to frighten me out of my pig. Having observed me passing towards Ford's just at night-fall, and suspecting the nature of my errand, they had followed me, seen me butcher and dress the porker, and start on my return. They had been pinched for food, and were driven to this extremity by necessity. Adam conveyed them to the parish jail, and was liberally rewarded.

Not unfrequently the runaway loses his life in the attempt to escape. Epps' premises were bounded on one side by Carey's, a very extensive sugar plantation. He cultivates annually at least fifteen hundred acres of cane, manufacturing twenty-two or twenty-three hundred hogsheads of sugar; an hogshead and a half being the usual yield of an acre. Besides this he also cultivates five or six hundred acres of corn and cotton. He owned last year one hundred and fifty-three field hands, besides nearly as many children, and yearly hires a drove during the busy season from this side the Mississippi.

One of his negro drivers, a pleasant, intelligent boy, was named Augustus. During the holidays, and occasionally while at work in adjoining fields, I had an opportunity of making his acquaintance, which eventually ripened into a warm and mutual attachment. Summer before last he was so unfortunate as to incur the displeasure of the overseer, a coarse, heartless brute, who whipped him most cruelly. Augustus ran away. Reaching a cane rick on Hawkins' plantation, he secreted himself in the top of it. All Carey's dogs were put upon his track—some fifteen of them—and soon scented his footsteps to the hiding place. They surrounded the rick, baying and scratching, but could not reach him. Presently, guided by the clamor of the hounds, the pursuers rode up, when the overseer, mounting on to the rick, drew him forth. As he rolled down to the ground the whole pack plunged upon him, and before they could be beaten off, had gnawed and mutilated his body in the most shocking manner, their teeth having penetrated to the bone in an hundred places. He was taken up, tied upon a mule, and carried home. But this was Augustus' last trouble. He lingered until the next day, when death sought the unhappy boy, and kindly relieved him from his agony.

It was not unusual for slave women as well as slave men to endeavor to escape. Nelly, Eldret's girl, with whom I lumbered for a time in the "Big Cane Brake," lay concealed in Epps' corn crib three days. At night, when his family were asleep, she would steal into the quarters for food, and return to the crib again. We concluded it would no longer be safe for us to allow her to remain, and accordingly she retraced her steps to her own cabin.

But the most remarkable instance of a successful evasion of dogs and hunters was the following: Among Carey's girls was one by the name of Celeste. She was nineteen or twenty, and far whiter than her owner, or any of his offspring. It required a close inspection to distinguish in her features the slightest trace of African blood. A stranger would never have dreamed that she was the descendant of slaves. I was sitting in my cabin late at night, playing a low air on my violin, when the door opened carefully, and Celeste stood before me. She was pale and haggard. Had an apparition arisen from the earth, I could not have been more startled.

"Who are you?" I demanded, after gazing at her a moment.

"I'm hungry; give me some bacon," was her reply.

My first impression was that she was some deranged young mistress, who, escaping from home, was wandering, she knew not whither, and had been attracted to my cabin by the sound of the violin. The coarse cotton slave dress she wore, however, soon dispelled such a supposition.

"What is your name?" I again interrogated.

"My name is Celeste," she answered. "I belong to Carey, and have been two days among the palmettoes. I am sick and can't work, and would rather die in the swamp than be whipped to death by the overseer. Carey's dogs won't follow me. They have tried to set them on. There's a secret between them and Celeste, and they won't mind the devilish orders of the overseer. Give me some meat—I'm starving."

I divided my scanty allowance with her, and while partaking of it, she related how she had managed to escape, and described the place of her concealment. In the edge of the swamp, not half a mile from Epps' house, was a large space, thousands of acres in extent, thickly covered with palmetto. Tall trees, whose long arms interlocked each other, formed a canopy above them, so dense as to exclude the beams of the sun. It was like twilight always, even in the middle of the brightest day. In the centre of this great space, which nothing but serpents very often explore—a sombre and solitary spot—Celeste had erected a rude hut of dead branches that had fallen to the ground, and covered it with the leaves of the palmetto. This was the abode she had selected. She had no fear of Carey's dogs, any more than I had of Epps'. It is a fact, which I have never been able to explain, that there are those whose tracks the hounds will absolutely refuse to follow. Celeste was one of them.

For several nights she came to my cabin for food. On one occasion our dogs barked as she approached, which aroused Epps, and induced him to reconnoitre the premises. He did not discover her, but after that it was not deemed prudent for her to come to the yard. When all was silent I carried provisions to a certain spot agreed upon, where she would find them.

In this manner Celeste passed the greater part of the summer. She regained her health, and became strong and hearty. At all seasons of the year the howlings of wild animals can be heard at night along the borders of the swamps. Several times they had made her a midnight call, awakening her from slumber with a growl. Terrified by such unpleasant salutations, she finally concluded to abandon her lonely dwelling; and, accordingly, returning to her master, was scourged, her neck meanwhile being fastened in the stocks, and sent into the field again.

The year before my arrival in the country there was a concerted movement among a number of slaves on Bayou Bœuf, that terminated tragically indeed. It was, I presume, a matter of newspaper notoriety at the time, but all the knowledge I have of it, has been derived from the relation of those living at that period in the immediate vicinity of the excitement. It has become a subject of general and unfailing interest in every slave-hut on the bayou, and will doubtless go down to succeeding generations as their chief tradition. Lew Cheney, with whom I became acquainted—a shrewd, cunning negro, more intelligent than the generality of his race, but unscrupulous and full of treachery—conceived the project of organizing a company sufficiently strong to fight their way against all opposition, to the neighboring territory of Mexico.

A remote spot, far within the depths of the swamp, back of Hawkins' plantation, was selected as the rallying point. Lew flitted from one plantation to another, in the dead of night, preaching a crusade to Mexico, and, like Peter the Hermit, creating a furor of excitement wherever he appeared. At length a large number of runaways were assembled; stolen mules, and corn gathered from the fields, and bacon filched from smoke-houses, had been conveyed into the woods. The expedition was about ready to proceed, when their hiding place was discovered. Lew Cheney, becoming convinced of the ultimate failure of his project, in order to curry favor with his master, and avoid the consequences which he foresaw would follow, deliberately determined to sacrifice all his companions. Departing secretly from the encampment, he proclaimed among the planters the number collected in the swamp, and, instead of stating truly the object they had in view, asserted their intention was to emerge from their seclusion the first favorable opportunity, and murder every white person along the bayou.

Such an announcement, exaggerated as it passed from mouth to mouth, filled the whole country with terror. The fugitives were surrounded and taken prisoners, carried in chains to Alexandria, and hung by the populace. Not only those, but many who were suspected, though entirely innocent, were taken from the field and from the cabin, and without the shadow of process or form of trial, hurried to the scaffold. The planters on Bayou Bœuf finally rebelled against such reckless destruction of property, but it was not until a regiment of soldiers had arrived from some fort on the Texan frontier, demolished the gallows, and opened the doors of the Alexandria prison, that the indiscriminate slaughter was stayed. Lew Cheney escaped, and was even rewarded for his treachery. He is still living, but his name is despised and execrated by all his race throughout the parishes of Rapides and Avoyelles.

Such an idea as insurrection, however, is not new among the enslaved population of Bayou Bœuf. More than once I have joined in serious consultation, when the subject has been discussed, and there have been times when a word from me would have placed hundreds of my fellow-bondsmen in an attitude of defiance. Without arms or ammunition, or even with them, I saw such a step would result in certain defeat, disaster and death, and always raised my voice against it.

During the Mexican War I well remember the extravagant hopes that were excited. The news of victory filled the great house with rejoicing, but produced only sorrow and disappointment in the cabin. In my opinion—and I have had opportunity to know something of the feeling of which I speak—there are not fifty slaves on the shores of Bayou Bœuf, but would hail with unmeasured delight the approach of an invading army.

They are deceived who flatter themselves that the ignorant and debased slave has no conception of the magnitude of his wrongs. They are deceived who imagine that he arises from his knees, with back lacerated and bleeding, cherishing only a spirit of meekness and forgiveness. A day may come—it *will* come, if his prayer is heard—a terrible day of vengeance, when the master in his turn will cry in vain for mercy.

XVIII

O'Niel, the tanner.—Conversation with Aunt Phebe overheard.—Epps in the tanning business.—Stabbing of Uncle Abram.—The ugly wound.—Epps is jealous.—Patsey is missing.—Her return from Shaw's.—Harriet, Shaw's black wife. —Epps enraged.—Patsey denies his charges.—She is tied down to four stakes.—The inhuman flogging.—Flaying of Patsey.—The beauty of the day.—The bucket of salt water. —The dress stiff with blood.—Patsey grows melancholy.—Her idea of God and Eternity.—Of heaven and freedom.—The effect of slave-whipping.—Epps' oldest son.—"The child is father to the man."

Wiley suffered severely at the hands of Master Epps, as has been related in the preceeding chapter, but in this respect he fared no worse than his unfortunate companions. "Spare the rod," was an idea scouted by our master. He was constitutionally subject to periods of ill-humor, and at such times, however little provocation there might be, a certain amount of punishment was inflicted. The circumstances attending the last flogging but one that I received, will show how trivial a cause was sufficient with him for resorting to the whip.

A Mr. O'Niel, residing in the vicinity of the Big Pine Woods, called upon Epps for the purpose of purchasing me. He was a tanner and currier by occupation, transacting an extensive business, and intended to place me at service in some department of his establishment, provided he bought me. Aunt Phebe, while preparing the dinner-table in the great house, overheard their conversation. On returning to the yard at night, the old woman ran to meet me, designing, of course, to overwhelm me with the news. She entered into a minute repetition of all she had heard, and Aunt Phebe was one whose ears never failed to drink in every word of conversation uttered in her hearing. She enlarged upon the fact that "Massa Epps was g'wine to sell me to a tanner ober in de Pine Woods," so long and loudly as to attract the attention of the mistress, who, standing unobserved on the piazza at the time, was listening to our conversation.

"Well, Aunt Phebe," said I, "I'm glad of it. I'm tired of scraping cotton, and would rather be a tanner. I hope he'll buy me."

O'Niel did not effect a purchase, however, the parties differing as to price, and the morning following his arrival, departed homewards. He had gone but a short time, when Epps made his appearance in the field. Now nothing will more violently enrage a master, especially Epps, than the intimation of one of his servants that he would like to leave him. Mistress Epps had repeated to him my expressions to Aunt Phebe the evening previous, as I learned from the latter afterwards, the mistress having mentioned to her that she had overheard us. On entering the field, Epps walked directly to me.

"So, Platt, you're tired of scraping cotton, are you? You would like to change your master, eh? You're fond of moving round—traveler—ain't ye? Ah, yes—like to travel for your health, may be? Feel above cotton-scraping, I 'spose. So you're going into the tanning business? Good business—devilish fine business. Enterprising nigger! B'lieve I'll go into that business myself. Down on your knees, and strip that rag off your back! I'll try my hand at tanning."

I begged earnestly, and endeavored to soften him with excuses, but in vain. There was no other alternative; so kneeling down, I presented my bare back for the application of the lash.

"How do you like *tanning?*" he exclaimed, as the rawhide descended upon my flesh. "How do you like *tanning?*" he repeated at every blow. In this manner he gave me twenty or thirty lashes, incessantly giving utterance to the word "tanning," in one form of expression or another. When sufficiently "tanned," he allowed me to arise, and with a half-malicious laugh assured me, if I still fancied the business, he would give me further instruction in it whenever I desired. This time, he remarked, he had only given me a short lesson in *"tanning"*—the next time he would "curry me down."

Uncle Abram, also, was frequently treated with great brutality, although he was one of the kindest and most faithful creatures in the world. He was my cabin-mate for years. There was a benevolent expression in the old man's face, pleasant to behold. He regarded us with a kind of parental feeling, always counseling us with remarkable gravity and deliberation.

Returning from Marshall's plantation one afternoon, whither I had been sent on some errand of the mistress, I found him lying on the cabin floor, his clothes saturated with blood. He informed me that he had been stabbed! While spreading cotton on the scaffold, Epps came home intoxicated from Holmesville. He found fault with every thing, giving many orders so directly contrary that it was impossible to execute any of them. Uncle Abram, whose faculties were growing dull, became confused, and committed some blunder of no particular consequence. Epps was so enraged thereat, that, with drunken recklessness, he flew upon the old man, and stabbed him in the back. It was a long, ugly wound, but did not happen to penetrate far enough to result fatally. It was sewed up by the mistress, who censured her husband with extreme severity, not only denouncing his inhumanity, but declaring that she expected nothing else than that he would bring the family to poverty—that he would kill all the slaves on the plantation in some of his drunken fits.

It was no uncommon thing with him to prostrate Aunt Phebe with a chair or stick of wood; but the most cruel whipping that ever I was doomed to witness—one I can never recall with any other emotion than that of horror—was inflicted on the unfortunate Patsey.

It has been seen that the jealousy and hatred of Mistress Epps made the daily life of her young and agile slave completely miserable. I am happy in the belief that on numerous occasions I was the means of averting punishment from the inoffensive girl. In Epps's absence the mistress often ordered me to whip her without the remotest provocation. I would refuse, saying that I feared my master's displeasure, and several times ventured to remonstrate with her against the treatment Patsey received. I endeavored to impress her with the truth that the latter was not responsible for the acts of which she complained, but that she being a slave, and subject entirely to her master's will, he alone was answerable.

At length "the green-eyed monster" crept into the soul of Epps also, and then it was that he joined with his wrathful wife in an infernal jubilee over the girl's miseries.

On a Sabbath day in hoeing time, not long ago, we were on the bayou bank, washing our clothes, as was our usual custom. Presently Patsey was missing. Epps called aloud, but there was no answer. No one had observed her leaving the yard, and it was a wonder with us whither she had gone. In the course of a couple of hours she was seen approaching from the direction of Shaw's. This man, as has been intimated, was a notorious profligate, and withal not on the most friendly terms with Epps. Harriet, his black wife, knowing Patsey's troubles, was kind to her, in consequence of which the latter was in the habit of going over to see her every opportunity. Her visits were prompted by friendship merely, but the suspicion gradually entered the brain of Epps, that another and a baser passion led her thither—that it was not Harriet she desired to meet, but rather the unblushing libertine, his neighbor. Patsey found her master in a fearful rage on her return. His violence so alarmed her that at first she attempted to evade direct answers to his questions, which only served to increase his suspicions. She finally, however, drew herself up proudly, and in a spirit of indignation boldly denied his charges.

"Missus don't give me soap to wash with, as she does the rest," said Patsey, "and you know why. I went over to Harriet's to get a piece," and saying this, she drew it forth from a pocket in her dress and exhibited it to him. "That's what I went to Shaw's for, Massa Epps," continued she; "the Lord knows that was all."

"You lie, you black wench!" shouted Epps.

"I *don't* lie, massa. If you kill me, I'll stick to that."

"Oh! I'll fetch you down. I'll learn you to go to Shaw's. I'll take the starch out of ye," he muttered fiercely through his shut teeth.

Then turning to me, he ordered four stakes to be driven into the ground, pointing with the toe of his boot to the places where he wanted them. When the stakes were driven down, he ordered her to be stripped of every article of dress. Ropes were then brought, and the naked girl was laid upon her face, her wrists and feet each tied firmly to a stake. Stepping to the piazza, he took down a heavy whip, and placing it in my hands, commanded me to lash her. Unpleasant as it was, I was compelled to obey him. Nowhere that day, on the face of the whole earth, I venture to say, was there such a demoniac exhibition witnessed as then ensued.

Mistress Epps stood on the piazza among her children, gazing on the scene with an air of heartless satisfaction. The slaves were huddled together in a little distance, their countenances indicating the sorrow of their hearts. Poor Patsey prayed piteously for mercy, but her prayers were vain. Epps ground his teeth, and stamped upon the ground, screaming at me, like a mad fiend, to strike *harder*.

"Strike harder, or *your* turn will come next, you scoundrel," he yelled.

"Oh, mercy, massa!—oh! have mercy, *do*. Oh, God! pity me," Patsey exclaimed continually, struggling fruitlessly, and the flesh quivering at every stroke.

When I had struck her as many as thirty times, I stopped, and turned round toward Epps, hoping he was satisfied; but with bitter oaths and threats, he ordered me to continue. I inflicted ten or fifteen blows more. By this time her back was covered with long welts, intersecting each other like net work. Epps was yet furious and savage as ever, demanding if she would like to go to Shaw's again, and swearing he would flog her until she wished she was in h—l. Throwing down the whip, I declared I could punish her no more. He ordered me to go on, threatening me with a severer flogging than she had received, in case of refusal. My heart revolted at the inhuman scene, and risking the consequences, I absolutely refused to raise the whip. He then seized it himself, and applied it with ten-fold greater force than I had. The painful cries and shrieks of the tortured Patsey, mingling with the load and angry curses of Epps, loaded the air. She was terribly lacerated—I may say, without exaggeration, literally flayed. The lash was wet with blood, which flowed down her sides and dropped upon the ground. At length she ceased struggling. Her head sank listlessly on the ground. Her screams and supplications gradually decreased and died away into a low moan. She no longer writhed and shrank beneath the lash when it bit out small pieces of her flesh. I thought she was dying!

It was the Sabbath of the Lord. The fields smiled in the warm sunlight—the birds chirped merrily amidst the foliage of the trees—peace and happiness seemed to reign everywhere, save in the bosoms of Epps and his panting victim and the silent witnesses around him. The tempestuous emotions that were raging there were little in harmony with the calm and quiet beauty of the day. I could look on Epps only with unutterable loathing and abhorrence, and thought within myself—"Thou devil, sooner or later, somewhere in the course of eternal justice, thou shalt answer for this sin!"

Finally, he ceased whipping from mere exhaustion, and ordered Phebe to bring a bucket of salt and water. After washing her thoroughly with this, I was told to take her to my cabin. Untying the ropes, I raised her in my arms. She was unable to stand, and as her head rested on my shoulder, she repeated many times, in a faint voice scarcely perceptible, "Oh, Platt—oh, Platt!" but nothing further. Her dress was replaced, but it clung to her back, and was soon stiff with blood. We laid her on some boards in the hut, where she remained a long time, with eyes closed and groaning in agony. At night Phebe applied melted tallow to her wounds, and so far as we were able, all endeavored to assist and console her. Day after day she lay in her cabin upon her face, the sores preventing her resting in any other position.

A blessed thing it would have been for her—days and weeks and months of misery it would have saved her—had she never lifted up her head in life again. Indeed, from that time forward she was not what she had been. The burden of a deep melancholy weighed heavily on her spirits. She no longer moved with that buoyant and elastic step—there was not that mirthful sparkle in her eyes that formerly distinguished her. The bounding vigor—the sprightly, laughter-loving spirit of her youth, was gone. She fell into a mournful and desponding mood, and oftentimes would start up in her sleep, and with raised hands, plead for mercy. She became more silent than she was, toiling all day in our midst, not uttering a word. A care-worn, pitiful expression settled on her face, and it was her humor now to weep, rather than rejoice. If ever there was a broken heart—one crushed and blighted by the rude grasp of suffering and misfortune—it was Patsey's.

She had been reared no better than her master's beast—looked upon merely as a valuable and handsome animal—and consequently possessed but a limited amount of knowledge. And yet a faint light cast its rays over her intellect, so that it was not wholly dark. She had a dim perception of God and of eternity, and a still more dim perception of a Saviour who had died even for such as her. She entertained but confused notions of a future life—not comprehending the distinction between the corporeal and spiritual existence. Happiness, in her mind, was exemption from stripes—from labor—from the cruelty of masters and overseers. Her idea of joy of heaven was simply *rest,* and is fully expressed in these lines of a melancholy bard:

I ask no paradise on high,
With caves on earth oppressed,
The only heaven for which I sigh,
Is rest, eternal rest.

It is a mistaken opinion that prevails in some quarters, that the slave does not understand the term—does not comprehend the idea of freedom. Even on Bayou Bœuf, where I conceive slavery exists in its most abject and cruel form—where it exhibits features altogether unknown in more northern States—the most ignorant of them generally know full well its meaning. They understand the privileges and exemptions that belong to it—that it would bestow upon them the fruits of their own labors, and that it would secure to them the enjoyment of domestic happiness. They do not fail to observe the difference between their own condition and the meanest white man's, and to realize the injustice of the laws which place it in his power not only to appropriate the profits of their industry, but to subject them to unmerited and unprovoked punishment, without remedy, or the right to resist, or to remonstrate.

Patsey's life, especially after her whipping, was one long dream of liberty. Far away, to her fancy an immeasurable distance, she knew there was a land of freedom. A thousand times she had heard that somewhere in the distant North there were no slaves—no masters. In her imagination it was an enchanted region, the Paradise of the earth. To dwell where the black man may work for himself—live in his own cabin—till his own soil, was a blissful dream of Patsey's—a dream, alas! the fulfillment of which she can never realize.

The effect of these exhibitions of brutality on the household of the slave-holder, is apparent. Epps' oldest son is an intelligent lad of ten or twelve years of age. It is pitiable, sometimes, to see him chastising, for instance, the venerable Uncle Abram. He will call the old man to account, and if in his childish judgment it is necessary, sentence him to a certain number of lashes, which he proceeds to inflict with much gravity and deliberation. Mounted on his pony, he often rides into the field with his whip, playing the overseer, greatly to his father's delight. Without discrimination, at such times, he applies the rawhide, urging the slaves forward with shouts, and occasional expressions of profanity, while the old man laughs, and commends him as a thorough-going boy.

"The child is father to the man," and with such training, whatever may be his natural disposition, it cannot well be otherwise than that, on arriving at maturity, the sufferings and miseries of the slave will be looked upon with entire indifference. The influence of the iniquitous system necessarily fosters an unfeeling and cruel spirit, even in the bosoms of those who, among their equals, are regarded as humane and generous.

Young Master Epps possessed some noble qualities, yet no process of reasoning could lead him to comprehend, that in the eye of the Almighty there is no distinction of color. He looked upon the black man simply as an animal, differing in no respect from any other animal, save in the gift of speech and the possession of somewhat higher instincts, and, therefore, the more valuable. To work like his father's mules—to be whipped and kicked and scourged through life—to address the white man with hat in hand, and eyes bent servilely on the earth, in his mind, was the natural and proper destiny of the slave. Brought up with such ideas—in the notion that we stand without the pale of humanity—no wonder the oppressors of my people are a pitiless and unrelenting race.

XIX

Avery, of Bayou Rouge.—Peculiarity of dwellings.—Epps builds a new house.—Bass, the carpenter.—His noble qualities.—His personal appearance and eccentricities.—Bass and Epps discuss the question of slavery.—Epps' opinion of Bass. —I make myself known to him.—Our conversation.—His surprise.—The midnight meeting on the Bayou bank.—Bass' assurances.—Declares war against slavery.—Why I did not disclose my history.—Bass writes letters.—Copy of his letter to Messrs. Parker and Perry.—The fever of suspense.—Disappointments.—Bass endeavors to cheer me.—My faith in him.

In the month of June, 1852, in pursuance of a previous contract, Mr. Avery, a carpenter of Bayou Rouge, commenced the erection of a house for Master Epps. It has previously been stated that there are no cellars on Bayou Bœuf; on the other hand, such is the low and swampy nature of the ground, the great houses are usually built upon spiles. Another peculiarity is, the rooms are not plastered, but the ceiling and sides are covered with matched cypress boards, painted such color as most pleases the owner's taste. Generally the plank and boards are sawed by slaves with whip-saws, there being no waterpower upon which mills might be built within many miles. When the planter erects for himself a dwelling, therefore, there is plenty of extra work for his slaves. Having had some experience under Tibeats as a carpenter, I was taken from the field altogether, on the arrival of Avery and his hands.

Among them was one to whom I owe an immeasurable debt of gratitude. Only for him, in all probability, I should have ended my days in slavery. He was my deliverer—a man whose true heart overflowed with noble and generous emotions. To the last moment of my existence I shall remember him with feelings of thankfulness. His name was Bass, and at that time he resided in Marksville. It will be difficult to convey a correct impression of his appearance or character. He was a large man, between forty and fifty years old, of light complexion and light hair. He was very cool and self-possessed, fond of argument, but always speaking with extreme deliberation. He was that kind of person whose peculiarity of manner was such that nothing he uttered ever gave offence. What would be intolerable, coming from the lips of another, could be said by him with impunity. There was not a man on Red River, perhaps, that agreed with him on the subject of politics or religion, and not a man, I venture to say, who discussed either of those subjects half as much. It seemed to be taken for granted that he would espouse the unpopular side of every local question, and it always created amusement rather than displeasure among his auditors, to listen to the ingenious and original manner in which he maintained the controversy. He was a bachelor—an "old bachelor," according to the true acceptation of the term—having no kindred living, as he knew of, in the world. Neither had he any permanent abiding place—wandering from one State to another, as his fancy dictated. He had lived in Marksville three or four years, and in the prosecution of his business as a carpenter; and in consequence, likewise, of his peculiarities, was quite extensively known throughout the parish of Avoyelles. He was liberal to a fault; and his many acts of kindness and transparent goodness of heart rendered him popular in the community, the sentiment of which he unceasingly combated.

He was a native of Canada, from whence he had wandered in early life, and after visiting all the principal localities in the northern and western States, in the course of his peregrinations, arrived in the unhealthy region of the Red River. His last removal was from Illinois. Whither he has now gone, I regret to be obliged to say, is unknown to me. He gathered up his effects and departed quietly from Marksville the day before I did, the suspicions of his instrumentality in procuring my liberation rendering such a step necessary. For the commission of a just and righteous act he would undoubtedly have suffered death, had he remained within reach of the slave-whipping tribe on Bayou Bœuf.

One day, while working on the new house, Bass and Epps became engaged in a controversy, to which, as will be readily supposed, I listened with absorbing interest. They were discussing the subject of Slavery.

"I tell you what it is Epps," said Bass, "it's all wrong—all wrong, sir—there's no justice nor righteousness in it. I wouldn't own a slave if I was rich as Crœsus, which I am not, as is perfectly well understood, more particularly among my creditors. *There's* another humbug—the credit system—humbug, sir; no credit—no debt. Credit leads a man into temptation. Cash down is the only thing that will deliver him from evil. But this question of *Slavery;* what *right* have you to your niggers when you come down to the point?"

"What right!" said Epps, laughing; "why, I bought 'em, and paid for 'em."

"Of *course* you did; the law says you have the right to hold a nigger, but begging the law's pardon, it *lies.* Yes, Epps, when the law says that it's a *liar,* and the truth is not in it. Is every thing right because the law allows it? Suppose they'd pass a law taking away your liberty and making you a slave?"

"Oh, that ain't a supposable case," said Epps, still laughing; "hope you don't compare me to a nigger, Bass."

"Well," Bass answered gravely, "no, not exactly. But I have seen niggers before now as good as I am, and I have no acquaintance with any white man in these parts that I consider a whit better than myself. Now, in the sight of God, what is the difference, Epps, between a white man and a black one?"

"All the difference in the world," replied Epps. "You might as well ask what the difference is between a white man and a baboon. Now, I've seen one of them critters in Orleans that knowed just as much as any nigger I've got. You'd call them feller citizens, I s'pose?"—and Epps indulged in a loud laugh at his own wit.

"Look here, Epps," continued his companion; "you can't laugh me down in that way. Some men are witty, and some ain't so witty as they think they are. Now let me ask you a question. Are all men created free and equal as the Declaration of Independence holds they are?"

"Yes," responded Epps, "but all men, niggers, and monkeys *ain't;*" and hereupon he broke forth into a more boisterous laugh than before.

"There are monkeys among white people as well as black, when you come to that," coolly remarked Bass. "I know some white men that use arguments no sensible monkey would. But let that pass. These niggers are human beings. If they don't know as much as their masters, whose fault is it? They are not *allowed* to know anything. You have books and papers, and can go where you please, and gather intelligence in a thousand ways. But your slaves have no privileges. You'd whip one of them if caught reading a book. They are held in bondage, generation after generation, deprived of mental improvement, and who can expect them to possess much knowledge? If they are not brought down to a level with the brute creation, you slaveholders will never be blamed for it. If they are baboons, or stand no higher in the scale of intelligence than such animals, you and men like you will have to answer for it. There's a sin, a fearful sin, resting on this nation, that will not go unpunished forever. There will be a reckoning yet—yes, Epps, there's a day coming that will burn as an oven. It may be sooner or it may be later, but it's a coming as sure as the Lord is just."

"If you lived up among the Yankees in New-England," said Epps, "I expect you'd be one of them cursed fanatics that know more than the constitution, and go about peddling clocks and coaxing niggers to run away."

"If I was in New-England," returned Bass, "I would be just what I am here. I would say that Slavery was an iniquity, and ought to be abolished. I would say there was no reason nor justice in the law, or the constitution that allows one man to hold another man in bondage. It would be hard for you to lose your property, to be sure, but it wouldn't be half as hard as it would be to lose your liberty. You have no more right to your freedom, in exact justice, than Uncle Abram yonder. Talk about black skin, and black blood; why, how many slaves are there on this bayou as white as either of us? And what difference is there in the color of the soul? Pshaw! the whole system is as absurd as it is cruel. You may own niggers and be hanged, but I wouldn't own one for the best plantation in Louisiana."

"You like to hear yourself talk, Bass, better than any man I know of. You would argue that black was white, or white black, if any body would contradict you. Nothing suits you in this world, and I don't believe you will be satisfied with the next, if you should have your choice in them."

Conversations substantially like the foregoing were not unusual between the two after this; Epps drawing him out more for the purpose of creating a laugh at his expense, than with a view of fairly discussing the merits of the question. He looked upon Bass, as a man ready to say anything merely for the pleasure of hearing his own voice; as somewhat self-conceited, perhaps, contending against his faith and judgment, in order, simply to exhibit his dexterity in argumentation.

He remained at Epps' through the summer, visiting Marksville generally once a fortnight. The more I saw of him, the more I became convinced he was a man in whom I could confide. Nevertheless, my previous ill-fortune had taught me to be extremely cautious. It was not my place to speak to a white man except when spoken to, but I omitted no opportunity of throwing myself in his way, and endeavored constantly in every possible manner to attract his attention. In the early part of August he and myself were at work alone in the house, the other carpenters having left, and Epps being absent in the field. Now was the time, if ever, to broach the subject, and I resolved to do it, and submit to whatever consequences might ensue. We were busily at work in the afternoon, when I stopped suddenly and said—

"Master Bass, I want to ask you what part of the country you came from?"

"Why, Platt, what put that into your head?" he answered. "You wouldn't know if I should tell you." After a moment or two he added—"I was born in Canada; now guess where that is."

"Oh, I know where Canada is," said I, "I have been there myself."

"Yes, I expect you are well acquainted all through that country," he remarked, laughing incredulously.

"As sure as I live, Master Bass," I replied, "I have been there. I have been in Montreal and Kingston, and Queenston, and a great many places in Canada, and I have been in New-York State, too—

in Buffalo, and Rochester, and Albany, and can tell you the names of the villages on the Erie canal and the Champlain canal."

Bass turned round and gazed at me a long time without uttering a syllable.

"How came you here?" he inquired, at length, "Master Bass," I answered, "if justice had been done, I never would have been here."

"Well, how's this?" said he. "Who are you? You have been in Canada sure enough; I know all the places you mention. How did you happen to get here? Come, tell me all about it."

"I have no friends here," was my reply, "that I can put confidence in. I am afraid to tell you, though I don't believe you would tell Master Epps if I should."

He assured me earnestly he would keep every word I might speak to him a profound secret, and his curiosity was evidently strongly excited. It was a long story, I informed him, and would take some time to relate it. Master Epps would be back soon, but if he would see me that night after all were asleep, I would repeat it to him. He consented readily to the arrangement, and directed me to come into the building where we were then at work, and I would find him there. About midnight, when all was still and quiet, I crept cautiously from my cabin, and silently entering the unfinished building, found him awaiting me.

After further assurances on his part that I should not be betrayed, I began a relation of the history of my life and misfortunes. He was deeply interested, asking numerous questions in reference to localities and events. Having ended my story I besought him to write to some of my friends at the North, acquainting them with my situation, and begging them to forward free papers, or take such steps as they might consider proper to secure my release. He promised to do so, but dwelt upon the danger of such an act in case of detection, and now impressed upon me the great necessity of strict silence and secrecy. Before we parted our plan of operation was arranged.

We agreed to meet the next night at a specified place among the high weeds on the bank of the bayou, some distance from master's dwelling. There he was to write down on paper the names and addresses of several persons, old friends in the North, to whom he would direct letters during his next visit to Marksville. It was not deemed prudent to meet in the new house, inasmuch as the light it would be necessary to use might possibly be discovered. In the course of the day I managed to obtain a few matches and a piece of candle, unperceived, from the kitchen, during a temporary absence of Aunt Phebe. Bass had pencil and paper in his tool chest.

At the appointed hour we met on the bayou bank, and creeping among the high weeds, I lighted the candle, while he drew forth pencil and paper and prepared for business. I gave him the names of William Perry, Cephas Parker and Judge Marvin, all of Saratoga Springs, Saratoga county, New-York. I had been employed by the latter in the United States Hotel, and had transacted business with the former to a considerable extent, and trusted that at least one of them would be still living at that place. He carefully wrote the names, and then remarked, thoughtfully—

"It is so many years since you left Saratoga, all these men may be dead, or may have removed. You say you obtained papers at the custom house in New-York. Probably there is a record of them there, and I think it would be well to write and ascertain."

I agreed with him, and again repeated the circumstances related heretofore, connected with my visit to the custom house with Brown and Hamilton. We lingered on the bank of the bayou an hour or more, conversing upon the subject which now engrossed our thoughts. I could no longer doubt his fidelity, and freely spoke to him of the many sorrows I had borne in silence, and so long. I spoke of my wife and children, mentioning their names and ages, and dwelling upon the unspeakable happiness it would be to clasp them to my heart once more before I died. I caught him by the hand, and with tears and passionate entreaties implored him to befriend me—to restore me to my kindred and to liberty—promising I would weary Heaven the remainder of my life with prayers that it would bless and prosper him. In the enjoyment of freedom—surrounded by the associations of youth, and restored to the bosom of my family—that promise is not yet forgotten, nor shall it ever be so long as I have strength to raise my imploring eyes on high.

Oh, blessings on his kindly voice and on his silver hair,
And blessings on his whole life long, until he meet me there.

He overwhelmed me with assurances of friendship and faithfulness, saying he had never before taken so deep an interest in the fate of any one. He spoke of himself in a somewhat mournful tone, as a lonely man, a wanderer about the world—that he was growing old, and must soon reach the end of his earthly journey, and lie down to his final rest without kith or kin to mourn for him, or to remember him—that his life was of little value to himself, and henceforth should be devoted to the accomplishment of my liberty, and to an unceasing warfare against the accursed shame of Slavery.

After this time we seldom spoke to, or recognized each other. He was, moreover, less free in his conversation with Epps on the subject of Slavery. The remotest suspicion that there was any unusual intimacy—any secret understanding between us—never once entered the mind of Epps, or any other person, white or black, on the plantation.

I am often asked, with an air of incredulity, how I succeeded so many years in keeping from my daily and constant companions the knowledge of my true name and history. The terrible lesson Burch taught me, impressed indelibly upon my mind the danger and uselessness of asserting I was a freeman. There was no possibility of any slave being able to assist me, while, on the other hand, there *was* a possibility of his exposing me. When it is recollected the whole current of my thoughts, for twelve years, turned to the contemplation of escape, it will not be wondered at, that I was always cautious and on my guard. It would have been an act of folly to have proclaimed my *right* to freedom; it would only have subjected me to severer scrutiny—probably have consigned me to some more distant and inaccessible region than even Bayou Bœuf. Edwin Epps was a person utterly regardless of a black man's rights or wrongs—utterly destitute of any natural sense of justice, as I well knew. It was important, therefore, not only as regarded my hope of deliverance, but also as regarded the few personal privileges I was permitted to enjoy, to keep from him the history of my life.

The Saturday night subsequent to our interview at the water's edge, Bass went home to Marksville. The next day, being Sunday, he employed himself in his own room writing letters. One he directed to the Collector of Customs at New-York, another to Judge Marvin, and another to Messrs. Parker and Perry jointly. The latter was the one which led to my recovery. He subscribed my true name, but in the postscript intimated I was not the writer. The letter itself shows that he considered himself engaged in a dangerous undertaking—no less than running "the risk of his life, if detected." I did not see the letter before it was mailed, but have since obtained a copy, which is here inserted:

Bayou Bœuf, August 15, 1852.

Mr. William Perry or Mr. Cephas Parker:

Gentlemen—It having been a long time since I have seen or heard from you, and not knowing that you are living, it is with uncertainty that I write to you, but the necessity of the case must be my excuse.

Having been born free, just across the river from you, I am certain you must know me, and I am here now a slave. I wish you to obtain free papers for me, and forward them to me at Marksville, Louisiana, Parish of Avoyelles, and oblige

Yours,

Solomon Northup.

The way I came to be a slave, I was taken sick in Washington City, and was insensible for some time. When I recovered my reason, I was robbed of my free-papers, and in irons on my way to this State, and have never been able to get any one to write for me until now; and he that is writing for me runs the risk of his life if detected.

The allusion to myself in the work recently issued, entitled "A Key to Uncle Tom's Cabin," contains the first part of this letter, omitting the postscript. Neither are the full names of the gentlemen to whom it is directed correctly stated, there being a slight discrepancy, probably a typographical error. To the postscript more than to the body of the communication am I indebted for my liberation, as will presently be seen.

When Bass returned from Marksville he informed me of what he had done. We continued our midnight consultations, never speaking to each other through the day, excepting as it was necessary about the work. As nearly as he was able to ascertain, it would require two weeks for the letter to reach Saratoga in due course of mail, and the same length of time for an answer to return. Within six weeks, at the farthest, we concluded, an answer would arrive, if it arrived at all. A great many suggestions were now made, and a great deal of conversation took place between us, as to the most safe and proper course to pursue on receipt of the free papers. They would stand between him and harm, in case we were overtaken and arrested leaving the country altogether. It would be no infringement of law, however much it might provoke individual hostility, to assist a freeman to rcgain his freedom.

At the end of four weeks he was again at Marksville, but no answer had arrived. I was sorely disappointed, but still reconciled myself with the reflection that sufficient length of time had not yet elapsed—that there might have been delays—and that I could not reasonably expect one so soon. Six, seven, eight, and ten weeks passed by, however, and nothing came. I was in a fever of suspense whenever Bass visited Marksville, and could scarcely close my eyes until his return. Finally my master's house was finished, and the time came when Bass must leave me. The night before his departure I was wholly given up to despair. I had clung to him as a drowning man clings to the floating spar, knowing if it slips from his grasp he must forever sink beneath the waves. The all-glorious hope, upon which I had laid such eager hold, was crumbling to ashes in my hands. I felt as if sinking down, down, amidst the bitter waters of Slavery, from the unfathomable depths of which I should never rise again.

The generous heart of my friend and benefactor was touched with pity at the sight of my distress. He endeavored to cheer me up, promising to return the day before Christmas, and if no intelligence was received in the meantime, some further step would be undertaken to effect our design. He exhorted me to keep up my spirits—to rely upon his continued efforts in my behalf, assuring me, in most earnest and impressive language, that my liberation should, from thenceforth, be the chief object of his thoughts.

In his absence the time passed slowly indeed. I looked forward to Christmas with intense anxiety and impatience. I had about given up the expectation of receiving any answer to the letters. They might have miscarried, or might have been misdirected. Perhaps those at Saratoga, to whom they had been addressed, were all dead; perhaps, engaged in their pursuits, they did not consider the fate of an obscure, unhappy black man of sufficient importance to be noticed. My whole reliance was in Bass. The faith I had in him was continually re-assuring me, and enabled me to stand up against the tide of disappointment that had overwhelmed me.

So wholly was I absorbed in reflecting upon my situation and prospects, that the hands with whom I labored in the field often observed it. Patsey would ask me if I was sick, and Uncle Abram, and Bob, and Wiley frequently expressed a curiosity to know what I could be thinking about so steadily. But I evaded their inquiries with some light remark, and kept my thoughts locked closely in my breast.

XX

Bass faithful to his word.—His arrival on Christmas Eve.—The difficulty of obtaining an interview.—The meeting in the cabin.—Non-arrival of the letter.—Bass announces his intention to proceed north.—Christmas.—Conversation between Epps and Bass.—Young Mistress M'Coy, the beauty of Bayou Bœuf.—The "Ne plus ultra" of dinners.—Music and dancing.—Presence of the Mistress.—Her exceeding beauty.—The last slave dance.—William Pierce.—Oversleep myself.—The last whipping.—Despondency.—The cold morning.—Epps' threats.—The passing carriage.—Strangers approaching through the cotton-field.—Last hour on Bayou Bœuf.

Faithful to his word, the day before Christmas, just at night-fall, Bass came riding into the yard.

"How are you," said Epps, shaking him by the hand, "glad to see you."

He would not have been *very* glad had he known the object of his errand.

"Quite well, quite well," answered Bass. "Had some business out on the bayou, and concluded to call and see you, and stay over night."

Epps ordered one of the slaves to take charge of his horse, and with much talk and laughter they passed into the house together; not, however, until Bass had looked at me significantly, as much as to say, "Keep dark, we understand each other." It was ten o'clock at night before the labors of the day were performed, when I entered the cabin. At that time Uncle Abram and Bob occupied it with me. I laid down upon my board and feigned I was asleep. When my companions had fallen into a profound slumber, I moved stealthily out of the door, and watched, and listened attentively for some sign or sound from Bass. There I stood until long after midnight, but nothing could be seen or heard. As I suspected, he dared not leave the house, through fear of exciting the suspicion of some of the family. I judged, correctly, he would rise earlier than was his custom, and take the opportunity of seeing me before Epps was up. Accordingly I aroused Uncle Abram an hour sooner than usual, and sent him into the house to build a fire, which, at that season of the year, is a part of Uncle Abram's duties.

I also gave Bob a violent shake, and asked him if he intended to sleep till noon, saying master would be up before the mules were fed. He knew right well the consequence that would follow such an event, and, jumping to his feet, was at the horse-pasture in a twinkling.

Presently, when both were gone, Bass slipped into the cabin.

"No letter yet, Platt," said he. The announcement fell upon my heart like lead.

"Oh, *do* write again, Master Bass," I cried; "I will give you the names of a great many I know. Surely they are not all dead. Surely some one will pity me."

"No use," Bass replied, "no use. I have made up my mind to that. I fear the Marksville post-master will mistrust something, I have inquired so often at his office. Too uncertain—too dangerous."

"Then it is all over," I exclaimed. "Oh, my God, how can I end my days here!"

"You're not going to end them here," he said, "unless you die very soon. I've thought this matter all over, and have come to a determination. There are more ways than one to manage this business, and a better and surer way than writing letters. I have a job or two on hand which can be completed by March or April. By that time I shall have a considerable sum of money, and then, Platt, I am going to Saratoga myself."

I could scarcely credit my own senses as the words fell from his lips. But he assured me, in a manner that left no doubt of the sincerity of his intention, that if his life was spared until spring, he should certainly undertake the journey.

"I have lived in this region long enough," he continued; "I may as well be in one place as another. For a long time I have been thinking of going back once more to the place where I was born. I'm tired of Slavery as well as you. If I can succeed in getting you away from here, it will be a good act that I shall like to think of all my life. And I *shall* succeed, Platt; I'm *bound* to do it. Now let me tell you what I want. Epps will be up soon, and it won't do to be caught here. Think of a great many men at Saratoga and Sandy Hill, and in that neighborhood, who once knew you. I shall make excuse to come here again in the course of the winter, when I will write down their names. I will then know who to call on when I go north. Think of all you can. Cheer up! Don't be discouraged. I'm with you, life or death. Good-bye. God bless you," and saying this he left the cabin quickly, and entered the great house.

It was Christmas morning—the happiest day in the whole year for the slave. That morning he need not hurry to the field, with his gourd and cotton-bag. Happiness sparkled in the eyes and overspread the countenances of all. The time of feasting and dancing had come. The cane and cotton fields were deserted. That day the clean dress was to be donned—the red ribbon displayed; there were to be re-unions, and joy and laughter, and hurrying to and fro. It was to be a day of *liberty* among the children of Slavery. Wherefore they were happy, and rejoiced.

After breakfast Epps and Bass sauntered about the yard, conversing upon the price of cotton, and various other topics.

"Where do your niggers hold Christmas?" Bass inquired.

"Platt is going to Tanners to-day. His fiddle is in great demand. They want him at Marshall's Monday, and Miss Mary McCoy, on the old Norwood plantation, writes me a note that she wants him to play for her niggers Tuesday."

"He is rather a smart boy, ain't he?" said Bass. "Come here, Platt," he added, looking at me as I walked up to them, as if he had never thought before to take any special notice of me.

"Yes," replied Epps, taking hold of my arm and feeling it, "there isn't a bad joint in him. There ain't a boy on the bayou worth more than he is—perfectly sound, and no bad tricks. D—n him, he isn't like other niggers; doesn't look like 'em—don't act like 'em. I was offered seventeen hundred dollars for him last week."

"And didn't take it?" Bass inquired, with an air of surprise.

"Take it—no; devilish clear of it. Why, he's a reg'lar genius; can make a plough beam, wagon tongue—anything, as well as you can. Marshall wanted to put up one of his niggers agin him and raffle for them, but I told him I would see the devil have him first."

"I don't see anything remarkable about him," Bass observed.

"Why, just feel of him, now," Epps rejoined. "You don't see a boy very often put together any closer than he is. He's a thin-skin'd cuss, and won't bear as much whipping as some; but he's got the muscle in him, and no mistake."

Bass felt of me, turned me round, and made a thorough examination, Epps all the while dwelling on my good points. But his visitor seemed to take but little interest finally in the subject, and consequently it was dropped. Bass soon departed, giving me another sly look of recognition and significance, as he trotted out of the yard.

When he was gone I obtained a pass, and started for Tanner's—not Peter Tanner's, of whom mention has previously been made, but a relative of his. I played during the day and most of the night, spending the next day, Sunday, in my cabin. Monday I crossed the bayou to Douglas Marshall's, all Epps' slaves accompanying me, and on Tuesday went to the old Norwood place, which is the third plantation above Marshall's, on the same side of the water.

This estate is now owned by Miss Mary McCoy, a lovely girl, some twenty years of age. She is the beauty and the glory of Bayou Bœuf. She owns about a hundred working hands, besides a great many house servants, yard boys, and young children. Her brother-in-law, who resides on the adjoining estate, is her general agent. She is beloved by all her slaves, and good reason indeed have they to be thankful that they have fallen into such gentle hands. Nowhere on the bayou are there such feasts, such merrymaking, as at young Madam McCoy's. Thither, more than to any other place, do the old and the young for miles around love to repair in the time of the Christmas holidays; for nowhere else can they find such delicious repasts; nowhere else can they hear a voice speaking to them so pleasantly. No one is so well beloved—no one fills so large a space in the hearts of a thousand slaves, as young Madam McCoy, the orphan mistress of the old Norwood estate.

On my arrival at her place, I found two or three hundred had assembled. The table was prepared in a long building, which she had erected expressly for her slaves to dance in. It was covered with every variety of food the country afforded, and was pronounced by general acclamation to be the rarest of dinners. Roast turkey, pig, chicken, duck, and all kinds of meat, baked, boiled, and broiled, formed a line the whole length of the extended table, while the vacant spaces were filled with tarts, jellies, and frosted cake, and pastry of many kinds. The young mistress walked around the table, smiling and saying a kind word to each one, and seemed to enjoy the scene exceedingly.

When the dinner was over the tables were removed to make room for the dancers. I tuned my violin and struck up a lively air; while some joined in a nimble reel, others patted and sang their simple but melodious songs, filling the great room with music mingled with the sound of human voices and the clatter of many feet.

In the evening the mistress returned, and stood in the door a long time, looking at us. She was magnificently arrayed. Her dark hair and eyes contrasted strongly with her clear and delicate complexion. Her form was slender but commanding, and her movement was a combination of unaffected dignity and grace. As she stood there, clad in her rich apparel, her face animated with pleasure, I thought I had never looked upon a human being half so beautiful. I dwell with delight upon the description of this fair and gentle lady, not only because she inspired me with emotions of gratitude and admiration, but because I would have the reader understand that all slave-owners on Bayou Bœuf are not like Epps, or Tibeats, or Jim Burns. Occasionally can be found, rarely it may be, indeed, a good man like William Ford, or an angel of kindness like young Mistress McCoy.

Tuesday concluded the three holidays Epps yearly allowed us. On my way home, Wednesday morning, while passing the plantation of William Pierce, that gentleman hailed me, saying he had received a line from Epps, brought down by William Varnell, permitting him to detain me for the purpose of playing for his slaves that night. It was the last time I was destined to witness a slave dance on the shores of Bayou Bœuf. The party at Pierce's continued their jollification until broad daylight, when I returned to my master's house, somewhat wearied with the loss of rest, but rejoicing in the possession of numerous bits and picayunes, which the whites, who were pleased with my musical performances, had contributed.

On Saturday morning, for the first time in years, I overslept myself. I was frightened on coming out of the cabin to find the slaves were already in the field. They had preceded me some fifteen minutes. Leaving my dinner and water-gourd, I hurried after them as fast as I could move. It was not yet sunrise, but Epps was on the piazza as I left the hut, and cried out to me that it was a pretty time of day to be getting up. By extra exertion my row was up when he came out after breakfast. This, however, was no excuse for the offence of oversleeping. Bidding me strip and lie down, he gave me ten or fifteen lashes, at the conclusion of which he inquired if I thought, after that, I could get up sometime in the *morning.* I expressed myself quite positively that I *could,* and, with back stinging with pain, went about my work.

The following day, Sunday, my thoughts were upon Bass, and the probabilities and hopes which hung upon his action and determination. I considered the uncertainty of life; that if it should be the will of God that he should die, my prospect of deliverance, and all expectation of happiness in this world, would be wholly ended and destroyed. My sore back, perhaps, did not have a tendency to render me unusually cheerful. I felt down-hearted and unhappy all day long, and when I laid down upon the hard board at night, my heart was oppressed with such a load of grief, it seemed that it must break.

Monday morning, the third of January, 1853, we were in the field betimes. It was a raw, cold morning, such as is unusual in that region. I was in advance, Uncle Abram next to me, behind him Bob, Patsey and Wiley, with our cotton-bags about our necks. Epps happened (a rare thing, indeed) to come out that morning without his whip. He swore, in a manner that would shame a pirate, that we were doing nothing. Bob ventured to say that his fingers were so numb with cold he couldn't pick fast. Epps cursed himself for not having brought his rawhide, and declared that when he came out again he would warm us well; yes, he would make us all hotter than that fiery realm in which I am sometimes compelled to believe he will himself eventually reside.

With these fervent expressions, he left us. When out of hearing, we commenced talking to each other, saying how hard it was to be compelled to keep up our tasks with numb fingers; how unreasonable master was, and speaking of him generally in no flattering terms. Our conversation was interrupted by a carriage passing rapidly towards the house. Looking up, we saw two men approaching us through the cotton-field.

* * * * * * * *

Having now brought down this narrative to the last hour I was to spend on Bayou Bœuf—having gotten through my last cotton picking, and about to bid Master Epps farewell—I must beg the reader to go back with me to the month of August; to follow Bass' letter on its long journey to Saratoga; to learn the effect it produced—and that, while I was repining and despairing in the slave hut of Edwin Epps, through the friendship of Bass and the goodness of Providence, all things were working together for my deliverance.

XXI

The letter reaches Saratoga.—Is forwarded to Anne.—Is laid before Henry B. Northup.—The statute of May 14, 1840—Its provisions.—Anne's memorial to the governor.—The affidavits accompanying it.—Senator Soule's letter.—Departure of the agent appointed by the governor.—Arrival at Marksville.—The Hon. John P. Waddill.—The conversation on New-York politics.—It suggests a fortunate idea.—The meeting with Bass.—The secret out.—Legal proceedings instituted.—Departure of Northup and the sheriff from Marksville for Bayou Bœuf.—Arrangements on the way.—Reach Epps' plantation.—Discover his slaves in the cotton field.—The meeting.—The farewell.

I am indebted to Mr. Henry B. Northup and others for many of the particulars contained in this chapter.

The letter written by Bass, directed to Parker and Perry, and which was deposited in the post-office in Marksville on the 15th day of August, 1852, arrived at Saratoga in the early part of September. Some time previous to this, Anne had removed to Glens Falls, Warren county, where she had charge of the kitchen in Carpenter's Hotel. She kept house, however, lodging with our children, and was only absent from them during such time as the discharge of her duties in the hotel required.

Messrs. Parker and Perry, on receipt of the letter, forwarded it immediately to Anne. On reading it the children were all excitement, and without delay hastened to the neighboring village of Sandy Hill, to consult Henry B. Northup, and obtain his advice and assistance in the matter.

Upon examination, that gentleman found among the statutes of the State an act providing for the recovery of free citizens from slavery. It was passed May 14, 1840, and is entitled "An act more effectually to protect the free citizens of this State from being kidnapped or reduced to slavery." It provides that it shall be the duty of the Governor, upon the receipt of satisfactory information that any free citizen or inhabitant of this State, is wrongfully held in another State or Territory of the United States, upon the allegation or pretence that such person is a slave, or by color or any usage or rule of law is deemed or taken to be a slave, to take such measures to procure the restoration of such person to liberty, as he shall deem necessary. And to that end, he is authorized to appoint and employ an agent, and directed to furnish him with such credentials and instructions as will be likely to accomplish the object of his appointment. It requires the agent so appointed to proceed to collect the proper proof to establish the right of such person to his freedom; to perform such journeys, take such measures, institute such legal proceedings, &c., as may be necessary to return such person to this State, and charges all expenses incurred in carrying the act into effect, upon moneys not otherwise appropriated in the treasury.

It was necessary to establish two facts to the satisfaction of the Governor: First, that I was a free citizen of New-York; and secondly, that I was wrongfully held in bondage. As to the first point, there was no difficulty, all the older inhabitants in the vicinity being ready to testify to it. The second point rested entirely upon the letter to Parker and Perry, written in an unknown hand, and upon the letter penned on board the brig Orleans, which, unfortunately, had been mislaid or lost.

A memorial was prepared, directed to his excellency, Governor Hunt, setting forth her marriage, my departure to Washington city; the receipt of the letters; that I was a free citizen, and such other facts as were deemed important, and was signed and verified by Anne. Accompanying this memorial were several affidavits of prominent citizens of Sandy Hill and Fort Edward, corroborating fully the statements it contained, and also a request of several well known gentlemen to the Governor, that Henry B. Northup be appointed agent under the legislative act.

On reading the memorial and affidavits, his excellency took a lively interest in the matter, and on the 23d day of November, 1852, under the seal of the State, "constituted, appointed and employed

Henry B. Northup, Esq., an agent, with full power to effect" my restoration, and to take such measures as would be most likely to accomplish it, and instructing him to proceed to Louisiana with all convenient dispatch.

The pressing nature of Mr. Northup's professional and political engagements delayed his departure until December. On the fourteenth day of that month he left Sandy Hill, and proceeded to Washington. The Hon. Pierre Soule, Senator in Congress from Louisiana, Hon. Mr. Conrad, Secretary of War, and Judge Nelson, of the Supreme Court of the United States, upon hearing a statement of the facts, and examining his commission, and certified copies of the memorial and affidavits, furnished him with open letters to gentlemen in Louisiana, strongly urging their assistance in accomplishing the object of his appointment.

Senator Soule especially interested himself in the matter, insisting, in forcible language, that it was the duty and interest of every planter in his State to aid in restoring me to freedom, and trusted the sentiments of honor and justice in the bosom of every citizen of the commonwealth would enlist him at once in my behalf. Having obtained these valuable letters, Mr. Northup returned to Baltimore, and proceeded from thence to Pittsburgh. It was his original intention, under advice of friends at Washington, to go directly to New Orleans, and consult the authorities of that city. Providentially, however, on arriving at the mouth of Red River, he changed his mind. Had he continued on, he would not have met with Bass, in which case the search for me would probably have been fruitless.

Taking passage on the first steamer that arrived, he pursued his journey up Red River, a sluggish, winding stream, flowing through a vast region of primitive forests and impenetrable swamps, almost wholly destitute of inhabitants. About nine o'clock in the forenoon, January 1st, 1853, he left the steamboat at Marksville, and proceeded directly to Marksville Court House, a small village four miles in the interior.

From the fact that the letter to Messrs. Parker and Perry was post-marked at Marksville, it was supposed by him that I was in that place or its immediate vicinity. On reaching this town, he at once laid his business before the Hon. John P. Waddill, a legal gentleman of distinction, and a man of fine genius and most noble impulses. After reading the letters and documents presented him, and listening to a representation of the circumstances under which

I had been carried away into captivity, Mr. Waddill at once proffered his services, and entered into the affair with great zeal and earnestness. He, in common with others of like elevated character, looked upon the kidnapper with abhorrence. The title of his fellow parishioners and clients to the property which constituted the larger proportion of their wealth, not only depended upon the good faith in which slave sales were transacted, but he was a man in whose honorable heart emotions of indignation were aroused by such an instance of injustice.

Marksville, although occupying a prominent position, and standing out in impressive italics on the map of Louisiana, is, in fact, but a small and insignificant hamlet. Aside from the tavern, kept by a jolly and generous boniface, the court house, inhabited by lawless cows and swine in the seasons of vacation, and a high gallows, with its dissevered rope dangling in the air, there is little to attract the attention of the stranger.

Solomon Northup was a name Mr. Waddill had never heard, but he was confident that if there was a slave bearing that appellation in Marksville or vicinity, his black boy Tom would know him. Tom was accordingly called, but in all his extensive circle of acquaintances there was no such personage.

The letter to Parker and Perry was dated at Bayou Bœuf. At this place, therefore, the conclusion was, I must be sought. But here a difficulty suggested itself, of a very grave character indeed. Bayou Bœuf, at its nearest point, was twenty-three miles distant, and was the name applied to the section of country extending between fifty and a hundred miles, on both sides of that stream. Thousands and thousands of slaves resided upon its shores, the remarkable richness and fertility of the soil having attracted thither a great number of planters. The information in the letter was so vague and indefinite as to render it difficult to conclude upon any specific course of proceeding. It was finally determined, however, as the only plan that presented any prospect of success, that Northup and the brother of Waddill, a student in the office of the latter, should repair to the Bayou, and traveling up one side and down the other its whole length, inquire at each plantation for me. Mr. Waddill tendered the use of his carriage, and it was definitely arranged that they should start upon the excursion early Monday morning.

It will be seen at once that this course, in all probability, would have resulted unsuccessfully. It would have been impossible for them to have gone into the fields and examine all the gangs at work. They were not aware that I was known only as Platt; and had they inquired of Epps himself, he would have stated truly that he knew nothing of Solomon Northup.

The arrangement being adopted, however, there was nothing further to be done until Sunday had elapsed. The conversation between Messrs. Northup and Waddill, in the course of the afternoon, turned upon New-York politics.

"I can scarcely comprehend the nice distinctions and shades of political parties in your State," observed Mr. Waddill. "I read of soft-shells and hard-shells, hunkers and barnburners, wooly-heads and silver-grays, and am unable to understand the precise difference between them. Pray, what is it?"

Mr. Northup, re-filling his pipe, entered into quite an elaborate narrative of the origin of the various sections of parties, and concluded by saying there was another party in New-York, known as free-soilers or abolitionists. "You have seen none of those in this part of the country, I presume?" Mr. Northup remarked.

"Never, but one," answered Waddill, laughingly. "We have one here in Marksville, an eccentric creature, who preaches abolitionism as vehemently as any fanatic at the North. He is a generous, inoffensive man, but always maintaining the wrong side of an argument. It affords us a deal of amusement. He is an excellent mechanic, and almost indispensable in this community. He is a carpenter. His name is Bass."

Some further good-natured conversation was had at the expense of Bass' peculiarities, when Waddill all at once fell into a reflective mood, and asked for the mysterious letter again.

"Let me see—l-e-t m-e s-e-e!" he repeated, thoughtfully to himself, running his eyes over the letter once more. " 'Bayou Bœuf, August 15.' August 15-post-marked here. 'He that is writing for me—' where did Bass work last summer?" he inquired, turning suddenly to his brother. His brother was unable to inform him, but rising, left the office, and soon returned with the intelligence that "Bass worked last summer somewhere on Bayou Bœuf."

"He is the man," bringing down his hand emphatically on the table, "who can tell us all about Solomon Northup," exclaimed Waddill.

Bass was immediately searched for, but could not be found. After some inquiry, it was ascertained he was at the landing on Red

River. Procuring a conveyance, young Waddill and Northup were not long in traversing the few miles to the latter place. On their arrival, Bass was found, just on the point of leaving, to be absent a fortnight or more. After an introduction, Northup begged the privilege of speaking to him privately a moment. They walked together towards the river, when the following conversation ensued:

"Mr. Bass," said Northup, "allow me to ask you if you were on Bayou Bœuf last August?"

"Yes, sir, I was there in August," was the reply.

"Did you write a letter for a colored man at that place to some gentleman in Saratoga Springs?"

"Excuse me, sir, if I say that is none of your business," answered Bass, stopping and looking his interrogator searchingly in the face.

"Perhaps I am rather hasty, Mr. Bass: I beg your pardon; but I have come from the State of New-York to accomplish the purpose the writer of a letter dated the 15th of August, post-marked at Marksville, had in view. Circumstances have led me to think that you are perhaps the man who wrote it. I am in search of Solomon Northup. If you know him, I beg you to inform me frankly where he is, and I assure you the source of any information you may give me shall not be divulged, if you desire it not to be."

A long time Bass looked his new acquaintance steadily in the eyes, without opening his lips. He seemed to be doubting in his own mind if there was not an attempt to practice some deception upon him. Finally he said, deliberately—

"I have done nothing to be ashamed of. I am the man who wrote the letter. If you have come to rescue Solomon Northup, I am glad to see you."

"When did you last see him, and where is he?" Northup inquired.

"I last saw him Christmas, a week ago to-day. He is the slave of Edwin Epps, a planter on Bayou Bœuf, near Holmesville. He is not known as Solomon Northup; he is called Platt."

The secret was out—the mystery was unraveled. Through the thick, black cloud, amid whose dark and dismal shadows I had walked twelve years, broke the star that was to light me back to liberty. All mistrust and hesitation were soon thrown aside, and the two men conversed long and freely upon the subject uppermost in their thoughts. Bass expressed the interest he had taken in my behalf—his intention of going north in the Spring, and declaring that he had resolved to accomplish my emancipation, if it were in his power. He described the commencement and progress of his acquaintance with me, and listened with eager curiosity to the account given him of my family, and the history of my early life. Before separating, he drew a map of the bayou on a strip of paper with a piece of red chalk, showing the locality of Epps' plantation, and the road leading most directly to it.

Northup and his young companion returned to Marksville, where it was determined to commence legal proceedings to test the question of my right to freedom. I was made plaintiff, Mr. Northup acting as my guardian, and Edwin Epps defendant. The process to be issued was in the nature of replevin, directed to the sheriff of the parish, commanding him to take me into custody, and detain me until the decision of the court. By the time the papers were duly drawn up, it was twelve o'clock at night—too late to obtain the necessary signature of the Judge, who resided some distance out of town. Further business was therefore suspended until Monday morning.

Everything, apparently, was moving along swimmingly, until Sunday afternoon, when Waddill called at Northup's room to express his apprehension of difficulties they had not expected to encounter. Bass had become alarmed, and had placed his affairs in the hands of a person at the landing, communicating to him his intention of leaving the State. This person had betrayed the confidence reposed in him to a certain extent, and a rumor began to float about the town, that the stranger at the hotel, who had been observed in the company of lawyer Waddill, was after one of old Epps' slaves, over on the bayou. Epps was known at Marksville, having frequent occasion to visit that place during the session of the courts, and the fear entertained by Mr. Northup's adviser was, that intelligence would be conveyed to him in the night, giving him an opportunity of secreting me before the arrival of the sheriff.

This apprehension had the effect of expediting matters considerably. The sheriff, who lived in one direction from the village, was requested to hold himself in readiness immediately after midnight, while the Judge was informed he would be called upon at the same time. It is but justice to say, that the authorities at Marksville cheerfully rendered all the assistance in their power.

As soon after midnight as bail could be perfected, and the

Judge's signature obtained, a carriage, containing Mr. Northup and the sheriff, driven by the landlord's son, rolled rapidly out of the village of Marksville, on the road towards Bayou Bœuf.

It was supposed that Epps would contest the issue involving my right to liberty, and it therefore suggested itself to Mr. Northup, that the testimony of the sheriff, describing my first meeting with the former, might perhaps become material on the trial. It was accordingly arranged during the ride, that, before I had an opportunity of speaking to Mr. Northup, the sheriff should propound to me certain questions agreed upon, such as the number and names of my children, the name of my wife before marriage, of places I knew at the North, and so forth. If my answers corresponded with the statements given him, the evidence must necessarily be considered conclusive.

At length, shortly after Epps had left the field, with the consoling assurance that he would soon return and *warm* us, as was stated in the conclusion of the preceding chapter, they came in sight of the plantation, and discovered us at work. Alighting from the carriage, and directing the driver to proceed to the great house, with instructions not to mention to any one the object of their errand until they met again, Northup and the sheriff turned from the highway, and came towards us across the cotton field. We observed them, on looking up at the carriage—one several rods in advance of the other. It was a singular and unusual thing to see white men approaching us in that manner, and especially at that early hour in the morning, and Uncle Abram and Patsey made some remarks, expressive of their astonishment. Walking up to Bob, the sheriff inquired:

"Where's the boy they call Platt?"

"Thar he is, massa," answered Bob, pointing to me, and twitching off his hat.

I wondered to myself what business he could possibly have with me, and turning round, gazed at him until he had approached within a step. During my long residence on the bayou, I had become familiar with the face of every planter within many miles; but this man was an utter stranger—certainly I had never seen him before.

"Your name is Platt, is it?" he asked.

"Yes, master," I responded.

Pointing towards Northup, standing a few rods distant, he demanded—"Do you know that man?"

I looked in the direction indicated, and as my eyes rested on his countenance, a world of images thronged my brain; a multitude of well-known faces—Anne's, and the dear children's, and my old dead father's; all the scenes and associations of childhood and youth; all the friends of other and happier days, appeared and disappeared, flitting and floating like dissolving shadows before the vision of my imagination, until at last the perfect memory of the man recurred to me, and throwing up my hands towards Heaven, I exclaimed, in a voice louder than I could utter in a less exciting moment—

"*Henry B. Northup!* Thank God—thank God!"

In an instant I comprehended the nature of his business, and felt that the hour of my deliverance was at hand. I started towards him, but the sheriff stepped before me.

"Stop a moment," said he; "have you any other name than Platt?"

"Solomon Northup is my name, master," I replied.

"Have you a family?" he inquired.

"I *had* a wife and three children."

"What were your children's names?"

"Elizabeth, Margaret and Alonzo."

"And your wife's name before her marriage?"

"Anne Hampton."

"Who married you?"

"Timothy Eddy, of Fort Edward."

"Where does that gentleman live?" again pointing to Northup, who remained standing in the same place where I had first recognized him.

"He lives in Sandy Hill, Washington county, New York," was the reply.

He was proceeding to ask further questions, but I pushed past him, unable longer to restrain myself. I seized my old acquaintance by both hands. I could not speak. I could not refrain from tears.

"Sol," he said at length, "I'm glad to see you."

I essayed to make some answer, but emotion choked all utterance, and I was silent. The slaves, utterly confounded, stood gazing upon the scene, their open mouths and rolling eyes indicating the utmost wonder and astonishment. For ten years I had dwelt among them, in the field and in the cabin, borne the same hardships, partaken the same fare, mingled my griefs with theirs, participated in the same scanty joys; nevertheless, not until this hour, the last I was to remain among them, had the remotest suspicion of my true name, or the slightest knowledge of my real history, been entertained by any one of them.

Not a word was spoken for several minutes, during which time I clung fast to Northup, looking up into his face, fearful I should awake and find it all a dream.

"Throw down that sack," Northup added, finally; "your cotton-picking days are over. Come with us to the man you live with."

I obeyed him, and walking between him and the sheriff, we moved towards the great house. It was not until we had proceeded some distance that I had recovered my voice sufficiently to ask if my family were all living. He informed me he had seen Anne, Margaret and Elizabeth but a short time previously; that Alonzo was also living, and all were well. My mother, however, I could never see again. As I began to recover in some measure from the sudden and great excitement which so overwhelmed me, I grew faint and weak, insomuch it was with difficulty I could walk. The sheriff took hold of my arm and assisted me, or I think I should have fallen. As we entered the yard, Epps stood by the gate, conversing with the driver. That young man, faithful to his instructions, was entirely unable to give him the least information in answer to his repeated inquiries of what was going on. By the time we reached him he was almost as much amazed and puzzled as Bob or Uncle Abram.

Shaking hands with the sheriff, and receiving an introduction to Mr. Northup, he invited them into the house, ordering me, at the same time, to bring in some wood. It was some time before I succeeded in cutting an armful, having, somehow, unaccountably lost the power of wielding the axe with any manner of precision. When I entered with it at last, the table was strewn with papers, from one of which Northup was reading. I was probably longer than necessity required, in placing the sticks upon the fire, being particular as to the exact position of each individual one of them. I heard the words, "the said Solomon Northup," and "the deponent further says," and "free citizen of New-York," repeated frequently, and from these expressions understood that the secret I had so long retained from Master and Mistress Epps, was finally developing. I lingered as long as prudence permitted, and was about leaving the room, when Epps inquired.

"Platt, do you know this gentleman?"

"Yes, master," I replied, "I have known him as long as I can remember."

"Where does he live?"

"He lives in New-York."

"Did you ever live there?"

"Yes, master—born and bred there."

"You was free, then. Now you d——d nigger," he exclaimed, "why did you not tell me that when I bought you?"

"Master Epps," I answered, in a somewhat different tone than the one in which I had been accustomed to address him—"Master Epps, you did not take the trouble to ask me; besides, I told one of my owners—the man that kidnapped me—that I was free, and was whipped almost to death for it."

"It seems there has been a letter written for you by somebody. Now, who is it?" he demanded, authoritatively. I made no reply.

"I say, who wrote that letter?" he demanded again.

"Perhaps I wrote it myself," I said.

"You haven't been to Marksville post-office and back before light, I know."

He insisted upon my informing him, and I insisted I would not. He made many vehement threats against the man, whoever he might be, and intimated the bloody and savage vengeance he would wreak upon him, when he found him out. His whole manner and language exhibited a feeling of anger towards the unknown person who had written for me, and of fretfulness at the idea of losing so much property. Addressing Mr. Northup, he swore if he had only had an hour's notice of his coming, he would have saved him the trouble of taking me back to New-York; that he would have run me into the swamp, or some other place out of the way, where all the sheriffs on earth couldn't have found me.

I walked out into the yard, and was entering the kitchen door, when something struck me in the back. Aunt Phebe, emerging from the back door of the great house with a pan of potatoes, had thrown one of them with unnecessary violence, thereby giving me to understand that she wished to speak to me a moment confidentially. Running up to me, she whispered in my ear with great earnestness,

"Lor a' mity, Platt! what d'ye think? Dem two men come after ye. Heard 'em tell massa you free—got wife and tree children back thar whar you come from. Goin' wid 'em? Fool if ye don't—wish I could go," and Aunt Phebe ran on in this manner at a rapid rate.

Presently Mistress Epps made her appearance in the kitchen. She said many things to me, and wondered why I had not told her who I was. She expressed her regret, complimenting me by saying she had rather lose any other servant on the plantation. Had Patsey that day stood in my place, the measure of my mistress' joy would have overflowed. Now there was no one left who could mend a chair or a piece of furniture—no one who was of any use about the house—no one who could play for her on the violin—and Mistress Epps was actually affected to tears.

Epps had called to Bob to bring up his saddle horse. The other slaves, also, overcoming their fear of the penalty, had left their work and come to the yard. They were standing behind the cabins, out of sight of Epps. They beckoned me to come to them, and with all the eagerness of curiosity, excited to the highest pitch, conversed with and questioned me. If I could repeat the exact words they uttered, with the same emphasis—if I could paint their several attitudes, and the expression of their countenances—it would be indeed an interesting picture. In their estimation, I had suddenly arisen to an immeasurable height—had become a being of immense importance.

The legal papers having been served, and arrangements made with Epps to meet them the next day at Marksville, Northup and the sheriff entered the carriage to return to the latter place. As I was about mounting to the driver's seat, the sheriff said I ought to bid Mr. and Mrs. Epps good-bye. I ran back to the piazza where they were standing, and taking off my hat, said,

"Good-bye, missis."

"Good-bye, Platt," said Mrs. Epps kindly.

"Good-bye, master."

"Ah! you d——d nigger," muttered Epps, in a surly, malicious tone of voice, "you needn't feel so cussed tickled—you ain't gone yet—I'll see about this business at Marksville to-morrow."

I was only a *"nigger"* and knew my place, but felt as strongly as if I had been a white man, that it would have been an inward comfort, had I dared to have given him a parting kick. On my way back to the carriage, Patsey ran from behind a cabin and threw her arms about my neck.

"Oh! Platt," she cried, tears streaming down her face, "you're goin' to be free—you're goin' way off yonder where we'll neber see ye any more. You've saved me a good many whippins, Platt; I'm glad you're goin' to be free—but oh! de Lord, de Lord! what'll become of me?"

I disengaged myself from her, and entered the carriage. The driver cracked his whip and away we rolled. I looked back and saw Patsey, with drooping head, half reclining on the ground; Mrs. Epps was on the piazza; Uncle Abram, and Bob, and Wiley, and Aunt Phebe stood by the gate, gazing after me. I waved my hand, but the carriage turned a bend of the bayou, hiding them from my eyes forever.

We stopped a moment at Carey's sugar house, where a great number of slaves were at work, such an establishment being a curiosity to a Northern man. Epps dashed by us on horseback at full speed—on the way, as we learned next day, to the "Pine Woods," to see William Ford, who had brought me into the country.

Tuesday, the fourth of January, Epps and his counsel, the Hon. H. Taylor, Northup, Waddill, the Judge and sheriff of Avoyelles, and myself, met in a room in the village of Marksville. Mr. Northup stated the facts in regard to me, and presented his commission, and the affidavits accompanying it. The sheriff described the scene in the cotton field. I was also interrogated at great length. Finally, Mr. Taylor assured his client that he was satisfied, and that litigation would not only be expensive, but utterly useless. In accordance with his advice, a paper was drawn up and signed by the proper parties, wherein Epps acknowledged he was satisfied of my right to freedom, and formally surrendered me to the authorities of New-York. It was also stipulated that it be entered of record in the recorder's office of Avoyelles.

Mr. Northup and myself immediately hastened to the landing, and taking passage on the first steamer that arrived, were soon floating down Red River, up which, with such desponding thoughts, I had been borne twelve years before.

XXII

Arrival in New-Orleans.—Glimpse of Freeman.—Genois, the recorder.—His description of Solomon.—Reach Charleston.

—Interrupted by Custom House Officers.—Pass through Richmond.—Arrival in Washington.—Burch arrested.—Shekels and Thorn.—Their testimony.—Burch acquitted.—Arrest of Solomon.—Burch withdraws the complaint.—The higher tribunal.—Departure from Washington.—Arrival at Sandy Hill.—Old friends and familiar scenes.—Proceed to Glens Falls.—Meeting with Anne, Margaret and Elizabeth.—Solomon Northup Staunton.—Incidents.—Conclusion.

As the steamer glided on its way towards New-Orleans, *perhaps* I was not happy—*perhaps* there was no difficulty in restraining myself from dancing round the deck—perhaps I did not feel grateful to the man who had come so many hundred miles for me—perhaps I did not light his pipe, and wait and watch his word, and run at his slightest bidding. If I didn't—well, no matter.

We tarried at New-Orleans two days. During that time I pointed out the locality of Freeman's slave pen, and the room in which Ford purchased me. We happened to meet Theophilus in the street, but I did not think it worth while to renew acquaintance with him. From respectable citizens we ascertained he had become a low, miserable rowdy—a broken-down, disreputable man.

We also visited the recorder, Mr. Genois, to whom Senator Soule's letter was directed, and found him a man well deserving the wide and honorable reputation that he bears. He very generously furnished us with a sort of legal pass, over his signature and seal of office, and as it contains the recorder's description of my personal appearance, it may not be amiss to insert it here. The following is a copy:

State of Louisiana—City of New-Orleans:

Recorder's Office, Second District.

To all to whom these presents shall come:—

This is to certify that Henry B. Northup, Esquire, of the county of the freedom of Solomon, a mulatto man, aged about forty-two years, five feet, seven inches and six lines, woolly hair, and chestnut eyes, who is a native born of the State of New-York. That the said Northup, being about bringing the said Solomon to his native place, through the southern routes, the civil authorities are requested to let the aforesaid colored man Solomon pass unmolested, he demeaning well and properly.

Given under my hand and the seal of the city of New-Orleans this 7th January, 1853.

[L. S.] Th. Genois, Recorder.

On the 8th we came to Lake Pontchartrain, by railroad, and, in due time, following the usual route, reached Charleston. After going on board the steamboat, and paying our passage at this city, Mr. Northup was called upon by a custom-house officer to explain why he had not registered his servant. He replied that he had no servant—that, as the agent of New-York, he was accompanying a free citizen of that State from slavery to freedom, and did not desire nor intend to make any registry whatever. I conceived from his conversation and manner, though I may perhaps be entirely mistaken, that no great pains would be taken to avoid whatever difficulty the Charleston officials might deem proper to create. At length, however, we were permitted to proceed, and, passing through Richmond, where I caught a glimpse of Goodin's pen, arrived in Washington January 17th, 1853.

We ascertained that both Burch and Radburn were still residing in that city. Immediately a complaint was entered with a police magistrate of Washington, against James H. Burch, for kidnapping and selling me into slavery. He was arrested upon a warrant issued by Justice Goddard, and returned before Justice Mansel, and held to bail in the sum of three thousand dollars. When first arrested, Burch was much excited, exhibiting the utmost fear and alarm, and before reaching the justice's office on Louisiana Avenue, and before knowing the precise nature of the complaint, begged the police to permit him to consult Benjamin O. Shekels, a slave trader of seventeen years' standing, and his former partner. The latter became his bail.

At ten o'clock, the 18th of January, both parties appeared before the magistrate. Senator Chase, of Ohio, Hon. Orville Clark, of Sandy Hill, and Mr. Northup acted as counsel for the prosecution, and Joseph H. Bradley for the defence.

Gen. Orville Clark was called and sworn as a witness, and testified that he had known me from childhood, and that I was a free man, as was my father before me. Mr. Northup then testified to the same, and proved the facts connected with his mission to Avoyelles.

Ebenezer Radburn was then sworn for the prosecution, and testified he was forty-eight years old; that he was a resident of Washington, and had known Burch fourteen years; that in 1841 he was keeper of Williams' slave pen; that he remembered the fact of my confinement in the pen that year. At this point it was admitted by the defendant's counsel, that I had been placed in the pen by Burch in the spring of 1841, and hereupon the prosecution rested.

Benjamin O. Shekels was then offered as a witness by the prisoner. Benjamin is a large, coarse-featured man, and the reader may perhaps get a somewhat correct conception of him by reading the exact language he used in answer to the first question of defendant's lawyer. He was asked the place of his nativity, and his reply, uttered in a sort of rowdyish way, was in these very words—

"I was born in Ontario county, New-York, and *weighed fourteen pounds!*"

Benjamin was a prodigious baby! He further testified that he kept the Steamboat Hotel in Washington in 1841, and saw me there in the spring of that year. He was proceeding to state what he had heard two men say, when Senator Chase raised a legal objection, to wit, that the sayings of third persons, being hearsay, was improper evidence. The objection was overruled by the Justice, and Shekels continued, stating that two men came to his hotel and represented they had a colored man for sale; that they had an interview with Burch; that they stated they came from Georgia, but he did not remember the county; that they gave a full history of the boy, saying he was a bricklayer, and played on the violin; that Burch remarked he would purchase if they could agree; that they went out and brought the boy in, and that I was the same person. He further testified, with as much unconcern as if it was the truth, that I represented I was born and bred in Georgia; that one of the young men with me was my master; that I exhibited a great deal of regret at parting with him, and he believed "got into tears!"—nevertheless, that I insisted my master had a right to sell me; that he *ought* to sell me; and the remarkable reason I gave was, according to Shekels, because he, my master, "had been gambling and on a spree!"

He continued, in these words, copied from the minutes taken on the examination: "Burch interrogated the boy in the usual manner, told him if he purchased him he should send him south. The boy said he had no objection, that in fact he would like to go south. Burch paid $650 for him, to my knowledge. I don't know what name was given him, but think it was not Solomon. Did not know the name of either of the two men. They were in my tavern two or three hours, during which time the boy played on the violin. The bill of sale was signed in my bar-room. It was a *printed blank, filled up by Burch.* Before 1838 Burch was my partner. Our business was buying and selling slaves. After that time he was a partner of Theophilus Freeman, of New-Orleans. Burch bought here—Freeman sold there!"

Shekels, before testifying, had heard my relation of the circumstances connected with the visit to Washington with Brown and Hamilton, and therefore, it was, undoubtedly, he spoke of "two men," and of my playing on the violin. Such was his fabrication, utterly untrue, and yet there was found in Washington a man who endeavored to corroborate him.

Benjamin A. Thorn testified he was at Shekels' in 1841, and saw a colored boy playing on a fiddle. "Shekels said he was for sale. Heard his master tell him he should sell him. The boy acknowledged to me he was a slave. I was not present when the money was paid. Will not swear positively this is the boy. The master *came near shedding tears: I think the boy did!* I have been engaged in the business of taking slaves south, off and on, for twenty years. When I can't do that I do something else."

I was then offered as a witness, but, objection being made, the court decided my evidence inadmissible. It was rejected solely on the ground that I was a colored man—the fact of my being a free citizen of New-York not being disputed.

Shekels having testified there was a bill of sale executed, Burch was called upon by the prosecution to produce it, inasmuch as such a paper would corroborate the testimony of Thorn and Shekels. The prisoner's counsel saw the necessity of exhibiting it, or giving some reasonable explanation for its non-production. To effect the latter, Burch himself was offered as a witness in his own behalf. It was contended by counsel for the people, that such testimony should not be allowed—that it was in contravention of every rule of evidence, and if permitted would defeat the ends of justice. His testimony, however, was received by the court! He made oath that such a bill of sale had been drawn up and signed, *but he had lost it, and did not know what had become of it!* Thereupon the magistrate was requested to dispatch a police officer to Burch's residence, with directions to bring his books, containing his bills of sales for the year 1841. The request was granted, and before any measure could be taken to prevent it, the officer had obtained possession of the books, and brought them into court. The sales for the year 1841 were found, and carefully examined, but no sale of myself, by any name, was discovered!

Upon this testimony the court held the fact to be established, that Burch came innocently and honestly by me, and accordingly he was discharged.

An attempt was then made by Burch and his satellites, to fasten upon me the charge that I had conspired with the two white men to defraud him—with what success, appears in an extract taken from an article in the *New-York Times,* published a day or two subsequent to the trial: "The counsel for the defendant had drawn up, before the defendant was discharged, an affidavit, signed by Burch, and had a warrant out against the colored man for a conspiracy with the two white men before referred to, to defraud Burch out of six hundred and twenty-five dollars. The warrant was served, and the colored man arrested and brought before officer Goddard. Burch and his witnesses appeared in court, and H.B. Northup appeared as counsel for the colored man, stating he was ready to proceed as counsel on the part of the defendant, and asking no delay whatever. Burch, after consulting privately a short time with Shekels, stated to the magistrate that he wished him to dismiss the complaint, as he would not proceed farther with it. Defendant's counsel stated to the magistrate that if the complaint was withdrawn, it must be without the request or consent of the defendant. Burch then asked the magistrate to let him have the complaint and the warrant, and he took them. The counsel for the defendant objected to his receiving them, and insisted they should remain as part of the records of the court, and that the court should endorse the proceedings which had been under the process. Burch delivered them up, and the court rendered a judgment of discontinuance by the request of the prosecutor, and filed it in his office.

There may be those who will affect to believe the statement of the slave-trader—those, in whose minds his allegations will weigh heavier than mine. I am a poor colored man—one of a down-trodden and degraded race, whose humble voice may not be heeded by the oppressor—but *knowing* the truth, and with a full sense of my accountability, I do solemnly declare before men, and before God, that any charge or assertion, that I conspired directly or indirectly with any person or persons to sell myself; that any other account of my visit to Washington, my capture and imprisonment in Williams' slave pen, than is contained in these pages, is utterly and absolutely false. I never played on the violin in Washington. I never was in the Steamboat Hotel, and never saw Thorn or Shekels, to my knowledge, in my life, until last January. The story of the trio of slave-traders is a fabrication as absurd as it is base and unfounded. Were it true, I should not have turned aside on my way back to liberty for the purpose of prosecuting Burch. I should have *avoided* rather than sought him. I should have known that such a step would have resulted in rendering me infamous. Under the circumstances—longing as I did to behold my family, and elated with the prospect of returning home—it is an outrage upon probability to suppose I would have run the hazard, not only of exposure, but of a criminal prosecution and conviction, by voluntarily placing myself in the position I did, if the statements of Burch and his confederates contain a particle of truth. I took pains to seek him out, to confront him in a court of law, charging him with the crime of kidnapping; and the only motive that impelled me to this step, was a burning sense of the wrong he had inflicted upon me, and a desire to bring him to justice. He was acquitted, in the manner, and by such means as have been described. A human tribunal has permitted him to escape; but there is another and a higher tribunal, where false testimony will not prevail, and where I am willing, so far at least as these statements are concerned, to be judged at last.

We left Washington on the 20th of January, and proceeding by the way of Philadelphia, New-York, and Albany, reached Sandy Hill in the night of the 21st. My heart overflowed with happiness as I looked around upon old familiar scenes, and found myself in the midst of friends of other days. The following morning I started, in company with several acquaintances, for Glen Falls, the residence of Anne and our children.

As I entered their comfortable cottage, Margaret was the first that met me. She did not recognize me. When I left her, she was but seven years old, a little prattling girl, playing with her toys. Now she was grown to womanhood—was married, with a bright-eyed boy standing by her side. Not forgetful of his enslaved, unfortunate grand-father, she had named the child Solomon Northup Staunton. When told who I was, she was overcome with emotion, and unable to speak. Presently Elizabeth entered the room, and Anne came running from the hotel, having been informed of my arrival. They embraced me, and with tears flowing down their cheeks, hung upon my neck. But I draw a veil over a scene which can better be imagined than described.

When the violence of our emotions had subsided to a sacred joy—when the household gathered round the fire, that sent out its warm and crackling comfort through the room, we conversed of the thousand events that had occurred—the hopes and fears, the joys and sorrows, the trials and troubles we had each experienced during the long separation. Alonzo was absent in the western part of the State. The boy had written to his mother a short time previous, of the prospect of his obtaining sufficient money to purchase my freedom. From his earliest years, that had been the chief object of his thoughts and his ambition. They knew I was in bondage. The letter written on board the brig, and Clem Ray himself, had given them that information. But where I was, until the arrival of Bass' letter, was a matter of conjecture. Elizabeth and Margaret once returned from school—so Anne informed me—weeping bitterly. On inquiring the cause of the children's sorrow, it was found that, while studying geography, their attention had been attracted to the picture of slaves working in the cotton-field, and an overseer following them with his whip. It reminded them of the sufferings their father might be, and, as it happened, actually *was,* enduring in the South. Numerous incidents, such as these, were related—incidents showing they still held me in constant remembrance, but not, perhaps, of sufficient interest to the reader, to be recounted.

My narrative is at an end. I have no comments to make upon the subject of Slavery. Those who read this book may form their own opinions of the "peculiar institution." What it may be in other States, I do not profess to know; what it is in the region of Red River, is truly and faithfully delineated in these pages. This is no fiction, no exaggeration. If I have failed in anything, it has been in presenting to the reader too prominently the bright side of the picture. I doubt not hundreds have been as unfortunate as myself; that hundreds of free citizens have been kidnapped and sold into slavery, and are at this moment wearing out their lives on plantations in Texas and Louisiana. But I forbear. Chastened and subdued in spirit by the sufferings I have borne, and thankful to that good Being through whose mercy I have been restored to happiness and liberty, I hope henceforward to lead an upright though lowly life, and rest at last in the church yard where my father sleeps.

Bibliographic Note

The best way to get into the subject of slave narratives is through the following excellent unpublished doctoral dissertations in the field of American literature: Marion W. Starling, "The Slave Narrative: Its Place in American Literary History" (New York University, 1946); Charles H. Nichols, Jr., "A Study of the Slave Narrative" (Brown University, 1948); and Margaret Young Jackson, "An Investigation of Biographies and Autobiographies of American Slaves Published Between 1840 and 1860: Based Upon the Cornell Special Slavery Collection" (Cornell University, 1954). One should also consult Charles H. Nichols, Jr., ed., *Many Thousands Gone: The Ex-Slaves' Account of Their Bondage and Freedom* (Leiden, 1963).

The following essays discuss the various narrative collections or aspects of the careers of some fugitives who wrote autobiographies: Norman R. Yetman, "The Background of the Slave Narrative Collection," *American Quarterly,* XIX (Fall, 1967), 534–553; B. A. Botkin, "The Slave as His Own Interpreter," *Library of Congress Quarterly Journal of Current Acquisitions,* II (1944), 37–63; W. Sherman Savage, "The Influence of John Davis and Lunsford Lane on the History of North Carolina," *Journal of Negro History,* XXV (January, 1940), 14–24; Edward M. Coleman, "William Wells Brown as an Historian," *Journal of Negro History,* XXXI (January, 1946), 47–50; William E. Farrison, "William Wells Brown in Buffalo," *Journal of Negro History,* XXXIX (October, 1954), 298–314; Samuel Shapiro, "The Rendition of Anthony Burns," *Journal of Negro History,* XLIV (January, 1959), 34–51; Alexander L. Murray, "The Provincial Freeman: A New Source for the History of the Negro in Canada and the United States," *Journal of Negro History,* XLIV (April, 1959), 123–135; W. B. Hargrove, "The Story of Josiah Henson," *Journal of Negro History,* III (January, 1918), 1–21; Fred

Landon, "Henry Bibb: A Colonizer," *Journal of Negro History,* V (October, 1920), 437–447.

A number of nineteenth-century works contain short descriptions of slavery by fugitives or writers who recorded their stories. Some illustrative and valuable books are: William Still, *Underground Rail Road Records . . .* (Philadelphia, 1883); Benjamin Drew, *The Refugee: Or, the Narratives of Fugitive Slaves in Canada* (Boston, 1856); Ephraim Peabody, "Narratives of Fugitive Slaves," *Christian Examiner,* XLVII (July, 1849), 61–93; Lydia Maria Child, *Isaac T. Hopper: A True Life* (Boston, 1853); Wilbur H. Siebert, *The Underground Railroad from Slavery to Freedom* (New York, 1898); Levi Coffin, *Reminiscences . . .* (Cincinnati, 1880); William Wells Brown, *The Black Man . . .* (New York, 1863); Wilson Armistead, *A Tribute for the Negro* (London, 1848).

The following are narratives collected in the twentieth century: James B. Cade, "Out of the Mouths of Ex-Slaves," *Journal of Negro History,* XXII (April, 1935), 294–337; B. A. Botkin, *Lay My Burden Down: A Folk History of Slavery* (Chicago, 1945); Federal Writers' Project, *Slave Narratives: A Folk History of Slavery in the United States from Interviews with Former Slaves* (typescript, Library of Congress, 1941), 17 vols.; Fisk University, *Unwritten History of Slavery* (Mimeograph, Nashville, 1945).

The three dissertations cited at the beginning of this bibliographic note should be consulted for detailed lists of slave autobiographies. Here is a sample of some of the more prominent full-length memoirs published before the Civil War: Charles Ball, *Slavery in the United States: A Narrative of the Life and Adventures of Charles Ball* (Pittsburgh, 1853); Leonard Black, *Life and Sufferings of Leonard Black . . .* (New York, 1847); Henry Box Brown, *Narrative of the Life of Henry Box Brown* (Manchester, 1851); L. A. Chamerovzow, ed., *Slave Life in Georgia: A Narrative of the Life, Sufferings and Escape of John Brown . . .* (London, 1855); Lewis and Milton Clarke, *Narratives of the Sufferings of Lewis and Milton Clarke . . .* (Boston, 1846); William Craft, *Running a Thousand Miles for Freedom . . .* (London, 1860); Noah Davis, *A Narrative of the Life of Reverend Noah Davis, a Colored Man* (Baltimore, 1859); Frederick Douglass, *Life and Times of Frederick Douglass* (New York, 1892); Olaudah Equiano, *The Interesting Narrative of the Life of Olaudah Equiano, or Gustavus Vassa, the African* (London, 1789); Moses Grandy, *Narrative of the Life of Moses Grandy* (Boston, 1844);

William Grimes, *Life of William Grimes, the Runaway Slave* (New Haven, 1855); William Hayden, *Narrative of William Hayden . . .* (Cincinnati, 1846); Josiah Henson, *The Life of Josiah Henson . . .* (Boston, 1849); Andrew Jackson, *Narrative and Writings of Andrew Jackson of Kentucky . . .* (Syracuse, 1847); Harriet Jacobs, *Incidents in the Life of a Slave Girl* (Boston, 1861); Lunsford Lane, *The Narrative of Lunsford Lane, Formerly of Raleigh, N.C.* (Boston, 1842); J. W. C. Pennington, *The Fugitive Blacksmith . . .* (London, 1849); Peter Randolph, *From Slave Cabin to Pulpit . . .* (Boston, 1855); Moses Roper, *A Narrative of the Adventures and Escape of Moses Roper from American Slavery* (London, 1840); Austin Steward, *Twenty-two Years a Slave and Forty Years a Freeman . . .* (Rochester, 1857); Peter Still, *The Kidnapped and the Ransomed . . .* (Syracuse, 1856); John Thompson, *The Life of John Thompson . . .* (Worcester, 1856); Sojourner Truth, *Narrative of Sojourner Truth . . .* (Boston, 1850); Sarah Bradford, *Scenes in the Life of Harriet Tubman* (Auburn, New York, 1869); Samuel Ringgold Ward, *Autobiography of a Fugitive Negro . . .* (London, 1855); Henry Watson, *Narrative of Henry Watson, a Fugitive Slave* (Boston, 1848).

71727387654

ABOUT THE AUTHOR

Gilbert Osofsky teaches history at the University of Illinois, Chicago Circle. He is the author of *Harlem: The Making of a Ghetto* and *The Burden of Race: A Documentary History of Negro-White Relations in America.*

Revised January, 1970

harper torchbooks

American Studies: General

HENRY STEELE COMMAGER, Ed.: The Struggle for Racial Equality TB/1300
CARL N. DEGLER: Out of Our Past: *The Forces that Shaped Modern America* CN/2
CARL N. DEGLER, Ed.: Pivotal Interpretations of American History Vol. I TB/1240; Vol. II TB/1241
A. S. EISENSTADT, Ed.: The Craft of American History: *Selected Essays* Vol. I TB/1255; Vol. II TB/1256
ROBERT L. HEILBRONER: The Limits of American Capitalism TB/1305
JOHN HIGHAM, Ed.: The Reconstruction of American History TB/1068
ROBERT H. JACKSON: The Supreme Court in the American System of Government TB/1106
JOHN F. KENNEDY: A Nation of Immigrants. *Illus. Revised and Enlarged. Introduction by Robert F. Kennedy* TB/1118
RICHARD B. MORRIS: Fair Trial: *Fourteen Who Stood Accused, from Anne Hutchinson to Alger Hiss* TB/1335
GUNNAR MYRDAL: An American Dilemma: *The Negro Problem and Modern Democracy. Introduction by the Author.* Vol. I TB/1443; Vol. II TB/1444
GILBERT OSOFSKY, Ed.: The Burden of Race: *A Documentary History of Negro-White Relations in America* TB/1405
ARNOLD ROSE: The Negro in America: *The Condensed Version of Gunnar Myrdal's* An American Dilemma. *Second Edition* TB/3048
JOHN E. SMITH: Themes in American Philosophy: *Purpose, Experience and Community* TB/1466
WILLIAM R. TAYLOR: Cavalier and Yankee: *The Old South and American National Character* TB/1474

American Studies: Colonial

BERNARD BAILYN: The New England Merchants in the Seventeenth Century TB/1149
ROBERT E. BROWN: Middle-Class Democracy and Revolution in Massachusetts, 1691–1780. *New Introduction by Author* TB/1413
JOSEPH CHARLES: The Origins of the American Party System TB/1049
WESLEY FRANK CRAVEN: The Colonies in Transition: 1660-1712† TB/3084
CHARLES GIBSON: Spain in America † TB/3077
CHARLES GIBSON, Ed.: The Spanish Tradition in America + HR/1351
LAWRENCE HENRY GIPSON: The Coming of the Revolution: 1763-1775. † *Illus.* TB/3007
PERRY MILLER: Errand Into the Wilderness TB/1139
PERRY MILLER & T. H. JOHNSON, Eds.: The Puritans: *A Sourcebook of Their Writings* Vol. I TB/1093; Vol. II TB/1094
EDMUND S. MORGAN: The Puritan Family: *Religion and Domestic Relations in Seventeenth Century New England* TB/1227
WALLACE NOTESTEIN: The English People on the Eve of Colonization: 1603-1630. † *Illus.* TB/3006
LOUIS B. WRIGHT: The Cultural Life of the American Colonies: 1607-1763. † *Illus.* TB/3005

American Studies: The Revolution to 1860

JOHN R. ALDEN: The American Revolution: 1775-1783. † *Illus.* TB/3011
RAY A. BILLINGTON: The Far Western Frontier: 1830-1860. † *Illus.* TB/3012
GEORGE DANGERFIELD: The Awakening of American Nationalism, 1815-1828. † *Illus.* TB/3061
CLEMENT EATON: The Growth of Southern Civilization, 1790-1860. † *Illus.* TB/3040
LOUIS FILLER: The Crusade against Slavery: 1830-1860. † *Illus.* TB/3029
WILLIM W. FREEHLING: Prelude to Civil War: *The Nullification Controversy in South Carolina, 1816-1836* TB/1359
THOMAS JEFFERSON: Notes on the State of Virginia. ‡ *Edited by Thomas P. Abernethy* TB/3052
JOHN C. MILLER: The Federalist Era: 1789-1801. † *Illus.* TB/3027
RICHARD B. MORRIS: The American Revolution Reconsidered TB/1363
GILBERT OSOFSKY, Ed.: Puttin' On Ole Massa: *The Slave Narratives of Henry Bibb, William Wells Brown, and Solomon Northup* ‡ TB/1432
FRANCIS S. PHILBRICK: The Rise of the West, 1754-1830. † *Illus.* TB/3067
MARSHALL SMELSER: The Democratic Republic, 1801-1815 † TB/1406

† The New American Nation Series, edited by Henry Steele Commager and Richard B. Morris.
‡ American Perspectives series, edited by Bernard Wishy and William E. Leuchtenburg.
α History of Europe series, edited by J. H. Plumb.
§ The Library of Religion and Culture, edited by Benjamin Nelson.
‖ Researches in the Social, Cultural, and Behavioral Sciences, edited by Benjamin Nelson.
Σ Harper Modern Science Series, edited by James A. Newman.
° Not for sale in Canada.
+ Documentary History of the United States series, edited by Richard B. Morris.
\# Documentary History of Western Civilization series, edited by Eugene C. Black and Leonard W. Levy.
Λ The Economic History of the United States series, edited by Henry David et al.
¶ European Perspectives series, edited by Eugene C. Black.
** Contemporary Essays series, edited by Leonard W. Levy.
* The Stratum Series, edited by John Hale.

LOUIS B. WRIGHT: Culture on the Moving Frontier TB/1053

American Studies: The Civil War to 1900

T. C. COCHRAN & WILLIAM MILLER: The Age of Enterprise: *A Social History of Industrial America* TB/1054
W. A. DUNNING: Reconstruction, Political and Economic: 1865-1877 TB/1073
HAROLD U. FAULKNER: Politics, Reform and Expansion: 1890-1900. † *Illus.* TB/3020
GEORGE M. FREDRICKSON: The Inner Civil War: *Northern Intellectuals and the Crisis of the Union* TB/1358
JOHN A. GARRATY: The New Commonwealth, 1877-1890 † TB/1410
HELEN HUNT JACKSON: A Century of Dishonor: *The Early Crusade for Indian Reform.* † *Edited by Andrew F. Rolle* TB/3063
WILLIAM G. MCLOUGHLIN, Ed.: The American Evangelicals, 1800-1900: An Anthology ‡ TB/1382
JAMES S. PIKE: The Prostrate State: *South Carolina under Negro Government.* ‡ *Intro. by Robert F. Durden* TB/3085
VERNON LANE WHARTON: The Negro in Mississippi, 1865-1890 TB/1178

American Studies: The Twentieth Century

RAY STANNARD BAKER: Following the Color Line: *American Negro Citizenship in Progressive Era.* ‡ *Edited by Dewey W. Grantham, Jr. Illus.* TB/3053
RANDOLPH S. BOURNE: War and the Intellectuals: *Collected Essays, 1915-1919.* ‡ *Edited by Carl Resek* TB/3043
A. RUSSELL BUCHANAN: The United States and World War II. † *Illus.*
Vol. I TB/3044; Vol. II TB/3045
THOMAS C. COCHRAN: The American Business System: *A Historical Perspective, 1900-1955* TB/1080
FOSTER RHEA DULLES: America's Rise to World Power: 1898-1954. † *Illus.* TB/3021
HAROLD U. FAULKNER: The Decline of Laissez Faire, 1897-1917 TB/1397
JOHN D. HICKS: Republican Ascendancy: 1921-1933. † *Illus.* TB/3041
WILLIAM E. LEUCHTENBURG: Franklin D. Roosevelt and the New Deal: 1932-1940. † *Illus.* TB/3025
WILLIAM E. LEUCHTENBURG, Ed.: The New Deal: *A Documentary History* + HR/1354
ARTHUR S. LINK: Woodrow Wilson and the Progressive Era: 1910-1917. † *Illus.* TB/3023
BROADUS MITCHELL: Depression Decade: *From New Era through New Deal, 1929-1941* ^ TB/1439
GEORGE E. MOWRY: The Era of Theodore Roosevelt and the Birth of Modern America: 1900-1912. † *Illus.* TB/3022
WILLIAM PRESTON, JR.: Aliens and Dissenters:
TWELVE SOUTHERNERS: I'll Take My Stand: *The South and the Agrarian Tradition. Intro. by Louis D. Rubin, Jr.; Biographical Essays by Virginia Rock* TB/1072

Art, Art History, Aesthetics

ERWIN PANOFSKY: Renaissance and Renascences in Western Art. *Illus.* TB/1447
ERWIN PANOFSKY: Studies in Iconology: *Humanistic Themes in the Art of the Renaissance. 180 illus.* TB/1077
HEINRICH ZIMMER: Myths and Symbols in Indian Art and Civilization. *70 illus.* TB/2005

Asian Studies

WOLFGANG FRANKE: China and the West: *The Cultural Encounter, 13th to 20th Centuries. Trans. by R. A. Wilson* TB/1326
L. CARRINGTON GOODRICH: A Short History of the Chinese People. *Illus.* TB/3015

Economics & Economic History

C. E. BLACK: The Dynamics of Modernization: *A Study in Comparative History* TB/1321
GILBERT BURCK & EDITORS OF *Fortune:* The Computer Age: *And its Potential for Management* TB/1179
ROBERT L. HEILBRONER: The Future as History: *The Historic Currents of Our Time and the Direction in Which They Are Taking America* TB/1386
ROBERT L. HEILBRONER: The Great Ascent: *The Struggle for Economic Development in Our Time* TB/3030
FRANK H. KNIGHT: The Economic Organization TB/1214
DAVID S. LANDES: Bankers and Pashas: *International Finance and Economic Imperialism in Egypt. New Preface by the Author* TB/1412
ROBERT LATOUCHE: The Birth of Western Economy: *Economic Aspects of the Dark Ages* TB/1290
W. ARTHUR LEWIS: The Principles of Economic Planning. *New Introduction by the Author°* TB/1436
WILLIAM MILLER, Ed.: Men in Business: *Essays on the Historical Role of the Entrepreneur* TB/1081
HERBERT A. SIMON: The Shape of Automation: *For Men and Management* TB/1245

Historiography and History of Ideas

J. BRONOWSKI & BRUCE MAZLISH: The Western Intellectual Tradition: *From Leonardo to Hegel* TB/3001
WILHELM DILTHEY: Pattern and Meaning in History: *Thoughts on History and Society.° Edited with an Intro. by H. P. Rickman* TB/1075
J. H. HEXTER: More's Utopia: *The Biography of an Idea. Epilogue by the Author* TB/1195
H. STUART HUGHES: History as Art and as Science: *Twin Vistas on the Past* TB/1207
ARTHUR O. LOVEJOY: The Great Chain of Being: *A Study of the History of an Idea* TB/1009
RICHARD H. POPKIN: The History of Scepticism from Erasmus to Descartes. *Revised Edition* TB/1391
BRUNO SNELL: The Discovery of the Mind: *The Greek Origins of European Thought* TB/1018

History: General

HANS KOHN: The Age of Nationalism: *The First Era of Global History* TB/1380
BERNARD LEWIS: The Arabs in History TB/1029
BERNARD LEWIS: The Middle East and the West ° TB/1274

History: Ancient

A. ANDREWS: The Greek Tyrants TB/1103
THEODOR H. GASTER: Thespis: *Ritual Myth and Drama in the Ancient Near East* TB/1281

A. H. M. JONES, Ed.: A History of Rome through the Fifth Century # *Vol. I: The Republic* HR/1364
Vol. II The Empire: HR/1460
SAMUEL NOAH KRAMER: Sumerian Mythology TB/1055
NAPHTALI LEWIS & MEYER REINHOLD, Eds.: Roman Civilization *Vol. I: The Republic* TB/1231
Vol. II: The Empire TB/1232

History: Medieval

NORMAN COHN: The Pursuit of the Millennium: *Revolutionary Messianism in Medieval and Reformation Europe* TB/1037
F. L. GANSHOF: Feudalism TB/1058
F. L. GANSHOF: The Middle Ages: *A History of International Relations. Translated by Rêmy Hall* TB/1411
HENRY CHARLES LEA: The Inquisition of the Middle Ages. || *Introduction by Walter Ullmann* TB/1456

History: Renaissance & Reformation

JACOB BURCKHARDT: The Civilization of the Renaissance in Italy. *Introduction by Benjamin Nelson and Charles Trinkaus. Illus.* Vol. I TB/40; Vol. II TB/41
JOHN CALVIN & JACOPO SADOLETO: A Reformation Debate. *Edited by John C. Olin* TB/1239
J. H. ELLIOTT: Europe Divided, 1559-1598 *a* ° TB/1414
G. R. ELTON: Reformation Europe, 1517-1559 ° *a* TB/1270
HANS J. HILLERBRAND, Ed., The Protestant Reformation # HR/1342
JOHAN HUIZINGA: Erasmus and the Age of Reformation. *Illus.* TB/19
JOEL HURSTFIELD: The Elizabethan Nation TB/1312
JOEL HURSTFIELD, Ed.: The Reformation Crisis TB/1267
PAUL OSKAR KRISTELLER: Renaissance Thought: *The Classic, Scholastic, and Humanist Strains* TB/1048
DAVID LITTLE: Religion, Order and Law: *A Study in Pre-Revolutionary England.* § *Preface by R. Bellah* TB/1418
PAOLO ROSSI: Philosophy, Technology, and the Arts, in the Early Modern Era 1400-1700. || *Edited by Benjamin Nelson. Translated by Salvator Attanasio* TB/1458
H. R. TREVOR-ROPER: The European Witch-craze of the Sixteenth and Seventeenth Centuries and Other Essays ° TB/1416

History: Modern European

ALAN BULLOCK: Hitler, A Study in Tyranny. ° *Revised Edition. Illus.* TB/1123
JOHANN GOTTLIEB FICHTE: Addresses to the German Nation. *Ed. with Intro. by George A. Kelly* ¶ TB/1366
ALBERT GOODWIN: The French Revolution TB/1064
STANLEY HOFFMANN et al.: In Search of France: *The Economy, Society and Political System In the Twentieth Century* TB/1219
H. STUART HUGHES: The Obstructed Path: *French Social Thought in the Years of Desperation* TB/1451
JOHAN HUIZINGA: Dutch Civilisation in the 17th Century and Other Essays TB/1453
JOHN MCMANNERS: European History, 1789-1914: *Men, Machines and Freedom* TB/1419
HUGH SETON-WATSON: Eastern Europe Between the Wars, 1918-1941 TB/1330
ALBERT SOREL: Europe Under the Old Regime. *Translated by Francis H. Herrick* TB/1121
A. J. P. TAYLOR: From Napoleon to Lenin: *Historical Essays* ° TB/1268
A. J. P. TAYLOR: The Habsburg Monarchy, 1809-1918: *A History of the Austrian Empire and Austria-Hungary* ° TB/1187
J. M. THOMPSON: European History, 1494-1789 TB/1431
H. R. TREVOR-ROPER: Historical Essays TB/1269

Literature & Literary Criticism

W. J. BATE: From Classic to Romantic: *Premises of Taste in Eighteenth Century England* TB/1036
VAN WYCK BROOKS: Van Wyck Brooks: The Early Years: *A Selection from his Works, 1908-1921 Ed. with Intro. by Claire Sprague* TB/3082
RICHMOND LATTIMORE, Translator: The Odyssey of Homer TB/1389
ROBERT PREYER, Ed.: Victorian Literature ** TB/1302

Philosophy

HENRI BERGSON: Time and Free Will: *An Essay on the Immediate Data of Consciousness* ° TB/1021
H. J. BLACKHAM: Six Existentialist Thinkers: *Kierkegaard, Nietzsche, Jaspers, Marcel, Heidegger, Sartre* ° TB/1002
J. M. BOCHENSKI: The Methods of Contemporary Thought. *Trans. by Peter Caws* TB/1377
ERNST CASSIRER: Rousseau, Kant and Goethe. *Intro. by Peter Gay* TB/1092
MICHAEL GELVEN: A Commentary on Heidegger's "Being and Time" TB/1464
J. GLENN GRAY: Hegel and Greek Thought TB/1409
W. K. C. GUTHRIE: The Greek Philosophers: *From Thales to Aristotle* ° TB/1008
G. W. F. HEGEL: Phenomenology of Mind. ° || *Introduction by George Lichtheim* TB/1303
MARTIN HEIDEGGER: Discourse on Thinking. *Translated with a Preface by John M. Anderson and E. Hans Freund. Introduction by John M. Anderson* TB/1459
F. H. HEINEMANN: Existentialism and the Modern Predicament TB/28
WERER HEISENBERG: Physics and Philosophy: *The Revolution in Modern Science. Intro. by F. S. C. Northrop* TB/549
EDMUND HUSSERL: Phenomenology and the Crisis of Philosophy. § *Translated with an Introduction by Quentin Lauer* TB/1170
IMMANUEL KANT: Groundwork of the Metaphysic of Morals. *Translated and Analyzed by H. J. Paton* TB/1159
WALTER KAUFMANN, Ed.: Religion From Tolstoy to Camus: *Basic Writings on Religious Truth and Morals* TB/123
QUENTIN LAUER: Phenomenology: *Its Genesis and Prospect. Preface by Aron Gurwitsch* TB/1169
MICHAEL POLANYI: Personal Knowledge: *Towards a Post-Critical Philosophy* TB/1158
WILLARD VAN ORMAN QUINE: Elementary Logic *Revised Edition* TB/577
WILHELM WINDELBAND: A History of Philosophy *Vol. I: Greek, Roman, Medieval* TB/38

Vol. II: Renaissance, Enlightenment, Modern TB/39
LUDWIG WITTGENSTEIN: The Blue and Brown Books ° TB/1211
LUDWIG WITTGENSTEIN: Notebooks, 1914-1916 TB/1441

Political Science & Government

C. E. BLACK: The Dynamics of Modernization: *A Study in Comparative History* TB/1321
DENIS W. BROGAN: Politics in America. *New Introduction by the Author* TB/1469
ROBERT CONQUEST: Power and Policy in the USSR: *The Study of Soviet Dynastics* ° TB/1307
JOHN B. MORRALL: Political Thought in Medieval Times TB/1076
KARL R. POPPER: The Open Society and Its Enemies *Vol. I: The Spell of Plato* TB/1101 *Vol. II: The High Tide of Prophecy: Hegel, Marx, and the Aftermath* TB/1102
HENRI DE SAINT-SIMON: Social Organization, The Science of Man, and Other Writings. || *Edited and Translated with an Introduction by Felix Markham* TB/1152
CHARLES SCHOTTLAND, Ed.: The Welfare State ** TB/1323
JOSEPH A. SCHUMPETER: Capitalism, Socialism and Democracy TB/3008

Psychology

LUDWIG BINSWANGER: Being-in-the-World: *Selected Papers.* || *Trans. with Intro. by Jacob Needleman* TB/1365
MIRCEA ELIADE: Cosmos and History: *The Myth of the Eternal Return* § TB/2050
MIRCEA ELIADE: Myth and Reality TB/1369
SIGMUND FREUD: On Creativity and the Unconscious: *Papers on the Psychology of Art, Literature, Love, Religion.* § *Intro. by Benjamin Nelson* TB/45
J. GLENN GRAY: The Warriors: *Reflections on Men in Battle. Introduction by Hannah Arendt* TB/1294
WILLIAM JAMES: Psychology: *The Briefer Course. Edited with an Intro. by Gordon Allport* TB/1034

Religion: Ancient and Classical, Biblical and Judaic Traditions

MARTIN BUBER: Eclipse of God: *Studies in the Relation Between Religion and Philosophy* TB/12
MARTIN BUBER: Hasidism and Modern Man. *Edited and Translated by Maurice Friedman* TB/839
MARTIN BUBER: The Knowledge of Man. *Edited with an Introduction by Maurice Friedman. Translated by Maurice Friedman and Ronald Gregor Smith* TB/135
MARTIN BUBER: Moses. *The Revelation and the Covenant* TB/837
MARTIN BUBER: The Origin and Meaning of Hasidism. *Edited and Translated by Maurice Friedman* TB/835
MARTIN BUBER: The Prophetic Faith TB/73
MARTIN BUBER: Two Types of Faith: *Interpenetration of Judaism and Christianity* ° TB/75
M. S. ENSLIN: Christian Beginnings TB/5
M. S. ENSLIN: The Literature of the Christian Movement TB/6
HENRI FRANKFORT: Ancient Egyptian Religion: *An Interpretation* TB/77

Religion: Early Christianity Through Reformation

ANSELM OF CANTERBURY: Truth, Freedom, and Evil: *Three Philosophical Dialogues. Edited and Translated by Jasper Hopkins and Herbert Richardson* TB/317
EDGAR J. GOODSPEED: A Life of Jesus TB/1
ROBERT M. GRANT: Gnosticism and Early Christianity TB/136

Religion: Oriental Religions

TOR ANDRAE: Mohammed: *The Man and His Faith* § TB/62
EDWARD CONZE: Buddhism: *Its Essence and Development.* ° *Foreword by Arthur Waley* TB/58
H. G. CREEL: Confucius and the Chinese Way TB/63
FRANKLIN EDGERTON, Trans. & Ed.: The Bhagavad Gita TB/115
SWAMI NIKHILANANDA, Trans. & Ed.: The Upanishads TB/114
D. T. SUZUKI: On Indian Mahayana Buddhism. ° *Ed. with Intro. by Edward Conze.* TB/1403

Science and Mathematics

W. E. LE GROS CLARK: The Antecedents of Man: *An Introduction to the Evolution of the Primates.* ° *Illus.* TB/559
ROBERT E. COKER: Streams, Lakes, Ponds. *Illus.* TB/586
ROBERT E. COKER: This Great and Wide Sea: *An Introduction to Oceanography and Marine Biology. Illus.* TB/551
WILLARD VAN ORMAN QUINE: Mathematical Logic TB/558

Sociology and Anthropology

REINHARD BENDIX: Work and Authority in Industry: *Ideologies of Management in the Course of Industrialization* TB/3035
KENNETH B. CLARK: Dark Ghetto: *Dilemmas of Social Power. Foreword by Gunnar Myrdal* TB/1317
KENNETH CLARK & JEANNETTE HOPKINS: A Relevant War Against Poverty: *A Study of Community Action Programs and Observable Social Change* TB/1480
LEWIS COSER, Ed.: Political Sociology TB/1293
GARY T. MARX: Protest and Prejudice: *A Study of Belief in the Black Community* TB/1435
ROBERT K. MERTON, LEONARD BROOM, LEONARD S. COTTRELL, JR., Editors: Sociology Today: *Problems and Prospects* || Vol. I TB/1173; Vol. II TB/1174
GILBERT OSOFSKY, Ed.: The Burden of Race: A Documentary History of Negro-White Relations in America TB/1405
GILBERT OSOFSKY: Harlem: The Making of a Ghetto: *Negro New York 1890-1930* TB/1381
PHILIP RIEFF: The Triumph of the Therapeutic: *Uses of Faith After Freud* TB/1360
ARNOLD ROSE: The Negro in America: *The Condensed Version of Gunnar Myrdal's* An American Dilemma. *Second Edition* TB/3048
GEORGE ROSEN: Madness in Society: *Chapters in the Historical Sociology of Mental Illness.* || *Preface by Benjamin Nelson* TB/1337
PITIRIM A. SOROKIN: Contemporary Sociological Theories: *Through the First Quarter of the Twentieth Century* TB/3046
FLORIAN ZNANIECKI: The Social Role of the Man of Knowledge. *Introduction by Lewis A. Coser* TB/1372